KILLER SMILE

RC Bridgestock

Fiction aimed at the heart
and the head..

Published by Caffeine Nights Publishing 2015

All character persons, living or dead to real

Published in Great Britain by
Caffeine Nights Publishing
4 Eton Close

British Library Cataloguing in Publication Data.
A CIP catalogue record for this book is available from the British Library

ISBN: 978-1-910720-06-6

Cover design by
Mark (Wills) Williams

Everything else by
Default, Luck and Accident

Also by RC Bridgestock

The D.I. Dylan Series

Deadly Focus
Consequences
White Lilies
Snow Kills
Reprobates

All available in paperback and eBook

Deadly Focus is available on MP3 CD
audiobook and as a downloadable audiobook

Consequences is available to download as an
audiobook

Acknowledgements

Our police and writing careers have both been eventful and fulfilling. We couldn't have done either without so many kind, dedicated and professional individuals who have walked into our lives and left footprints on our hearts... Our special thanks go to our publisher Darren Laws, Caffeine Nights Publishing for seeing the potential in us and our writing in the first instance and his continued loyalty and support. David H. Headley our new literary agent from DHH Literary Agency, London who in a short time has already has made such an impact on us and our work as you will see in this 6th DI Dylan, 'Killer Smile'. And to Sarah Jarvis, co-owner of The Gate Manchester for settling the option to hopefully turn the Dylan crime novels into a TV series. We are very excited to be presently working with The Gate along with Claire Lewis and Mervyn Watson, both of whom are BAFTA award winning TV Producers.

Thanks, too, to Yin & Phil Johnson, JJ Associates for sharing in-depth knowledge of International Private Investigative work and Claire Booth, Leeds Dental Nurse, who educated us in oral health and dental instruments and practices. All this factual knowledge helps us to give our readers the most realistic experience possible in our fictional tales.

To all those who bid to The Forget Me Not Children's Hospice to name a character in the book we can't thank you enough and hope you enjoy how we have portrayed your character(s) in 'Killer Smile'.

We will be forever thankful for the love and support of Betty and Ray Jordan (Carol's Mum and Dad) who have looked after us when we have 'forgotten' to eat or Belle and Vegas needed walking whilst we work to a deadline.

And to our children and grandchildren who remain in our thoughts every hour of everyday for their love and support in what we do even though this means we get less time with them...

Finally, but by no way least to our followers #TeamDylan and Kath Bainbridge-Keith, Jeannette Bainbridge-Steinson whose idea it was to knit the DI Dylan dolls we now auction to raise funds for The Forget Me Not Children's Hospice.

Thank you from the bottom of our hearts...

To

Our family for their love, support and patience when we constantly disappear into 'Dylan's' world...

All emergency service personnel around the world for putting us all before themselves to make the world a much safer place.

And last but not least a charity that is close to our hearts. Forget Me Not Children's Hospice, Huddersfield a special place that supports children with life shortening conditions and their families throughout West Yorkshire.

'Teeth are nice and white when new.
  They make a smile and help you chew.
  In your skull long after you're dead,
  I'd like to remove them from your head...'

Killer Smile

Chapter One

The month of June had been a hot one. However, rain had spread from the north-west for the fifth consecutive day in July, windless rain, straight and heavy. So, it was no surprise for Detective Inspector Jack Dylan to see the mandatory amber flood warning at Tandem Bridge, on the Chief Constable's daily Log. Crime had been relatively quiet across the Division but for the Senior Investigative Officer who had worked the previous weekend it had nevertheless been an eventful one, in the CID department at Harrowfield Police Station.

A domestic incident had dominated Dylan's Sunday. The deceased was found slumped back in a dining chair at the kitchen table and to all intents and purposes looked asleep. The only telltale sign to the fatal stabbing, through the heart, was an old bone-handled carving knife hanging from the old man's chest. There was nothing but a speck of blood on his pristine long-sleeved white shirt that was finished off with a smart blue tie.

'After sixty years you'd think I'd feel something, wouldn't you?' said his wife with a look on her face that told the experienced SIO a different story. 'Truth be known, I never was more than his cook and bottle washer. And those teeth... He would insist on displaying his bloody dentures, like precious ornaments, in my finest crystal. Look, over there... ' The lady pointed her arthritic index finger towards the bonbon dish on the mantelpiece. 'They grin at me like they possess a smugness of their own,' she said glaring at the offending objects over her glasses. 'His dinner was dried up,' she said matter of factly as she turned to Dylan. 'Well, it would be, wouldn't it? He never did know when to come home from the pub,' she said with a nonchalant shrug of her shoulders.

'Thank God for the microwave,' Dylan thought as he addressed his own lifestyle. A police officer's life was an unpredictable one, and getting home on time was not one of his priorities, especially when he was dealing with a murder. Being a civilian worker with Harrowfield Police Station's administration department helped his wife, Jen, understand the need for flexibility of his job.

Dylan picked up the portrait photograph from his desk and a little sigh escaped his lips. He felt a lucky man. He'd never known a woman like Jennifer Jones before. As much as he loathed Avril (Beaky) Summerfield-Preston the pretentious, devious Divisional Administrator who was also Jen's boss, she had indirectly been responsible for bringing them together and for this he would be eternally grateful, although he'd never dream of telling her.

'Beaky' continued to make life difficult for her staff, goodness only knew why... In Dylan's experience a happy office was a productive one.

Jen, sensitive and trusting, struggled to be supervised by someone like her and Dylan put that down to her being brought up on a small Island, within a close village community and in a loving home. He'd recognised immediately that she needed protecting soon after she'd arrived in Harrowfield. It was pretty obvious to him, in those early days that Jen was vulnerable and naive because her supervisors used her like a dogsbody. How different the two women were. You wouldn't catch Jen wearing sloppy high-heels, tight ill-fitting clothing or smelling of heady nauseous scent. Dylan coughed as the thought of the pungent smell caught in his throat. Jen wouldn't dream of wearing fake eyelashes and big jewellery. What attracted him to Jen was not only the calming way she had about her but her bubbly personality, bouncing blonde ponytail and her sing song tone of her southern accent, and that was before he was ever the recipient of her kind, caring nature. He remembered how grateful he had been to Jen when he walked into the station after a particularly busy week of 'call outs', albeit only from his bachelor cell at the divisional police flats that were named 'Heartbreak Hotel', which provided a roof over the heads of single and separated officers. Jen had brought him hot coffee and a plateful of warm toast into his office. He wanted to spend the rest of his life with this leggy blonde. Spending time with her and getting to know her had made him realise that after all the knockbacks of promotion he'd had in recent years and the pressure he was under being a Senior Investigative Officer he'd been melting into the shadows, and he didn't recognise himself anymore. He had been living to work, not working to live...

It came as a complete and utter shock to Dylan that Jen singled out the rugged Yorkshire detective inspector, nine years her senior. The attention she gave him made him feel sharper and more alive than he'd done in years. 'Where did the time go when you were enjoying yourself?' It would be Maisy, their daughter's third birthday very soon and she was growing fast. The only 'fly' in the domestic 'ointment' was Jen's worry for her dad, Ralph. His living alone in the large family home on the Isle of Wight, since her mum's untimely death, often gave her cause for concern. However, recently he had acquired a lady friend to occupy his time and they heard from him less and less. The parent child thing appeared to be on the other foot for Jen and Ralph, and Dylan knew she wouldn't settle until she had met Thelma Moore.

There was a gentle knock on his office door and Detective Sergeant Vicky Hardacre popped her head around it. 'Sorry to disturb you boss but our attendance is being requested on the cycle path behind the Anchor Inn, Tandem Bridge. The only information I have at the moment is that a female has been found dead, and her bike has been located a few feet away. Initially, her death was thought to be as a result of a fall. However, the paramedics in attendance are concerned about an injury to her neck that they're pretty satisfied is non-accidental.'

'Sounds ominous,' said Dylan. 'Get HQ control to speak to uniform to ensure that access to the area is stopped so the scene remains sterile. Tell them we'll be with them in about fifteen minutes?' he said, looking at his watch. 'We'll need a Crime Scene Supervisor, the body tent and some weights to hold it down should the wind pick up like it's forecast. Otherwise it could be blown into Lancashire,' he said as he rose from his chair. Vicky withdrew from the doorway, back into the CID office.

Dylan took his suit jacket from the back of his chair and reached for his old leather coat. Standing in front of his office window showed him a world of wet, grey, gloom, dripping drainpipes and soaked tarmac of the police yard. So low was the sky it seemed to rest on the rooftops of the town beyond. Fingers of grey mist trailed across the car park. 'British summer?' he murmured.

'All done boss!' said Vicky as she re-entered the office, breaking his reverie. 'The couple of cyclists who discovered her, are still at the scene. The taking of their witness statements is in progress.'

'I hope they're sheltering somewhere,' he said with an explanatory nod over his shoulder towards the window pane.

'The landlord has opened The Anchor for us. I've got DC Ned Granger coming with us as exhibits officer.'

'Well, in that case what are we hanging about for, let's get the show on the road.' Dylan pulled up his collar and like a racehorse wearing blinkers he marched out through the office with one focus in mind. His CID entourage in tow.

So large were the drops of water that Dylan could feel their individual impact on his face and hands as he ran towards his car. He hugged his coat to him. The deluge soaked his hair and ran down into his eyes. Solace was found in his vehicle, but not for long he feared. He turned on the windscreen wipers and switched on the blower to clear the condensation from the windows. Vicky opened the passenger door and flopped down beside him.

'Jesus wept,' she said, shaking her long blonde hair.

'Is Ned taking the CID car?' he asked.

She pointed to the dashboard. 'Yes, you'd better turn on your lights, boss.'

'Yes, ma'am,' Dylan said with a raised eyebrow and a nod of his head.

***

Dylan drove off the main road and into the pub car park. An ambulance, its doors wide open, blocked the intended route. Paramedics could be seen scurrying around inside the vehicle. One indicated to him that they knew he was waiting. Dylan tapped on his steering wheel and waited. Outwardly he appeared patient, inwardly a thousand questions regarding the scene he was about to witness whirred though his mind.

'It probably isn't unreasonable to expect to see a pub named Anchor on the coast,' said Vicky looking quizzically up at the swaying pub sign. 'But, why do you think they'd name a pub in Tandem Bridge The Anchor Inn?' she said.

'I don't know, it may have been named by a sailor who wanted to attract sailors to use it?'

'I wouldn't have thought there'd be many sailors in Tandem Bridge would you?' she said turning to look at him with knitted brows.

Dylan shrugged his shoulders. 'Come to think of it I once read an article about the emergence of the canal network in the early days of the industrial revolution which led to a growth of pubs named Anchor further inland...'

'Is that another gem from the encyclopedia of Dylan? Mind you, my grandpa did use to tell me that on a clear day you can see Blackpool Tower from our very own formidable Wainhouse Tower.'

Yeah, I heard that myth too,' he said.

The ambulance driver jumped down from the back of the vehicle, secured the doors, waved a hand at Dylan and proceeded to climb into the cab. He drove forward to allow Dylan access. Dylan steered his car slowly into a vacant parking space. He was pleased, not only because the rain had abated but because he could see that the scene had been protected by the copious amounts of crime scene tape. When he emerged from the car he could hear it also flapping noisily in the wind. Dylan was pleased someone had taken the initiative to preserve the area and any evidence.

A rendezvous point had been established and a uniformed police officer with a clipboard, albeit a soggy one, was checking the identity and recording the names of everyone attending and leaving.

As he looked past the uniformed staff at the entrance of the taped cordon he could see the high level, fast flowing canal beyond the cycle path.

'If the rain continues to fall at the pace it has over the last few hours,' Vicky said tilting her head up towards the threatening dark clouds, 'our crime scene will be underwater before much longer.'

'We're going to have to act fast on the inner cordon, just in case,' Dylan said. With his trained eye he scanned the wider taped outer cordon, an area to search later should the inclement weather allow.

Now he knew the outer cordon was already sealed he could concentrate on the inner scene. This wasn't always possible at some murder investigations and preparatory work had to be started on his instruction, when he arrived. This care to detail was something he was very thankful for and there was no doubt in his mind that Inspector Peter Reginald Stonestreet must be working. He smiled to himself – there was nothing like having an old timer on your shout.

Dylan ripped open the polythene packet that contained his protective clothing feeling a little relieved. Vicky gave the Police Loggist her details. DC Duncan 'Ned' Granger joined them carrying the major incident holdall. Booted and suited the three trudged, heads bowed, against the wind along the tarmac track towards the area where the body lay. They were feet away but Dylan was still conscious that behind them other members of the team were arriving and preparing to follow their route.

The rural cycle path was used on a daily basis for pleasure, exercise and getting to and from work as it led directly to Harrowfield town centre from outlying villages and hamlets. The Anchor Inn was an old established pub, known locally for its good food in more recent times rather than its ales; frequented by locals and visitors alike.

The group passed a light blue coloured Dawes Mountain bike which was in disarray on a wet, muddy, grass verge.

'That's a serious piece of kit,' Vicky said with a slight tilt of her head in Dylan's direction.

'Nothing like the Hercules Jeep bike I had as a lad. That hard saddle, crunchy gears...'

'Remember those awkward handlebars?' said Ned. 'I went over them a time or two.'

Approximately ten yards away lay the body of the female rider. She could quite clearly be seen laid on her back, dressed in a black and white cycling jersey.

'ASSOS,' said Vicky.

Ned gave a long low whistle. 'She takes her sport seriously by the look of that gear.'

'And she's not short of a bob or two if she can afford it,' said Vicky.

Police Inspector Stonestreet walked towards them. A small duck sat contentedly in his hat.

'Victor!' exclaimed Vicky genuinely happy to see the tall uniformed officer. 'What on earth have you got there?'

'It's got an injured wing, I couldn't leave it to suffer now could I?' he said handing his hat and duck to a special constable who was guarding the scene, with instructions to take it to the RSPCA.

Peter, known to his colleagues as 'Victor Meldrew' was an ex-detective. He wore a flat cap, could display the grumpiest of faces but he had a heart of gold and his knowledge of crime scene procedure was second to none. Dylan was Peter Stonestreet's aide in CID and Stonestreet his sergeant.

'Morning sir,' Peter nodded. Dylan met his greeting with a slight shake of his head and a knowing smile. Peter was a true gentleman, calm and kind and had been very much missed by Dylan when he had gone back into uniform to take up the rank of uniform Inspector.

'I know, it does nothing for my street cred...' Peter said, pulling a cursory comedic frown. 'Bah humbug!'

Vicky laughed at the older man.

'What've we got here?' said Dylan.

Stonestreet turned his attention to the dead body.

'A female discovered by a married couple who are also cyclists, whose accounts are being documented at this moment, in the pub.' He took a step towards the deceased. 'They contacted paramedics via mobile, who in turn informed us. Basically, their initial thoughts were that she had taken a tumble and was unconscious. The husband, being trained in first aid felt her neck for the carotid pulse but couldn't find one, which was when he made the emergency call. That waterproof cape that's flapping about her is one which they used to try and give her some protection from the rain. First impressions given to us from the paramedics having pronounced her dead were that she'd gone over the handle bars. Her mouth is a bloody mess and some of her teeth appear to be missing. But when they looked closer, as you will see for yourself, they discovered a fine line around her neck which is a very thin, deep cut to her throat. My first thoughts were that it was consistent with someone putting wire across the track? However, a quick visual check round hasn't proven anything of that nature which may have caused the injury lying around. The pathways are clear.'

'And the paramedics? Where are they now?'

'Responding to another call but arrangements have been made to get their written statements later today.'

'Good. And we've requested Crime Scene Investigation Supervisor?'

Peter nodded.

'What we did find in close proximity to the body is a used knotted condom which I've left in situ for you to see.'

Dylan raised his eyebrows and looked towards the nearby shrubbery that Stonestreet pointed at.

'As always, your team never ceases to impress me,' Dylan said. He looked up and down the canal path and appeared to be pondering over something. His eyes narrowed. His thinking process was tangible. 'Something across the path you think?' he muttered. 'But what would have caused those injuries that has now disappeared?'

'It is possible that whatever it was, was removed before she was discovered,' said Vicky.

'Maybe the person who did this to her took whatever it was with them?' said Peter brushing a hand over his head.

'... I'm not sure... Wouldn't wire drag her backwards off her bike?'

'Never assume,' said Peter to Dylan. The uniformed Inspector winked at Vicky.

'Why, that's his favourite saying,' she said throwing her head in Dylan's direction.

Peter raised an eyebrow and gave her a little cheeky nod.

'Mmm... Do we have any idea who she is?' said Dylan.

18

'Not yet boss, as you can see she has a hip pouch around her waist. Which might give us further clues but I didn't want to disturb the body more than was necessary, until you arrived.'

'Why would anyone do that? What could their motive be?' said Vicky.

Inspector Stonestreet hunched his shoulders. 'Your guess is as good as mine.'

***

Dylan looked up at the darkening sky. The investigation was off to a good start in spite of the weather. Light rain sprinkled his face and he screwed up his eyes for an instant. It was obvious there was no time to waste. He bent down to look closely at the deceased's face. Her cycle helmet had already been removed, by the paramedics, and it lay on the floor to her left.

'Perfect crime scene preservation,' Vicky said to Peter.

'Something that you never forget, the way to protect a crime scene.'

'Why did you leave CID?'

'We had to go into uniform to get the next rank and I got put in charge of public order control at football grounds,' he grinned from ear to ear.

'Don't be fooled by his cool, mild mannered persona. You should see him at a football match,' said Dylan. He turned to look at the pair. 'The poor ref...' he said shaking his head.

'I'm a passionate man,' said Peter. 'A red blooded male... Nothing wrong with that.'

'Way too much information,' said Vicky.

'We're talking football here,' said Peter. 'I'm no Don Juan.'

'Who?' said Vicky.

Dylan cocked an eyebrow at his colleague. 'Yes, but I'll have you know he's been known to try and sneak a full hip flask into football grounds with him.'

Vicky gave Peter a wry smile. 'Well, I guess he can't abuse referees any worse than the hierarchy did you Dylan.'

Peter looked inquisitively at Dylan. 'Why what's happened?'

'Oh, me and another lad scored the highest at the recent Chief Inspector boards but the powers that be decided not to put anyone through this time round.'

'How come?'

'They raised the benchmark, after the event,' said Vicky.

'Can they do that?'

'Presumably so, when it's in-house. We're in a disciplined service after all,' said Vicky.

Peter's mouth hung open for a moment – in a silent oh. 'Ah I see and you and this other person were not on their list of officers the bosses wanted to be promoted?'

'That about sums it up,' said Vicky.

'We can only speculate,' said Dylan wearily.

'Yeah, whatever,' said Vicky. 'Talking of mild manners, is it true you took the Assistant Chief Constable to task about the system?' Dylan looked sheepish.

'Dylan?' Peter growled. Vicky watched Dylan's face. His was serious.

'Just leave it,' he said. 'We've a job to do. Karen Ebdon CSI Supervisor is here.'

Ned was on hand to help carry her load.

***

Low, black clouds hovered directly above now threatening heavy rain. It was a clear warning to everyone that the brief respite was over and the weather was about to worsen.

'Don't bother with the tent Karen,' Dylan said as Ned threw the bag to the ground at his feet. 'I think we had better concentrate on getting the necessary photographs and samples.' He pointed out the condom. 'Seize that will you.'

Dylan needed to make quick decisions. As if someone above was listening in on his thoughts hailstones, as big as golf balls, hurtled down from the sky. They bounced off the already sodden ground and quickly created a thin white covering across their path. The team ran under a nearby tree that was luckily in full bloom and provided them shelter. Coveralls were not rainproof.

'Talk about raining cats and dogs,' said Vicky shaking herself. Control room shouted for Inspector Stonestreet over the radio and he turned his back on the others to hear what was said.

'Did you know Shakespeare would have said haddocks and bloaters?'

'What's that to do with the price of fish?' said Ned.

'It's called educating yourself numbskull.'

'You're so full of shit.'

'It's true!'

'We'll give it another minute or two and if there's no sign of the weather improving, we'll have to brave the elements until we've got what's necessary from this scene,' Dylan said raising his voice to be heard. 'Then let's get her body to the mortuary. In drier conditions I'd have had that tent erected and the Home Office pathologist out but it looks like we're not going to be that fortunate today.'

Peter tapped Dylan on the shoulder. 'I don't want to add to your problems but the canal is known to overflow at this stretch and I've just been told it's reached its maximum.'

'I saw the amber warning on the Chief's Log.' He looked at the others. 'Let's just do what we can.'

Within seconds the hailstones had stopped and the sun shone through the fast moving clouds spasmodically. Sadly Dylan could see the thorough scene protection he had been so impressed with was losing its effectiveness fast. Soaked to the skin they worked industriously. Vicky arranged for the body and the bike to be recovered as the photographs were being taken.

'How old do you think she is?' said Dylan.

'Early twenties,' said Karen.

'Any rings on her fingers?' Dylan said.

Karen held up the left hand of the deceased.

'Slight indent on her ring finger,' said Vicky.

'Thank you,' Dylan said. His gaze not wandering far from the dead girl's face.

'Let's have a look inside that bag round her waist Karen,' Dylan said.

The Scenes of Crime Supervisor carefully unzipped the pouch. A mobile phone, a ten pound note and a letter addressed to Harrowfield Council, sealed and stamped were carefully extracted between Karen's gloved finger and thumb. Ned Granger held out a plastic exhibit bags for her to drop the articles in. 'That's the total contents,' she said.

21

'The letter; correspondence ready to post en route do you think?' Vicky said.

'Maybe, probably, but it's not necessarily hers. Can you open it for us Karen? Inside an exhibits bag please, otherwise the rain could destroy it.'

There was a moment or two when everyone appeared to hold their breath. 'Let's see what this tells us,' said Dylan. 'The mobile should be a help to us if nothing else...'

Everyone's eyes were on Karen. They watched as her gloved hands fumbled about inside a transparent plastic bag. Eventually she managed to open the letter and read the contents out loud. 'It's regarding a planning application signed by a Davina Walsh of 4, Spring Bank Road, High-town, Harrowfield.'

'Make the look at the Burgess Roll a priority Vicky. Can you also check to see who's working that's a trained Family Liaison Officer too,' said Dylan.

The scene wouldn't be abandoned. The tape would remain in situ and the covered area would be thoroughly searched but not until the weather was more settled. Dylan was happy for the uniformed officer guarding the crime scene to remain at the scene inside a vehicle. Offenders had been known to return to the scene of their crime and people notoriously ignored the crime scene tape unwittingly destroying evidence. Although how anyone could miss the police 'DO NOT CROSS' instruction was a mystery.

The Anchor Inn, being the nearest building to the incident would be a priority line of early enquiries.

Ned signalled to the others that the private ambulance had arrived and collectively they moved the deceased very carefully into a body bag. Karen was about to fasten it up when Dylan held his hand out to stop her. He wanted one last look at the neck injury. The cut to the deceased was so clean it could have been done with a cheese wire. Her mouth was agape. Dylan spoke aloud as he studied the wound. 'Tell me, wouldn't you expect her teeth to be chipped or broken, not actually missing completely if she had fallen?'

'Yes, yes I guess I would,' said Karen.

'The cavities are very clean as if she has had teeth extracted. Look, the loss of that tooth has left such a hole you can see actually see up to her sinuses... And if they have come out due to the fall where on earth are they?' he said looking about them. 'Zip her up, we'll find out more hopefully at the post-mortem.'

'Is there a chance that she had been to the dentist?' Vicky said.

'Dressed as she is?' Dylan sighed, 'I'm not convinced. Let's get back to the nick.'

'Are you thinking the killer has pulled out her teeth?' Vicky said as she hurried to keep up with Dylan to his car. He stopped suddenly, she nearly walked into him, he looked over his shoulder. 'You are aren't you?' she said. 'You think it was a deliberate act don't you?'

Chapter-Two

'It's at times like this when you appreciate the car has air conditioning,' Dylan said. He sat back in his car seat, undid his shirt collar and pulled at the knot of his tie.

'I couldn't agree more,' Vicky said as she wiped her damp forehead with the back of her hand.

The pair sat in silence as police radio informed them of a road collapse due to the heavy rainfall, causing a power cut at Tandem Police Station, who were now on emergency generator.

'God forbid that cloud had carried the rain a few more miles up the valley, we'd have lost the scene completely,' said Vicky.

'And the body with it,' said Dylan.

Vicky was unusually quiet as they drove back to the station.

'So, what're your thoughts?'

'I think it was pre-planned. The injury to the neck... The person or persons who did it must have known what they were doing and brought along the equipment to carry out the act. But, it's the teeth thing that bothers me... that's totally weird,' she said, screwing up her nose. 'Unless she had just been to the dentist.'

'Well, you know what they say. See how a person lived and you'll find out how they died,' said Dylan as they drove into the back yard of the police station. 'She was someone's target, for some reason, that's for sure. Once we've got dry we'll grab a coffee and wait for the family liaison officer to contact us before we go any further. With Ned Granger gone with her body to the mortuary for continuity, I guess we've got a while before the Home Office Pathologist gets there. We need to use that time to get the incident room up and running. Then we'll see what we can find out about Davina Walsh and the address on the letter, prior to making a visit. We also need someone to go and speak to the landlord at the Anchor.'

'The killer must know her or her routine. Surely no one would put wire across a footpath on the off chance that some stranger would come along on a bike to garrotte them, would they?' said Vicky.

'If that's what it was, wire?'

'Well, it has to be mighty strong to cause that sort of damage to the poor woman's neck. What else could it be?' Vicky lifted her shoulders, tilted her head and gestured with her palms up.

'And the condom... Connected to the killing do you think?'

'God knows!' said Vicky.

'I'm glad somebody does,' said Dylan.

***

The CID office was empty apart from Lisa who was attending to her administration duties. She raised her head above her computer screen, lifting her eyes to see who had entered the office and continued to type when she saw it was Dylan and Vicky.

Vicky sat down with a thump on her chair and switched on her computer. Dylan continued down the centre aisle of desks to his office, opened the door and switched on the lights that juddered into action.

Dylan heard DC Andy Wormald's voice in the outer office. He was talking to Vicky. A few minutes later she knocked at Dylan's door and walked in. 'There's nothing on the intelligence system in relation to a Davina Walsh. The only info we have on the address is on the Burgess Roll.'

'At least it's good for something...'

'What is?'

'The Burgess Roll; at one time conmen used to go into the post office to look at the Burgess Roll to see where the elderly lived, and who lived on their own. Fortunately for us the criminals weren't that bright and left their fingerprints all over the paper which put them into the frame for the offences.'

'The Burgess Roll shows her living alone. Andy says the house is a two bed semi-detached in a nice area.'

'Send Andy into my office will you, I need him to go to The Anchor Inn to get a statement from the landlord.'

The phone was ringing in the outside office. Lisa picked up. Dylan could see her grab Andy Wormald's arm as he passed her desk and she slipped a piece of paper in his hand; he read it, opened Dylan's door and walked in.

'Home Office Pathologist Professor Bernard Stow will be attending the mortuary at four o'clock today to carry out the post-mortem examination, sir,' he said

Dylan was thoughtful. 'Thanks. Sit down. Vicky got you up to speed?'

Andy nodded his head.

'Good. So tell me this. If our victim is Davina Walsh and she lives alone, as the Burgess Roll suggests, then why do you think she didn't have a house key on her?'

'She does live with someone but they just haven't updated the Electoral Register yet?'

'Mmm... you're probably right. I want you to find out who was at the Anchor Inn last night. Find out whatever gossip you can glean from the landlord and see what CCTV you can gather for us, and seize it? Is Ned back yet?'

'I believe the body has been handed over to the Coroner's Officer and booked in and he's on his way back from the mortuary, sir.'

'Take him with you and tell him from me if he comes back from The Anchor smelling of alcohol he'll be back on the beat quicker than he can say Sir Robert Peel.'

As if the mention of his name conjured him up Dylan saw DC Ned Granger walk into the outer CID office. Andy, signalled his colleague to join them.

'What's up boss?' Ned said with a painfully wide cartoon smile upon his face.

Dylan picked up his jacket. 'I'll leave it with you Andy, I'm off to visit the address with Vicky.'

Dylan's tone was serious. As he walked out of his office past Ned, the detective grimaced at Andy. 'Who's rattled his flaming cage?' he said.

Dylan stopped and swung around to face the detectives and they both stood perfectly still. 'Get me samples of the condoms they sell in the pub while you're at it,' he said.

'Any particular flavour boss?' said Ned in a hushed tone.

'Just do it smart arse,' Dylan said, his expression unchanged.

***

It was known in the force as the 'Death Notice'. Dylan marched out of the police station with a walk of a man who was going to deliver that knock on the door, by a police officer, that no one wanted to hear. DS Vicky Hardacre followed solemnly in his footsteps.

PC Bullock, the designated Family Liaison Officer, opened the gate of number 4, Spring Bank Road and strode head down with the CID officers up the path.

Dylan stopped at the glossy red front door, checked the number and before he knocked he glanced over his shoulder at the two women. The knock, when it came, was loud and clear. There was a humming of insects. Dylan stared at the door for a moment or two waiting for it to be answered. After a moment or two Vicky noticed his broad, taut shoulders visibly drop. He knocked again and this time it wasn't as forceful. He tilted his head upwards slightly, raising his eyes sufficiently to be able to see through the small arc of a window. Still there was no reply. Dylan tried the handle. The door was secure. A path directly under the lounge window appeared to continue around to the rear of the house and the three walked it in a singular line, taking a cursory glance through the window pane as they passed. All looked quiet inside. At the back door Dylan knocked again but his knocking was met with silence.

Dylan stepped down from the doorstep and at that moment a lady suddenly appeared on the doorstep of the adjoining house. 'What's all the banging about?' she shouted.

The three officers held up their warrant cards and before they could speak she had walked to the chest-high privet hedge and continued in a softer voice.

'Who are you looking for? Davina's out on her bike and you've just missed her partner Gary. Can I give them a message?'

'There's been a serious incident on the canal cycle path which has proven fatal. We need to speak to Gary as a matter of urgency,' he said.

The lady's face drained of colour and her eyes filled with tears. 'Oh my,' she said.

'Stay where you are and we'll come around to you,' said Dylan, locating the iron gated access to her garden.

Vicky stayed talking to the neighbour as Dylan and the FLO made their way next door. With a light touch of her fingers PC Bullock guided her indoors. She felt a faint tremor go through her. 'They're in training to do a sponsored bike ride to raise money for the children's hospice,' she said.

'What's your name dear?' asked PC Bullock pulling out a kitchen chair.

'Mrs Crowther,' she said. 'Jean, Jean Crowther.'

Davina's next door neighbour appeared to be having difficulty breathing. 'Shall I pop the kettle on?' said PC Bullock.

The four sat around a breakfast table by the window. 'It's this weekend, the Three Peaks Cyclo-Cross.' Mrs Crowther half smiled briefly, as she wiped a lone tear that had escaped her watery eyes.

***

The team had been given a positive identification of their victim and the clothes she wore when training. There was no doubt in Dylan's mind their victim was Davina Walsh. Mrs Crowther stood, walked to her dresser and picked up a teddy bear key fob. She held one hand to her breast and the other out towards the police officer. 'Gary gave me this so she could get in the house. You will probably need this now?'

Giving someone distressing news was hard and so was leaving them alone but, satisfied that Mrs Crowther was okay the three officers thanked her for her help and headed towards Harrowfield Fire Station.

***

The fire station was devoid of its fire engines. 'They're out on a shout,' Frank Jessop the officer in charge of the watch told Dylan. 'Do you want to come in and wait?'

'I'd like to have a word with you first if I may?' said Dylan.

Dylan could see the older man's eyes fill up as he sat opposite him in his office explaining the reason for their visit.

'Bloody hell, what a shock. Davina... She's a grand lass... Murdered you say? Christ Almighty... Davina's only recently lost her mum and that's why they're doing the bike ride to raise money in her memory, quite a few of the lads from here are involved. Do you want me to stay with you whilst you break the news to Gary?'

'If you would? There is never an easy way to break news like this but sometimes a familiar face helps.'

Frank Jessop looked at Dylan with eyes full of sorrow. 'Have you got the bastard who did it?' he said, shaking his head gently to and fro. 'This is going to destroy him... I'm ... I feel... What can I say?'

'No, we've no suspects at the moment. Is there anything else you can tell us about Davina? Has she any other family?'

'No not that I know of. Her dad, he's been dead a long while. She's had it rough; a young lass looking after her poorly mum. Look, let me try and get Gary back here a bit quicker if I can. Let's get this done. I'll get Harrowfield Outer Station to pick up our calls for now...'

***

Gary was a pleasant looking young man. He had a ruddy, weathered face and was clean shaven. At some stage in his past it was apparent from looking at him that he had his nose broken; in fact his lean, strong body could have been that of a boxer. Dylan stood and introduced himself and the other officers to him. Understandably he looked puzzled. 'What's all this about?' he said. He was still dressed in his weatherproof trousers, minus his jacket but he still held his helmet at his hip. 'What's up,' he said meeting their serious faces with a frown. 'I submitted my report for the fatal fire weeks ago, Frank?'

Gary's boss got up from behind his desk, pulled up a chair for Gary to sit down and closed his office door.

'Now you're worrying me,' he said with a nervous laugh. Frank couldn't look Gary in the face. Gary followed his boss's shaky movements back to his seat.

Dylan detested this part of his job. He knew the next few words that came from his mouth would change this young man's world forever. They would cause him unimaginable pain no human being should ever have to endure. For Dylan, telling someone their loved one was dead, murdered, never got any easier. People reacted differently, he could never predict the response. He took a deep breath. 'Gary, it's not about the fire. I've got some terrible news for you and there is no easy way... The body of a young lady was found earlier this morning on the cycle path near the Anchor Inn. We believe it to be that of Davina.' Dylan could hear his own voice shaking.

Gary's face became contorted, his complexion turned the colour of milk. He sat still. He blinked his eyes. 'It can't be. Why are you saying that?' His eyes had a blind look as though his vision had turned inwards.

Dylan talked, although he knew by Gary's expression he heard very little of what he said. Dylan explained what Davina had been wearing when she was found, described her bike and revealed the contents of the waist pouch found strapped to her body – almost as if Dylan himself needed reassurance that the body that had been found was Davina Walsh. He told of how he and the officers present had visited at his home address, and he relayed the conversation they had had with their neighbour Mrs Crowther. Lastly he passed Gary the key they had been given. 'There will have to be a formal identification of Davina's body but we wouldn't be sitting here telling you this unless we were sure it was her, Gary.'

'I told her not to go training today,' Gary's eyes lifted from where they had focused, on the wooden floor, between his legs. The keys dangled loosely from his hand. He looked directly into Dylan's eyes with a pleading stare Dylan was accustomed to from victim's families.

'Why's that?' said Dylan.

'A cold... she's full of cold...' Gary's voice grew louder and bitter. 'Why did she have to be so pig-headed? She was so determined to keep up with her damn training because she didn't want to let the team down,' he said. He brought his hands up to his head and grasped it as though it would explode. 'I shouted at her.' His voice cracked. 'Can you believe I told her she'd kill herself?' His voice became a whisper. 'I'm sorry... I just can't... She didn't listen, she never bloody listened...' he said. Unchecked tears ran down his face. 'Cycling's second nature to Davina. She frightens the hell out of me how fast she goes...' his focus flew up to the ceiling, he shut his eyes and was still. For a few moments Gary was quiet and he appeared to be holding his breath.

'You don't have to apologise. Never apologise. We can only imagine how you're feeling. Davina died instantly, but Gary, I have to tell you this wasn't an accident. It wasn't her fault. We believe Davina was murdered.'

'Murdered?' Gary's eyes grew wide. 'Murdered? Why? Why would anyone want to murder Davina?' He sprang up from his chair. Overturned it lay between him and Dylan. His face crumpled. 'It can't be her ... It just can't be... you must be wrong. She's my world.' Gary looked as if something had broken within him.

'Gary, I'm heading a major investigation to find out why and by whom,' Dylan said.

'I don't understand? Am I missing something? Did they think she was carrying money?'

Dylan could only raise his shoulders. He sighed deeply and shook his head slightly from side to side. 'At this point I don't have an answer for you.'

'How did she die?' Gary appeared to be more composed as he made a groping gesture towards the desk and he rested for a moment when he found it. His hands spread out upon it, he faltered for a moment or two.

'She died of a serious injury to her throat,' said Dylan.

Gary turned.

'Someone cut her throat?' Gary's eyebrows knitted together and he looked over his shoulder to his station officer. 'I can't cope with this Frank,' he said, panic flashed across his eyes.

Frank Jessop rested his elbow on his desk, put his hand to his forehead and covered his eyes. 'You and me both lad,' he replied wiping his eyes with a handkerchief that was swiftly retrieved from his trouser pocket, 'you and me both.'

'I'm sorry. We have to tell you what happened because we need to ask you some questions about Davina,' Dylan said.

Gary swallowed hard and waited in anticipation. Dylan righted the chair and gestured that he should sit down.

'It appears that Davina has teeth missing and we are wondering if they came out when she fell from her bike?' Dylan continued.

'Must have,' Gary said reaching inside his pocket for his wallet. 'Look,' he said pulling out a picture of Davina and pointing to her perfect smile. 'She had beautiful white teeth, no fillings, no nothing.' Gary stared at his girlfriend's picture that he held so tightly that the top of his thumbnail turned white.

'He's right, it was one of the first things you noticed about her when you met her, her beautiful smile,' said Frank.

Gary looked agitated. He sat bolt upright and looked Dylan straight in the eyes. 'I have to see her. Where is she?' He jumped to his feet once again as if his chair was on fire.

'Of course,' Dylan said gently. 'We need you to officially identify her. She's in the mortuary at Harrowfield Hospital. Being a fire officer you'll know it can only be brief, through the viewing room window at this stage. Again, I'm probably teaching you to suck eggs but this allows us to secure uncontaminated evidence which is very important to help us catch who did this to Davina. As soon as she has been examined by the pathologist you'll be able to spend more time with her.'

'I can take you to the hospital,' said Frank. 'I don't want you riding your bike.'

'We will arrange transport for you both,' said Dylan.

Gary's eyes were agonised and questioned Dylan. It was apparent that he was in shock and in a very lonely place with his thoughts.

'We know Davina's parents are not alive but does she have any family that we need to inform? And what about you Gary? Do you have someone who we could contact to be with you?'

'No... My parents... they're local. God, this is going to give them a heart attack, she was a daughter they never had... Davina was the kindest, loveliest, most thoughtful person that ever walked the earth...' Gary's tears freely rolled down his cheeks. He began shaking uncontrollably. Frank got up from behind his desk and walked towards him, stopping only to wipe away his own tears. He put a comforting arm around Gary's shoulders.

'Come on son,' he said.

'Why Frank? Why Davina? She wouldn't hurt a fly. Who would want to kill her?'

The sadness in the room left no one untouched. Dylan focused on the job in hand and nodded at Vicky and PC Bullock. They stood.

'DS Hardacre and myself will be at the hospital to meet with you shortly,' said Dylan. 'After the post-mortem I will sit with you and explain what we know. I can assure you that I won't keep anything from you throughout the enquiry no matter how upsetting it maybe.'

'Thank you,' said Gary softly. 'I appreciate it.'

'PC Bullock here is your family liaison officer and she will be available to you at all times. She will be in constant touch with me and the rest of the team throughout the investigation.'

'I can take you in my car to Harrowfield Hospital Mortuary Gary, Frank ?' said PC Bullock.

'Thank you,' said Gary, looking at Frank.

Frank nodded as he wiped his eyes. 'Yes.'

***

Dylan walked out of the fire station a different man from the one that went in. Each death notice took its toll. That was one thing that wouldn't be disputed by any of his colleagues.

On the way to the mortuary Vicky was unusually quiet. 'The bastard who did this needs catching and fast,' she said through gritted teeth. 'I'm glad you did that. I don't think I could have talked to him without bursting into tears myself,' she said as she looked across at Dylan.

'Murder causes devastation for families and friends of the victim... and,' he sighed, 'the survivors are the ones who are left serving a life sentence.'

Dylan was deep in thought.

'We need to speak to the coroner's officer before Gary and Frank get to the hospital. I want him to get a sheet draped on top of the body bag. Have it opened just enough so Gary can see the upper part of Davina's face to identify her. Tell Geoff Painter he'll need to get the lights dimmed in the viewing room. I don't want Gary to see her toothless, swollen mouth. After the post-mortem, when she's been cleaned up, then he can see her.'

PC Bullock was an experienced officer and she had spent hours with bereaved families. Dylan was pleased he had her on board for this investigation. He made a mental note to ask her to obtain a photograph of Davina for the press and one that Gary liked. He knew that once he gave it to the media it would appear in all the newspapers and be shown on the TV news.

Dylan parked in the hospital car park and whilst Vicky went to get a parking ticket he took the opportunity to ring Jen. Maisy had banged her leg at the play gym, he was told, but his wife had kissed it better and she was straight back on the apparatus.

'That's my girl,' said Dylan smiling. 'Tough as old boots.'

'You had time to speak to Hugo-Watkins yet about the promotion board results?' Jen shouted over the screams of the tots at Jimmy Tumble Gym.

'No, not yet but I have a date for my debrief at HQ with the Assistant Chief Constable.'

'How they can profess, in all honesty, to having a transparent, equal opportunity police service is totally beyond me,' said Jen

Dylan smiled. 'Me neither, but we're in a disciplined service and they can do pretty much what they want, so for now I'm still an Inspector and I'm happy doing what I do,' said Dylan.

'You're too bloody soft. You know what they've done borders on corruption.'

'Yes, well, right now I need to be focused on this murder enquiry and not some pointless paper exercise. Seeing a young corpse on a post-mortem slab has a way of bringing home to you just what matters, and that's definitely not worrying about what rank anyone holds in the police force. I don't know what time I'll be home tonight. I'm at the mortuary waiting for the PM to start.'

'Really? Oh, God, the girl on the canal, it's murder?'

'Yeah.'

'That's my day mapped out tomorrow too then when I'm back at work.'

'We are in the process of getting the incident room up and running. Just for your info I've pulled Vicky in on it. DC Ned

Granger as Exhibits Officer, PC Bullock Family Liaison Officer and DC Andy Wormald is working on it too for now.'

'I heard snippets about it on the radio but there was no suggestion of a murder enquiry.'

'The press office will be putting a statement out very soon I expect. We're just waiting for her boyfriend to ID her.'

'You got some mints for the PM and a bottle of water?'

Dylan's eyes flew to the compartment in his car door and put his hand in his pocket to ensure his mints were ensconced. 'I have yes, thanks,' he said.

Extra strong mints were Jack Dylan's way of dealing with the putrid smell of the mortuary. He knew only too well how he could be stood for hours at the side of an examination table once the post-mortem began.

***

The identification of Davina Walsh was positive. Gary was only saved from collapsing on the floor by Frank his station master and friend. Tears were shed and now PC Bullock was with them in a private room at the hospital whilst he answered the coroner's officer's questions. A formal written statement of identification was required.

Dylan spoke to Gary briefly.

'I couldn't see all of her face,' said Gary to Dylan. 'I suppose that was on purpose. PC Bullock said she needs cleaning up.'

'You didn't need to see any more of Davina to recognise her did you?'

'No... no... I didn't,' he said sadly.

'You will be able to go and see her and touch her, spend some time with her later, I promise.'

'Thank you,' he said.

***

Experienced Family Liaison Officers like PC Bullock were an invaluable asset to Dylan. The role took such a burden off the SIO's shoulders and for the victims' families to have someone on hand whom they could ask questions, at any time, it was most necessary.

Senior Crime Scene Investigator Sarah Jarvis was made aware that her presence was also required imminently, as were the other officers nominated to work on the investigation.

'Although this sounds really morbid boss, I'm interested to see what the PM tells us about how her teeth were removed,' said Vicky.

'Me too Vicky, post-mortems are never pleasant but it may be what helps us to catch the killer and put the bastard away for life, that's why we endure them.'

Chapter Three

It was four o'clock and Dylan was pleased that Professor Stow was predictably punctual.

Dylan had to look twice as the pathologist walked through the door of the mortuary. The usually rotund, loud and jovial pathologist displayed the signs of a poorly man; he was concerned.

'Hey, slim Jim!' Vicky called. 'Care to share your secret?' she said grabbing the spare tyre around her middle.

'Kidney stones,' he said flatly. His face was ashen.

Vicky cringed. She bit her lip.

'Trust you. Feet first as usual,' said Dylan.

'Sorry,' said Vicky quickly.

'Worst bit is not being able to drink my usual fix of strong coffee. Caffeine supposedly causes one to lose fluid too quickly,' he said in a stern deep voice and with a scowl. He looked over his half-rimmed glasses. 'And in turn it makes me bloody dehydrated! But there's always a positive. Since I've stuck to the low fat diet and drunk more water the cramping in my legs seems less frequent.' Professor Stow's eyes held Dylan's and a twinkle of his old self was present. He stepped into his protective clothing and held his gloved hands in the air whilst his splash apron was tied behind his back. He winked at Vicky. 'It's nothing to look forward to, getting old lass,' he said in his thick Yorkshire accent. 'But at least now they've been broken up they've passed through successfully.' He put his chin to his chest as the neck tape was secured.

'Too much information,' she said with a little gasp, for Dylan's ears only.

Dylan related the facts of the case to the Professor as the group stood around the examination table in the mortuary.

Davina's body was still inside the body bag. He told him of the attendant circumstances.

Professor Stow was as methodical and thorough as ever, taking care of every detail that needed to be accounted for and asking for all photographs that were required, along the way. All was done in the usual chronological order that the team present was able to follow.

The task of removing the body bag was completed with the utmost care. It was passed intact to DC Granger the exhibits officer to bag and tag, record and retain, and further photographs were taken of all that the action revealed.

Dylan watched Professor Stow scan the front of the body first. He took tapings, fingerprint impressions and nail scrapings. In silence, he stopped and indicated where necessary more photographs were required. Davina's clothing was removed layer by layer. The tiny framed, naked body of Miss Walsh now lay before him. At first glance, apart from a thin dark line on the neck and dried blood crusted around the mouth, that looked like it could be dirt, nothing else seemed unusual. More tapings were taken, vaginal and rectal swabs, head and pubic hair samples, which were both cut and pulled, before the mortuary assistant was asked to assist him to turn her body over on to her stomach.

'There is nothing obvious to suggest she has been subjected to a sexual assault,' Professor Stow said. 'No bruising,' he continued for the purpose of the tape recording. Standing perfectly still, his head moved from her head to her toe. 'Now what do I see here?' he said stopping at her left shoulder. Stow's gloved hand hovered above the marble looking skin. 'We have what looks like it could be a bite mark on her left shoulder. Can you see it? It's not very visible, but that may be because it was done through her clothing.' Stow never lifted his head. 'And what else do we have? In the middle of her lower back I believe we have some bruising. Already I can see a partial mark in the shape of a foot appearing. Can you?' he said, following the outline of the imprint with his finger. 'Her clothing might give you more... but I don't need to tell you that Inspector,' he said with a quick glance up at Dylan.

Dylan gave him a slight nod of his head.

Senior CSI Supervisor Sarah 'Jarv' Jarvis's camera flashed and there were several clicks in quick succession. More photographs were asked for, after which the naked body of Davina Walsh was turned on its back once more.

'Body block please,' Professor Stow said as he looked around for the assistant who handed him the necessary equipment.

The block in place under the body caused Davina's arms and neck to fall backwards, whilst pushing her chest upwards. This would make it easier for Professor Stow to cut her open and give him maximum exposure of the trunk.

'Okay, let's look at the neck wound because I think it's pretty obvious this little lady has been the victim of a garrotte,' he said very matter-of-fact.

Vicky winced.

'The representation of the footmark on her back suggests to me that this was how the perpetrator tightened this ancient execution device to slit her throat.' He stopped and looked up from the body and pushed his half-rimmed glasses further up his nose. Sweat glistened on his brow. 'Did you know the garrotte has been around in some form or other since the first century BC?' Stow said. His head dropped down and he was quickly back to the job in hand which was carefully swabbing the wound. 'There is also evidence that this ligature had a knot at the centre, look, here,' he said pointing to a slightly bigger indentation near the larynx. 'This comes from the Indian version of the assassination device which aids in crushing the larynx when the perpetrator applies pressure to the victim's back, usually as in this case with a foot but the same amount of pressure can be applied from a bended knee. Her neck has been sliced as easily and neatly as a piece of cheese by a cheese wire, in fact I can confirm by her injuries, that this has been done by a handheld ligature but not by a rope, scarf, chain, telephone cord, cable tie as is often used but by a thin wire or catgut,' he said screwing up his face. 'The evidence we have before us suggests that only one ligature was used however a typical garrotte used by soldiers of the French Foreign Legion had a double-loop, referred to as *la loupe*, where a double coil is dropped around a victim's neck and then pulled taut. You didn't happen to find any sticks or pieces of wood with a wire around them at the scene did you?' he said looking up at the officers. 'Pieces of wood at each end of the wire would have helped to tighten the ligature,' he said acting out the action with his gloved hands.

Dylan looked at DC Granger, the exhibits officer who silently shook his head.

'No, and it was Peter Stonestreet's team who sealed the scene, so I'm pretty confident there was nothing left lying around, even though we lost it pretty quickly to heavy rain.'

'Okay then,' Stow said with a little dry cough. 'So let's move on to look inside the mouth and at her teeth.' He carried on speaking whilst gently washing away the blood from her lips. 'Humans like other mammals are diphyodonts, which in simple terms means we have two sets of teeth,' Professor Stow allowed himself to take a breath. 'Human beings lose their milk teeth at around six years of age.' The professor stopped, looked up from the corpse and pondered for a moment. 'What a lovely sounding word diphyodonts is, don't you think?' he said to Dylan before continuing the examination.

Dylan saw another glimpse of the old mischievous Professor Stow and Vicky noted that the professor's smile reached his eyes.

'First the lower jaw or the mandible and then we'll move to the upper – the maxilla, its prime function is to hold our teeth in place.' Blindly Professor Stow searched inside the mouth with his gloved index finger. His eyes found the fluorescent light fitting on the ceiling and remained there while he silently counted. 'Twelve... and in the upper jaw... ten, eleven. Well, her remaining teeth appear to be firmly attached but... as I'm sure you know, humans have thirty-two teeth, sixteen in the maxilla and sixteen in the mandible... so we've lost nine here in total.'

Professor Stow opened the mouth wide and peered inside.

'We're told the first thing that you noticed about Davina was her brilliant white teeth. According to her boyfriend she's never had any dental work done,' Dylan said.

'Lucky girl, but that's not the case now,' he said. Standing upright he stretched his back. 'Four central incisors and an upper molar have been extracted from the upper jaw and four incisors from the lower jaw. And when I say extracted I mean just that.'

'So they weren't knocked out by the fall?' said Vicky.

'No, I would suggest they've been neatly removed, using possibly dental instruments such as an elevator to lift upwards and forceps to take each one out. Your attacker knew what they were doing.'

Vicky looked at Dylan. 'But why would they do that, to sell?'

'Like most things teeth are a saleable commodity. A famous film star just sold his kidney stone for fourteen thousand pounds to an online casino, to raise money for a housing charity.'

'Really?' said Vicky.

'Really,' said Stow. 'Maybe I should try...?' He stopped and considered. He leant against the examination table as if he had suddenly felt giddy. His face was suddenly the colour of clay.

'Get an action raised to ascertain how much teeth are worth on today's market and where someone might sell or buy them?' Dylan said to Vicky although his eyes were fixed on the professor.

'A friend of mine makes jewellery out of teeth,' said Ned thoughtfully.

Vicky gave him a wide stare. 'That is actually gross,' Vicky said.

Professor Stow pushed himself away from the table and carried on.

'Do you know where your friend gets them from Ned?' said Dylan.

'No, I never thought to ask.'

'Find out will you.'

Ned gave a nod of his head.

'May be of little comfort to her loved ones; she wasn't tortured. The teeth have been pulled after she died,' said Professor Stow.

'How can you be sure of that?' Vicky said.

'If she'd been tortured they would have been ripped out, we would see damage here,' he said, pointing to the cavity in the jaw bone that went through to the sinus. 'This act has been done, dare I say, professionally,' said Professor Stow.

'So the teeth came out whole do you think?'

'Oh yes, absolutely, it strikes me you have a planner here. Someone who is focused and determined.'

The room was silent as relevant samples were taken from around and inside the mouth – more photographs were taken.

The post-mortem continued to be executed and Professor Stow opened up the body with a simple scalpel blade. It was a large and deep Y-shaped incision starting at the top of each of Davina's shoulders and met at the lower part of the sternum.

The bleeding of the cut was minimal. The pull of gravity producing the only blood pressure at this point, related directly to the complete lack of cardiac functionality. Professor Stow opened up her chest cavity and sawed through her ribs on the lateral sides to allow the sternum and attached rib to be lifted out as one chest plate. He placed it to the side to be replaced at the end of the examination; this done the heart and lungs could be seen in situ. He proceeded to remove the organs in a systematic fashion and the weighing plus more detailed examinations of each organ took place. Samples in the form of slices were taken from each organ. There were no clots found in her heart. Her left lung was removed by cutting the bronchus, artery, and vein at the hilum. The right lung taken from its rightful place in the body was followed by abdominal organs which were plucked one by one. Next her stomach and intestinal contents were examined and weighed.

At the bursting of the sac to allow the stomach contents to be revealed Dylan popped a mint in his mouth. Vicky closed her eyes briefly. Jarv clicked the camera and Ned held the evidence bag open.

'This may seem unnecessary as we have a definite window of time when she died and we know the cause, but by doing this procedure we can glean more exact information by the areas in the intestines that are empty,' he said with his hand cupped under the bowel. This tells me approximately how long the deceased has gone without a meal,' said Professor Stow studiously.

The body block that was used earlier to elevate the chest cavity was moved to elevate the head so that Stow could examine the brain. An incision from behind her left ear, over the crown of her head, to a point behind her right ear, was made with precision. The scalp was pulled away from the skull in two flaps with the front flap falling over the face and the rear flap over the back of the neck. Professor Stow was handed a Stryker saw to create a cap in the skull that he pulled off to expose the brain, examining it in situ before lifting it out for further examination and weighing. In this case there was no need for Davina's brain to be preserved so the container of formalin that stood waiting on the side was not required.

The reconstruction of the body could now take place. Davina's body looked like an empty vessel; open and void of its internal organs. The chest was a casket ready for the contents to be returned. The chest flaps lay open on both sides. The top of the skull was missing, and the skull flaps were still over the face and neck.

'There is no need to examine arms, hands or legs internally,' said Professor Stow.

By this time in the examination the smell wasn't as much of a problem, standing on the cold floor with the air conditioning on constantly was. The chill went through the soles of Dylan shoes and he could feel the cold creeping up his legs and his muscles tightened. His calves ached. He knew the others felt the same as he watched them step from foot to foot and shuffle on the spot.

It was time for the team to leave Davina's body in the hands of the mortuary assistant and Dylan knew when he had finished his work, Gary would not be able to tell the procedure had been done or what Davina's body had been subject to, which was ultimately a blessing.

The team left Senior CSI Jarvis taking the final post-mortem pictures. Last of the officers to leave the room, Dylan stopped and looked back over his shoulder to see Davina's face being reconstructed. Vicky stepped back and stood with him.

'Remarkable isn't it?' he said.

'What is?' said Vicky.

'The skin on the face goes back perfectly on the skull, like a mask. Or as long as the skin is still attached at the tip of the nose it does,' said Dylan.

Cotton wool was sourced by the mortuary assistant who proceeded to pack the chest cavity. The organs were placed in a plastic bag, to prevent leakage, and they too were returned to the body before the chest flaps were closed and sewn together. The skull cap would be replaced and the body wrapped in a shroud ready for make-up to be applied to cover abrasions and bruising on Davina's face.

Post-mortems always left Dylan with a renewed impetus – if ever one was needed to catch the perpetrator of such a heinous crime.

***

Professor Stow sat behind the desk in the office. 'I can't see anything else untoward, Dylan. All the visual checks show me that Davina Walsh was a healthy young lady. It would appear the attacker, as I said in the post-mortem, used a garrotte, with a foot in her back and as she was down on the ground the attacker bit her shoulder. In my experience that is something usually more commonly seen in a sexual attack. But, we can never presume, nothing surprises me anymore, and it looks like in this case, the murderer has gone on to remove her teeth instead.'

'A fetish you think?' said Dylan.

'Who knows, as I said earlier there is no doubt in my mind the perpetrator knew exactly what they were doing. This is someone with a practical knowledge of tooth extractions. Dentist, medic? She hasn't been sexually assaulted.'

'Which leaves the mystery of the used condom that was found close by her body,' said Dylan? 'Unless it's his in which case if he is on our system we'll have him.'

'What the hell could be the motive? Teeth are his trophies perhaps?'

***

The day had been a long one, but he still needed to debrief the staff, do a press release and Davina's boyfriend needed updating. He picked up the phone to speak to the Family Liaison Officer to find their present location. PC Bullock and Gary were at his home address, Gary's station sergeant Frank Jessop was still with them, Dylan was informed.

Dylan dropped Vicky off at the police station to arrange for the officers who had been identified to work on the murder to be in the incident room within the hour for him to update them. Dylan then drove on to Spring Bank to update those present with the findings of the post-mortem. No matter how unsavoury the task was, he knew from experience, Davina's boyfriend would be on the edge, waiting for news.

44

***

Like giving the death notice there was no easy way of sharing results of a post-mortem examination to tell someone how their loved one had died. In this case it was to tell Gary how his girlfriend had been murdered.

'This is going to be hard for you to take in right now,' Dylan told Gary. 'But I want you to hear this from me, first hand and not at a later date at an inquest or a trial.'

Dylan sat opposite Gary and painstakingly he went through the details of each injury Davina had sustained. He knew he had to be open and honest, no matter how uncomfortable the conversation was. It was important that Davina's family had confidence in him, the person in charge of the investigation, so that in the future they could also trust him implicitly.

***

Back at Harrowfield Police Station the investigation team had assembled together for the first time. The drone of voices from the room could be heard by Dylan as he moved briskly along the corridor towards the incident room. The group immediately fell silent the moment he walked in.

It took an hour and a half standing at the front of approximately thirty serious-faced police personnel to outline the discovery of Davina Walsh's body and the attendant circumstances. His briefing was supported by a plethora of photographs of the body in situ and of the surrounding area that CSI Ebdon had taken. He shared with them the findings of the post-mortem of Davina's body and told them what background he knew of the deceased and her boyfriend. There were more pictures taken by CSI Sarah Jarvis. So thorough were the initial stages of the investigation, but there was only one person on the enquiry who knew as much as the perpetrator or perpetrators at this stage and that was Dylan. Dylan concluded the briefing, 'Our victim, was a young woman in the process of training for a bicycle challenge to raise funds for charity. This killer should not be underestimated; he has no doubt pre-planned this crime. This is not someone who has done this on the hoof or panicked at the scene of an accident. We need to find our murderer and we need to find them as soon as possible.'

Afterwards he spoke with Inspector Stonestreet who had been on duty since the body was discovered. 'The Anchor is a regular spot for people to drink and eat. Locals use it as well as visitors to the area. I've asked the manager to go through the till receipts, which I thought may help trace people who had been at the pub in the last forty-eight hours. I'll revisit him tomorrow when I'm back on duty and see what he has come up with for us.'

'You can take a police officer out of the CID but you can't take the investigator out of 'em,' said Dylan patting his colleague on the back. 'Thanks mate. I really appreciate it.'

Peter Stonestreet pretended to stagger away down the corridor in a comical fashion. 'By the way boss the lads got you the assortment of condoms that the pub sells from the toilets,' he said, with a salute to his brow.

It brought a smile to Dylan's tired looking face.

***

As he typed up a press release for the press office he looked at his watch. No doubt Maisy and Jen would be sound asleep in bed.

The press release was brief and to the point: The body of a female cyclist was discovered this morning on the cycle path just off Waterford Road, Harrowfield. A murder investigation is underway led by Detective Inspector Jack Dylan after her injuries are found to be non-accidental. This was followed by the usual appeal for anyone in the area, at the time, or with any information to get in contact with the incident room. The relevant direct dial and the crime stoppers numbers should anyone wish to offer information anonymously would be added by the press office.

***

When Jen hadn't heard from Dylan by nine o'clock she talked herself into having an early night. With Maisy tucked up in bed and fast asleep, Jen picked up the phone to ring her dad, Ralph, on the Isle of Wight before turning in. It was great to hear him in good spirits. Thelma's son who was staying with them, in-between his travels, had set up a window cleaning round in the village to earn money for his next big adventure and subsequently had saved the life of a pensioner when he had discovered her post-stroke and lying on her bedroom floor. It was a feel-good story for the local press and Jen felt pleased her dad was moving on with his life after her mother's untimely death.

'And I've got a little job for myself down at Sandown Pet Stores,' he said with more than a hint of a small boy's excitement in his voice.

'But you retired donkey's years ago Dad,' she said. 'How'd that come about?'

'Well,' he chuckled. 'I went in for my tropical fish food and found they'd only gone and knocked through into next door and were putting in fish tanks. As you can imagine I was overjoyed and told the owners, Paul and his wife as much. Paul asked me if I'd consider going in to help out, just a few hours a week to look after the tropical fish, and train up his staff.' Jen could see in her mind's eye, her dad smiling from ear to ear.

'That sounds like a grand job for you.'

'I know I've no certificates to say I know what I'm doing but experience is what Paul was after so he said I was his man.'

'What did you say?'

'I bit his bloody hand off. What do you think I said – and I'm getting paid too.' He chuckled again. 'I'd have done it for nothing truth be told. And it gets me out of the house.'

'Why do you need to get out the house Dad?' Jen said, a little worried. 'It's your house after all.'

'Ozzy's young and I'm not as patient as I was,' he said.

Jen hadn't met Thelma or her son and was looking forward to doing so as soon as the Dylan household could get away for a long over-due break. She looked at the clock as she got into bed and sighed. She had learnt very early in her relationship with Jack Dylan that it was no use sitting up like an outraged wife when he was on a major incident, or she could be waiting forever.

A few fireworks were popping in a neighbouring garden. 'Someone must have been having a party,' she thought. With a book in her hand Jen climbed in between the cool cotton sheets but she couldn't concentrate on reading as her eyes and ears fought for supremacy, and in the end her ears won as she listened intently for a car on the driveway or Dylan's key in the lock.

Maisy had woken three times since Jen had put her to bed. She had been irritable and clingy after tea. Jen tried to relax. Maisy had no temperature and hadn't been sick so Jen assumed she might be coming down with a viral infection, something she had been prone to since she started mixing with other children at the childminder's. Jen put her book on her bedside table, switched off the lamp and heard the dining room clock strike eleven as she lay down. She looked at the roundness of Dylan's pillow and felt its coolness with her hand. All was silent for a moment or two and Jen's heavy eyes closed only to shoot open again at the melancholy howling that quickly escalated to a clawing and spitting cat fight outside. The felines shuffled about noisily on the gravelled path for some time before someone shouted at them. Silence returned and she drifted off to sleep until a muffled cry woke her, she listened intently, Maisy was no doubt dreaming. Her thoughts turned to Dylan once more and beside her the bed was still empty.

Chapter Four

Dylan was buttoning up his shirt when Jen woke the next morning. She watched him pull his suit trousers from the clothes hanger and put a foot in a leg before he noticed she was watching him. He smiled, a tired smile. 'Everything okay?'

'Maisy was a bit off after her fall. She complained of her leg aching last night but otherwise... yeah. I made up some sandwiches. They're in the fridge next to the bottles of water ready for you. Grab a couple of bananas from the fruit bowl,' she said sleepily. 'What time did you get in?'

'Late.'

'You mean early?'

'I mean early, yes.' Dylan forced a smile.

'How was it?'

'It was tough. All the evidence points to it being a "runner". There are no obvious leads so we're concentrating on covering the ground beneath our feet and getting the incident room up and running.'

Dylan looked in on Maisy. Jen softly padded down the steps before him and put the kettle on.

'She's still sleeping,' he said as he took a bowl of cereal from her outstretched hand.

'Not surprising, she took ages to settle and was talking in her sleep.'

'Takes after her mummy...'

'I never... I did as a kid though and I used to sleep walk.'

Dylan smiled at his wife, pulled her close and kissed her forehead. 'I do love you,' he said.

***

Dylan saw few cars on the road as he travelled into work, until he got to the front of the police station. TV satellite vans lined the route, waiting for the next update.

Arriving in the backyard he looked at his watch; it was barely seven o'clock.

No sooner had he entered his office he heard the office door bang behind him and it continued banging as incident room personnel arrived for work. One of his first tasks was to prioritise samples to go to Forensic. They needed to be at the laboratory for lunchtime. Glancing at the duty sheet, staffing levels seemed reasonable and he had every intention of using the Operational Support specialist search team for the scene examination, sending a message to Sergeant Simon Clegg. He was thankful that the day was dry and bright, in complete contrast to the previous twenty-four hours.

Next Dylan listed the lines of enquiry that he wanted to cover:

1. Victims's background
2. Use of her telephone
3. Timeline for her movements over the last few days
4. Customers at the Anchor Inn to be identified and traced
5. Intelligence unit to scrutinise the national database to look for evidence of possible similarities in other murder enquiries, i.e. use of a garrotte and/or the offender removing teeth
6. Names of recent releases from prison
7. Offenders who were known to leave a condom at the scene of a crime
8. What could the experts do to identify the bite/foot mark on the body
9. Was there any traces of saliva on the clothing where the offender had bitten the victim – possible DNA?

Dylan's fingers were struggling to type quick enough to keep up with the speed of his thoughts and he knew it would be a working list of a document. He would make sure the officers on this enquiry were kept busy with meaningful enquiries – the pressure to achieve results and move on to the next action would be constant. His next job was to write up his policy log, his own bible of events and actions that he had already instructed the team to carry out. It was a laborious task now to date, time and sign every entry but he knew it would be a godsend to him at a trial.

His telephone rang with the internal tone and instinctively he thought it would be the press office but it wasn't, it was Jen. His smile on hearing her voice soon turned to a frown.

'It's Maisy,' she sobbed. 'I've just dropped her off at the childminder's and she cried, screamed, begged me not leave her. What do you think I should do?'

'That's not like her, she usually bounds in and doesn't give us a second glance. Were her friends not there?'

'Yes, Annabelle, Hermione, Cameron were all there. What worried me was Chantall noticed a small cluster of red spots on her neck. I know, I'm a drama queen. I panicked, I automatically thought it was something serious.' Jen gave a little laugh.

'And, it's not meningitis then?'

'No, Chantall was brilliant, as always. She did the usual checks, looked to see if it disappeared under pressure, and it did, so we came to the conclusion that it must be some sort of viral infection she's picked up.'

'No other symptoms?'

'No, her temperature is fine, she hasn't been sick... Oddly though she is still complaining of her leg aching. We looked but there is nothing to suggest anything's wrong.'

'So you left her?'

'If it was anyone else other than Chantall I'd have had to ring in sick and bear Beaky's wrath, but Maisy's known Chantall long enough and I know she's in safe hands. She'll sleep it off no doubt. She can have Calpol again at twelve o'clock and Chantall said she'd keep me updated but...' Jen's voice turned into a whisper. 'Why I'm ringing, Beaky, Ms Avril Summerfield-Preston, the Divisional Administrator, that God forbid MUST be obeyed is on the warpath. She's just given Rita a right rifting about taking a private call on her mobile and demanded we all turn them off.'

'Oh, for god's sake, why?'

'I don't know. Some bee in her bonnet about the noise, we actually think she's over indulged on the G and T's last night by the looks of her. I've texted Chantall to tell her to ring you. Is that okay?'

'Yes, of course.'

***

The media briefing was planned for eleven o'clock. 'Will that give the Family Liaison Officer enough time to get a recent picture of Davina from Gary for us to give it to the media present?' Dylan asked.

'Yes, a police motorcyclist is on route to HQ now with it and they will do the necessary,' said Vicky.

'Good, it should make the lunchtime news with any luck,' said Dylan. 'By the way, will you tell the team I've decided not to divulge to the media that the victim's teeth were extracted just yet.'

***

The microphones were lined up before Dylan on the far side of a long trestle table in-between him and the national media that filled the room where the press conference was to take place. Dylan took a seat offered to him by the press officer.

It was warm, humid and the feeling of anticipation hung in the air. A presenter from the community radio station caught his eye. Maggie Currie was on the front row with her Vectis Radio roving microphone. A one-to-one interview with her was on Dylan's agenda. He knew there was no way of getting news out faster to the local community than via the local station.

Behind this staged scene of police banners and reporters a structured and well-versed incident room was up and running below in the bowels of Harrowfield Police Station. The operation had been given the name Operation Walnut by headquarters. Every action or inaction was being documented and stored on the computer databases including HOLMES for easy comparison, recollection and ultimately disclosure, and the massive criminal file that would ultimately make *War and Peace* look like a pamphlet in comparison, had begun.

Not only the arena where the press conference was being held, or the incident room but the whole station was also a hive of activity. When a murder investigation broke it appeared to breathe new life into the old building as well as into the personnel within, and the whole community at large. It was that supportive drive, joint co-operation, and determination that found the killers.

To outsiders the initial stages of an investigation must seem to move forward at nothing more than a snail's pace, but the solid foundation was essential so that nothing was overlooked or discarded.

Forensic as requested had treated the examination of the condom found at the scene as a priority and on leaving the press conference Dylan was told that they had obtained a DNA profile from the contents.

'They've told me that it will be run through the National database today,' said Vicky. At this point Dylan knew that the forensic department would contact him immediately if they had a 'hit'. He could feel the adrenalin run through his veins as he walked into the next room for the one-to-one interviews with the media. If the user of that condom was recorded on the system they could potentially have a major suspect in the case in for questioning. However, Dylan also was more than aware that unless the user was known to the police the DNA profile could lie on the system waiting to be identified, ultimately forever.

'I want the samples of condoms from the Anchor Inn sending over to them. We need to check if any of those could match the exhibit,' Dylan said.

***

Dylan sat at his desk, pen in hand, coffee in front of him, willing the phone to ring and it did but not with the news he had expected.

'Why the hell didn't you answer your mobile? You promised me! It's Maisy ...' Jen screamed.

'What? I didn't turn it off. It was on silent... I was in the press conf...' Dylan pulled his mobile from his pocket. It showed him over a dozen missed calls.

'Get out of my way!' shouted Jen. Dylan heard someone in the background swear.

'What the hell's going on?'

'I bumped into... Shit! Sorry.' Dylan could hear mumbled angry voices, the clatter of crockery and then the pitter-patter of Jen's hurried footsteps continue on a hard floor surface.

'Where are you?' he said trying to stay calm. His heart beat fast, his mouth dry.

'I've just arrived at A and E...' Jen's voice was shaky. She was breathless. 'Where will they be?' she muttered under her breath?

'Where will who?'

'Maisy and Chantall!'

'Head for the reception. I'll be with you soon as soon as I can,' he said scooping his car keys from his desk drawer.

'Boss?' Vicky stood up with a quizzical frown upon her face as Dylan rushed through the office, towards the exit.

'Maisy's in hospital. You're going to have to hold the fort until I know what's happening.'

'But, but... What do you want me to do?' she shouted at the retreating Dylan. The door banged behind him.

The office came to a standstill, some people mumbled a few words to the person closest to them. 'I know as much as you,' she snapped with eyes wide. 'Get back to work.'

***

It was lunchtime. Chantall heard hurried, heavy footsteps come to a standstill behind her in the corridor; she turned, her red-rimmed eyes flashed upwards and found Dylan's cold and blue. He could see that unchecked tears had fallen on her silk blouse and dried upon her face. He put an arm around her shoulder and heard a faint crackling sound. She handed him a piece of paper. 'Poor baby...' she sobbed.

'What happened?' he said. His eyes scanned the detailed account of the mornings' events.

'The doctor is examining her. We have to wait here. Jen is with her. I tried to get hold of you, honestly I did. When I couldn't, I thought it best to bring her straight here.' Dylan looked through the half glass door of the small examination room. Periodically the curtain flashed open for a moment and he caught glimpses of the back of a tall man in dark green attire.

'She wasn't herself, the rash, it started to spread to her shoulders but, the rest of her body was fine. Her temperature was 37.5 when Jen left her with me and although it was a little high it wasn't too worrying since she looked a little under the weather. What worried me was her lethargy. I rang you to ask you what you wanted me to do but when you didn't pick up I made her a bed in the playroom, so I could keep an eye on her. When she started to shake I covered her with a blanket. I rang you again. I've looked after poorly children before, but this was very different. Maisy felt cold and clammy and the shaking got worse, so much so that I was worried she might have a fit. I tried to call you again and again. When you didn't answer I did another top to toe check. The rash was unchanged, her hands and feet were like ice but her temperature had risen. I rang you again. I panicked, so I rang Jen at the police station and they put me through to the admin office. I know Jen said to ring you but I'm sorry, I didn't know what else to do ... Her meds... The Calpol wasn't due for another forty minutes you see...' A sob caught in her throat as fresh tears trickled down her cheek. 'The lady I spoke to, Avril, Jen's boss? She told me Jen was in a meeting, she didn't know how long she would be and I had to ring back. What a horrible woman... Oh, God I hope I haven't got her into trouble?'

Dylan shook his head. 'No, no, not at all.'

'I tried Jen again about ten minutes later and luckily this time I got another lady who got Jen straight away. I can't believe it's got to this after a couple of hours...'

'What have the doctors said?'

'Nothing... They're still doing tests.'

'Go home. There is nothing more you can do here. I will ring you the minute we have any news I promise.'

'You sure?'

Dylan nodded his head.

Chantall turned to go.

Dylan grabbed her arm. 'I... we can't thank you enough for what you've done,' he said with tears in his eyes.

Dylan knocked on the door, put his hand on the handle and opened it slowly. The nurse appeared from behind the curtain.

Her white, leather plimsolls made no sound as she softly walked towards him.

'I just hope and pray it was enough,' Chantall whispered into the tissue as she walked a few steps down the corridor. All of a sudden she felt dizzy and sick. She stood facing the wall, her burning forehead touched the cold surface, her hands twisted the tissue she held in her hand, but she made no sound and the hospital inhabitants walked past her unseeingly.

Jen sat close to the bed. She looked to Dylan as if she had been there for hours; upright, solid and still. Dylan put her hand on her shoulder but she didn't acknowledge him. 'I'm Maisy's dad,' Dylan said to the doctor in a hushed tone. The doctor had a high, bald forehead and staring eyes in a face with a complexion the colour of raw meat.

'Mr Dylan,' he said with a nod of his head.

Maisy was shaking violently. 'Temp forty point one,' said the nurse to the doctor.

The doctor had a puzzled look on his greasy face as he examined Maisy's leg that had begun to swell. 'Toxic shock,' he said, abruptly.

Jen looked up at him. 'She fell yesterday... I kissed it better and sent her back to play,' Jen stuttered and began to weep again, quietly. 'Bless her,' she said, stroking her small flaccid hand that lay on the bed sheet. The sun suddenly shone through the window and rested on Maisy's pale, serene face.

'This little graze here,' he said pointing to a tiny mark on her knee with one forefinger and a mechanical grimace, 'is probably how the virus got into her bloodstream and Maisy appears to be having an allergic reaction to it. You have a very poorly little girl. I'm going to arrange to have her taken down to the operating theatre immediately to drain the toxins from her blood.'

Jen reached out to her daughter and stroked to one side the fine strands of damp hair that were stuck to her forehead.

'I want samples sent to infectious diseases for analysis,' he said the nurse who made notes. Then he turned to Dylan and Jen, 'We won't have the results back for at least forty-eight hours,' he said. 'In the meantime we will put her on antibiotics. Is she allergic to penicillin?'

Jen shook her head. 'I've no idea,' she said. She looked at Dylan.

'She's never had to take anything like that before,' he said.

The doctor was thoughtful, he looked at Maisy and then back at Dylan. 'We have to make a decision and quickly.'

'Do whatever you need to,' he said. Reassuringly he gripped Jen's shoulder and looked at the doctor with disbelieving eyes.

Jen's hand lay on the pillow next to her daughter's face, her wedding ring shone in the sunlight on her long, slender finger. She lifted it and touched Maisy's cheek, stroking it intermittently, and her touch was featherlight.

'We need to get her temperature down,' said the doctor. His face was sombre and Dylan recognised the adorning of his 'professional mask'. A 'mask' that Dylan himself used when delivering bad news. A sob caught in his throat but he nodded at Jen's upturned face and hoped that his 'professional mask' fooled his wife in her moment of need.

Jen eyes were fixed on the hospital gown that rose and fell gently with every breath Maisy took and Dylan watched Jen as fresh tears tumbled periodically down her face. The nurse offered her a box of tissues and she accepted it with a wan smile.

***

Detective Sergeant Rajinder Uppal walked into the incident room and Detective Sergeant Vicky Hardacre who was new to the role of supervisor was uncharacteristically silent; it was such a pleasant shock it left her speechless. 'Thank God,' she said silently. Dylan hadn't returned and the pressure was building as actions flooded in. Whether Dylan had arranged Rajinder's attendance or there really had been some divine intervention Vicky might never know but the relief that flooded over her was immeasurable.

Raj gave Vicky a knowing smile when she saw the younger woman's face and the smile reached her big brown eyes. Raj was a bit older than Vicky and had considerably more experience in the role, and Vicky had been lucky enough to work with her on previous enquiries. There would be none of that awkwardness, none of the 'getting to know you' and it was a good job as DS

Raj, as she was affectionately known, senior Detective Sergeant seconded on this enquiry, was going to have to hit the ground running and take ultimate charge, in the absence of Dylan.

Raj's shoulder length hair was tied up in a neat knot; a stark contrast to Vicky's blonde, wild mane. She sported a slight olive tone to her skin as opposed to Vicky's fairness, and although she was Indian she could easily be taken for being of Mediterranean origin.

'Lisa, Raj can have the desk next to mine – it's free,' Vicky said as she jumped to her feet and wheeled over a nearby vacant chair. Leaning over the work station she briskly swept the contents into the middle of her desk; the only free space available. Several discarded, dirty mugs were swiftly moved by the younger of the women to the top of the filing cabinet behind and the remaining disregarded stationery was finally scooped up and thrown into Vicky's overflowing drawer.

'I see you haven't changed,' said Raj, putting her briefcase down next to her chair. She took off her suit jacket, walked to the coat stand at the far end of the office and took a duster out of her bag.

The office personnel looked on as she very deliberately unfolded the duster and wiped the desk. Vicky saw her take a new notepad, pen, mug, blotter and desk tidy out of her bag and place them neatly on her desk alongside a pile of post-it-notes in different colours and sizes.

'Lists, she loves lists,' Vicky whispered to Lisa. 'Nor have you,' Vicky said louder this time and with an eyebrow raised. 'You ready to hear the facts?'

'I've read the facts,' said Raj.

Raj sat down, crossed her legs and opened her notepad. Accepted a cup of tea from Lisa, picked up her pen and turned her attention to Vicky. 'Right where are we at kid?' she said. 'And have we heard from Dylan how his daughter is?'

***

Maisy was dressed for theatre. There was an agonising silence. The consent forms that Dylan had signed lay on top of her hospital file. Her body looked tiny enveloped in the bed with its

58

cot sides up. Although it was a nice gesture, the characterised Princess trolley was lost on Maisy, who was thankfully fast asleep and unaware of what was happening. Jen stood, holding onto her daughter's limp hand. Jen's heart hammered against her chest. The nurse checked Maisy's hospital wristband, and that her drip was stable. She nodded her head when the porter arrived before once more flicking through the paperwork in her arms. Jen felt sick, faint, she looked at Dylan's face for reassurance but all she saw the mask of the detective.

'Can I go with them?' Dylan asked.

'Sorry,' said the doctor. 'We can only allow one person to go with her.'

The nurse walked in front. Jen clung to the cot side. The porter pushed Maisy along the corridors. Each time they turned a corner the next looked exactly the same. They were all long, They were all mostly empty. However, when they encountered people they invariably moved to the side to let them pass. Jen looked down at the floor to avoid the sympathetic looks. She couldn't bear to see the compassionate faces. The floor covering was highly polished. Her heels pitter-pattered. The echo bouncing off the stark white, glossy walls. The hospital was terribly warm and Jen was thankful for the breeze of cool air from a door opening to the outside world. Down in the lift, through the bowels of the old building they buffered their way through the tightly sprung doors before finally arriving at their destination. Silently Jen, alongside her sleeping daughter, stood in a room with no windows and two doors. A masked anaesthetist awaited them, he didn't speak but immediately got on with the job he was tasked to do. A member of the theatre staff jovially exchanged pleasantries with nurse. The porter left. One side of Maisy's cot was dropped unceremoniously. The noise was loud to Jen's ears. She looked at Maisy with horror in her eyes. Please don't let her wake up in this place, she thought. The anaesthetist was busily putting plastic pads in place to monitor the sleeping child.

'Has she any allergies' he said as the surgically clad theatre staff member took the patient's notes from the nurse and checked Maisy's wristband against the notes.

'Not that we're aware of, no,' said Jen quietly.

'Is she on any prescribed medicines?'

'Only the medicines that she has been given whilst she has been here but she did have a dose of Calpol about eight o'clock this morning.' The anaesthetist dismissed this interaction without a look but a wave of his hand. Jen's voice was shaking and the nurse looked at her through thick brown eyelashes. Touching her arm she gave her a comforting little smile.

'We won't be administering Maisy with the anaesthetic until she is in theatre, through the cannula that is already in place,' said the anaesthetist to Jen.

As Jen was steered out of the room by the nurse Maisy was pushed through the swinging doors of theatre. Jen turned to the nurse and sobbed into her open arms as though her heart would break.

'Try not to worry. Maisy is in excellent hands Mrs Dylan,' said the nurse as she gave her a squeeze. 'It's likely she will go into Intensive Care after she leaves Recovery and I will be the one taking her there.'

'When will we be able to see her?'

'You will see her as soon as we have her settled.'

***

Dylan was on the phone to the incident room. The nurse and Jen arrived back in the examination room where they were told to wait until they had news that Maisy was out of theatre. The nurse closed the door behind her. Dylan walked over and held Jen's hands in his. She sat on one chair, he sat on the other, she reached for Maisy's teddy on the bedside cabinet and held it to her face, inhaling the comforting smell of home. There was a huge bed sized void in front of them.

Dylan's voice seemed to bounce off the walls as if he was in an empty cave. Jen looked around for something to read, there was nothing, no newspapers, no magazines, nothing on the walls. He eventually turned off his mobile. 'Okay?' he said. Jen nodded.

'I have to make a few calls,' he said. Jen closed her eyes momentarily and shrugged her shoulders. 'Jen, I have to do something. I'm going out of my mind with worry too for God's sake.' He got up and stepped outside into the corridor and the door remained slightly ajar. She heard his voice growing quieter and quieter as he walked away. The only sound Jen could hear after a while was the rustling of paper under the cushion of her chair when she changed her seating position. Dylan didn't return. Her eyes hung on the hands of the clock on the wall yearning to hear footsteps along the corridor that would enter the room. She began to wish Dylan had not left her alone but neither did she want to leave the room to look for him in case the doctor returned. Surely Dylan would be back soon?

Eventually the nurse returned and it was obvious to Jen that Dylan had been watching from a distance as within moments he followed her into the room. He closed the door behind him.

'I'm taking you to Intensive Care Unit where Maisy is now comfortable. The doctor will come see you,' she said. 'Maisy is being administered antibiotics. Don't be alarmed by the tubes, wires and cables, it's our way of monitoring her. You may also hear alarms and bleeps in Intensive Care which again are nothing to worry about in most cases. If you are unsure about anything there are always specialist nurses and doctors on hand to answer your questions. Don't be afraid to ask. Most of the patients in ICU are asleep because they're more than likely on painkillers or sedatives which make them drowsy.'

Jen walked alongside the nurse, Dylan behind. He checked his phone.

'Is everything okay?' said the nurse. 'Your husband...?'

'He's heading a murder enquiry.'

'A murder enquiry?'

'Yes.'

'My goodness, as if he doesn't have enough on his plate.'

The nurse held the door of ICU open for Jen and Dylan. The walls in the ward were too white, too shiny, the beds were aligned too neatly, the beeping of the monitors too regular, the sheets too starched. Even the sun shining through the window was not enough to soften the harsh, sterile practicality of the room. The doctor who was by her side looked up at Dylan and Jen. 'The operation went as well as could be expected.' Jen let out a sigh of relief. Dylan put his hand around her waist and she wiped the tears from her eyes.

'How long will she stay in here?' Jen said.

'As long as we feel it necessary. We need to stabilise her, her temperature still remains higher than we would like so, until that time we want to keep a close eye on your daughter.'

'Can I stay?'

'Of course,' said the nurse. 'We have a room where you can sleep or we can bring you a chair to sleep at her bedside.'

Unspeaking, Dylan and Jen sat either side of their daughter. Jen could see tears in Dylan's downcast eyes. She slid her small warm hand on top of his.

'You should go home and rest,' said Dylan.

'No, you go home and see to Max, he'll be crossing his legs bless him,' said Jen. 'I want to stay here...'

'You heard the doctor they're going to monitor her. There is nothing we can do.'

Jen shook her head. 'I'm not going anywhere.'

'Okay, if you don't want to leave her alone I'll stay. After all I'm used to being awake all night.'

Jen sat back in her chair and crossed her arms. Dylan could see in her eyes that there was no way his wife would be leaving the hospital that night.

'You sure, you're okay?' said Dylan as stood up to leave. She walked him to the door. 'She's going to be fine now. Look,' he said raising his chin to look at Maisy over Jen's shoulder. 'Her colour is coming back already. She's a little fighter.' Dylan gave Jen a hug. He pulled back and looked into her face, caught a lone tear that had broken free of her closed eyes and kissed her. Her face crumpled.

'The last time I was in ICU was after mum's accident.' Jen inhaled sharply as her bottom lip wobbled. 'They told me she'd be okay then and... She died.'

'That is not going to happen this time.'

Jen gulped back the tears.

'Ring me if you need anything.' Dylan handed Jen his handkerchief.

Jen nodded her head and wiped her eyes. She breathed in deeply. 'Yes, yes, I'm fine,' she said giving him a weak smile.

Dylan walked out of ICU reluctantly alone, he looked back twice and saw Jen watching him from the head-high small window in the door. It was at times like these that he knew Jen desperately missed her mum and no matter what he did that was one wish he couldn't grant her but, he knew something that would make her feel a whole lot better. He put his hand in his pocket and looked at the list of missed calls as he walked down the hospital corridor. But, there was something he needed to do first – call Jen's dad Ralph.

***

A sharp, shrill ring pierced the silence. Dylan woke with a jolt in his armchair. Too damn early was how his brain interpreted the neon-green digital numbers on the clock. He swiped a hand roughly over his face; the stubble lining his jaw rasped softly on the palm of one hand and he picked the phone up with the other.

'Hello,' he said.

'Dylan?'

'It is.' Dylan's mouth was extraordinarily dry. He looked at the empty wine bottle and the glass on the table at his side.

'Control Room sir, we've got a body. I'll ring you back when you're awake.' The phone went dead and Dylan held it away from his ear, looked down at the hand piece and growled. He flopped backwards only to feel his heart beating furiously in his chest. 'Who do you think answered the bloody phone?' Dylan said, through clenched teeth.

***

By the time he had begun to feel fully awake Dylan found himself standing on a dark, draughty street corner in Harrowfield town centre. He looked up to the name of the street on the soot stained brick wall of the Council offices. The blue flashing lights lit it up for him to read. 'Viaduct Street'. A Dragon Lamp was being set up by the Crime Scene Investigators a sure sign the circus had already arrived. He opened his car boot, took out his coveralls and booted and suited was putting on his gloves when Vicky arrived.

'How's Maisy?' she said as she walked towards the inner scene cordon with him.

'The operation went well, we're told,' he said.

'And Jen?'

'At the hospital, she's sleeping there.'

'And this morning?'

'A little early to ring don't you think?' he said, looking at his watch. He stood, sallow and solid looking at her with dull, blue eyes, his face impassive.

His attention turned to DS Rajinder Uppal immediately they caught up with her. 'It's good of Calderdale Division to let you come quickly,' he said. 'Glad to have you on board. You know Vicky, that's a bonus. Have you got an update for me?'

'What do you already know, sir?'

'Brief circumstances as you'd expect from a call out by the Control Room in the middle of the night.'

'Okay, so we've got a body of a young lad, approximately twenty years old. It appears he may have been in a fight or he could have been robbed,' she said. 'He has a serious depressed head injury which is consistent with him being hit with force, by a hard object. Paramedics have pronounced him dead at the scene and his body is still in situ. The outer cordon is being sealed at this moment,' she said pointing to the hive of activity before them.

'How was it reported?' said Vicky.

'Key-holder from Mushies rang it in – we've established that he was the last to leave the nightclub,' said Raj.

'Mushies? Why on earth would anyone give a night club a street name for drugs?' said Vicky.

'Magic Mushrooms,' said Raj with the raising of her eyebrows. 'What time do they close?'

'Oi Andy, what time does Mushie's turf them out?' Vicky shouted across to Andy Wormald who stood at the open rear doors of the CSI van.

'About twoish,' he said struggling into the small sized disposable suit CSI had provided.

'Haven't you got any bigger sizes?' he said.

'Sorry, that's all we have left mate,' said Stuart, digging deep into a CSI holdall.

Andy discarded his jacket and took off his tie. Coverall pulled up over his head he looked like someone had inflated him.

'Bloody hell,' he said with a groan as he bent down to enter the cordon and the suit split under his legs. He stood up directly and faced Dylan and the two women.

Dylan's eyes, that showed above his mask lost their flatness and crinkled at the sides. 'Go to the boot of my car, there's some large disposable suits in a carrier bag to the left hand side.' He looked back at the DS's. 'I guess there's little else open at this time of night, morning, around here, to attract the punters, apart from the nightclub?'

'There is the China House Chinese take-away and Park and Ride Taxis,' said Vicky.

'I guess,' he said, his nose now more sensitive to the smell oozing from the Indian takeaway a street away.

'We're lucky Stonestreet's team are on duty,' said Vicky.

'I think you mean Inspector Stonestreet is the duty inspector?' said Dylan.

'I just said that didn't I?' she said with a quizzical frown.

'You might try, but you'll never change her,' said Raj with a sigh and a shake of her head.

'I know,' he said.

There was a deep depression in the victim's skull. His mouth was open, swollen and bloodied. An open wallet lay a few yards away, propped up against a low, red brick wall. Across the pathway was a heavy metal pole that looked like a piece of scaffolding.

'Discarded murder weapon maybe?' said Raj.

'More than likely,' said Dylan.

'Robbery seems like the obvious motive to me,' said Vicky.

Raj screwed up her eyes. 'Yes, but there is still money in it.'

'Maybe whoever did it got disturbed, threw away the weapon and the wallet and legged it,' said Vicky.

'Any CCTV about that we know of?' Dylan said.

'The database is being checked,' said Andy who had just returned suitably suited and booted. 'The nightclub doesn't appear to have had their CCTV on out front.'

'No surprise there then? Let's face it that would record the fact they had underage drinkers in, and cut down half of their trade,' said Vicky. 'They're not bloody daft.'

'And the rest it could be recording,' said Dylan. 'I want a picture of the wallet in situ.'

'No problem,' said on duty CSI Supervisor Karen Ebdon, who had been busily and quietly snapping away in the background.

The wallet photographed, Karen picked it up in between her finger and thumb and carefully opened it. 'The wallet belongs to a Carl Braithwaite, twenty-two years old and he lives locally at 26, Moorlands Road. If he's known to us we'll have an ident,' she said.

'Good, when you've finished here, let me know. I want him to go straight to the mortuary.'

'Joy, another post-mortem to look forward to tomorrow,' said Vicky.

'Today hopefully,' said Dylan. 'We'll need some of that scaffolding pipe at the mortuary for comparison of size and shape of the wound. We also need to know who Mr Braithwaite lives with. Check the Burgess Roll. We'll have to go and break the news to his family. Once the body is away I want you to head back and look at the resources we can draw from, the officers working today and not those on Operation Walnut if at all possible. Andy, I want you to follow the body to the mortuary for continuity will you and then everyone, we'll reconvene back at the office for a scrum down later.'

As they were walking away from the scene Dylan's phone rang. 'Jen?' he said.

'Where are you? I've been calling home,' she said.

'I've picked up another murder.'

'Maisy is allergic to penicillin and the doctors are telling me that if they can't get the meds right Maisy might lose her leg.'

'Oh my God, I'm on my way,' he said turning round into Vicky who was standing right behind him.

'What's up?'

'Maisy's serious,' he said. 'I've got to go. Just do what I've said. You two are more than capable of spinning the plates. I'll be back as soon as I can.'

'Do you want us to inform HQ and get another SIO?' shouted Vicky.

'Don't you dare, not yet!' shouted Dylan as he ran backwards towards his car. 'We can do this. I have every faith in you.'

From beside the bed where Maisy lay desperately ill Jen looked up at Dylan with hooded eyes that held no focus. Her face was contorted; her fingers pale where knuckles stretched skin as she clung to Maisy's soft toy upon her knee. Dylan felt wretched and helpless as he watched the medical team prepare their daughter for a second operation to remove the infected tissue.

Maisy was wheeled out of ICU quickly this time with no fuss or delay. Dylan enveloped Jen in his arms and held her tightly as the doors closed behind her. She sobbed uncontrollably, her nails digging deep into Dylan's arms. The second banging of the door made her open her eyes. She blinked away her tears once, then twice, pulled back from Dylan, wiped the tears from her wet cheek. Dylan let her go and turned to see what she was looking at over his shoulder that had rendered her silent, to see Ralph, Jen's dad standing at the door. Jen unbelieving looked at Dylan, then at Ralph and moved quickly across the room as if gliding and into her dad's open arms. Ralph soothed her like Dylan imagined he would have done as a child.

'Shh... she's going to be okay,' he said. 'Don't cry... we've got to be strong for Maisy.'

'Dad you shouldn't have travelled all this way.'

Dylan and Ralph exchanged glances. Dylan looked sheepish.

'You rang him didn't you?' she said to Dylan.

He nodded.

'But Dad...'

'But nothing. Tell me who's going to look after Max if you and Dylan need to be here?' he said. 'Thelma's son is home so she'll not be missing me and there is nowhere else I want to be than with my girls right now.'

'Thanks,' said Dylan. 'I really appreciate.'

'What are dads for?' said Ralph.

***

Tension was building in the CID office. 'He's on the system Raj,' said Vicky with a note of excitement in her voice. 'Cautioned for possession of cannabis two years ago,' she read from the computer screen. 'But other than that we've no more intel on him.'

'Electoral List shows an Albert Braithwaite, Ivy Braithwaite and Carl Braithwaite living at the address,' said Raj.

'Another family's lives destroyed and we've got to go tell them. Dylan's not here to deliver it... It's up to us,' Vicky said with a look of angst on her face.

'I know a retired police officer who went to work for Camelot, the lottery people. Her job is now handing over the cheque to the lucky winners, in a variety of exotic locations. How's about that for a job that gives job satisfaction?' said Raj.

'That's one knock at my door I wouldn't mind,' she said.

'But you and I are realists aren't we? So we will roll our sleeves up and get on with it shall we? Do you want me to break the news?'

'Will you? Dylan will not be happy he can't do this himself. Well I mean...'

'Don't worry, I know what you mean but his family comes first Vicky. Remember that. Family must always come first...'

***

Mr and Mrs Brathwaite sat on the sofa in their towelling dressing gowns, hand in hand. They looked at the two CID officers expectantly.

'It's Carl isn't it?' said Mrs Braithwaite.

Raj nodded and looked down preparing herself to break the news and outline the circumstances of their son's death. Initially the couple were calm and appeared stilted, even accepting but experience told the police officers they were in shock. Ivy Braithwaite's lip trembled, she brought both hands up over her pale lips and closed her eyes. Her whole body appeared to sag and as her shaking hands slipped down to her chest she gasped. Tears spilled from the corner of the father's grey watery eyes. He had a way of sniffing as though he suffered from nasal catarrh; his voice was monotone when he eventually spoke.

'He was nothing but a lad...' Mr Braithwaite pointed to a framed photo of handsome young man on the sideboard. 'Even

68

as a nipper Carl was always smiling... We've only just stopped listening for his key in the door before we go to sleep.'

'You might have,' whispered Carl's mother.

'We will need you to come to the mortuary and identify your son,' said DS Raj.

Albert Braithwaite nodded his head. His mouth was open but no words came out.

'Is there anyone we can contact for you? There will be a Family Liaison Officer coming to see you. They will be able to answer all your questions and will support you. In the meantime if you are sure there is nothing we can do, here's my card with my contact details on,' Raj said handing it to Albert Braithwaite, who took it from her with a shaking hand.

***

Harrowfield was waking up.

The press release had gone out from the press office and a police spokesman said:

'Officers were called to Viaduct Street at around two a.m. The body of a man was discovered. Officers remain at the scene and inquiries are continuing. Anybody with any information should call the police on 101.'

The incident room for the murder of Carl Braithwaite was being set up, at a pace. Raj and Vicky knew that this needed to be done as a matter of urgency to support the various strategic approaches that would follow.

The investigation needed to be kept separate from the Davina Walsh murder. Each incident was given a unique name so that they could not be mistaken for another.

The team now in attendance waited for the Braithwaite murder's operational name to be allocated by HQ.

***

Ralph Jones pulled a face at his daughter. 'Has Dylan got a problem?' he said in a whisper.

Maisy had been removed to a side ward and was off ICU, much to her parents' and grandfather's relief.

The three had been sitting around Maisy's bed waiting for her to wake for what seemed like hours. Frequently Dylan would jump at his phone vibrating and he would excuse himself.

Jen smiled despite their predicament and her tiredness.

'No dad, he's picked up another murder, that's why he keeps nipping out to get the updates from his team,' she said just as Maisy opened her eyes.

'Ah,' he said. 'I thought he was a bit young to have bladder trouble.' Ralph smiled at Maisy and she scowled. Her bottom lip out she moaned. 'I'll go and get us a drink shall I?'

'If you must. I'm awash with tea,' Jen said, not taking her eyes off her daughter's face. 'Hello sweetie, how are you feeling,' she said.

Chapter Five

In the foyer of the hospital Dylan was talking in hushed tones. 'Thank you for ringing me back Detective Inspector Dylan,' Beryl from Forensic said. 'I have good news for you. I've a hit on the system for Operation Walnut.'

'Let me just... get a pen and paper, I'm... at the hospital,' he said feverishly feeling in the inside pocket of his jacket for his notebook and pen. Back to the wall he leant his notebook on the door jamb. 'Go ahead.'

'On the system for the first, and indeed the only time, last year Roger Briggs appears for a drink-drive offence.'

'Can you email me his reference number and any other details you might have?'

'Of course.'

'Have I ever told you, you're one amazing woman Miss Knight?' he said.

Dylan put his phone back in his pocket and turned around to face Ralph who was standing directly behind him.

'Who's this Miss Knight then lad?' he said. Dylan looked at him with his lips tightly pressed together. 'Just in case you wished to know, your daughter... remember your daughter Maisy? Well, she's just woken up from the anaesthetic.'

Dylan set off quickly and pushed past his father-in-law. Maisy was awake? He had to get to her.

He walked hurriedly past a doctor and a nurse who appeared to be swapping notes; brushed past a patient being pushed along the corridor in a wheelchair and zig zagged in-between two food trollies that held the patients' tea.

Maisy had nodded back to sleep when he went into the ward but she looked peaceful. Jen was holding her hand but her head was laid on the bed, her eyes were closed. Dylan watched from the doorway for a moment or two not wanting to break the peace of the scene after the trauma they had suffered in the last forty-eight hours. Jen must have sensed a presence as she raised her head slowly, opened her eyes and focused on his face. She smiled broadly. 'The results are in,' she said, waving a piece of paper; then sighed with relief. 'The virus that caused the toxic shock was streptococcus A.'

Dylan walked towards them. Bent down and kissed Maisy's forehead. 'The common cold?' he said. With a puzzled expression he tilted his head towards Jen.

'Yes, It appears Maisy is allergic to it. However the operation was successful and now they know what they are dealing with she'll remain on antibiotics via the intravenous drip for a while, but she's out of the woods.'

Dylan put a hand to her daughter's head and held it there for a moment or two. He could no longer hold back the tears that found their way from the corners of his eyes. 'She's not going to lose her leg?'

'She is not going to lose her leg. Her temperature has already stabilised,' Jen said. She looked questioningly at the notebook Dylan held in his hand.

'News from Forensic,' he said. 'We've a hit on Operation Walnut.'

'You'd better get going.'

Dylan bent down and kissed Jen on the top of her head. 'You know I love you both more than anything...'

'I know you do. If I was in need of an SIO right now there is no one else I'd rather have on my side,' she said tiredly. 'Go, go,' she said waving him away. 'I'll keep you updated.'

Dylan smiled down at his wife and bent down for a kiss. Jen kissed him on the lips and pulled playfully at his tie, holding it firm for one more.

'Not the green one?' she said, with a frown. 'Whilst the cat's away the mouse wears his old ties.'

'I'm going to a post-mortem I don't think they will really care at the mortuary what tie I am wearing,' he said.

'I care,' she said. Dylan backed out of the room towards the door and blew her a kiss.

'Keep me updated,' he said. At that moment Ralph appeared, head down, carrying two cups of tea.

'Hey, steady on,' he said as Dylan walked into his path. 'Where's the bloody fire?'

The tea slopped over into the saucers. 'I suppose you'll want one now you're here,' he said putting the drinks down on the bedside unit. He mopped the overspill with a tissue. 'I'll go and get you one,' he sighed gruffly as he handed Jen her cup and saucer.

'No, not for me thanks,' Dylan said. 'I've got to go, look after them both for me.'

Ralph's jawline twitched. 'And I thought you were different... You're all the same you bloody coppers...'

'Dad?' Jen said with a frown. 'What's that about?'

'Him, he's no different from that other policeman you were in love with... that Shaun Turner,' he said.

Jen looked puzzled.

'He heard me on the phone to Beryl,' Dylan said.

Jen smiled at Dylan. 'Beryl... ah, yes, Miss Knight – the other woman?' Dylan was pleased to see Jen raise a smile.

'You'd better not keep her waiting,' she said, her face now showing no emotion. She shook her head slowly from side to side and tutted.

'That's it? Do you mean you're just letting him ... I don't know how you put up with...' Dylan heard Ralph chuntering as he walked down the corridor.

Jen turned to Ralph. 'Sit down; here beside me,' she said tapping the chair next to her. Jen's dad sat beside her and she turned to face him. 'Dylan,' she said, 'is hurting just as much as we are.' She took his aged hand in hers. 'You might think I should be screaming and shouting at him, but really? You know me better than that Dad. I have to accept that he is married to his job as well as to me and I do.'

'But, I heard him telling another woman she was amazing. Your mother... she would never have put up with that.'

'His "other woman" is the job dad. It's not other women that take Dylan away from us. You can't simply take time out whilst you're heading a murder enquiry – the murderer will never be caught and what's more others may end up dead.'

Ralph lowered his head.

'I appreciate what you're saying Dad, really I do. Don't think I don't have tantrums, sometimes, especially when I'm tired. But I know beyond doubt that Dylan loves me and Maisy, and I also know how difficult his job is. That is not going to change until he retires and I have to accept that. Anyway talking of other women, how're things with you?'

***

'Thank you God for Jen, Maisy, the doctors and Beryl!' Dylan said, looking up to the bright blue sky. The cold breeze that hit him was welcomed. He was overtaken by a wave of emotion and it gave him a lump in his throat. He walked out of the hospital and towards the car park. For an instant he couldn't remember where he had parked his car. Tears blurred his eyes. He stood, then it came to him and he turned left and headed directly up a pathway. The vehicles swam in front of his eyes. He had a strange feeling that the cars, the hospital, the people were nothing more than an illusion, dream figures. He touched his face, it felt wet. He was crying.

By the time he had reached the Sibden Valley his heart felt lighter. The grass appeared greener. He could see the children playing on the swings in Sibden Park, from the road. The boats were on the lake, dogs were running. What was life all about? He sat and stared at the traffic light that was at red. A moment later there was a blare of car horns that broke his reverie. Dylan waved his hand, an apology to the driver behind, and carried on.

Dylan's mind was on ensuring that the Braithwaite murder had got off the ground and the post-mortem of Carl Braithwaite was arranged. But part of him also wanted to know everything about Briggs and to ensure he was well and truly locked up. The adrenalin might have kicked in but he also knew that only fools rushed in.

***

Dylan caught a glimpse of Vicky entering the incident room and waved her over.

'You're back?' she said with a smile on her face. 'How's Maisy?'

'She's going to be okay,' he said with a huge sigh of relief. Dylan's shirt collar was opened his tie drawn down. He needed a shave.

'Thank goodness. And Jen?'

'She's good. Come into my office will you? Shut the door behind you,' he said sliding into his old leather chair behind his desk. He turned on his computer, input his password and pressed a few keys.

'The Braithwaite incident room is up and running. DS Raj has taken charge. Andy, DC Wormald is working with her and the HOLMES team are up and running – staffing levels are getting there – it's all good. We've got PC Michelle Mitchell as Family Liason Officer. I'm sure Raj will update you thoroughly, as soon as. The post-mortem is later today.' Vicky fidgeted, she spoke quickly.

'Yes, I'll speak to Raj afterwards. So, you're staying on Operation Walnut with Ned, DC Granger is exhibits and the incident team remain the same,' he said without taking his eyes off the computer screen. Dylan's face was grey and drawn but the hunger to catch up on developments on the enquiries was tangible.

Vicky nodded, 'Yes.'

Dylan's face was expressionless. She sat for a moment and watched him read the computer screen.

'Good,' he said turning to her.

'What is?'

'For a start we have an identification, off the DNA database, for the contents of our condom at the Davina Walsh murder scene. Beryl Knight from Forensic rang me at the hospital and has sent over details on email.' He turned the screen to face her.

'Really?' she said her eyes wide. 'Some pervert we know?'

Dylan raised an eyebrow.

'Well, it must be for us to have a hit so quickly,' said Vicky.

'They call him Roger Briggs, he's forty-two years old, his Criminal Records Number is 197/5366 and his PNC Nominal 562231. I want to know all about him. Every little bit of intel we have on him. And I want you to keep this under your hat for now.'

'You're joking aren't you? You know what it's like in an incident room, if they get wind of me checking a suspect out it'll be around the station quicker than a dose of salts!'

'I know and that's why I want you to do this for me. If we can keep it close to our chests until we have more information... then we'll spill the beans together.'

Vicky gave him a lop-sided smile.

'Oh, and Vicky,' he said as she put her hand on the door. She turned to face him.

'Yeah.'

'Thanks for keeping the plates spinning with Raj whilst I was at the hospital, I really appreciate it, you did good kid.'

Dylan thought he saw a slight blush to her cheeks. 'Oh shucks, thanks boss. That means a lot. But let's face it, it's better the devil you know rather than working with a jerk of an SIO who doesn't have as much service as I do,' she said with a wink.

She turned to leave. Dylan shook his head. 'And Sarg.'

'Yes, boss.'

'I think that bit of good news I've just shared with you is well worthy of a cup of coffee, don't you?'

'I should have known better than walking into your office without a brew shouldn't I?'

'Truth be known, I need the caffeine. I've got that PM to go to yet today.'

'Yeah, well rather you than me,' she said leaving the room. 'Lisa!' Dylan heard Vicky shout out in the outer office. 'Boss wants a coffee – make it a strong, sweet one!'

Dylan couldn't help but raise a smile.

***

Dylan had succeeded in keeping the press at bay. He had caught up with the ongoing enquiries but when satisfied he was on top of the situation his clock told him the media would have to wait until after he'd attended Carl Braithwaite's post-mortem.

Five minutes to go and now with an emergency energy drink in hand he picked up the phone and dialled Jen's number.

'Wouldn't you know, her first words to me when she woke up just now were, when is Father Christmas coming?'

'She must have had a nice dream, bless her.'

'So far so good... I'm staying at the hospital with her. Dad has gone to get me some clean clothes and he is walking Max. Thank you for ringing him... that was very thoughtful.'

'Thoughtful? No, selfish, I want to know you're both okay and if I can't be with you twenty-four seven then; there's no one better than your dad.'

'Praise indeed. Although, the feeling's not mutual, he didn't have a high opinion of policeman after Shaun and now he thinks you've got a roving eye,' she said with a little chuckle.

'Ah well, I've got broad shoulders. How's Maisy?'

'She's sleeping again. The doctor says she'll sleep a lot.'

'I should be there... I wish I was ...'

'You don't need to be here. She's doing okay. All her obs. are good. There isn't anything you could do if you were here that I'm not, so please don't feel guilty – just keep in touch.'

'I'll be over as soon as I can after the post-mortem. Give her a kiss from me.'

'Okay,' she said wistfully.

***

DS Raj Uppal was already at the mortuary. Dylan found himself standing at the preparation room door. He grabbed the handle. In distance he could hear footsteps, muffled voices and the sound of a door being opened and closed. On entering the prep room he could see the pathologist looked brighter than he had a few days ago. Stow was his usual jovial self and he was sparring with his assistant in front of Raj. Seeing Dylan he walked over to greet him.

'I'm going to have to change my duty rota to avoid you Dylan,' he said. 'We are meeting far too often for my liking.'

'The feeling's mutual,' he said.

'What delight have you got for me today then? Raj here tells me we have a piece of scaffolding pole and a discarded wallet at the scene of the young man's body. Carl Braithwaite,' he said, reading from his paperwork. He looked at Dylan questioningly over his half-rimmed glasses.

'That's right. Over to you.'

Professor Stow looked inside Carl Braithwaite's pockets before removing his outer clothing. His mobile was still on his person, as was his watch. 'I thought someone might have been late night shopping, but it would appear not. Perhaps only cash would do?'

'But that's it, there was still money in his wallet,' said Raj.

Stow passed the exhibits to the exhibits officer, who in turn put the items into bags which he sealed. The evidence label attached to each item would be signed at the end of the post-mortem by the professor.

At the head Professor Stow examined the injury. 'That's one hell of a blow Inspector. There is no chance that that's been done accidentally. It's smashed through the young lad's skull. He'd know nothing about it. There is a slight curve at its lower edge like the crescent of a moon. Can you see?' he said pointing to the indentation. 'This mark looks to me as if it is consistent with your piece of scaffold pipe. I'll measure so we can check. It's caused a massive fracture to the skull exposing the brain. To put it simply it's like cracking the top of a hard-boiled egg with a spoon. That would give you the same sort of effect, but with the force that has been used here, if it had been an egg the egg would have been completely shattered. There's just the one blow with no evidence here of any more attempts. The attacker was sure that the damage in that singular strike would do the intended job. It is possible that you will find skin and blood on the weapon... the scaffolding pole.'

Professor Stow and his assistant turned Carl Braithwaite onto his back and sponged away the dried blood from Braithwaite's lips.

'Is this a test?' he said. Stow looked left and right and then all about him. 'There is no eminent surgeon hiding in the wings waiting to assess me is there?'

Raj looked at Dylan with a puzzled expression. 'No, what makes you say that?'

'Teeth, the young man's teeth have been extracted... not knocked out but look here, carefully removed.'

'You're winding me up,' said Dylan.

'I most definitely am not. Come here,' he said.

The professor pulled the lower lip down with his gloved hand exposing the gums. He then did the same with the upper lip and counted four teeth had been extracted from the top and four from the bottom.

'Not the same teeth as Davina Walsh?' said Raj.

'No,' Dylan said. 'Different teeth....'

Raj watched his jawline tense.

'Extracted just as professionally though,' said Stow.

'I knew the scene was too good to be true,' said Raj. 'Do you think it's the same person?'

'This is unique,' said Stow. 'This is not a coincidence. The murderer has just linked the two crimes for you.' Stow swabbed the area. Pictures were taken to conclude. 'There is nothing else untoward. Carl Braithwaite was otherwise a healthy young man,' he said concluding his findings. 'I said at the end of the Walsh post-mortem you had someone who likes to kill for the thrill. But in all my years in this job I've never seen anything so bizarre. Teeth extraction and thrill in the same sentence?' The professor's fat, pink cheeks wobbled when he took off his mask.

'Well, I always say if there is no other obvious explanation of a crime it's usually to do with some sexual perversion or fetish,' said Dylan

***

Dylan walked to the pathologist's office alongside Professor Stow. 'The DNA national database has struck lucky with a hit on a name from the contents of a condom we found at the scene near Davina Walsh's body.'

'Well, I don't need to tell you how to do your job Inspector. But I suggest you tread with caution. Do you think the person who has done this would make it that easy for you?'

Dylan shrugged his shoulders. 'God knows.'

'Well, I've got to go, I've got people dying to see me, and all that jazz,' he chuckled. 'I'll be seeing you. But hopefully not too soon.'

Professor Stow turned at the door of the mortuary office.

'If you get any more similar cases I'd like to know about them. No, I should say when you get any similar cases I'd like to do the post-mortems personally, for continuity.'

'You're that sure?' said Dylan.

'I'd bet my career on it,' Stow said.

***

Dylan drove back to the station with Raj in the car. 'It looks like we have a psycho on our hands.'

'Local, do you think?'

'I don't know what I think. There is no obvious link with the locations the killer has chosen.'

'That murder scene was good enough for a training school exercise,' said Raj.

'I want you to look at offender profilers. Call Boscombe for me. See if he can shed any light on the type of individual we are looking for and check with the National Crime Faculty to see if teeth extractions have featured in any past crimes. This is a new one on me.'

'If the person who used that condom is known to us and this enquiry is now known to be linked to the Davina Walsh murder, we could potentially have our man in custody real soon,' said Raj with a glint in her large brown eyes.

'Talking of the Braithwaite murder, I must go and meet his family. But for now, let's not get ahead of ourselves. Most importantly we must not stray from the tried and tested methodical investigative strategy. Even cool and calculated killers are prone to mistakes. Usually by being over confident you'll find, in my experience, a killer will give something away and at every opportunity, as with the gift of the condom, we'll be ready to strike like a coiled snake.'

***

The CID office, incident room, was now also doubling up as the investigation briefing room. The HOLMES team were already in their seats, at desks that were covered with computer terminals, trays and an abundance of paperwork. More chairs had been brought in to house the extra staff at the meeting but even then people stood by the filing cabinets that ran around the periphery of the office. The numbers of the team were building day by day.

Dylan sat with Raj and Vicky at the front of the office. Raising his head from his notes he looked around him. People were coming in from all directions and the noise grew louder and louder. He could feel the buzz of anticipation in the air. Although incident rooms had changed over the years, mostly due to the introduction of computers, that didn't deflect from what they were used for. This room was adequately modern, its decor nothing like the leather topped desks, dark mahogany walls and paper index systems of yesteryear.

When Dylan stood the room's inhabitants were instantly silent and with a nod of his head the door was closed shut and only then did he speak to his team to outline the circumstances of the latest murder and reveal the findings of the post-mortem.

'So far I have not confided to the media about the skilful removal of the teeth from our victims. I want to hold that information back as long as possible and at this moment Operation Walnut and the latest Braithwaite murder which has now been given the operational name of Tapestry, will not be officially merged. The purpose of this is to allow investigations into each to remain focused for the next few days. As far as the media are concerned they have been given an update regarding the young man who has died that he sustained a severe head injury, in what appears to us to be a robbery. An appeal for witnesses has been made. Vicky, can you update the team in relation to Operation Walnut please?'

Vicky took centre stage. Her revelation of the DNA hit released a silent cheer and punch in the air from more than one of the audience.

'We will be making a visit to Mr Roger Briggs at seven o'clock tomorrow morning. Just so you are aware he is a family man with two small children of school age,' said Vicky.

'I am in no doubt, after being involved in many murder investigations that coincidences do occur. So, tomorrow we will pursue our suspect rigorously and professionally. Remember we deal with evidence at all time, not speculation,' said Dylan.

Chapter Six

The good news that greeted Dylan at the hospital was that Maisy had been taken off the intravenous drip and was now taking antibiotics orally. This was to be continued for the next four weeks to ensure the virus had been defeated but it was anticipated that she would be allowed home within the next forty-eight hours.

'I had squashed peas for tea Daddy,' Maisy said sleepily. Dylan looked at Jen.

'She means she had mushy peas for tea,' said Jen stroking her daughter's arm.

***

With the worry of Maisy's illness taken from him Dylan was looking forward to a good night's sleep. However, the house was too quiet. The bed too empty. His father-in-law too pre-occupied to be party to any meaningful conversation, when he arrived home.

'Drink?' Dylan said to Ralph as he reached over the ironing board and switched on the kettle. Ralph was letting Max out of the back door. Dylan was pressing a shirt – one of his pet hates: creases in a collar. Ralph grunted in the affirmative.

'Something wrong?'

'Wrong? There's nothing wrong with me,' Ralph snapped, shovelling a heaped spoonful of sugar into his mug of Horlicks.

'Everything all right at home?'

'Why shouldn't it be?'

'Is Thelma okay?'

'What you asking me that for?'

83

'Just trying to be sociable... it might be strange having her son living in your house too. You are pretty much strangers,' Dylan said.

'What're you saying?'

'Nothing,' Dylan raised a smile, his voice shifted up an octave. 'I'm just showing an interest.'

'Young men these days,' Ralph tutted. 'Smoking and drinking in bed. At his age I was working from six o'clock in a morning until six o'clock at night and then I went to college to try and better myself,' he muttered under his breath.

Call him a cynic, Ralph's mood and the tone of his voice told Dylan a different story to what he was telling his son-in-law. But, maybe Ralph still hadn't accepted Dylan's explanation about the phone call he'd overheard with Beryl at Forensic. Or was Ralph missing his home comforts? Then maybe, Dylan, tired as he was, was imaging things...

***

The good night's sleep Dylan had been looking forward to evaded him; his thoughts were in turmoil. Keeping an open mind about murder investigations was an art in itself, without doubt. His gut feelings told him a dangerous predator was trying to make his mark in Harrowfield and Dylan's fear was that this was only the start. 'Tomorrow/today,' he told himself as he looked at the neon lit numbers of the alarm clock, 'he would contact Doctor Francis Boscombe, the Offender Profiler himself.' Perhaps he could steer Dylan towards the type of individual he was looking for.

Francis Boscombe worked for the Home Office in London. His present role was to examine those in prison for murder; trying to understand the reason for their actions and their subsequent incarceration. Dylan had used Boscombe on the Daisy Charlotte Hinds and Christopher Spencer murder enquiry. Although, in truth he knew all the ologist's in the world alone couldn't catch a killer but they could give him expert advice. And whether Dylan took it and acted on it was down to him. The offender profiler could at least confirm that the detectives were on the right track. There was nothing to lose in talking to him.

As soon as the grey daylight began to filter through the bedroom curtains Dylan got up showered, shaved and dressed in silence. Only the creaking of the floorboards outside the bedroom door told him that someone was on the landing. Dylan stood quietly whilst he tied his tie, a frown upon his face, looking momentarily from mirror to door, fully expecting his father-in-law to knock upon it and enter. But after a few minutes he realised he must have changed his mind and noiselessly have crept down the stairs because when he reached the kitchen Ralph was there too.

Jen's dad was talking on the phone. He was sitting in his dressing gown and slippers and looked all of his seventy-six years. His pallor was as grey as the day outside. He held a hand to his brow. 'You must report it to the police,' he said in hushed tones. 'There's bugger all I can do from up here is there?'

***

It was shortly after seven a.m. and the team of six officers were outside the home of Roger Briggs. The house was a smart looking detached, brick built property with climbing roses around the doorway. A pottery sign reading 'The Heights' was fixed to the five-bar gate, that opened onto a driveway, where a car was parked.

Dylan walked up the path. CID officers followed. Uniformed officers stood back at the entrance to the garden path. Dylan rang the doorbell. Westminster chimes rang out. They appeared to go on forever and ever.

Eventually the door was answered by the man of the house himself. A lady, whom Dylan took to be his wife, was in the hallway, a few feet behind him. She peered over his shoulder to see who the caller could be at that time of day.

'Mr Briggs, Roger Briggs?' said Dylan.

'Who's asking?' he said. Roger Briggs looked the suited detective inspector up and down. 'Double glazing, Jehovah's witnesses? Whatever you're selling we don't want it,' he said looking briefly at his watch. He began to close the door with a force that would have made it slam shut if Dylan's size ten booted foot was not in the way.

'Detective Inspector Jack Dylan, Harrowfield CID, this is DS Vicky Hardacre and DC Duncan Granger,' he said, indicating by way of his thumb to the CID officers behind him. 'May we come in?'

It was apparent by the look on Roger Briggs's face that Dylan now had his full attention. 'We are investigating the murder of Davina Walsh, the young lady who was killed recently on the cycle path, behind the Anchor Inn,' he said.

Mr Briggs gave Dylan a veiled look. He stepped backwards and directly into the woman behind him. He stumbled but didn't turn round, or apologise, but remained locked in eye contact with the detective.

'We have evidence to prove you were in that area around that time and in close proximity to where the body was found.'

'You've evidence to prove I was in the area and in very close proximity to where the body was found?' Briggs said. He swallowed hard. 'Is this your idea of a sick joke?' he said, turning around abruptly on his wife. You, you fucking bitch! What have you been saying?'

Mrs Briggs's hand went to her face. A look of distress flashed across her eyes. 'I didn't... but, why would I?' she said staring up at her husband. Dylan saw Roger Briggs's wife was physically shaking, her mouth remained open. If she had fallen at his feet she couldn't have begged harder for him to believe her. 'No, no, honestly... I don't know of ... please, you've got to believe me... this is nothing to do with me.'

'I'm arresting you under suspicion of murder,' said Dylan, and before Roger Briggs knew what was happening he was handcuffed and being frogmarched to the waiting marked police vehicle.

DS Vicky Hardacre entered the house and taking Mrs Briggs by the elbow she led her into the kitchen. 'Let's put the kettle on shall we?' she said to DC Granger and nodded towards the children who were sitting quietly at the table, toast on their plates, hands by their sides. 'I'll explain what is happening Mrs Briggs. Come on now take a seat. Louisa isn't it?'

Mrs Briggs nodded.

'Is it okay if I call you Louisa?'

Ned Granger steered the children into the hallway.

'Do you want to go upstairs and get yourself ready for school?' he said kindly. 'We just need to speak to your mummy. She's okay, don't worry, she's just a little shocked that we came this early that's all.'

The oldest reached out to hold the youngest's hand. Together they walked up the steps, looking back at regular intervals to see Ned standing on the bottom step. Each time they did so he hurried them on with a wave of his hand and a smile. 'Go on,' he said. 'Mum is okay, don't worry, we'll look after her.'

There was no missing the hole in the staircase wall which was the size of a fist.

'Is there anyone we can call for you; a family member, friend? Someone who could take the children to school for you and pick them up?' said Vicky.

Louisa Briggs sat on a wooden kitchen chair, her elbows on the table, her head in her hands. She looked up at Vicky and it was only then that the detective saw the bruise down the side of her face.

'My neighbour will be here soon, she takes them to school,' she said. Sitting up she caressed the side of her neck which was deep red in places, mottled and bruised.

'He did that,' said Vicky softly.

Mrs Briggs looked down at the floortiles under her stockinged feet. 'Yes,' she said quietly with a little hesitation. She looked directly into Vicky's eyes. 'Yes, yes he did, but it was my fault,' she said with more vigour. 'I'm a terrible nag and the children and I are so untidy,' she said, apologetically.

'Do you think your husband is capable of murder Louisa?' Vicky said.

Roger Briggs's wife looked at Vicky long and hard without releasing the eye contact. Then she blinked and shook her head. 'No, no I don't think he is capable of murdering anyone else...' she said.

***

The children were collected. It was a fraught exchange. The Briggs children didn't want to leave their mum, the neighbour was clearly puzzled by the attendant officer's presence.

'Could you pick the children up and keep them at yours after school, until Mrs Briggs can collect them please?' said Ned.

'Yes, of course.' She tried to peer around Ned. 'Louisa!' she called out. 'Are you okay?'

'I'm okay,' Louisa Briggs said. 'Don't worry. I'll pick the girls up as soon as I can Sonia.'

Ned nodded, smiled sympathetically and shut the door behind her.

Louisa Briggs ran to the kitchen sink and retched as if she might be sick. 'Have a sip of tea,' said Vicky. She turned and started at Vicky with big round empty eyes.

'We need to search your house. I'm sorry. I know it is very... intrusive... but it's an essential process in our investigation.'

'The hole in the wall. Did your husband do that?' said Ned Granger. Louisa nodded. 'But, it was me that... He was going out and I hadn't ironed his best blue shirt.'

***

Roger Briggs stood by the Custody Suite counter being booked in, protesting his innocence and demanding to speak with his MP.

'At this moment a solicitor will have to do,' said the Custody Sergeant.

'This is damn ridiculous! Heads are going to roll! Mark my words... heads will roll. I demand to see the man in charge of the investigation,' he said.

'But, you've already seen him,' said the Custody Officer with an eyebrow raised.

'I certainly have not. When?' said Roger Briggs. He stood erect. His chin was raised and both sides of his mouth turned down.

'When he locked you up,' said the sergeant with a little smirk.

'Now, do you have a solicitor you wish me to call out to represent you? Or would you like me to ring the duty solicitor?' he said, his voice was monotone.

***

Ms Perfect, duty solicitor, sat alongside Roger Briggs in an interview room. The formalities were complied with. It was now three hours after his custody clock had begun. DI Dylan and DS Hardacre watched the prisoner intently from the opposite side of the table. The two more than aware that there were twenty-one hours left before they would have to ask for a further extension to his detention to continue interviewing, from the Divisional Commander. Should they not have enough evidence to charge him with at that stage for the offence the courts could afford them a further thirty-six. But, once the seventy-two hours was up, they knew that they would have to charge Mr Briggs or release him.

In turn those present in the interview room spoke their names, for the purpose of voice recognition for the interview recording. This done the search for the truth could commence.

Dylan was pleased. Roger Briggs was talking to them. In fact he was loud, arrogant and bullish with his responses to questions put to him by the two officers, and it appeared he thought he was in charge, at this early stage. The officers let him; but how wrong he was.

He denied knowing Davina Walsh. He denied being in the area at the time of her murder and stated that he had a watertight alibi, his wife.

'Louisa will confirm I was at home, with her all weekend,' he said without hesitation. So sure of himself it appeared.

'You seem very confident your wife will give you an alibi given you've hit her, bruising her face badly and at the same time we understand you also knocked a hole in the wall with your fist, at your home, her home, the family home?'

Lin Perfect intervened. 'That is totally unacceptable Inspector. My client is here on suspicion of murder, not for a domestic incident between him and his wife.'

'Really? Well, I'd have to disagree. You see your client is putting his wife forward as an alibi and because of the history between them, I think it's more likely that she would be compelled, through fear, to say what he wants. He even blamed her wrongly for his arrest this morning, but let's move on shall we?'

'What do you know about my relationship with my wife?' Briggs said. He looked at them through slit eyes. 'How dare you? I have been nowhere near the Anchor Inn recently.'

Dylan ignored his outburst and continued, 'Very close to Davina Walsh's body there was a condom.'

'Sorry to disappoint but I don't use condoms. Never have. You can ask my wife. This is such a pathetic attempt at a stitch up. Can't you do something?' he said raising his voice at his solicitor. He banged his fist on the desk. 'For fuck's sake.'

Lin Perfect didn't shy away but blinked momentarily at the continued emphatic waving of his hands.

'If you let me finish,' said Dylan, '... very close to the body of Davina Walsh, who was brutally murdered, a condom was discovered...'

'Are you bloody deaf? What don't you understand about I-do-not-use-condoms!' Briggs threw himself back in his chair and let out a huge sigh.

Dylan stared at Briggs intently. If he thought the detective inspector was intimidated he was wrong. Dylan continued in a calm, unhurried fashion. 'The condom had been discarded. It had been recently used.'

Roger Briggs was sweating profusely. He ran his fingers through his hair. He shuffled in his seat. Annoyingly for him he couldn't move it as it was bolted to the floor.

Dylan waited for a moment or two for the prisoner to calm down. Briggs leant forward and tapped under the table with busy fingers, emphatically.

'The contents of the condom have been forensically examined and a DNA profile obtained which resulted in your arrest. The contents have proven positive, beyond any doubt, as being yours. So now, would you like to explain to us how that can possibly be, if you don't use condoms and have not been near the Anchor Inn recently?'

Briggs recoiled from the table. His head bowed. There was silence...

'You're very quiet suddenly?' said Dylan

'I want to speak to my solicitor, in private,' he said.

His solicitor agreed after the disclosure that it was timely to consult with her client.

Dylan couldn't argue, it was their right to do so, he terminated the interview.

***

Back in the office Dylan hoped that an update from the team at Briggs's home address would give them a find of relevance that they could use in the next interview. Ultimately, as time passed the next call he got could be from the custody suite informing him that Briggs and his solicitor were ready to resume.

'We know he's a wife beater and is lying through his back teeth. Arrogant git,' said Vicky.

'He's lying alright but about what? For all his arrogance, I am not getting a feeling he's our murderer.'

'He beats his wife and his DNA is inside a used condom next to Davina's body. What more do you want?'

'I'm not disputing what it looks like... but before we get carried away let's see what he's got to say in the next interview.'

'That's if he carries on talking. It's just our luck that he'll "no reply" to everything after speaking with his solicitor.'

'Now who's being negative?' said Dylan.

Ned Granger walked in Dylan's office. 'We have it confirmed that Roger Briggs's credit card was used at the Anchor Inn on the night before Davina was murdered, boss,' he said.

Vicky's eyes lit up. 'I thought he said he hadn't been near the Anchor Inn?'

***

The solicitor was with her client for over an hour before the call came in to say they were ready to reconvene. Briggs was noticeably calmer and his body language suggested he was in a more receptive mood.

'The last interview was halted at your request, so you could consult with your solicitor after we disclosed to you that your DNA had been found in a condom next to the body of Davina Walsh. Do you now wish to say anything about that?

There was a brief pause. Briggs turned to look at his solicitor. No longer did he stare at the officers with intent.

'Okay, look, I have no idea how it got next to the victim's body, but I do accept it's my DNA. I'm sorry but I can't help you any more than that.'

'Let's rewind to the previous interview. You said you hadn't been out the night before Davina Walsh's body was found or the morning of the discovery of her body. You said your wife could verify that you were at home. Was that a lie?' said Dylan.

'I told you that because I know I am one hundred per cent not involved in the murder of that woman.'

'Let's start at the very beginning shall we? Are you still saying you were at home on the morning it is believed Davina Walsh's murder took place?'

'I don't know.'

'Were you at work?'

'I don't know, maybe. I don't know. I'm confused. I work shifts?'

'Okay so is there someone we can check what shift you were working that day?'

'You can check with our admin department.'

'Good. We will.'

Vicky remained silent as Dylan continued.

'Where were you on the Sunday night – the night before Davina Walsh was murdered?'

'I was at the Anchor Inn. But, that was the night before she was murdered for goodness sake.'

Vicky looked sideways at Dylan.

'Who were you with at the Anchor Inn?'

'Look I'd argued with the wife, which is not unusual and I'm not proud of it but, I did hit her that night and I punched a hole in the wall of the staircase. I get frustrated. The children had gone to bed. I stormed out and went for a few beers.'

'What time did you leave?'

'I don't remember.'

'Was it before midnight, after midnight?'

'Before.'

'What were you wearing that night?'

'Oh, I don't know... Probably my jeans and a jumper.'

'Did you drive there?'

'No, I caught the bus.'

'Really?' said Dylan.

'I've been done once by your lot for drinking and driving. I don't risk it now.'

'So, tell me about the condom... You told us quite emphatically that you didn't use them in the last interview.'

'I don't usually. I do sometimes, on occasions... I got it at the pub.'

'And?' said Dylan. 'We seem to be going around the houses don't we? Let's cut to the quick, did you have sex with someone or did you masturbate into the condom?'

Roger Briggs blushed profusely. 'I do not masturbate into condoms. I had sex with someone.'

'Someone you know? A stranger?'

'No, not a stranger, what kind of person do you think I am? I rang a friend and I met them outside the pub.'

'And you had sex with this, friend?'

'You must have anticipated having sex with your friend, otherwise why would you buy the condoms?'

'I hoped we'd... yes ... we usually do when we ... but we don't often. They were working, which is why I didn't know...'

'We are investigating a murder. All we are doing is trying to ascertain the truth of what took place. So if there is someone out there who can confirm what you are saying and therefore a reason for your DNA being close to the body of a murdered person, would you please tell us who it is and we can stop wasting valuable time and move on?'

'We didn't have sex on the cycle path. We had sex in a car so I don't understand how the condom could have possibly got onto the cycle path?'

Vicky broke her silence. 'You're the type of person who at his own admission assaults his wife. You've threatened your wife in our presence and lied to us constantly since your arrest. So tell me why should we believe you now? Did you kill Davina Walsh and is this just another lie?'

'No, no, I swear on my children's lives. I did not murder the woman. That's the honest truth.'

'Well, if you give us your friend's name, we will speak to them and confirm what you are telling us is the truth.'

'That might be difficult.'

'So is a murder investigation Mr Briggs. At this moment you are not helping yourself, or anyone else.'

'Can I speak to my solicitor again, in private please?'

The interview was terminated.

***

Lunchtime was looming and Lin Perfect made a comment that her client had not had breakfast. Dylan knew the next interview would be deemed oppressive and could result in it being thrown out of court at a future trial if they continued without allowing Briggs to have some sort of nourishment.

Vicky and Dylan sat with sandwiches from the vending machine in the room that used to be the station canteen. Times were changing in many aspects of the police force and many of them not for the good.

'This will be office space before long,' said Dylan as he looked about him at the demolition work that had already cleared the police station's bar area. 'No more quick drinks together for the team, in the privacy of the station, after dealing with the aftermath of an incident or a post-mortem,' said Dylan.

'They'll be expecting us to not only eat on the hoof but do our paperwork in cafés before long,' said Vicky.

'So you've heard?'

'Heard what?'

'The powers that be are expecting officers to do their paperwork, albeit now on computers but in cafés, on their patch, where they can be seen and approached by the public at any given time during their shift.'

'You're joking?' Vicky said. The detective sergeant shook her head. 'Jeez,' she said.

'I kid you not.'

Vicky took a bit of a soggy roast beef salad sandwich. A small tomato popped in her mouth and its juice ran down her chin. It was Dylan's turn to shake his head.

'Just think Briggs is probably tucking into fish and chips, with salt and vinegar and tomato sauce that some police officer has gone out and got for him, whilst we're eating a wretched sandwich from a bloody machine,' she said wistfully as she

94

pulled a flaccid piece of lettuce from in-between two slices of bread. 'He wouldn't get bread and water if it was up to me never mind a warm meal.'

Dylan smiled, 'You'd also have him dangling from the gallows.'

'Probably,' she said.

'Do you know one of the most obvious questions that isn't asked in an interview is, 'did you do it?'' he said.

'I know, that's why I asked him,' she said smugly, 'it doesn't mean that the prisoner will answer the question honestly though does it? Do you think he did it boss?'

'No, I don't. You know what we're forgetting?'

Vicky looked puzzled.

'The teeth extraction. There is nothing in his background that we know of that suggests he has the know-how to remove teeth with the expertise he'd require to be the murderer.'

'Ah but who knows what other secrets he has if he's capable of having a secret relationship with another woman behind his wife's back?' she said with a twinkle in her eye.

There was a message left for Dylan in the incident room to contact the local radio station, no doubt what they wanted was an update. It was right for them to keep asking to try and keep the public up-to-date as to what was happening on their turf and also from the detective inspector's point of view the frequent broadcasts kept the murders at the forefront of everyone's mind. They would have to wait.

***

The next interview with their prisoner took place as scheduled. Ms Perfect, Roger Briggs's solicitor spoke first.

'After discussions with my client he has agreed to co-operate fully. When you have heard what he has to say. I think you will understand his earlier reluctance in offering the explanation until he feels he has had no alternative Inspector.'

Briggs spoke hesitantly. 'I admit I did meet someone and have sex with them the night before the lady was murdered. I have known this person for a long time but we do not see each other often. Now I see that I have no option but to tell you who it is.'

He took a deep breath, looked at his solicitor who nodded once at her client. 'This is very awkward because it's a police officer,' he said.

Dylan felt Vicky flinch.

'We will need you to name her,' said Vicky.

'Him,' he said. 'It's him...'

Dylan could see Vicky out of the corner of his eye. She hadn't let her face change or her body language show that Roger Briggs's revelation had surprised her. He was pleased with how she had handled the disclosure by the prisoner, as he knew only too well that it had come as much of a shock to her as it had to him.

'His name is Geoffrey... Wiley. He was the one who arrested me when I got stopped for the drink driving offence. He's going to be in serious trouble isn't he and it's the last thing I wanted...'

'Why should he be in any trouble?' said Dylan.

'Like I said, he was on duty. He came to help me. I was in a mess...'

Dylan looked intently at Briggs but remained silent.

'Honestly, I didn't know when I called him he was working... I told him I hated myself for what I had done to my wife and I... threatened to kill myself. He talked to me. He came straight away.'

'Okay, so back to the used condom?' Dylan said.

'I must have thrown it out of the car.'

'His car?' said Vicky.

Briggs shook his head. 'You're going to find out anyway. The police car.'

'You do understand that we will need to check what you have told us,' Dylan said.

'Yes.'

'Will you now be releasing my client and "refusing charge" Inspector?' said his solicitor.

'Not so fast, we still need to verify what we have been told, until then Mr Briggs remains in custody.'

The interview was terminated.

Dylan and Vicky walked back to the incident room.

'I didn't see that coming,' said Vicky. Her eyes were wide.

'And he now appears genuine. We need to speak to PC Wiley as soon as possible. Bloody fool. This isn't something that can be swept under the carpet. This will ultimately be disclosed to any future defence team and therefore on the court file... Find out who his inspector is will you. I need to speak to him as a matter of urgency.'

Vicky sat at her desk. Dylan's hand rested on the back of her chair. The computer system was being slow. 'As luck would have it, according to the box Wiley should be on duty,' she said.

'Good. Professional standards will be involved. His behaviour whilst on duty is for somebody else to investigate. All we're interested in is that PC Wiley can corroborate what Briggs is saying, so we can eliminate him from the enquiry and move on. We will need a written statement from him.'

Lisa handed Dylan a piece of paper which he read.

'Forensic confirming that the condom is similar to the type sold in the Anchor Inn,' he said to Vicky. 'Thanks for that Lisa. That ties in nicely.'

***

The conversation with PC Wiley's Inspector regarding the enquiry, just over an hour later, was not a pleasant one.

'I've had a very tearful officer in my office who has confirmed to me the relationship between himself and Roger Briggs,' he said. 'He also can corroborate their meeting on the night in question at the Anchor Inn car park. He has reluctantly also confirmed the use of the police vehicle. A written statement will follow for your records marked "strictly confidential" for your personal attention Dylan. I am waiting on the officer's federation representative to be present due to the fact it is a disciplinary matter.'

Dylan thanked his opposite number for the promptness of his response.

'The team have finished at the Briggs's home address. Louisa Briggs is staying at her mother's address with the children and the domestic violence issue is now in the hands of officers at the Safeguarding Unit,' said Vicky.

'She's asked for help?' said Dylan.

'She has,' said Vicky

'Good. One good thing that has come out of this sorry mess is that she and the children are now on our radar. I'll telephone Perfect & Best to save them a trip back to the station and Briggs can be released from custody. Give me a minute and I'll come with you to see him.'

***

Roger Briggs stood in the foyer talking to a plain clothed police officer when the detective arrived. The officer nodded at Dylan and Vicky and walked away.

'All the relevant details of the assault on your wife will be passed on to the Safeguarding Unit where they deal with the domestic violence issues, for follow-up enquiries,' said Vicky.

Roger Briggs nodded but without speaking turned to leave the custody suite. He stopped and turned at the door. 'You wouldn't do me a favour and speak to Geoff Wiley for me would you, let him know I had no choice but to tell you about me and him?'

'Your relationship with Geoff Wiley is for you to deal with. I don't have time to pass on personal messages. It may have slipped your mind Mr Briggs but we are investigating a murder and time wasters saving their own skins are very unhelpful,' said Dylan.

Appearing disgruntled rather than ashamed Roger Briggs left the building.

There were a few raised eyebrows. Dylan knew the information about the officer, like most things in a police station, wouldn't remain confidential for long. The news would spread like a bush fire and the Chinese whispers would enhance it beyond recognition Dylan was in no doubt. But like anything else, for PC Wiley it would soon become yesterday's news.

A further note to ring Maggie Currie from Vectis Radio was waved in front of Dylan as he approached his office. He picked up the telephone.

'Maggie, Jack Dylan, sorry for the delay, how can I help?' he said.

'Can I come see you? I've had an anonymous call that's freaked me out a bit. The caller asked the receptionist if he could speak to me. When she put him through all he said was that I had to ask the murder cops about teeth? I don't know if this means anything to you but I thought I'd better ring you.'

'I think I need to see you urgently,' said Dylan.

'I'm on my way,' said Maggie.

Chapter Seven

Maggie caused a few heads to turn as she breezed through the incident room behind a uniformed civilian officer. Radio presenter Ms Currie was in her mid-twenties, tall with long blonde hair. She wore black leather biker trousers, a white t-shirt and black biker boots. Her jacket was thrown casually over her shoulder.

'Stop drooling saddo. She's young enough to be your daughter,' said Vicky in a flat quiet tone of voice.

'Nothing wrong with a sugar daddy is there?' said Ned with an over exaggerated wink at Dylan's visitor from where he languished in his chair.

'Bless him... Don't worry he's harmless,' said Vicky extending her hand out to Maggie. 'Nice to see you,' she said.

Dylan heard the exchange and saw the radio presenter walking towards his office. He stood and walked to greet her at the door.

'Sorry about the natives, they don't get out as often as they should,' he said, his mouth turned up at one corner.

DC Granger nearly fell off his chair laughing. Vicky turned and stuck one finger up at him. 'Swivel,' she said sitting heavily back down in her seat.

Lisa appeared with two drinks on a tray and a plate of biscuits. She walked up the aisle between the desks. Ned reached over and took a biscuit from the plate, Vicky took another. Lisa scowled at them over her shoulder. Ned blew her a kiss. Vicky raised an eyebrow. Lisa knocked at Dylan's door.

'Come in,' he called.

Dylan and Maggie were no strangers. She had volunteered with Jen to fundraise for the local children's hospice.

'I'm intrigued by your caller and what was actually said,' said Dylan.

'You can listen yourself. All our calls to the radio station are recorded as a matter of course these days.' Maggie removed her iPad from her rucksack.

Dylan moved to sit next to her. She put the tablet on her knee and tapped in her password. 'We get a lot of crank calls,' she said looking at Dylan for a brief moment. 'But there was just something about this one...' Maggie pressed the arrow on the illuminated screen and their heads almost touched as they leant in further to listen to the gruff, slightly muffled, male voice.

'Maggie, why don't you ask the cops what they know about the dead people's missing teeth?' said the caller.

She replayed the piece over and over again at Dylan's request.

Maggie looked puzzled. 'I play the news every hour on my programme and I'm pretty sure I'd have picked up on that idiosyncrasy if you had given that information to the press.

Dylan was quiet and thoughtful. For a moment or two they sat in silence. Eventually Dylan sat back in his chair. 'Look, what I'm going to share with you must remain totally confidential,' he said.

Maggie took a gulp of her drink and a bit into a biscuit.

'The murderer is removing teeth from his victims and that information is not in the public domain. and I purposefully have not made any mention of the murdered victims having teeth missing,' said Dylan.

'Shit,' she said with a cough and a splutter.

'You okay?' Dylan said.

'Fine,' she said. 'So...' She took a sip of her tea. 'So, that could actually be the voice of the murderer?'

'Could be. It doesn't mean it is though. It would be wrong of us to assume anything in an enquiry without having proof, but what I do know is our murderer appears to like playing tricks.'

'What to try and throw you off the scent?' she said.

'Who knows? What we do know is that he removed the teeth when they are dead and he does it with a certain amount of skill.'

'Oh, my God! Do you think it's a dentist? How bloody frightening...'

Dylan laughed. 'That I can't tell you. But now you know why I'm interested in your caller.'

'If he calls again what do I do?' said Maggie.

'If he calls again, we will have our technical people on the job to trace it. Another option is we don't wait to see if he calls again but I come on your programme and make an appeal for him to come forward.'

'Do you want to?'

'I think that might be a good idea. It might encourage him to ring again sooner than he anticipated and it would give us an opportunity to try and trace the call if he does. I'll have a confidential chat with your management team so that they are aware of what's going on and see what they say.'

'Wow, if this results in an arrest that'd be dead cool. My boss would be well chuffed.' Maggie's excited face suddenly clouded over and she put her hand to her mouth. 'OMG I've just remembered I'm due at the dentist next week. I think I might postpone.'

Dylan laughed, 'I suggest you just carry on as normal.'

Maggie stood to leave.

Dylan shook her hand. 'Thanks for bringing this to my attention and for coming in today. I'll be in touch, and to save you from our resident vulture,' he said nodding in Ned Granger's direction. 'I'll walk you to the door.'

The incident room was filling up with people ready for the day's debriefing.

Maggie said hello to people she knew and smiled at the ones who acknowledged her. Dylan couldn't help but note that Ms Currie had nice teeth and a lovely smile. The last thing he wanted was for her to be the focus of a killer's attention. Was he asking her to be their bait?

***

The debrief proved to be a full and informative one, but there was nothing new that gave them any leads towards a suspect. Tomorrow Dylan would make enquiries into the possibility of tracing calls that were made to Vectis Radio station. He was still waiting for information from the national database involving crimes by offenders who were known to extract teeth from their victims and the document promised by offender profiler, Dr Francis Boscombe outlining the possible type of individual they were looking for. The intel at this time told Dylan that the killer was likely to be a middle-aged local man due to nothing more than the knowledge he had of the area and the skill he had acquired in dentistry.

***

Dylan left the police station. With any luck he would get to the hospital in time to read Maisy her bedtime story.

Jen was waiting for him outside Maisy's room. 'Dad's leaving tonight,' she said solemnly.

'So soon, why?'

'Seemingly Thelma has had her purse pinched and before she was aware it had gone missing a considerable amount of money has been withdrawn from her account.'

'How?'

'Cash card withdrawal at the max each day.'

'Someone knew her number?'

Jen shrugged her shoulders. 'Watched her pin it in at some time maybe?'

'How long before she was aware it was missing?'

'A few days, it has only been reported to the police today after she told Dad.'

'When did she last use it?'

'She recalls having it last at the post office last week.'

'And they've checked with them?'

'Yes, she didn't leave it there. Vince remembers her being in that particular day though because she collected her pension, paid for her papers and got quite a few groceries which is why she used her debit card. Her son Ozzy carried the bags home for her.'

Ralph opened the door and walked into the corridor. He looked sad. Dylan shook his hand. 'At least the little 'un is due home tomorrow, God willing,' Ralph said.

'Jen's told me about the money. I'm sorry. I'll make a call to the local nick to see what's going on.'

'There's not a lot that can be done in reality though is there? The money, we're not going to see that again. I don't know

103

what's going on down there. They've had an attempted break-in at the post office this week too.'

'How'd you know?'

'Well, like I said I rang Vince to see if anyone had handed in Thelma's card. I've known him and Jacqui his wife for years,' Ralph's eyes were watery. 'They don't deserve this bad luck, not with everything they do for our local community.'

'But the culprits won't have got anything. The safe, that's on a time lock surely?'

'Yes, the thieves didn't get any money. They took cigarettes and drinks and left one hell of a mess trying to open the safe. The coppers are trying to obtain clues but it appears futile – they wore gloves.'

'Crime Scene Investigation will be in there gathering any possible forensic.'

'Frightening thing is that rumour has it they used a gun to shoot the lock out. A gun in Godshill for pity's sake! Whatever next?'

'I'll go home with Dad to pack up his things if you're okay here for a while? I'll bring back some clothes for Maisy to leave hospital tomorrow,' said Jen.

'You do that. I'm fine here with Maisy.'

Dylan sat beside Maisy. She was drawing and humming quietly to herself.

'Time to go to sleep pet?' he said looking at his watch.

She nodded her pretty, tired, little head then looked up at Dylan and scowled. 'I'm not a pet. I'm a big girl,' she said. Maisy jumped under the covers, laid her head on her pillow and closed her eyes tight. A cheeky little grin spread across her face.

Dylan watched and waited. A few seconds later she opened them. 'Can you read me Hansom and Gretel please Daddy,' she said. 'I'm going home to see Max tomorrow you know.'

'Hansel and Gretel darling. Yes, of course I can,' he said as he fingered the books on her bedside table to find the chosen story. 'I bet Max can't wait to see you.'

***

Dylan knew before long that both the murder enquiries would be subjected to an internal force review. This elected team would scrutinise what had taken place so far in the investigations. They would look at Dylan's strategies and possibly assist with advice on future lines of enquiry they collectively deemed necessary to pursue.

The review team consisted of an assistant chief constable, a detective superintendent, the divisional commander, a scenes of crime supervisor and a supervisor from the HOLMES team (the computer system used in all major incidents). Would their expertise assist in the investigation? Only time would tell.

The team had been briefed and updated by Dylan. They were of course under no pressure in their deliberations as the detective and his team were. Their job was to look from the outside without physical contact, nor being on the 'battlefield' itself.

The verdict they arrived at was in the form of a question. Why hadn't Dylan given the media details of the victims' teeth being extracted?

Dylan had given this considerable thought from the outset and explained why when he gave his brief. He had gone to some lengths to assert the 'for' and 'against' argument in doing so. Dylan wondered if they had listened to a word he'd said.

If the caller to the radio station was the murderer, what did he want, publicity, notoriety? Dylan thought about revisiting his earlier decision of updating the media on the teeth extraction subject. If he told the media that in his view the extractions had been less than professionally done, would that declaration annoy or anger the caller sufficiently enough to make him ring again? Once he had decided the way forward he would write up his policy book explaining his reasoning in relation to this matter. The policy log always felt such an inconvenience at a time that offered no respite, but Dylan knew what an advantage a well-documented policy log would mean to him, for court purposes, some eighteen months down the line when this murder investigation would be a distant memory, due to more recent cases.

***

Dr Francis Boscombe entered Dylan's office the next day with gusto! 'What an interesting case,' said the five foot eight, fifty something rotund man. Boscombe threw down his briefcase, slung his tweed jacket over the chair and proceeded to adjust his khaki green coloured baggy cord trousers. 'This is not the norm, everyday serial killer Dylan,' he said, sitting down opposite him. He leant forward. 'This killer I feel will be taking the teeth as trophies and getting a great deal of satisfaction by removing them no doubt. In my opinion, the killer is thoroughly enjoying the thrill of this chase with you and trying to mislead the enquiry by sending you on these wild goose chases.'

'You've confirmed my thoughts but what could the motive be? Based on what we already know?' said Dylan.

'The offender is, no doubt in my mind, a male with good local knowledge who also knows how to kill. Best educated guess would be probably that he has some military background or some connection to the services. I don't believe that this is the first time he has killed and if you were to suggest that he was less than professional, I believe that yes, you'd get a response. What that would be, I hasten to add, I don't know. What I am confident about is that he will kill again. The motive? I think it has to give him some sort of satisfaction. Why? I don't know.'

**

An 'Action', in police terms, is a paper enquiry. The action that Dylan would now create for this would be fed into the computer system to record the discussion with Dr Boscombe. The category created would be titled 'Profiler's Comments'. A line of enquiry is a paper trail that is recorded by the HOLMES system for comparison, retrieval, disclosure and ultimately preparation of a murder file.

Victimology of the two deceased revealed very little, they had nothing in common in their lifestyles. They were a different sex. The attendant circumstances and cause of death were not the same and the location was fifteen miles apart. The obvious link was the teeth extraction.

Dylan concluded from the available data that the victims were randomly selected, possibly due to their isolation at the time of their death. Was the killer an opportunist, did he know his victims or spend time observing his prey before moving in for the kill?

Homicide is the supreme test for the investigator and this offender had started in earnest. He knew exactly what he was doing in Dylan's mind. He was throwing down a gauntlet to Dylan, whilst pursuing some misguided self-indulgent fetish. In Dylan's thoughts the killings were not the main focus, merely the vehicle to gain access to the trophies – teeth. The attempts to disrupt the subsequent enquiries was all part of the killer's game plan.

'Chilling, ultimate, and full of menace with the dark suspicion that no one is safe until the killer is caught; murder calls out like no other...' Dylan read from the plaque on his office wall. A gift from Peter Stonestreet when he had been promoted to Detective Inspector.

The suspect criteria was wide open, all Dylan felt that could be reliably recorded was that the offender was a male, due to the strength required to render the victims helpless and he was most likely to be over the age of twenty-one, a calculated guess, based on his expertise.

The various suspect categories were building in the computer system, recent releases from prison, people with mental challenges who had returned to the community, dentists that had been 'struck-off', local dentists, including those who had retired, sex offenders... the list continued as Dylan scanned the screens. This done Dylan was satisfied that the net was cast far and wide; he was working through the investigations methodically keeping to the tried and tested strategies. Dylan agreed with the offender profiler it wasn't about, 'if he killed again, but when'.

Since the murderer had struck the first time there had been no breakthrough, other than the call made to the radio station. The good news from his initial telephone enquiries was that the call was found to be from a local phone booth which was situated midway between murder scenes.

***

Dylan's mood was sombre but significantly lightened by the fact that Maisy was home.

'Six, seven, eight, nine, ten, eleventeen,' she squealed, counting her stickers when Dylan walked in. She was pale but her eyes were bright and she was clearly very happy to be home. She leant up against Max, throwing her arms lovingly around his, big, thick Golden Retriever neck periodically. Being the accommodating soft animal he was he soaked up the adoration.

No matter how Dylan tried to be upbeat Jen could tell by her husband's persona that he was making no headway in the murder enquiries.

'Every line of enquiry completed, every person eliminated is one step closer to catching the killer. That's what you tell me,' Jen said to him when Maisy had gone to bed and they sat together on the settee that night.

'You're right,' he said, relaxing in her arms. 'It's good to have you back home where you belong.'

'I wonder how Dad is getting on? He should have arrived home, but he hasn't let me know. That is so unlike him.'

'No doubt he's enough on his plate. He'll be in touch as soon as he is fully appraised as to what's gone on,' said Dylan.

The longer the investigations remained undetected the more the pressure increased for Dylan and his team. The feeling in the community was as if a dark cloud hung over them. People were nervous. No one felt safe, not until the killer was caught. The fear seemed to be gathering momentum day by day.

***

Dylan, Jen and Maisy's annual dental check-up was upon them and Jen gently reminded Dylan at breakfast.

'I don't think I can make it. I'm far too busy. Give my apologises,' Dylan said as he popped a piece of toast in his mouth. He gave a piece of crust to Max who sat at his side.

'Oh yes you can. You can spare half an hour today. I checked with Lisa. You have nothing pressing in your diary this morning. And stop spoiling the dog. Toast is not good for him. Have you seen the size of his belly.'

Dylan moaned. 'But, you know I hate going to the dentist.'

'No, you don't, do you?' Jen said between clenched teeth. Maisy looked up at her mum's face and then to her dad's. Dylan pulled a funny face at his daughter and she giggled.

'Actually,' said Dylan to Maisy, 'Daddy is really looking forward to going to the dentist today.' His smile stretched from ear to ear.

'Nah... Not convincing... Try harder,' said Jen. 'You are such a whimp Dr Eklund is lovely.'

***

Dylan held Maisy in his arms. The smell he associated with the dentist hit him as soon as Jen opened the door and his stomach clenched. He must have flinched as Maisy looked at him, took his face in her little hands, turned his head towards her and kissed him. 'It'll be okay Daddy,' she said, holding him tight. Jen offered their names to the receptionist. Maisy patted Dylan on his back soothingly, like she would her baby doll.

Jen shook her head and smiled.

'Aww... She's so cute,' the receptionist mouthed.

Dylan and Maisy found the contents of the display cabinets in the dentist's waiting room fascinating. Maisy because there were some huge animated teeth on display in one and Dylan because there were some antique dentistry instruments in another.

'Bet you're glad you came now aren't you?' said Jen looking over his shoulder.

'Gruesome looking aren't they?'

With the antique dentistry implements in mind, Dylan took an unprecedented interest in the present day tools Karl Eklund was using. They were thinner, shinier, smaller.

The dental assistant put a bib on Dylan which Maisy found highly amusing, laid him back in the chair and Dr Eklund, with his mask firmly in place hovered over him. 'Open wide for me,' he said.

Dylan looked at the map of Harrowfield and surrounding areas on the ceiling above him. He concentrated on the areas they were covering on the murder enquiries. The dentist prodded a few of Dylan's teeth, mumbled numbers and letters to the dental assistant who was inputting the data onto the computer. No sooner had Dylan located Tandem Bridge on the map than Dr Eklund started to raise Dylan's chair to the sitting position.

'All done,' said the dentist displaying a brilliant white, toothy smile.

Dylan was unusually quiet as he sat with Maisy on his knee and watched Karl Eklund working on Jen. Were there any striation marks on the victims' gums, jaws or lips which may determine a size and or age of the tools the killer had used, he wondered? If they found the tools the murderer had used could they match the tools to the victims? His mind was buzzing as they stood at the counter to pay. Jen used her debit card. There wasn't any craft for the robbers of today to learn. There was nothing hard about standing over an unsuspecting victim and noting the number they tapped in.

***

With a fresh focus Dylan marched through the incident room, sat at his desk and picked up his phone.

Professor Stow wasn't available but the pathologist at the mortuary confirmed it was possible to get striation marks from tools that had been used to extract teeth from victims if they could find the tools used.

Dylan created the necessary action to be put on the incident room computer system – HOLMES.

The new line of enquiry lifted Dylan and the team when in debrief he announced that Professor Stow had agreed to re-examine the victims' jaws and the sockets where the teeth had been removed for possible fresh evidence.

'I will meet you at the mortuary tomorrow morning and bring CSI Jarvis along with you,' Stow had said.

The debrief otherwise was an insignificant one, with nothing of note and the TIE enquiries (trace interview and eliminate) were a continuous stream of lines of necessary, prioritised investigations.

***

The next morning, booted and suited with Professor Stow at the examination table in the mortuary the two bodies were brought out of their respective fridges.

Dylan spoke to Stow about Dr Eklund's cabinet, displaying the antiquarian dentistry tools.

'I wondered if there was a possibility that we could age the tools that the murderer used?' said Dylan.

'You don't want a lot, do you?' said Stow.

'I know it's a lot to ask,' said Dylan. 'But, if you could just indicate to us if the striation marks that are present on the gum and jaw are the same, this means we can link them based on the same principle as marks found at scenes are from the same knife, screwdriver...'

'The odontologist could no doubt help us further but I've brought a rather nifty piece of equipment with me with a rather powerful magnifying eye piece. Additional lighting Jarv might help?' he said.

CSI Jarvis manipulated the lights to give Professor Stow the best sight of the wound.

'I'll remove the mandibles, the lower jaws, take them back with me to the lab and dependant on how that goes I may need to examine the maxilla cavities too.'

The stance that Stow took could only be likened to a jeweller examining the quality of a diamond. All the pair heard from him was the occasional grunt. Dylan and Sarah Jarvis waited patiently.

Fifteen minutes later Professor Stow asked for two exhibit bags as he independently dislocated and cut through adjoining tissue to release the mandibles. He now had two lower jaws in plastic bags which were clearly marked.

'I hope I don't get stopped en route Inspector. They'll think I regularly break the jaw if they find these two.' He laughed at his own joke heartily. 'Break the jaw! Get it?'

***

The three sat in the office, a cup of tea in hand. Dylan was happy to see Professor Stow had regained his sense of humour. Albeit very corny.

'Well?' Dylan said. 'What are your thoughts?'

'I don't want to build your hopes up, they need to be looked at with a keener eye I would suggest but what is interesting for me, from this initial examination, is that there may be, and I emphasise may be, some reoccurrence with the way the teeth have been extracted and what they have been extracted with... there is definitely something different about the particular instruments used that's pretty unique.'

'Good, that's good,' said Dylan.

'The lab at Sheffield will invoice you for the work Inspector, and my guess is that the work that has now to be done will be time consuming.'

'What you're saying is that this is going to cost me. I'm sure I will blow my budget with this enquiry but in my mind providing we have results it is money well spent.'

'And that we will never know until we try.'

'Just get me a result then I can justify the expenditure to the hierarchy,' Dylan said with a slight grimace.

'Be assured it will be given priority. This one is interesting, very interesting... I'll be in touch.'

***

How could anyone put a cost to a murder investigation? If there was an open line of investigation on Dylan's enquiries it would be completed. He knew however that the powers that be wouldn't agree. Structure in place, Dylan would now have to be patient but anyone who knew Jack Dylan would say he wasn't a particularly patient man. The days rolled by and the machinery of the incident continued to churn out enquiries or 'actions' as they are commonly known. Every action had to be completed in order of urgency and written up as completed, or not as the case may be, and for what reason. The golden rule for DI Dylan was each action was as important at the last because the last action could be the one that led to the perpetrator. Each member of the team was invaluable to the SIO. Dylan's theory being, a team was only as good as the weakest link and Dylan wouldn't tolerate, under any circumstances a weakened chain.

An audit would be carried out by the HOLMES sergeant at regular intervals which would look at staffing levels, workloads and actions completed. This would make sure that everyone was pulling their weight, this ensured nothing and no one were overloaded and urgent enquiries not missed, buried under a mountain of paper.

A murder investigation has no capacity to carry passengers and anyone Dylan believed was slacking he would personally speak to, if he had to speak to them twice they would be off the investigation and never work on another.

People said he was ruthless. As far as Dylan was concerned it was a professional approach. He also had to justify the continued high staffing levels to Divisions who provided those officers for the initial support. Their Divisional Commanders were always looking to get their staff back. The knock on effect of this, for them, was less bobbies on their beat which reflected in their performance figures. Dylan was constantly reminded that a murder, no matter how violent was recorded as just one crime for the commanders. Dylan was more than aware. But that one crime would create uncertainty and fear in a community as well as what devastation it caused to the families involved. They deserved professional commitment and whilst he was in charge that's what they would get from him and his team.

Jen was back at work and Maisy returned to her child minder's, Dylan hadn't heard from Professor Stow and here had been no major leap forward with either of the murder investigations.

'It's time to share with the media the fact that the victim's teeth have been extracted,' he said at the briefing. 'PC Bullock and PC Mitchell as the family liaison officers I want you to make sure the families are aware of the content of the press release before it goes out.'

***

Dylan parked his car outside the radio station on the industrial estate in Harrowfield. It was nestled in the middle of other light industrial, warehouse type buildings, singled out by its huge masts that reached high into the brilliant blue sky. On entering he was led into the Green Room by the show's producer. He had an earpiece in one ear and headphones draped around his neck.

'I will take you through to the studio in a few minutes,' the producer said. 'Would you like a cup of tea, coffee?'

Dylan smiled at Maggie who he could see in her goldfish-bowl like studio. She put her thumbs up at him.

'Coffee please,' he said making himself comfortable in a big, red chair that was designed in the shape of a hand. Fingers and a thumb comfortably supported his back. The music played softly in the background and Maggie Currie announced his arrival at the station, on air. He looked up at the opening of the door and the producer came in with a mug in his hand.

'Would you like to follow me and I'll take you through to the studio?' he said.

The huge desk Maggie sat behind engulfed her small frame. Dylan was guided to a seat opposite her. The producer positioned a microphone in front of him. He looked around him at the thick fibreglass lined walls as Maggie flicked switches, pressed buttons and hit keys on a keyboard. When she had completed her tasks she looked up at him and put her headphones to the back of her head as the news played.

'Dylan,' she said standing up and leaning towards him to peck him on the cheek. 'Lovely to see you again. I will be speaking to you just after the weather, is that okay?'

The producer disappeared and the On Air light above the door was immediately illuminated.

The room was full of monitors, speakers, digital audio equipment.

'Joining me this afternoon is Detective Inspector Jack Dylan from Harrowfield CID who is with us to make a direct appeal in relation to the recent murders in Harrowfield. And you have some interesting information to share with us today haven't you Inspector?'

'Thank you for having me on your show Maggie. The investigations into the brutal murders of Davina Walsh and Carl Braithwaite continue to move forward at pace. Today, I'm here to primarily make an appeal to anyone with information to contact the incident room at Harrowfield Police Station or if they don't feel they can do this for any reason they can anonymously contact Crimestoppers on 0800 555 111 who will pass on the information on their behalf.'

'And you have news on those investigations for us don't you?'

'Yes, today we are releasing information which we hope will encourage people to come forward. It has become apparent that there is a macabre and bizarre twist in both crimes. The killer randomly and roughly removed some of the victims' teeth which is linking both these enquiries for us.'

The interview finished, the producer came back in to the studio and whisked Dylan out before the next item was broadcast.

'Thank you,' he said. 'That was great. Let's hope we get some response.'

'I'll let you know,' said Dylan. 'I'd have liked for the appeal to be stronger but I didn't want to strike more fear in the community.'

'Hopefully it will have the desired effect.'

'Well, if he rings here the trace is set up and static obs are in place at the previously used telephone booth, mobile patrols ready to respond.

Dylan was back at the police station but within the hour the caller had bit.

'Good girl Maggie,' said the caller. 'Glad you did as I asked. But, now ask him why he's lying? He said the extractions were random when he knows they were not.' The caller's voice was irate towards the end.

Dylan and the team waited with bated breath.

'Sorry boss,' came the call. 'He didn't use the same phone booth.'

'I guess that's not a surprise,' said Dylan. 'Don't worry Vicky.'

'Wait on. He did use a call box within a five mile radius and the response was quick, just not quick enough. The drive past proved the box to be empty and there was no one in the immediate vicinity.'

'I wonder where he lives,' said Dylan. 'What we do know is that he listens to the local radio station.'

'Does that suggest he lives in the locality?' said Vicky.

'At one time I'd have said yes, but these days, especially with the availability of being able to listen in on the internet, I'm not so sure...'

Dylan put down the phone and immediately it rang again.

'Professor Stow!' said Dylan.

'We've linked the striation marks and we are now trying to date the implement with the odontologist by its size if that's at all possible,' he said.

Dylan began to structure more press releases, anything he could think of that would keep the murders in the public eye and would be relevant enough for the media to pick up and run with. Using the family members at a conference, photographs of the deceased and going over their last movements before their deaths. He hoped one of these would jog someone's memory.

'Human teeth and dental instruments are available on the internet, Amazon, eBay...' said Ned Granger. 'That's where my friend gets them from.'

'Enquire with Amazon and eBay and see if they have ways and means to see if they can tell us if any have been delivered to Harrowfield or surrounding areas recently. I don't want anything left to chance if we are able to obtain that sort of information,' said Dylan.

'I've a list of prison releases and other institutions for people arriving or returning to the Harrowfield area. These are being worked through, traced, interviewed and eliminated where possible,' said DS Raj.

Debrief over Dylan dismissed the officers. Everyone needed a good night's sleep.

Dylan's respite was brief as he was awoken at four o'clock the next morning by the control room which required Dylan's attendance at the scene of a taxi driver who had been robbed and murdered. It was on his patch and he was the on call senior investigative officer.

Chapter Eight

Dylan travelled the main road that linked Harrowfield to Breland his thoughts in disarray. Had the taxi driver been killed for his cash? Or could this latest murder be connected to the others? Part of him hoped it would be linked. The early hour meant that typical of a Sunday morning he passed people staggering, brawling and crawling home – literally. Some would be under the influence of drink and others drugs. Age nor creed, drink and drugs did not appear to be discriminatory as to the influence it had on humans.

He stopped the car at a red traffic light. Alongside, a traffic officer was standing at the driver's side of a sports car. It was apparent by his stance, and pad in hand, that he had given the young driver a tug, for motoring offences.

'Do you know who my father is?' Dylan heard the driver say. Dylan looked his way. He knew that arrogance would not go down well with his colleague.

'No, didn't your mother tell you? Now do as you're told and get out,' the officer snarled.

So much for the kid's bravado Dylan thought with a smile on his face as the lights turned green.

'If only your fathers could see you now,' Dylan said shaking his head at a group of girls, laughing hysterically after collapsing in a heap at the pavement edge of a zebra crossing.

Dylan knew only too well that sadly amongst these were potential victims. Harrowfield, like many towns and cities provided numerous opportunities for predators who were out and about, like foxes in the night, scouring for isolated, incapacitated prey.

He wished he had a pound for every time he'd heard a parent say, 'If only I'd picked them up.' 'If only I had told them they couldn't go.' Or the victims cry, 'If only I'd got a taxi.' 'If only I had credit on my mobile phone.' If was a little word with a big meaning and hindsight, as everyone knew, is a wonderful thing.

Dylan was almost at his destination. He drove slowly so he didn't miss the road sign. The tripe factory and a cattle market of yesteryear had long gone. As a young PC Dylan would chase rats around the wasteland, loading bays andcar parks on nights. He could still smell the pungent odour that was worse during the night shift. Cow heel, elder and tripe, was considered a tasty treat in those days. His parents and grandparents might have succumbed to the delicacies but he never had. He shuddered at the thought of them.

He saw blue flashing lights in the distance and headed towards them. Adrenaline started to pump through his veins. Had the killer struck again, so soon? If so his workload had just increased – three undetected murders which in police terms meant that the attacker had just gained himself the title of serial killer. Should this be the case, things would change in the investigations. An Assistant Chief Constable would be assigned to overlook the investigations as per Home Office guidelines – albeit this ACC did not have to have any investigative skills. The financial cost to the Force would be a huge implication as would the impact on Divisions; more staff would be seconded to the investigation with immediate effect. There was no doubt he would be heading this enquiry, even though he had two more murder investigations on the go. He knew the Force had no one available to step in to take charge, they hadn't even advertised for senior investigating officers this time around. This wasn't an oversight on their part but an intention to keep to the overall budget, which was at an all-time low, to achieve government targets. The thin blue line was almost non-existent and it worried Dylan where it would all end. As for the Assistant Chief Constable no matter who he or she was he would be more than happy for them to deal with the policies and press. This was a positive role they could take on without being hands on in the investigation. It was an opportunity for the person in the ACC role to use their vocal skills that had been developed extensively in training. 'In the theatre of operations' was always a good line for them to make use of or 'no one will penetrate the ring of steel' another. Phrases like this made Dylan smile. There was nothing surer than he and his team would carry on as normal, with their shirt-sleeves rolled up in the arena doing battle.

Dylan was no stranger to dealing with serial killers but he worried about the effect the label for the killer would have on the community. It gave him and his team another chance to obtain evidence against the killer. The other part of him hoped it wasn't. Whatever, one thing he knew for certain was that another family on his patch would be awoken with the same horrendous, life changing news. A loved one was dead.

Dylan waited at a crossroads. He felt the knot in his tie and ran his finger under his collar. He knew some of his colleagues turned out in the middle of the night to incidents in jeans but what sort of image did that portray to the public, he thought? Especially ten hours later when they stood in front of the media. He was confident in his own mind that perpetrators watched the news to see what the person looked like that was leading the hunt for them. The public, he felt, also needed to have confidence in the Senior Investigator and first impressions for both were of no doubt important.

Decidedly buzzing and anxious to get on with the job in hand he steered his car into the side of the road and parked directly behind a marked police car. Beyond the crime scene tape he could see a yellow cab with the taxi sign illuminated on its roof. His mind was focused on what was in front of him. He got out of the car and walked towards a small group of people. He could make out DS Vicky Hardacre, Ned Granger and DC Wormald amongst others who were unrecognisable due to already being booted and suited. Uniformed officers were guarding the scene. Crime Scene Investigators were setting up, handing out coveralls from the back of their van and unloading equipment. It was unprecedentedly quiet. Everyone was doing the job they were trained for and with the minimum of fuss. The best way to deal with a heinous sight as a murder usually was, in his experience, to concentrate on what needed to be done to preserve the evidence to catch the person responsible. To let emotion get in the way was asking for trouble. There was nothing else that could be done for the poor soul who had died but justice would prevail if it was anything to do with Dylan's team and they would put the perpetrator behind bars. As Dylan got closer to the scene his eyes looked beyond the team and to the taxi cab. The driver's door was open and the cab was positioned neatly at the side of the kerb. The weather was not a concern so no evidence should be lost this time to the elements.

Vicky left the group and walked towards Dylan. Very carefully she carried two white plastic cups.

'Coffee boss?' she said. 'Crap vending machine stuff from the foyer of Bentley's Mill over there,' she said indicating the imposing soot-blackened building opposite, 'but it's better than nothing.'

'Looks like the soup we used to get at the swimming baths as a kid. Kind of them though,' he said taking a sip. He winced. 'So what have we got?'

'Alan Bell, cab driver, forty-five years old... Been doing the job for going on twenty years according to his mate Micky, so he was no stranger to the game. He's a bachelor and we're told he is known to his friends as "Film Star" because of his love of cosmetic surgery – all he spends his money on. Well, that and his foreign holidays.'

Dylan raised his eyebrows at Ned who joined them. '...yes, before you ask. He's had his teeth whitened boss.'

'He also has a gym membership and is never without a tan,' Vicky said.

'Whatever floats your boat,' Ned said.

'Maybe you could take over his gym membership Ned?' Vicky pulled her jacket tightly around her. 'What are you looking at me like that for? I don't need to go to the gym,' she said.

'If the cap fits,' said Ned. One dark eyebrow lifted and a corner of his mouth tipped up.

'Fit for his age,' said Vicky.

'Well, not anymore,' said Dylan studiously.

'His mouth is open and it looks like teeth are missing,' said Ned.

'So, we think our man has struck again do we?' said Dylan his eyes scanning Vicky's face.

'It certainly looks that way. Paramedics have pronounced life extinct. Mr Bell appears to have been garrotted in a similar way to Davina Walsh,' said Vicky.

'Last sighting of him?' said Dylan.

'Just after midnight; he was in George Square, Harrowfield. At the taxi rank chatting with late night revellers, according to Micky. He found him. Apparently, according to his mate Film Star liked to think of himself as a bit of a ladies man.'

'So he may have picked up his fare, the killer, from the rank?' said Dylan. 'How come his mate raised the alarm?'

'Micky was dropping off a fare about an hour later when he saw Mr Bell's, taxi here, with its lights on and the driver's door wide open to the pavement. He didn't think anything of it, but on his return from dropping off his fare it was still here.'

'Where is he now?'

'Micky? He's gone back to the rank but I've got his details.'

Dylan nodded his head.

'I'm on with Control to see what CCTV coverage or speed cameras we have between here and George Square. Sarah Jarvis is your crime scene manager and DC Wormald exhibits, boss.'

'Thanks Vicky, you seem to have everything covered so let me have a closer look at what we have and then we'll get things moving before the town awakes.'

Dylan, Vicky and Andy walked towards the inner cordon. Jarv came towards them.

'Have you taken all the pictures we need before we go ahead?' Dylan said.

'Yes, and the footplates are in situ.'

'Good, we'll do this together then, shall we?' said Dylan turning to the others.

'According to Micky, he thinks Alan Bell has an internal camera covering the backseat of his taxi,' Vicky said.

'Now that's what I like to hear,' said Dylan. 'Get onto HQ I want screens around this site and this road blocked. The last thing I want to see is a picture of the cab on the TV or in some daily newspaper, unless we give it them.'

'You can imagine the headline can't you, "Film Star murdered in Harrowfield."'

The lifeless body of Alan Bell was slumped in the driver's seat. A faint line around his throat showed Dylan the fatal wound. With the help of the Dragon Lamp he could see that the cut on his neck stretched from ear to ear, and due to there not being a vast amount of blood Dylan knew that Mr Bell had bled internally. The downside of this was that there would not be a lot of opportunity to find blood staining on the attacker, or his clothing should they trace a suspect.

'Aha! Maybe today is going to be your lucky day Dylan?' said Jarv who had opened the back door and was on her haunches closely surveying something she had found in the footwell.

'How do you figure that one out?' Dylan said uncurling himself from the passenger side of the taxi. 'I've been woken in the early hours, dragged out of my warm bed to see this horrific sight and I now find our murdering bastard has gained the label of serial killer which means I'm going to very soon have an ACC on my back.'

'One thing's for certain it's going to be a long day,' said Vicky.

'Well, when you put it that way...' said Jarv. 'But look what we have here, on the floor. It's a garrotte. Could that be our murder weapon?' she said. Clicks and flashes resulted in her squeezing her camera into the footwell with her and photographing her find in situ before it was removed as evidence.

'Left behind intentionally or dropped accidentally?' said Dylan.

'It looks like a guitar string and it also looks to have blood on it,' Jarv said, looking up into Dylan's eyes.

'Okay, I'll give you it's a good start. But I want someone arrested and charged, then and only then will I feel like we've had a stroke of luck today.'

'Do you reckon it was always his intention to be branded a serial killer?' Vicky said.

'Oh my,' said Jarv. 'I think we might have also had a visit from the tooth fairy.' The CSI Supervisor was shining her torch onto the back seat. 'Look there.' She pointed to a large tooth. 'It's an upper molar.'

'How do you know that?' said Vicky.

'Because it has three roots, lower molars have only two,' said Jarv.

Dylan returned to look with greater interest into the victim's mouth. It was quite clear, as Ned had pointed out that there was a number of teeth missing.

'Is it one of his do you think?' said Vicky.

'I don't think so. It looks like he has taken different teeth once again from this victim... Although we will have to wait to get him to the mortuary to be sure.'

'He'll have a set soon...' said Vicky.

'His intention do you think?' said Jarv.

It was apparent from the noise that the crime scene was now proving to be of interest to nearby residents who appeared at the cordon in all different states of undress.

'I want the body and the taxi away from here as a matter of urgency. We need to be aware of prying eyes.'

Traffic was relatively light and being diverted, but some people's curiosity Dylan knew would encourage them to get as close as they could to the scene.

'Vicky, have we an ETA for those screens we requested?'

She shook her head. 'No, not yet, sir.'

'Will you ask HQ to arrange for a low-loader to come and pick up this vehicle and tell them to send a protective covering for its transportation? I want the taxi lifted and taken to the lab to let the scientists have the best chance inside and out for securing evidence.'

'Will do boss,' said Vicky.

Within minutes she was back. 'ETA of the screens, twenty minutes; low-loader within the hour.'

'Thanks, we'll need someone to oversee the covering and lifting of the vehicle. Jarv perhaps you and another from CSI would probably be the best for the job? Did I see Stew somewhere around?'

'Yes boss,' said Vicky pointing in the CSI's direction.

'Will you two liaise with forensic in these initial stages?'

'Consider it done,' she replied.

The body of Alan Bell and his taxi cab would be examined in detail later.

'Notify Professor Stow Home Office Pathologist will you?' Dylan said. 'I want him to carry out the post-mortem. He is aware that I will be contacting him should we have another,' Dylan said to Control. 'Vicky, I want the length and breadth of this road checked for any evidence.'

Dylan's thoughts were in free fall. Did the killer have transport or had he walked away? He stood quietly and surveyed the killer's options. Was there an exit that was more appealing due to the fact he could disappear quickly? What direction was that from the scene? The location was a built up area, main road. Was this the killer's intended location for a victim from the outset; if so, why? Dylan could leave nothing to chance. Anything lying around chewing gum, cigarette butts, sweet wrappers, crisp packets, cans, bottles, everything that was recently discarded he wanted photographed in situ then bagged and tagged and retained as potential evidence.

'If there is a chance of getting DNA then preserve it,' he told Simon Clegg, from the search team who had now arrived on site. 'It might be a slow process but it's a vital one.'

A press conference was arranged by the press office for him from Harrowfield Police Station for eight thirty.

'We will supply the press with brief details and some distant photographs of the scene can be taken,' Dylan said.

'Will you be giving them pictures of the victim's vehicle?' said the press officer.

'Yes, we will have pictures taken and I'll ensure you get them as soon as possible.'

'I want to appeal to anyone out in the town centre last night using or seeing the distinctive yellow taxi to contact me. It's likely that the press will interpret the scene as that of a robbery and I will allow them to take that route at this stage as it appears that money is missing. I won't drop the bombshell of the killer striking again until a later press conference once we have established all the facts,' Dylan said.

The detectives moved away from the inner scene. 'What I need right now is a full English breakfast,' said Vicky.

'Trust you to always think of your stomach,' said Ned.

'Come on, my shout,' said Dylan. 'I want to clear my head before we brief the teams and the inevitability of an Assistant Chief Constable arriving.'

Chapter Nine

Murder was at the forefront of Dylan's mind. DS Raj waited for him and DS Hardacre in the incident room. Standing at the window she saw Dylan's car flash out of the shadows and pull up in his space directly under the incident room window. He got out and appeared to stand and survey his surroundings as he waited for Vicky to alight. Rajinder heard the beep of the car alarm and she watched them turn the corner of the building and head for the police station entrance. From her position she saw not two detectives but two colleagues with the same purpose climb the stairs in silence, each with their own thoughts. Dylan and Vicky gave her a knowing nod as they approached, the strain of the enquiries and tiredness etched on their faces.

'The name given to the Alan Bell murder enquiry is Operation Saturn,' she said as they walked together briskly through the incident room's doors. Dylan saw her take a few deep breaths, no doubt in his mind this was the body's protest against the long suspense.

As luck would have it the incident rooms for Operation Walnut, Davina Walsh murder and Operation Tapestry, Carl Braithwaite murder were on the same floor at Harrowfield Police Station. The virtual screens had been taken down in what seemed like a dramatic unveiling of the two being merged and a third murder enquiry that of Alan Bell, Operation Saturn taken on board. The collective teams awaited the head of the enquiry with anticipation.

DS Rajinder Uppal, as were many others, had been called in before dawn to get the incident room up and running.

Direct sunlight did not penetrate the incident room but it was well lit with artificial lighting. This was a place that would never sleep until the perpetrator was apprehended and charged.

Dylan noticed that at the end of the incident room another visual aid board had appeared alongside that of the first two murder enquiries. These were of major importance to allow the team easy retrieval of salient points being added, as and when the information came in. Used like a classroom whiteboard they held pictures of the victims, the crime scenes, names, dates, reference numbers, known facts about them and the crimes, suspects and their associates. Dylan had some sixty staff in the room that were ready to hang on his every word. Some were working at their work stations. Others who didn't have a desk in the incident room sat on extra chairs that had been brought in, drinking coffee, exchanging notes, reacquainting themselves with colleagues they had not seen in a while. This body of people, the best available to him, were drafted in from neighbouring divisions, or further afield for their expertise to help him find the killer.

'Since the killer has now linked the murders for us all three operations are now officially merged,' said Dylan, looking around the incident room. 'We have an individual, who is putting us all to the test. Very quickly we need to let him know that he is dealing with the professionals that we are. We will be taking onboard the murder overnight of Alan Bell, better known to his friends as Film Star. This tried and tested practice will enable us to see things as a bigger picture in the hunt for what Home Office Guidelines now class as a series of Category A murders linking to one perpetrator, a premeditated killer. There is a possibility for more staff to be brought onto the enquiry as and when we need them and of course an ACC will be taking overall charge which will mean that we won't have to wait as long for decisions, from the top, to be made.' The onlookers exchanged silent glances, raised eyebrows, shared a few muted words. Dylan forced a smile, a smile that concealed a slight anguish.

The telephones in the CID office rang intermittently. They were answered immediately.

Being a career detective Dylan had reached a realisation of a human attachment that was somehow elemental and subconscious. His training and experience kept him detached from the horrific sights and emotion in his work. He might not appear to show emotions, but he was desperate to catch the person responsible for the crimes, before he struck again. Trouble was, first and foremost Dylan was a human being beneath the mask and he did care. He cared a lot about man's inhumanity to his fellow man.

***

Dylan checked his mail box, he saw that he had been notified that PC Wiley had been suspended. He took a deep breath and sighed. Vicky sat silently opposite writing in the policy book. She looked across the desk at him. Her blue eyes fixed on Dylan. 'What?' she said.

'Wiley, he's been suspended...'

'Why does it shock you?' she said. 'He won't be the first to be found with his trousers around his bloody ankles on duty, and I very much doubt he'll be the last, do you?' she said. Her head bowed and she carried on regardless.

'I don't know how they find time to... When I was a probationer, I remember a uniformed sergeant and a policewoman on our shift getting caught in a compromising position on a golf course. Their goal, I heard afterwards was to have sex on a different green every night of their night week.'

'Classy,' she said. 'What happened?'

'Complaints from the public and hints to the duty inspector meant they were eventually caught at Hole six. '

'It took the Inspector a week to catch them at it?' she said. 'One of my shift inspectors was nicknamed Dustin.'

Dylan sat back in his chair, his eyebrows knitted together and he ran his hand tentatively over his chin. 'Why?'

'Dustin Hoffman; The Graduate? He was a graduate entry, bright but fucking useless... Theory-wise he was shit hot and very eloquent both orally and in writing, but when it came to practical application he was found seriously wanting.'

'What happened to him?'

'Which ACC are we getting?' she said with a smile spreading across her young, pretty face.

'Oh Christ, no, don't say...' said Dylan.

DS Raj walked in the CID office, sat down at the desk and instantly tided up Vicky's clutter that had spread into her personal space. Files were put back in the filing cabinet, pens in the drawer, coffee cups placed on the tray and moved to the kitchen. She put her shopping bag on the chair and pulled out sandwiches, drinks, fruit and crisps.

'Hey, Mary Poppins, you got anything in there for me?' shouted Vicky from inside Dylan's office.

'I might not like exercise, but I know someone who likes it even less,' said Raj with a flick of her head.

'I have to conserve my energy for more pressing matters. You know, I think I might have a male brain,' said Vicky wandering through Dylan's office door, into the main office, empty cups in her hands. 'Seriously, I've been reading this article...'

'Let's get on shall we ladies? Bring a pen and paper with you.' Dylan called as he fingered the pages of the updated policy book. 'I want you to check with the incident room staff that all enquiries into dentistry are prioritised. Dental practices and hospitals, must be checked in relation to employees for those known to have left at any stage of their with dentistry training. Army medics... you get the drift?' he shouted.

Vicky looked at Raj, put the cups down on Raj's desk and turned on her heels. Raj's eyes looked at the offending drinking vessels defeated, picked up her pad and pen and followed Vicky into Dylan's office. They sat down - pen poised.

'I know it's a long shot but it would be naive of us to ignore the fact that he has acquired some skill in dental extractions and that enquiry will, I know, be pretty open ended but we know for a fact our man has some experience in dentistry, we just don't know to what extent. Raj, I've already upset the Press Office because of my delay in getting to them, will you give them an update? I want to speak to Maggie at the radio station to let her know there has been another murder and warn her that another call should be anticipated. Vicky, make sure the action to trace and observe phone boxes in the vicinity of the ones we already know have been used by the caller, is ongoing. Check that covert cameras are in place at those telephone kiosks and I want plain clothes observations on them, today.'

Alan Bell's home was searched but revealed nothing obvious to assist the investigation. There was only one known living, distant relative in Scotland who was informed of the death. It appeared that he had never met Mr Bell and therefore was unable to assist them in their enquiries.

**

The press officer was relieved to see Jack Dylan arrive at the press conference which was packed full of journalists. So much so that the detective inspector imagined the numbers probably breached all health and safety regulations.

Dylan stood behind the chair indicated for him to sit upon. Nodding to a few familiar faces he put his finger between his neck and his shirt collar and cleared his throat. He pulled his shirt cuffs from under the arms of his suit jacket and opened the button on his jacket before sitting down behind a table which held a jug of water, a glass and a plethora of microphones, perched precariously in all directions. The flash of the cameras was a hundred times more intense than a photo booth and although from experience he expected it to happen on his sitting down, it still caused him to blink in quick succession several times. They subsided a little in anticipation that he was to start speaking. Then the room fell silent.

Dylan outlined to those present firstly the circumstances of how the body of Alan Bell was discovered in his taxi in the early hours of the morning. He told them Mr Bell had received a serious injury to his throat and that he had been robbed. He went on to say that the investigation was still in its infancy and a post-mortem had yet to be carried out, after which time he would hopefully be able to tell them more. Before they got chance to ask questions in respect of the other two murders he informed the assembled press that in respect of the murders of Davina Walsh and Carl Braithwaite he would be holding a press conference at eight o'clock tomorrow morning to update them on developments. He assured the media more resources were being drafted into the area and that all the investigations were moving at pace. Dylan concluded, 'Ladies and gentleman as you can see I am extremely busy, therefore if you have any questions with regard to those incidents, of which I'm sure there are plenty, I will make myself available in the morning.' He reinforced the appeal for witnesses in respect of the brutal murder of the local taxi driver before leaving the room.

Dylan had purposely not mentioned at the conferences the teeth extractions hoping that it would encourage the anonymous caller to open dialogue with the radio presenter. He was sure that the perpetrator would be watching for an update and media coverage of his latest crime.

***

Professor Stow was on his way to carry out the post-mortem on Mr Bell. Forensic had taken receipt of the taxi cab and Beryl Knight assured Dylan that it was presently undergoing tests in the lab.

'I need to know as a matter of urgency as much about the tooth that was found on the back seat and the string we believe our killer may have used as the garrotte,' said Dylan.

'Don't worry,' said Beryl. 'You now have a dedicated team of scientists on the case and I am taking the lead.'

***

Dylan stood at the side of Crime Scene Supervisor Sarah Jarvis at the post-mortem. DC Wormald bagged and tagged the exhibits handed to him by Professor Stow who confirmed to Dylan that the cause of death for Alan Bell was in no doubt by way of a garrotte and that the teeth had been neatly extracted following the pattern of the previous two murders. On this occasion however the killer had for some reason chosen to take a couple of premolars.

'In brief, my expert opinion is that the dental implement used to extract this persons teeth is one and the same as was used in the other two murders. Here look,' Professor Stow said, pointing into the open mouth of the deceased, 'the same size, the same shape, the same indentation marks can quite clearly be seen, now I know what I'm looking for. I'll send you a written report in due course with relevant photographs,' he said at the exact moment that Jarv took another photo. Professor Stow flinched. 'Simply, this dentistry tool comparison will be of as much use to you as

130

the indents of a specific jemmy mark used to force windows or doors during a burglary, but obviously on a much, much smaller scale. Find me the implements Inspector and I'll tell you if they were responsible,' he said with a flaccid grin.

Dylan wondered if the killer had been disturbed to have only taken two of the victim's teeth this time? Or was the purpose of this crime to leave a tooth and the garrotte for the detectives to find?

***

On his return from the mortuary Dylan read the message that had been left on his desk, it was from Assistant Chief Constable Wendy Smythe. 'I have been given the task of overseeing the murders, please ring my secretary on your return from the mortuary to arrange for you to attend HQ. I will require an up to date briefing from you as soon as possible.'

Well, well, Windy-Wendy was to take charge. She was well known for her reluctance to make a decision or sign her name to anything. Which Dylan had to admit was an art in itself.

'Why the hell couldn't she come here?' Dylan said out loud.

'Who?' said Vicky.

'ACC Smythe.'

'Windy-Wendy,' said Vicky. 'I've heard she never comes out of her office. Maybe that rumour is actually true?'

Dylan scowled.

'Ah, don't moan. You can't have it all ways, at least she won't interfere with the enquiry will she?' said Vicky.

'I wouldn't mind if an ACC would show an interest in an enquiry, for the team's sake,' he said. 'All the information I'm going to need to brief her is here,' he said waving his arm around the room. '... and the rest easily retrievable whilst she is here with the qualified personnel for her to talk to.'

'Ah but... what would you rather do? Stay in your own carpeted office, with the most up to date computer, your personal assistant on hand to bring you drinks and food and air conditioning or have your batman sitting in traffic in this heat, albeit in your nice car the force provides for you...' Vicky stopped as if to think on that, 'and come to this hell hole?

131

Anyway, she's no bloody experience in CID so she'd be pretty darn useless to us anyway.'

'She could make the coffee?' said Ned.

'I'll get her out here to show support for the team if it bloody kills me,' said Dylan picking up the phone.

Ned raised his eyebrows, Vicky pulled a face, Dylan turned his back on them both.

'Assistant Chief Constable's office how can I help you?' said ACC Smythe just as Lisa came into his office flapping an A4 piece of paper in front of him.

Urgent: 'Maggie Currie has received another call at Vectis Radio,' she had written. 'Officers have a suspect in view and are about to strike.'

Chapter Ten

Dylan immediately cut the phone call to the ACC's office. He looked serious and sat perfectly still as if considering his next move. He blinked. Opened his mouth as if to say something when the phone rang. He picked up instead. 'Dylan,' he snapped.

'DC Sue Philburn, sir, surveillance unit,' said the plain clothes detective. Dylan was aware of all eyes upon him. His eyes locked onto Vicky's face.

It was apparent to her the message had thrown Dylan. None of them had expected the mysterious caller to contact the radio station again so quickly.

'Was it the same kiosk do you know that was used last time?' Vicky whispered to Lisa who shrugged her shoulders in return.

'Boss, we've just nicked a thirty-year-old white male by the name of Michael Hook,' DC Philburn said.

Dylan's face was expressionless. He listened intently. 'Go on.'

'He made the call to the radio station and was still speaking to the presenter when we collared him. I don't know the exact details of the conversation but apparently I am told he was asking for a meet and there was some intimation about being paid for the information. We're about ten minutes away from the nick so once we've booked him in we'll come up to your office.'

'Right thanks for that, and Maggie?'

'We've spoken to her and she'll be ringing you to arrange to come in to make a statement.'

Ned Granger came to the door, eating a Pot Noodle, and making rather a mess of it.

Rajinder turned, scowled and shooed him away.

'Okay thanks for that Sue and well done,' Dylan said, his eyes strangely bright.

No sooner had he replaced his phone, it rang again. Maggie Currie was on the line. Dylan picked up his pen and twiddled it between his fingers as he spoke to her, making notes when applicable on his blotter. Vicky leant across the table to try and see what he had written. She screwed her nose up and shook her head at Raj – Dylan's writing was legendary and was illegible when it suited.

'I told you about the teeth. See, I was right wasn't I? I can give you more but tell me what's in it for me?' the mystery caller had said to Maggie. 'He wanted me to meet up with him and suggested he might have a reward for the information he could give you?' she said. Maggie sounded anxious.

'He did, did he?' Dylan said thoughtfully.

'We've got the conversation taped so I'll pop the recording over to you.'

'There was no specific mention to this morning's murder?' said Dylan.

'No,' Maggie said.

'That's interesting,' he said. Dylan scratched his forehead. 'That's very interesting.'

There being no specific talk about Alan 'Film Star' Bell's murder led Dylan to believe the caller was not the person they were looking for.

'If he was our murderer,' said Dylan, to the attendees of the briefing. 'I'm sure given the timeliness of the call he would have used the latest killing and the detail of the teeth removal as credibility to taunt us. Like people say, if something appears to be too good to be true, it usually is.'

The atmosphere was sullen, his officers looked deflated, it was Dylan's job to raise their spirits.

The post-it note that asked him to ring ACC Wendy Smythe stared up at him from his desk. He peeled it from the surface, felt its sticky back on his fingers and stuck it back down on his telephone. The call would keep for a while longer. The last thing he wanted was to get off to a bad start with the ACC but he needed to speak to the officers who had apprehended Michael Hook. He wanted to hear more about the call from the radio presenter and the arrest first-hand. Only then could he give ACC Smythe the full picture, as he saw it.

DC Sue Philburn and DC Howard Atkin were followed into his office by Maggie Currie.

The recording was played in its entirety finishing with DC Philburn taking over the call and confirming who she was speaking to.

The caller seemed to be excited about his previous call and his knowledge of the extraction of teeth and as Maggie had told Dylan on the phone he had suggested he could assist further in their enquiries if he could possibly meet with her. The radio presenter had done extremely well to keep him on the line for long enough for them to trace the call. She cleverly had cajoled him into a sense of security.

'I think we can safely say the calls will now stop,' Dylan said to Maggie. 'I don't think for a minute this Michael Hook is our man, he's just some chancer trying to get some money. He's the proverbial time waster. Unfortunately all enquiries attract one nutter or other. We will soon find out for sure when these two have interviewed him,' Dylan said nodding his head towards DC Philburn and DC Atkin.

Dylan turned to the detectives. 'You ready to go into interview?'

'We are, after we have taken a statement from Ms Currie' said DC Philburn who stood, and taking the lead she walked to the door. She turned to see the others behind her. 'We will update you as and when sir,' she said.

***

The day was a sunny one but none of it could be seen from Dylan's office at the rear of the police station. Detective Inspector Dylan had been on the phone to ACC Wendy Smythe for less than a minute. 'Maggie Currie will be at the press conference here representing the radio station tomorrow ma'am, so the plan is that you could meet her here?'

Jack Dylan could hear a phone ringing in the background and Wendy Smythe seemed distracted.

'Sorry Jack, can you just... hold the line for one moment. I must take this call.'

Dylan could hear a one-sided conversation. 'So to confirm the flight departs London Heathrow twenty-one twenty-five hours and arrives Chep Lap Kok at seventeen forty? Yes, thank you.'

He heard the turning of pages, a closing of a zip and perhaps the putting down of a handbag.

'Okay Jack I'm back. So, in relation to me overseeing the trio of homicides you are dealing with. I need to be briefed fully about each incident and we need to plan our strategic way forward.'

'Regarding that briefing, can I suggest that it would be far better to do it at the incident room where we have all the data at our fingertips? We also have display boards for early recollection and depicting the deceased and the scenes.'

She was silent for one moment.

'And of course if you come tomorrow morning it is a major press conference which you might feel you need to be at?'

'Yes, alright. I have to pick up my currency. Might as well do it in Harrowfield as anywhere else. How long will it take to do you suppose?'

'A couple of hours max I would have thought.'

'Oh, so long? Mmm...'

'It's highly likely it will take me so long to take you through all the strategic lines of investigation and bring you up to speed.'

Again Dylan heard the rustle of paper, pages being turned over? This time more slowly as if the book was somewhat larger.

'Yes, of course. I will have to have a meeting with the Chief Constable first.'

'The press conference is planned for eight o'clock tomorrow morning. Will you be spearheading that from an operational point of view? I can deal with the actual incident briefing and questions for you?' said Dylan

'Yes, I'd better had, hadn't I? We need to reassure the public that everything is being done that can be done. It needs someone of my rank to do that. Tell you what, let's do the press conference. I can meet with the radio presenter, then I can come to the incident room for you to brief me. I know it's the wrong way round in terms of procedure but it's probably the best course of action due to the press conference planned for so early in the day.'

'Good. I'll be at Harrowfield Police Station from seven o'clock tomorrow morning so if want to come earlier to be briefed beforehand?'

'No, no, I will be there for the press conference. That's plenty early enough for me.'

'As you are aware ma'am after the main press conference I'll have to do the one-to-one interviews which may take some time. Therefore our incident briefing will be delayed until I've finished doing them,' said Dylan.

'That's fine, it will give me a window to look in on the District Commander Walter Hugo-Watkins and perform an ad-hoc performance review, that will save me time later,' he could hear the smile in her voice. 'I'm off to Hong Kong for a fortnight, staying at the Metro Park Hotel, my brother works for the chain, although he isn't in Hong Kong at the moment. Have you ever been to Hong Kong Jack?'

Vicky came to the door. He waved her in. She sat on the chair at the other side of his desk.

'No, we haven't,' he said. 'I really must go,' he said cupping his hand over the mouthpiece. 'ACC,' he mouthed. His eyes looked up towards the ceiling. Vicky chuckled.

There was a pause at the other end of the phone, the sound of an opening and a closing of a door a clink of a spoon stirring liquid in a cup. In his mind's eye he saw ACC Smythe reclining back in her large leather chair and dreaming of her trip with the brochure in hand.

'You should Dylan,' she said. 'It really is beautiful.'

'Yes, I'd love to. But I doubt that will be happening anytime soon...'

'I've been before. I flew from Heathrow with Virgin Atlantic. Although the return journey was a bit of a nightmare. We flew through storms, got diverted to Leeds/Bradford because of the fog, and then sat on the runway not half a mile from my home for two solid hours, without an alcoholic drink in sight and no air con,' she continued.

Dylan rolled his eyes at Vicky. 'Oh dear, well... let's hope your journey is a lot less eventful this time,' he said. 'I must go...'

'When the fog eventually lifted we took off for Heathrow, and I had to wait four hours for a flight back to Leeds/Bradford!' Wendy Smythe groaned. 'It was just awful.'

'Yes, well hopefully it won't happen again. Now I really must get...'

'Hong Kong airport is actually on the very edge of an island named Lan Tau , it's reclaimed land and some distance from the city, you immediately can't help but be impressed with the terminal and the transport over the suspension bridge as to just how clean it is, clinically clean in fact.'

'Well that's good... Look, I've got to go...'

'Yes, of course. I'll tell you all about it tomorrow. I can bring some photographs with me. I've got some lovely pictures of bauhinia flowers, they are wonderful and just about everywhere in Hong Kong. Sadly we don't see the likes of those exotic flowers growing here even in this heat.'

'Goodbye ma'am. See you tomorrow,' he said and put the phone down, looked up at Vicky and his shoulders slumped. 'I sometimes wonder if those at headquarters live on the same planet as we do,' he said.

'Okay Bye, bye, bye,' she said. ACC Wendy Smythe sat up abruptly in her leather recliner chair and took the phone away from her ear when she heard the dialling tone. She looked at the telephone handset as if it had offended her. She shook it. Had Detective Inspector Jack Dylan just put the phone down on her? She scowled. He really needed to lighten up.

***

'Her eye is NOT on the ball.' Dylan said to Vicky.

'Well you can hardly blame her if she's off on her jollies now can you? '

'Considering what she gets paid, yes?'

'Take it as a compliment that she knows the job is in a safe pair of hands.'

'How much of the briefing tomorrow is going to go over her head too? She is involved for a reason, not just as a bloody figurehead.'

'But like I said she's no CID background has she? Cut her a bit of slack.'

'On a positive note it is an ACC's visit to an incident room and to see anyone at that rank is on our team will lift the others, won't it? At Command level she is on our side in terms of help with resources and financial issues should we have any problems. It can't do the enquiry any harm.'

'And by the sound of it she won't try to take over the day to day running of the investigation and she will leave it to us to get on with it. So it's all good.'

'Do you know you talk a lot of sense sometimes DS Hardacre. You impress me. One day I want to see you sitting behind that desk at headquarters, do you hear me? Now what did you want?'

'Maggie Currie has just left the building. I have taken her statement she has given to be uploaded onto the HOLMES system and DC Philburn and Atkin are in interview at present with Michael Hook. So, I thought it would be a good time for me to find out what's likely to be happening at tomorrow's press conference.'

'I'll be introducing Wendy Smythe as the Commander overseeing the enquiry, with her approval and she will make some sort of statement. I don't know if she will do it before or after the update from me, whichever she feels appropriate. We will have to take her lead on that. I'm sure she will be speaking to the press office later today after her meeting with the Chief. For my part I will confirm that taxi driver Alan Bell is being linked to the previous two murders, that of Davina Walsh and Carl Braithwaite and I'll divulge at that time the common theme throughout the murders which is the removal of teeth. I'll reassure the public that we are working around the clock to catch the murderer and assure them he will be caught.'

Dylan's telephone ringing disrupted his train of thought.

'Dylan,' he said. His eyes appeared to darken.

'Beryl Knight.'

'Beryl, what have you got to tell us? Something good I hope'

'The tooth from the back of the taxi?'

'Yes.'

'It doesn't belong to your taxi driver murder victim, Alan Bell.'

'Who does it belong to? I don't suppose you know?'

'I do actually, yes. I took the liberty of doing some quick checks pre-empting your question.'

Dylan looked across the desk into Vicky's face. His eyes twinkled.

'So, what you're telling me is that it isn't Alan Bell's tooth in the back of the taxi but you know whose it is? Come on Beryl, stop teasing?'

Chapter Eleven

Why would the killer leave Davina Walsh's tooth at the scene of Alan Bell's murder? It didn't make sense. But what it did do in Dylan's mind was reinforce the murderer pre-planned the murder, before setting out.

'He knows exactly what he is doing and it's quite apparent he is very calm in completing his task. What puzzles me is why would he leave Davina's tooth and not Alan's at the scene?' said Raj.

'To link the crimes or to test our investigative skills,' said Dylan.

'Do you think he carries his previous trophies with him when he sets out to murder?' said Vicky.

'He'll be aware that women's teeth are smaller than men's so... Maybe, he wondered if we would pick up on the little clue he obviously left for us?' said Raj.

'He's playing with us,' said Vicky, eyebrows raised.

'He thinks he's in control,' said Raj.

'What concerns me is that he is gaining confidence. It seems to me that he will go on killing until we find him?' said Dylan.

***

At the debriefing that evening he shared with the team the update from forensics and made them aware just what a brutal, manipulative serial killer they were dealing with.

'I'll be breaking to the media tomorrow morning that we have a serial killer on the loose who extracts teeth at the scene of the crimes. ACC Wendy Smythe will join us and because of the serial killer status of the enquiry she will now be in overall command of the investigations into the three murders. Collectively these serial murders will now be known under the official police operational name of 'Operation Tangent'.

***

It was dark and raining when he drove out of the police station yard. The lights in the incident room lit up the second floor of the building and he knew they would continue to burn throughout the night.

Dylan arrived home and here too the lights in the house burned brightly upstairs and down. That could only mean one thing – Maisy was still up. He parked the car and alighted from his vehicle with a spring in his step. If he was lucky he would get to read her a bedtime story. He put his key in the latch feeling happy and opened the door. A feeding cup landed at his feet. Splashes of milk fell on his trouser leg. Maisy squealed. Jen shouted at her. Max who had been about to greet Dylan turned on his paws in the hallway and headed for the kitchen, his flag of a tail in-between his legs. Dylan calmly put his briefcase down and picked the cup up. He threw his jacket over the chair.

Jen was down on her knees facing Maisy, she had a hold of her arm and was also engaged in a conversation on the phone. Her eyes were like hard blue pebbles that matched those of their daughter, who promptly on seeing her daddy burst into tears. Jen let go of her arm and Maisy ran to Dylan, holding her arms up for him to pick her up. He obliged by swiftly sweeping her off her feet. She clung to him and sobbed into his shoulder. He looked at Jen questioningly soothingly rubbing Maisy's back. He stepped over toys that littered the floor.

'Dad,' Jen mouthed, shaking her head. 'There has been a break-in.' Holding the phone between her ear and her shoulder she scooped some bricks up and put them in a container.

'At home?' he said.

'No, at his friends, it's not good, the husband, he's in hospital, he's had a heart attack.' She turned away. 'Yes, Dad I'm still here,' she said.

Dylan took Maisy to bed, her sobs calmed when he started to read to her. He closed her bedroom door quietly behind him when she fell asleep, clinging to her favourite soft toy. Hearing

Jen still on the phone Dylan headed for the bedroom, took off his shirt and tie and put on his jeans. With any luck he wouldn't be called back out.

When he finally got downstairs Jen was in the kitchen pouring them both a glass of wine. She looked tired. The tea she had started preparing, some time ago, languished on the worktop. Maisy's half-eaten supper was in a bowl on the corner of the table. Max had his back to them, his head buried in the cushion of his basket but his tail swished to and fro when he heard Dylan's footsteps on the tiles.

Jen picked up Dylan's large glass between floury fingers, turned and held it out to him. He held it up. 'That bad?' he said.

'Worse,' she said, her shoulders drooping. She turned back towards the worktop, picked up the rolling pin and began rolling out the pastry that had hardened around the edges. 'Supper won't be long,' Jen said wiping the back of her hand across her forehead.

Dylan came up behind her, put his head on her shoulder and hugged her from behind.

'You don't have to...' he said. 'Shall I go and fetch us fish and chips?'

Jen put her head back to his, looked up at the ceiling and then closed her eyes for a moment. 'It's no good letting perfectly good stewing steak go to waste,' she said with a sigh. 'It's not like we can do anything to help them is it?'

Jen turned rolling pin still in hand. 'Is there nothing you can do?'

A weary smile crossed Dylan's face. 'What do you think I can do?' he said. 'Anyway don't you think I have enough on here?'

'Of course,' she said sullenly. 'It's just if I was ever in their position there is no one I'd rather have taking charge of the enquiry but you.'

'I don't know about that. I feel pretty damn useless at the moment. I think I'm getting too bogged down with the killer's motive, rather than the evidence,' he said.

***

Dylan sat quietly in the lounge, ostensibly reading the evening paper, in effect he was going over the details of the murders. Each victim's background was different. They used different dentists. They didn't know each other and they had nothing in common with each other, until their untimely deaths.

The only apparent common denominator was they all had good, strong, white teeth. Was this really the only thing that led the killer to them and if so how? Dylan was still in deep thought when Jen arrived with his dinner on a tray.

'You look troubled,' she said as she sat down beside him. 'Do you want to talk about it?'

'Ah, I was just wondering whether or not I should let the Divisional Commander know that the Assistant Chief Constable is intent on doing an impromptu "performance check" on Harrowfield Division tomorrow.'

'Well she'll be left wanting if she's expecting Hugo-Watkins to know what's happening. He was out with Avril Summerfield-Preston all day today looking for a new painting he could buy for his office.' Jen tutted. 'You're not really thinking about forewarning him are you? Let the bugger reap what he bloody sows.'

Dylan ate his food in silence. He licked his lips and handed her the tray when she stood.

'Pudding,' she said.

'Mmm... give me a minute.' Dylan picked up his phone.

'You're going to warn him aren't you?' She stood to go into the kitchen but turned at the door.

'He gets paid three times as much as you, does half the hours you do and they promoted him two ranks above you, you're crackers,' she said.

'Better the devil you know. If they move him, the Divisional Commander that comes out to cover will only want to make his mark and change things, probably not for the better and then they will move back to whence they came before the implications of the changes impact, so they aren't around to pick up the pieces. But we are there and left to suffer the consequences. At least Hugo-Watkins does care about Harrowfield Division.'

'Only because he lives on the Division.'

Dylan tossed his mobile around in his hand thoughtfully then proceeded to key in a number.

'Walter, I'm just ringing to let you know...' Jen heard Jack say as she went into the kitchen to wash up.

Chapter Twelve

Dylan arrived at work to find television satellite vans and journalists with their gear causing traffic congestion at and around Harrowfield Police Station. It was barely seven a.m. The media frenzy was building towards the press conference and he knew from experience it would only get worse. The town's serial killings would today become national headlines. Murder assured interest. Bad news travelled fast.

It was known that a national news broadcast automatically brought about increased telephone calls to the incident room and staffing levels had been raised in anticipation.

Before the working day began Dylan sat in the tranquil quietness of his office updating his policy book. He was more than prepared for the deluge of questions that would accompany the conference. Although some of his colleagues tried their utmost to avoid being interviewed by the media Dylan didn't mind they, like he, had a job to do and journalists knew how to spread the word and had the platform to do it efficiently and effectively. It was getting them to sustain their interest that he had a problem with. The appeals he had written were about to reach a nationwide audience and who knew what or who that may bring to their attention.

The door swung open and Vicky tumbled in his office and took a few wobbly steps towards his desk in her high heeled shoes. 'Was it you who tipped old Walter off that Windy-Wendy was coming?' she said.

'Why?'

'Him and Beaky have just followed me into the back yard.' She took one look at his face for her answer. 'I guessed you had. It was either that or they'd both pee'd the bed. I don't know why you bother?' Vicky scowled. 'What's he ever done for you?'

He pointed to invisible sergeant's stripes at the top of her arm. 'We've got a short memory haven't we Vicky?'

'Well yeah, but he knew he was getting a good deal when he helped me with my sergeant's boards.'

'Maybe, but he didn't have to help you. Tell Lisa that the ACC will be here at anytime now will you and ask her if we can have a pot of tea; cups and saucers would be nice please.'

'Tea? Have you completely lost the plot?' she said screwing her nose up. 'What's up with coffee?'

'Tea, it's what she has requested,' said Dylan.

'Oooo it's what she requests now is it?' she repeated parrot fashion just as Rajinder entered the incident room with ACC Wendy Smythe in tow.

The ACC looked very smart in her uniform. Dylan rose to greet her. She carried with her a shiny black leather briefcase that was in slightly newer condition than Dylan's old, battered one. He kicked his under his desk and out of sight.

'Jack arrr,' she said.

Dylan's eyes flashed from Wendy Smythe to Raj. The ACC giggled like a school kid. 'Don't mind me - just practicing my chinese. Ney Ho!'

Dylan couldn't hide his disapproval at her inappropriate manner.

***

The conference room was full. Reporters sat with their notebooks and pens on their laps. Television cameras, lights and shades adorned each end of the room along with their operators, all were trying to get the best angle for their TV footage. Microphones of all shapes and sizes stood alongside, or lay haphazardly upon the table that the ACC and Dylan would sit at. Large banners with the police logo stood upright at the back of the chairs and covered the door where they would walk in from the corridor beyond, that ultimately led into the heart of the police station. Dylan was impressed with Wendy Smythe's approach. She didn't profess to know everything about the investigation or about investigative procedure and neither was she afraid to ask – unlike some officers of the same rank. The strategy was agreed between her and Dylan and she asked if she could meet with Dylan for lunch afterwards.

'Looks like you'll be finding out more about the Hong Kong expedition boss,' said Vicky out of the corner of her mouth. Dylan scowled at her but found himself nodding in agreement at the ACC's request.

It was eight-thirty a.m. exactly when they sat united behind the desk. Only at this point did the flashing from the cameras cease. Wendy Smythe spoke clearly and with an air of calm. The gathered audience hung onto her every word. She had the full room under her spell and there was recognition for her faith in the Senior Officer Detective Inspector Jack Dylan and an endorsement for his track record in solving homicide enquiries.

It was now Dylan's turn to speak of the enquiry itself.

'I will remind you of the three murders in their order of discovery, why and how they are being linked followed by an appeal,' he said. 'Thereafter, there will be time for questions and one-to-one interviews with me that have been requested in advance afterwards.'

Dylan went on to share with the attendees the fact that Alan Bell was locally known as Film Star and that it may be that many people would only know the taxi driver by his nickname. He ended with an appeal. 'I ask that anyone with any information about any of the incidents, or anyone who was in the area at the time, used the taxi that day or have information of someone collecting human teeth, no matter how trivial you think the information is to please contact Harrowfield Police or Crimestoppers. I will now open up the room to questions,' he said.

'Joel Duncan. *Harrowfield Times*. Does the community of Harrowfield need to be worried? Three murders in a matter weeks and the killer is still stalking our streets.'

'Patrols have been increased and I would suggest the community needs to be vigilant as opposed to being worried. I cannot impress upon you how important, as Detective Inspector Dylan has outlined this morning, that any information should be passed on,' said ACC Smythe

'Evie Wallace, *Yorkshire Star*. Are these murders all about the teeth?'

ACC Smythe nodded for Dylan to take the question. 'It's wrong to assume at this stage exactly what the motive is, but all the deceased did have very white teeth some of which have been removed, only time will tell the relevance of that fact.'

'Jason Costello, *The National Imperial Press*. From what you have told us, the victims' teeth are extracted after death and this is done with some degree of skill you say?'

'Yes that's correct,' Dylan said.

'So the murderer will have a background in dentistry?' Jason continued.

'May, is the word I'd use Jason. We should never assume anything. I am keeping an open mind as to the background of the killer, but obviously it is a line of enquiry and I hasten to add it's just one line of enquiry.'

The questions flowed in the same vein for ten minutes. Dylan ended the press conference and whilst some of those from the media left quickly, no doubt to get back to their respective outlets for a deadline, others waited for pre-planned one-to-one interviews.

As Dylan went to speak to national radio he saw the ACC speaking to radio presenter Maggie Currie.

***

A little hoarse from repetitive conversations Dylan sank into his old leather office chair and selfishly enjoyed a large cup of coffee undisturbed, wondering what headlines the media would run with. He would find out in due course as the HQ press office recorded and retained all publicity with regard to murder enquiries and he and the incident room would get a copy sent through the internal post for their knowledge should they wish to respond, and their retention. The reason for this also being that at any given time they all knew exactly what had, or had not been said in the media.

He saw Wendy Smythe talking to incident room staff as she made her way through the large room to his office and he was pleased. Although the respite had been brief the break had allowed his mind to settle.

'Come on Inspector, I need something to eat and we can have that little chat you promised me,' she said. 'Bye, bye, bye,' she shouted to the team.

'Yes ma'am,' he said.

'We will have to eat out. This idea of closing canteens is a bloody nuisance,' she said. 'Chinese okay with you?'

'I guess you're going to show me your skill of eating with chopsticks?'

'Of course.' Wendy Smythe laughed and when she laughed she looked ten years younger than her fifty-two years.

***

Dylan picked up his chopsticks and used them adequately enough. It was Wendy Smythe's turn to be impressed. 'Full of surprises aren't we Dylan,' she said.

'Always keep a lady guessing my dad used to say.'

'Makes a difference to treat 'em mean, keep 'em keen I guess,' she said. 'Which is what my dad used to say.'

Now and then the restaurant staff burst into a sing-songy noisy melody of arrr and laaa's as they greeted their diners. 'They's such lovely friendly people,' Wendy said. 'Did you also know the invention of chopsticks reflects the wisdom of the Chinese?'

Dylan's concentration was on eating. He shook his head.

'Although they look simple they can nip, pick, rip and stir food and are considered to be lucky gifts for marriage and other important ceremonies. I'm quite used to them now. Taken years of practice though.'

'I can't say I have mastered them,' said Dylan as he chased a piece of rice around the bowl.

'Where did you learn to eat with them if you've never ventured to China?'

'Jen and I have friends who work regularly in Hong Kong... Yin is originally from Hong Kong, Phil comes from Bradford. They are private investigators. I'll give you their contact details if you like?'

'Yes, I will drop in on them if I have time. Although my schedule is rather full. I used to live in Bradford. Do you remember the trams?'

'No, I don't but my mother often talked about them.'

'Touche. Well, in Hong Kong people use them daily as a mode of very cheap transport. They're known as "ding dings". Lovely that name don't you think?'

'Sounds like something Maisy would play with,' he said.

'You'd enjoy the markets in Mong Kok most people do, perhaps it's a place you'd like to go when you retire?'

Dylan looked across the table at his dinner companion. 'Markets are not really my cup of tea,' he said putting his fingers in the finger bowl. 'Anyway, I've quite a few years to go yet before I can retire.'

Their table was next to the window which looked out onto the taxi rank in George Square.

'In Hong Kong taxi drivers spend most of their downtime cleaning and waxing their vehicles and keeping them spotlessly clean. You don't see that here do you?'

Dylan thought about Alan Bell's taxi; the empty crisp packets, empty cans and sweet wrappers. 'No definitely not,' he said.

The meal finished, the pictures she had promised were taken from her bag. There was no doubt in Dylan's mind this woman had a great deal of love for China, he just wished she had more passion for finding the murderer.

'... and I'm presently studying Cantonese,' she said. 'Hence my using the words and phrases whenever I can.'

Coffee arrived and she asked for the bill. 'So Jack, back to reality,' she said with a big sigh. 'What about these murders? Have we any potential suspects in the frame at all?'

'I wish I could say yes but I can't. The arrest of the man who telephoned the radio station was the only positive lead we had, but it looks like he was just out to get some money.'

'And I also believe he has a bit of a thing about Ms Currie,' said Wendy Smythe.

'Yes, that's right. They've extended his detention but he's likely to be released later today. As we speak I'm awaiting an update from the DCs dealing with him.'

'So in brief, we are no nearer now than when the first murder was committed?'

'We've gathered a lot of evidence, linked the other crimes, spoken to a profiler and ultimately I've no doubt in my mind we'll find him. What we know for sure is that he must spend time at a crime scene carefully removing the teeth. We also believe he is testing us by leaving evidence at murder scenes to see if we pick that up.'

'I like your positive attitude Jack, but what if he strikes again?'

'Well let's be realistic. The likelihood is that he will strike again and all we can do for now is keep doing what we are doing and like I said at the press conference ask people to be vigilant. The increased patrols and high visibility policing will hopefully make it more difficult for him, so perhaps, maybe, he'll lie low for a while and allow us to chew through all the gathered data and hope the investigation keeps moving forward at pace.'

'I will be contactable when I am in China, so you can update me at all times. I am au fait with Skype and FaceTime should we need to use it. Of course you may arrest the perpetrator before I go. I'd really like to be here when you do.' Wendy Smythe's eyes lit up.

'You would?' Dylan looked shocked.

'Yes, I'd love to see what the murderer looks like and see him interviewed first hand.'

Dylan was pleased that she was taking such an interest. Never before had he known any ACC interested in a murder investigation until it was over and they could shine their uniform buttons and come out for the photo call. 'You can be assured I'll update you with any developments,' he said with a slow smile that reached his eyes.

'Jack you must. As you are well aware I'm in overall charge and decisions will have to made about certain strategies and I will need to write and endorse policy. That sounds impressive doesn't it?' Wendy Smythe chuckled. 'But, don't worry,' she said laying her hand over his. 'I know I'm just a figurehead to appease the media and assure the public that someone at the top, or as near the top as to show enough of my arse, pardon my French, has a grip on the investigation. I also like to think it lets the officers out on the street see how serious the Force is taking the investigations with the ACC rank involved. Joy geen,' Wendy said as they left the restaurant.

'Joy geen,' the staff echoed.

'Joy geen?' said Dylan.

'See you again,' said Wendy.

***

Dylan was back in the incident room and his first priority was to find out what the situation was with Michael Hook who was still in police custody.

'Nice lunch,' said Vicky.

'Interesting,' said Dylan.

'Another ACC pretending to be interested?'

'No, I don't think so Vicky. I was pleasantly surprised at how grounded she is for an ACC with no background in CID. Not as passionate about the enquiry as I'd like her to be as an ACC of Crime but we lost that rank years ago sadly,' he said with a lopsided smile.

'What did he have to say for himself?' Dylan leant with his elbows on the table, his chin cupped in his hand.

'He said the only reason he knew about the teeth was that he had been in the Anchor pub, when he had overheard a man talking to the landlord about the Davina Walsh murder and they must have said that the killer had knocked her teeth out. He knew him to be a police officer, Ned Granger. He played football with him some years ago in the Sunday league. The guy fancies the radio presenter so the numbskull saw it as a chance to meet her, and make a bob or two, so he thought.'

'Bloody time-waster,' said Dylan. 'You haven't mentioned to him about his girlfriend and the drugs?'

'No, not yet.'

'Just make sure Hook understands the seriousness of his actions will you and how bloody angry I am,' Dylan said. His expression was tense and strained.

'I will do sir,' she said heading to the door.

'And Sue?'

'Yes, sir,' she said with her hand on the door handle.

'Give him a bit of advice. Tell him to stay away from Ms Currie, she's a witness.'

'Will do. I'll bail him then sir?' she said.

Dylan nodded. 'Pending further enquiries to confirm his movements and check out alibis he's put forward. You happy he's not got anything to do with the murders?'

'Well, I'm more or less certain he isn't our killer but he is guilty of trying to obtain monies by deception and by purporting that he had valuable information.'

'Any more drugs found in the house?

'Not that we could see from the initial look around but it's a hell of a mess. How people live like that I don't know. It'll need a further search to ascertain what's beneath all the clutter.'

'Send Ned Granger into my office will you? I want a word with him. If he had been more discreet this would be one line of enquiry we wouldn't have had to investigate, and I could have used the resources elsewhere.'

DC Philburn closed Dylan's office door quietly behind her. He saw she had stopped at Vicky Hardacre's desk. 'Ned!' Vicky yelled a few moments later. 'Get your backside into the boss's office, you're in for a right bollocking.'

***

The integrity of an enquiry was of utmost importance and that should be at the forefront of the minds of the officers who worked on it. Dylan had removed officers from major investigations in the past for a number of reasons. It wasn't something he relished or did lightly, but he wouldn't allow any individual's behaviour to compromise detraction from the focus of catching the murderer.

All investigations went through a lull, and brought about external enquiries, or so it seemed, but the daily grind of the murder incident room was continually in motion. Every minute, every hour, every day they were gathering and recording vast amounts of information, just none of it seemed to point towards any one suspect which was mightily frustrating.

Whether relevant or not, a prime function of an investigation was to record, retain and reveal evidence to comply with future disclosure issues, for court purpose. Dylan knew it was early days in piecing this particular jigsaw together and he knew, as always, there would be plenty of pieces of 'blue sky' to fill in before they got to the rich rewards of the full picture. However he remained upbeat. They had to be patient and the evidence would come.

He started a list of questions that needed answering.

a) Did the killer select his victims because of their white teeth or was it an incredible coincidence all three victims had exceptional white teeth? Dylan pondered. He leant towards the first option and this would also mean that the killer may have been watching them and waited for an opportunity to strike.

b) Was there some other common link between the victims? Had they visited the same place at different times during the lead up to their murder? There had to be a common theme of how he identified his victims, but what?

c) Dr Francis Boscombe told him that access and opportunity were imperative to serial killers, and historical data suggested they usually started near to where they lived.

Dylan decided to take a drive around the area surrounding the cycle path where Davina's body was discovered. Then he would head over to where Carl Braithwaite's body was found and last he would tour the last known route Alan Bell travelled. He hoped by doing this that he would get a feel for the immediate areas around the scenes. It also allowed him to take a breather from the confines of the police station.

***

The cycle path along the canal was a twenty mile link between Harrowfield Town, Tandem Bridge and the village of Brelland which was an alternative to the roadway via foot, bicycle or boat. In fact, the scene of the murders of Carl Braithwaite and Alan Bell were also only a short walk away from the path and Davina was killed on the twenty mile stretch of pathway. Was this the killer's chosen route? If he used the direct pathway Dylan found that there was little or no lighting in most areas other than at the bridges that crossed the canal at various points. These were used by vehicles. To make his journey quicker, and to make his approach relatively quiet, the killer could have used a boat, a bicycle, or a horse he considered, as a horse and its rider trotted over the bridge to join him on the path. The rider courteously waved to him. There was no politer road user than a horse rider. From what Dylan did know of the killer's modus operandi he did not need a vehicle to carry his murder weapons. Dylan decided he would initiate enquiries at the Braithwaite and Bell murder scenes to ascertain the shortest route from the scene to the cycle path. Then he would arrange with PS Clegg to have the operational support team do a visual search of all routes leading off the canal path to them. He wanted an aerial photograph depicting all three scenes and one showing all three in the one frame. He knew the helicopter pilot and the observer would ask him if he wanted to fly with them. He also knew a lot of people would jump at the chance to have a ride in the police helicopter, but the very thought of it made his stomach flip. His dislike of heights and the fact he was prone to travel sickness meant he would certainly be declining the offer.

He looked up from the canal banking where he stood quietly, and surveyed his surroundings. He was amid a line of barges. A couple of disused, crumbling cottages nestled between trees not too far away. The housing for the mill workers still stood in a unique relation of 'double decker' houses, clinging to the hills. There were one or two large stone properties set above and beyond the canal that overlooked the cycle track, high on the hillside of Norland. The original stone that they were built from had been smoke-blackened by the mills, the dye works and the textile mills – relics of the industrial revolution.

It was no doubt this canal was once one of the best networks of rights-of-way in the country. Increasingly these abandoned buildings had recently begun to be renovated, and the chimneys now reached like sandblasted fingers to the sky. The mills had taken on a new identity, brought back to life as flats and small business complexes. In some the old waterwheels still turned. How clean these premises looked up against the buildings that had not been given that makeover.

In the renovated flats groups of strangers lived – many he knew from other enquiries did not know who lived next to them on the same corridor. Never mind on the floors above and below. Gone were the days of a good old gossip over the garden wall. He smiled at the thought of his grandmother and her friends and the black and white pictures he loved looking at as a child. He wondered briefly where those were... Maybe with one of his siblings. He wondered briefly what they were up to too. There was no time to reflect on past times. He'd ensure that routine house enquiries were carried out in all the houses that overlooked the canal from the hillside beyond and the flats in the mill complex. He would also have a static information seek carried out on the canal path from midnight to six a.m. over a period of a week to discover who if anyone used the cycle path during the night. An action plan would need to be drawn up in the event of another murder taking place. He would instruct officers to take up Stop And Check points immediately.

Dylan pulled his mobile phone out of his pocket. 'Get everyone together, I want a debrief at six,' he said to DS Raj. 'Can you arrange for someone to create a map on which we can show entry and exit points to the canal cycle paths? I want it to include the unofficial as well as the official ones, the snickets, the ginnels, the man made paths. What I'm looking for is the feasibility to have units immediately cover the entry and exit paths in the event of another murder or an attack happening. I'm looking at a five mile radius of where Davina's body was found. Then we can work out what staffing levels we will need to achieve our plan,' he said. 'The killer may be a resident of the area or a past resident. He appears to have a local's knowledge of the area and that has become more apparent to me on the recce. I'll see you in an hour,' he said.

Dylan stood quietly for a while longer, his phone was still in his hand. He looked at his watch and dialled home. 'How long does it take for a kettle to boil?'

'Around a minute, I guess why?' Jen said.

'In that case I'll be with you in ten,' he said. He walked to the car.

***

'You okay Jack?' Jen said when he walked in the door and planted a kiss on her cheek.

'I am now,' he said with a smile on his face.

Chapter Fourteen

Dylan reached for his pen and signed the documents that Vicky had placed in front of him. His phone rang. She picked it up. 'DI Dylan will be with you in two shakes of a lamb's tail,' she said, smiling as she took the papers from Dylan's outstretched hand and he took the phone off her. 'Forensic,' Vicky mouthed and left him alone.

'Beryl! How lovely to hear from you; what've you got for me today,' he said with genuine warmth in his voice.

'Macabrely good news, I think...' she said.

'That sounds ominous,' said Dylan draining his coffee cup. It was cold. He grimaced as he looked into the empty vessel and replaced it on his desk.

'The line from the garrotte found in Alan Bell's taxi has been identified as a piece of braided fishing line.'

'Anything specific about it, can you give us the make? It would help us source suppliers in the area?'

'I'm working on it,' she said. 'But, my fishing expert colleague says it's very old. Braid was first developed in England during the early twentieth century and in the nineteen thirties, the first braided synthetic. Since then there has been significant steps forward as it became popular amongst fishing enthusiasts.'

'Sadly my knowledge of fishing could be written on the reverse of a postage stamp and then there would still be space left, but it'll give us another line of enquiry.'

***

Dylan walked into the incident room. 'We must have other reported incidents over the years connected to the canal cycle path? What about other cycle paths and walkways in

Harrowfield? This killer must have committed offences prior to these murders,' he said.

'He might have but were they reported?' said Raj.

'Or did he commit the offences here, in this county, or country even?' said DC Wormald.

'Boss, there is someone interesting here that's just come onto the system,' said Vicky waving a sheet of paper in the air, like a flag in a breeze. 'It's a dentist who was struck off for misconduct. Trouble is its over five years ago.'

All eyes were upon Vicky. 'Go on,' Dylan said looking at her and patiently waiting for more. 'What was he struck off for?'

'Sexual assault of a patient and theft.'

'Theft?' said Dylan.

'Theft?' said Ned screwing his nose up as if an undesirable smell had wafted under it.

'Theft of teeth,' she said with an undeniably satisfied smirk upon her face.

Dylan held out his hand for the paper. He studied it in silence.

Timothy Woodcock was fifty-eight years of age at the time.

Vicky turned her head to the computer screen and gently tapped at the keys, 'And... the ... address shown for him is approximately a mile from where Davina's body was found,' said Vicky.

'And his place of work,' said Dylan. 'Brelland Dental Practice; at the time he was a senior partner, according to this.'

Ned's face took on a look of surprise 'No, way!' he said. 'I went there when I was a kid. What did you say his name was?'

'Timothy Woodcock.'

'Jesus Christ,' he said holding his hand to his mouth. 'I think he might have been our dentist.'

'Explains a lot,' Vicky said, grabbing her colleague's chin and turning his face to look at her. Ned bared his teeth and snapped them together.

'Daft bugger,' she said, jumping away from him.

'Says here that Woodcock denied all the allegations but could offer no explanation...' said Dylan.

'It also says the complaint was by a patient and his partner in the practice.'

'Why would a dentist take teeth from a dental practice?' said Ned.

'According to this he said, for research,' said Vicky.

'That's it, that's his defence?' said Ned.

'His defence to the theft allegation was that "he had no intention to permanently deprive the practice of the teeth,"' said Vicky.

'An intention to permanently deprive the owner of property, an important point to prove in the definition of theft,' said Dylan. 'There must have been more to it than that?'

'He said he had every intention of returning them to the practice,' said Vicky. 'Asked to put a value on them he also classed them as "rubbish with no value."'

'Interestingly enough, two of the teeth belonged to the woman who had made allegations of indecent assault against him,' said Dylan. 'And he had administered gas to relax her, she claimed, prior to the tooth extractions. He hadn't been pursued for misconduct as he had resigned, but part of the enquiry looked at the excessive number of extractions he had carried out in comparison with other dentists in the district. The inference here being that some of his patients' healthy teeth may have been unnecessarily removed, by him. Well, he's certainly just earned himself a place at the top of our actions. Prioritise the research into him Vicky, Raj, get back to me asap.'

'I notice he only got a suspended sentence which expired ages ago,' said Raj.

'Just out of curiosity I'm interested to know where our lot found the teeth. I'd like to know if they were secreted?' said Dylan.

'Another one of Harrowfield's pervs,' mumbled Ned.

'Hey, don't talk about Mr Dylan like that DC Granger. He'll have you thrown off this enquiry quicker than you can say Jack Flash!' said Vicky with a grin.

He put his middle finger under her chin this time. 'Swivel,' he said.

'Come on, back to work,' said Dylan with a shake of his head.

'It made you smile though boss,' said Vicky. 'And you haven't been doing a lot of that lately.'

Chapter Thirteen

Michael Hook's home had been searched but nothing had been found to link him to any of the incidents, although the task hadn't gone without a drama.

'His girlfriend's locked up sir,' said DC Philburn.

'She kick off?' said Dylan, his concentration was firmly on the document he was completing for interview strategy.

'Well, not exactly, she stood in the porch when we arrived, well I say stood, she leant on the door jamb ... and was drunk as a skunk.'

He stopped what he was doing and looked DC Philburn's way.

'We must have made her jump, she... well she, lost control of her bladder. She thought it was hilarious for some reason and collapsed on the floor laughing.'

'She did what?' Dylan said, then uttered a curse under his breath. 'What did you do?'

'Offered to help her inside, if she gave me her key. She struggled to her feet, with a little help from us and asked Howard to hold onto something she had in her hand whilst she looked for the key in her pocket.' A smile spread across Sue Philburn's face.

'What?' said Dylan. Her smile was infectious. 'What?'

'She only went and placed a bag of cocaine into his hand. You ought to have seen the look on her face when she realised what she'd done, it was priceless, sir.'

'So she's in the cells too.'

'Yes sir, sleeping off whatever it was she had taken. We'll speak to her later.'

'And you've interviewed him now in relation to the Maggie Currie saga?'

DC Philburn nodded.

Dylan sat down in front of his computer. He didn't realise he had been walking around with such a serious face but he was in no doubt the troops had picked up on his mood. He told himself he had to make a conscious effort to be more upbeat and smile outwardly no matter how flat he felt. He didn't want them to think the pressure was getting to him, but how could it not be with a dangerous serial killer on the loose?

The incident room was a hive of industry. On a daily basis, from his office Dylan could see it working like cogs turning in a well-oiled machine. Dylan had access, from his office computer link to read and sign off, in some cases, the daily glut of enquiries. Each action had a unique number given to it at source. A hard copy of that enquiry was printed off and allocated to an investigator on the enquiry team to complete. This document informed them what action was required of them and they would write up the result which then was typed into the computer database. Then the SIO had the ability to see instantly the officers' work rate in terms of the enquiries/actions issued to them and completed. He would expect the team supervisor, often the sergeant or detective sergeant in the incident room to pick up on anyone who was not pulling their weight, but if they didn't, he certainly would. Most of the enquiries/actions had to be completed within a maximum of seven days' duration and if not they would be resubmitted for an extension. This allowed an audit trail and also made sure that no enquiry/action was left dormant. After all, any one of them could potentially change the direction of the enquiry in an instant and no one had the foresight to know which enquiry/action that would be.

The exhibits category on the HOLMES system allowed Dylan to review the list of exhibits seized and which had been forwarded to Forensic so he was able to review the forensic strategy. All the information was there at his fingertips, including his own policy log. This incorporated, where appropriate, the need for a risk assessment.

A couple of hours sitting at the computer in one session were enough. He got up and stretched his legs. He was pleased to see that the office was almost empty apart from the specialist HOLMES team who were tapping away on their individual keyboards. This signified to him that the investigators were out doing what they got paid for. He slipped a five pound note in the tea fund jar on Lisa's desk.

'Is that a subtle hint that you're thirsty boss?' Lisa said.

'Well, now you mention it a coffee would be nice. Tell you what. Shall I make one for you for a change?'

'Nice of you to offer boss, but if you just switch the kettle on I'll see to it,' she said with a pleasant smile on her face.

Dylan strolled over to the display boards. There was a separate one set up for each murder which continued to be updated daily with essential details. This visual, quick reference was an instant reminder of vital information for everyone's purpose. There were now photographs of dental tools, 'elevators' and 'forceps' plus a human teeth chart. He studied it closely.

Lisa brought his coffee mug over. 'It's not that long ago they used to torture people by pulling their teeth out, is it?' she said.

'A bit before my time,' he said. 'Although come to think of it you could probably class our school dentist as a torturer.'

'Pity it isn't part of the interview skills allowed today. Then we could instantly identify our regulars by the lack of their teeth.'

'Trouble is Lisa, you'd get people admitting to the crime even if they hadn't done it so they didn't have to suffer toothache and it was free to get them removed. Others would probably enjoy it, bizarrely, it appears.'

'Yeah, well it's just a shame, when you look at the innocent faces of the victims that we can't still make the evil gits who've done it actually suffer for what they've done. Mind you, we'd have to have alternative punishment because some of our prolific offenders wouldn't have any teeth left by the time there were adults.' Lisa's young face looked sad.

'You can imagine a solicitor's face can't you? The use of body language and other interview techniques have failed, we now intend to extract one of your client's incisors.'

'They wouldn't be able to tell their client to keep their mouth shut then would they?' Lisa laughed heartily.

'Just out of interest has anyone on this enquiry asked for time off for a dental appointment?'

Lisa laughed. 'No, that's bizarre in itself and it's probably due to the fact that everybody's a suspect, and on this job dentists more than most.'

Dylan felt more relaxed. He walked back into his office carrying his coffee. No sooner had he sat down but his telephone rang.

'Sorry to trouble you sir, but the body of a middle-aged man has been discovered hanging from a tree in the middle of Shrogg's Wood. Officers at the scene are asking for you to be notified as the deceased's teeth are apparently missing.'

Chapter Fifteen

Dylan, followed the well-trodden path. Pushed open a sagging gate and waded through tall grasses to the copse where the body had been found. The officers who stood guarding the scene were doing what was required of them. Another body, with teeth missing, but this time found hanging in a wood? Could this really be another in the series of murders or the murderer himself?

Inspector Stonestreet met him at the outer cordon. PC Tracy Petterson nodded to Dylan. 'Apparently the body was discovered by a local walking group. One member required hospital treatment so shocked was she by the discovery,' Stonestreet said.

'Still in situ?'

'Of course sir.'

'Top man. Your thoughts?'

'It doesn't appear to fit the criteria for your serial killer, but you did say that you wanted notification of any suspicious death which occurred included people with missing teeth in your action plan,' Peter Stonestreet said studiously 'and quite rightly so...'

'You taught me to never assume,' Dylan said with a wry smile on his face.

'Exactly.'

Dylan walked with him through the cordon once they were booted and suited. The body was hanging from a lower branch of the tree about ten feet from the ground. A rotting fence that had collapsed lay on the ground below and as Dylan tried to walk around the swinging corpse his foot went through the rotting wood. It was smothered in moss and green growth. He looked at the piles of wood around him. A ladder was propped against the tree.

'His?' said Dylan pointing to the ladders.

'Ours,' said Inspector Stonestreet.

'How did he get up there then?'

Inspector Stonestreet shrugged his shoulders. 'Your guess is as good as mine.'

'Have we got the Crime Scene Investigation Supervisor out?' said Dylan.

'She's here now sir,' said the PC Petterson.

Dylan saw the arrival of the CSI van that carried the CSI's.

'We might need his muscles,' said Dylan, nodding towards Stewart who was uncurling himself, grimacing as he did so, from the small white van's passenger seat.

'When you've taken the pictures in situ let's get him cut him down and lay him on a sterile plastic sheet to see what's what,' shouted Dylan to the CSIs.

Karen raised her arm in acknowledgment.

The uniformed officers looked from Dylan to their Inspector, both supervisors looked at each other and together Dylan and Peter produced a pocketknife from their pockets; much to the relief of the younger officers and the CSIs. Peter Stonestreet and Dylan shared a knowing look.

The carrying of a penknife was a lesson Dylan had learnt from Inspector Stonestreet many years before when he was a young PC. He too had been called to a person who was hanging from a tree and he had no implement to cut the person down. Luckily for Dylan that person was already dead and there wasn't a panic to preserve life but it could have been a very different story if the person had only just jumped.

The expression on a person's face when they had died through hanging was not a pretty sight. Even from a distance Dylan could see that the man's face was a grey, purple colour, his jaw hung down and his swollen tongue extruded.

'He needs to be lowered,' said Dylan, as tempting as it was to cut the rope and let him fall to the ground.

The youngest PC's face seemed to darken, and then grow pale and serious under the shadow of his helmet. He took off his hat, and wiped his sweating forehead, flies buzzed around him. He flicked a flustered hand at the pests; like a signal of distress.

'Tony's first dead body sir,' said PC Petterson. 'I'm a tutor now, sir,' she said, giving Tony a glimmer of a smile. 'You okay?' she said.

Dylan saw a proud look cross her face, her feet were planted far apart, her fists clenched.

Tony's gaze fell. He turned about and walked slowly back towards the police car. Once or twice his knees appeared to buckle.

'Go, make sure he's alright,' said Dylan. 'And bring him back when he's feeling better. I want him to see there is no harm in a dead body, no matter how bad it looks.'

Tracy nodded.

Inspector Stonestreet took off his cap and scratched his head. 'That was a nice thing to do,' he said.

'I remember my first dead body only too well,' he said.

'Me too,' said Inspector Stonestreet with a wink of his eye. He chuckled.

'Yeah, well, it was the smell, and the fact the house was littered with piles of dog faeces that did it,' said Dylan.

'That's what they all say,' Peter Stonestreet said with a grin.

'Come on. The guy had been rotting in a house with the heating on full for two weeks,' protested Dylan.

'If I remember, wasn't his body almost putrified? Sitting on the sofa, his right arm extended outwards as if he was pointing to something.'

'We never did find out what that was, did we? Although it may have been the cannabis on the shelf on the wall ... it looked like oxo cubes didn't it? Do you recall his ears and nose being missing and so were most of his fingers,' said Dylan.

'Aye, his glasses had slid halfway down his face. Well, they would do wouldn't they if you had lost your nose?' said Stonestreet.

'He still looked human though.'

'Yes surprisingly... I felt sorry for the dogs,' said Peter.

'They had to be put down didn't they? Once they've tasted human flesh they have to be destroyed. Hardly seems fair does it? It's not their fault they'd had nothing to eat,' said Dylan. 'For all your bravado, you're an old softy Peter.'

'So are you Dylan,' he said nodding at the young PC who they watched was being led back to the scene slowly by his mentor, his face still bleached and frightened looking.

'Okay now mate?' Dylan said.

Tony nodded sheepishly and looked slightly embarrassed.

'Don't worry. It happens to us all. Here, have a mint, it helps,' Dylan said giving the young PC a pat on the back.

The mint was eagerly accepted.

'I'm ready now to look closely at the body,' said Karen Ebdon. 'You okay with that Dylan?'

The team stood over the body. Karen leant into the face of the deceased with her lens and took the pictures required before they made a closer inspection of the mouth.

'The front teeth, both upper and lower are missing, but they're not recent extractions,' said Karen.

The unknown deceased was approximately forty years of age, thin build, balding with a high forehead and a ginger, woolly beard.

The gloved, uniformed officers, led by PC Petterson, searched his pockets for any item that may assist in his identification. Inside his coat pocket they found two gum shields with four front teeth on each.

'It appears this one was a waste of your time Dylan,' said Stonestreet.

'You know me better than that Peter. Nothing is ever a waste of time. I'm just pleased we've found the denture plates though, it rules out foul play.'

'There's a wallet too,' said Tracy. 'In his trouser pocket.'

Tony took the wallet from her and looked inside. 'Abbott, Neil Abbott, forty-seven years old,' he said.

'Is there an address?' said Stonestreet.

'There is sir, yes and pictures of a woman and children.'

'We will do the death notice,' he said to Dylan.

Tony bent down to his tutor who handed him a piece of paper she had retrieved from inside the jacket pocket.

'The pain was too bad. I can't carry on,' Tony read. 'That's so...'

'Sad,' said Dylan. 'Yes, it is.'

***

In the late afternoon heat of the summer's day Dylan walked back to his car alone. Reaching the car park he heard the gravel beneath his feet crunch loudly. For him it was another dead body dealt with but yet he was no nearer catching the Harrowfield serial killer. A moment of panic rose in him. He felt no hero; something was lacking. He was poignantly aware of fear and failure.

He lowered his car windows to let the fresh air blow through the car. He hoped it would help clear his head. Along the Sibden Road he passed a row of newly painted cottages. The houses were like brilliant white teeth, below their thatched roofed gums, flashing an ironic grin at him. Teeth! Teeth and dentists were taking over his every thought.

Parking outside his house he watched the sky grow more blue. He thought of the family of Mr Abbott and he felt sad for around now they would be getting the knock on the door from a police officer that no one wanted. 'Seize the day,' he said to himself. 'Carpe Diem.'

Maisy ran to greet him, a picture in her hand. 'Daddy's home,' she squealed. Dylan lifted her up into his arms and held her tightly for a moment or two.

'I love you sooo big,' he said, nuzzling his head into her little neck. She giggled.

'No daddy,' she exclaimed. 'I love you sooo much!'

Chapter Sixteen

Dylan and Vicky watched Rajinder walking towards his office door, knock, open it and walk in. She held papers in her hand.

'Walk around with a bit of paper and folks will think you're busy Raj,' Vicky said. She crossed her legs and folded her arms over the paperwork upon her lap.

DS Raj gave her a tight lipped smile and turned to speak to Dylan. 'Timothy Woodcock.'

'Yes, Rajinder,' Dylan said, his eyes gazing upon her face.

'The teeth he took from the dental practice were found displayed on green felt, in a presentation case.'

'I don't look after my jewellery that well,' said Vicky with a tut.

'Exactly,' said Raj. 'Thirty-two teeth in total.'

'A full set?' said Dylan.

Raj nodded.

'I guess although we should never assume, we can perhaps presume in this case that the others are from clients at Brelland Dental Practice?' said Vicky.

'He told the investigating officers at the time that they were at his home for research purposes but wouldn't go on to explain what. It's surely not credible that he'd display the objects as an ornamental piece, is it?' said Raj.

'Who knows. Can we house him?' said Dylan.

'His address on the file is 15 Rock Villas and I've checked the up to date Electoral List and it shows one occupant, which is a Timothy Woodcock,' said Raj.

'That's one of those big houses near The Moor isn't it, overlooking the valley towards the hillside of Norland?' said Vicky.

'That's perfectly central to our murders,' said Dylan thoughtfully. 'Get your coats on we'll have a quick look around the area and knock on the door.'

***

Dylan parked on the opposite side of the road to Rock Villas. The three officers got out of the car. He crossed the wide flagged pavement and stepped over the small wall that he had done so many times as a small boy having being brought up in the area. Standing on the unkempt patch of grass he surveyed the steep drop over huge, craggy rocks. The spot offered a glorious view. Directly ahead and to his right was a well-worn, unlit footpath that he knew continued down through the wood that was full of bluebells in spring, because he had picked them year after year with his granddad. This path led out onto the main Waterford Road, which led to the cycle path of the canal. As a kid he'd hurtled down that path, as fast as he could on his bike more times than he cared to remember. The journeys resulting in many a scraped knee. The exposed tree roots had proven no fear for him as a young lad. 'JB Priestley, on his travels for *English Journey* declared this terrain, "the hilliest of any town of its size in England,"' he said. Dylan's voice was momentarily lost in the wind. He continued for a moment or two to silently consider the view and the ladies chattered. The main road directly to the left also dropped down to the valley and eventually to the canal. Buildings, factories and rows of houses seemed to strike out among trees at all angles in the craggy hillside below. He turned around and looked back at the large houses with windows that looked over the scene and seeing the properties, and taking into account the location.

When there was no answer to their knocking and it was obvious that no one at home. Dylan turned to Raj. 'So, plan of action; get hold of Sergeant Clegg. We need the operational support team to do a house-to-house around the area. If they have no joy I want them to create a questionnaire asking the occupants if they knew any of the deceased. If they use the cycle path or the canal, I want to know. And, is there anything that you haven't been asked about which you think may assist the police... we can't presume people will tell us. We need to locate Timothy Woodcock and speak to him.'

'I'll get someone in the incident room onto that now,' said Raj.

'Get them to do a quick draft. I want to see it before they print hundreds.'

Raj nodded in the affirmative.

They drove back to the police station via the road which ran adjacent to the canal. 'Is there any local fishing done around here?' he said.

'You're thinking about the garrotte aren't you?' said Vicky.

'Yes. Have we got someone looking at where fishing line can be sourced around here?'

'We have,' said Raj. 'It appears that particular type appears to be rather antiquarian now.'

***

Every day Dylan awoke he was relieved to know that there had not been another murder. But, he was more than aware that if the killer wasn't caught it was only a matter of time before he struck again and that made him anxious.

Forty-eight hours after Dylan had visited Rock Villas, the Operational Support Unit were knocking on the doors of the homes situated in the vicinity of Rock Villas. A team of ten were doing the footwork, speaking to people and completing pro forma. Each day the information was fed into the system; the HOLMES team having created a separate category for this house-to-house information seek. A member of the team had called at 15 Rock Villas each day but no one had answered their knocks. They confirmed with neighbours that the occupant was a man they knew to be Timothy Woodcock.

Woodcock's neighbour, at number seventeen, told us that since his wife had left him the retired dentist has been ill. He was taken into hospital about two months ago with a bad foot, diagnosed with cirrhosis of the liver and ended up having his leg amputated below the knee,' said PS Clegg. 'Since then he's been looked after in a nursing home.'

'Anyone else live at the property?' said Dylan.

'Not according to the neighbours or the Burgess Roll, sir,' said Simon Clegg

'And do we know where his wife lives?'

'Ex-wife, she lives in Lytham St Annes with her daughter and son-in-law. The Woodcocks also have an adopted younger son but he hasn't lived at home since he went away to university.'

'The neighbours know a lot about the family?'

Sergeant Clegg chuckled. 'Yeah, and so it seems they've also now given Mr Woodcock a watertight alibi for the murders,' he said. 'They also supplied us with contact details for his next of kin.'

Vicky walked hurriedly into Dylan's office. Her rush took Dylan and Simon by surprise.

'I've been checking the system and there's a recent report of a burglary at Woodcock's address, sir,' said Vicky.

'Really,' said Dylan. 'But there has been no one living there...'

Chapter Seventeen

From his office Dylan witnessed many comings and goings. DCs Andy Wormald and Ned Granger were about to leave the incident room for Lytham St Annes. Their Action brief by Dylan was to visit Mrs Edna Woodcock and find out more about the Woodcock family. Dylan needed to clear the ground beneath his feet before he moved on. It was possible to get local officers to do an enquiry out of the force area. But he wanted his officers to go and see Timothy Woodcock's ex-wife and daughter in person as they would have more idea of what information was relevant to the case.

'Be thorough. Find out what you can and Ned don't let me catch you sending pictures to the team of you eating ice cream on the beach, wearing Kiss Me Quick hats or riding the Big Dipper, do you hear me?' said Dylan with a beady glare.

Ned lowered his head and turned to go. 'As if,' he said, to Vicky under his breath.

'As if what?' Dylan said loudly in a growl of a voice. Ned stopped in his tracks.

'As if, sir,' he said turning on his heels and saluting Dylan.

Dylan couldn't help but raise a smile.

'You missed riding a donkey sir?' said Vicky.

'He wouldn't dare?' said Dylan.

Vicky raised her brows. 'You think not?' she said.

There was always a feeling of great satisfaction for Dylan when he could update his policy log with 'an elimination criteria' for possible suspects. If it could be proven that on one of the dates, for any one of the murders, a suspect could be accurately placed elsewhere, Dylan knew he could rule them out of the enquiry. Albeit the team would still need to obtain a reliable alibi or get some evidence and have it verified.

'The younger adopted son?' Vicky said.

Dylan's eye brows knitted together. 'Whose son?'

'The Woodcocks' son – Jim?'

Dylan lifted his head. 'Yes?'

'I've contacted him and he's going to call in to see me.'

'Good.'

She slipped into a seat opposite Dylan. 'When I was an aide, I once went with a detective to Hull on an enquiry and he called in at the docks on the way home to bring back some fresh fish to sell to his mates in the pub. Trouble was he left his share in the boot of the CID car and it was locked in the garage. We didn't half get a bollocking off the boss,' Vicky said.

'They used to take orders before they set off on an out of force enquiry in my younger days. If you went to Northampton it was shoes, Scotland was haggis but don't tell Ned that,' Dylan said winking at her.

***

Edna Woodcock's home was an interesting place and disappointingly for Ned away from the hullabaloo of the seaside town. The two detectives paused at the gateway and looked up the driveway at the grand old building. A uniformed police car was parked outside the big old green, glossy, painted door with its brass ornaments; several bicycles, one with a basket upfront were parked under a bike shelter. Ned walked ahead of Andy, up the big steps, in-between the large stone pillars; he rang the doorbell. It was answered by a tall, well-built young woman in medical scrubs with a face mask still hanging about her neck. On seeing their warrant cards the detectives were invited into the hall and asked to wait. The woman's bare feet made no noise on the rich wool carpet as she vanished swiftly through one of the large wooden doors that led off the vestibule. Ned and Andy were silent as they looked first at each other and then about them.

The house was pristine. Rays of sunshine filtered through the stained glass window and fell on the table filled with vases of flowers in the centre of the room.

A few moments later a uniformed officer beckoned them into the lounge.

'We're just in the middle of taking a statement from Mrs Gillard. It appears Mrs Woodcock is suffering from dementia. We've been here an hour,' he said. He tossed his head in the direction of another officer who was busily taking notes. 'She says she's been burgled.'

'Has she?' said Andy.

'When we arrived she showed us a safe full of expensive jewellery, diamonds, rubies, gold, silver, the lot. She insisted the robbers had taken away the real stuff and left her with fakes and she wanted us to take it away. We had to contact her daughter at work.'

Edna Woodcock was sitting on a chair by the big bay window. She had a white, translucent complexion and a little red beak of a nose. Her green eyes were very bright but vacant. She got up to greet her newly arrived visitors, whom she seemed delighted to see, but the young woman who had opened the door to them, gently coaxed her back to her seat to continue her conversation with the police officer.

Once she had settled her, Mrs Woodcock's daughter joined them. 'I'm sorry, I'm Ginny Gillard, Mrs Woodcock's daughter. I must have appeared very rude,' she said to the detectives. 'As you can see... well.... What can I do for you?'

DC Wormald explained that they had come from West Yorkshire to speak to Mrs Woodcock about her ex-husband.

'Dad? You have?' said Ginny.

'Yes, we arranged it with her yesterday but I can see you have other pressing matters. Is it okay if we come back later in the day?'

'I'm sorry. I fear you have had a wasted journey. Mum is getting progressively worse. We really are going to have to do something about this,' she said. She looked irritated and then apologetic. 'She loves all the attention you see. She gets lonely when Devlin and I are out at work and so she would have been highly delighted if you rang to say you wanted to come and see her. Then she forgets...'

Mrs Woodcock was left alone, fiddling with the buttons of her cardigan as the woman police officer who had been speaking to her joined them. 'The safe is now locked Mrs Gillard,' she said.

'If you could just check nothing is missing when you've a minute.'

'Yes, thank you,' Ginny said.

'We'll see ourselves out,' the officer said.

The uniformed officers nodded in the detectives' direction and left them alone.

'Please take a seat and I'll go and make us all a drink. It's the least I can do for your trouble,' Ginny said to Andy and Ned.

They sat side by side on the sofa facing Mrs Woodcock. She smiled sweetly, happily humming to herself. She proceeded to wet the corner of her handkerchief with spittle to polish the chrome on the handle of her chair.

'My daddy was a dentist you know,' she said.

'Was he?' said Andy.

'Yes,' she said. 'What did your daddy do?'

'My dad was a fisherman,' said Andy.

'Oh, that's nice,' she replied, excitedly. 'My daddy loved fishing too, how jolly,' she said. 'Maybe they fished together?'

'Maybe,' said Andy.

Andy looked at Ned and he shrugged his shoulders. All was quiet except for the clinking of utensils on china that they assumed came from the kitchen. The grandfather clock struck the hour and Edna Woodcock counted the chimes.

'Mum, what on earth are you doing?' Ginny scolded Edna the moment she reappeared. She put the tray laden with china cups and saucers on the coffee table and whipped the stained, lace handkerchief from her mother's hand, replacing it swiftly with a cup and saucer. She offered her mother a biscuit and she took it.

'Now be careful. It's hot,' she said. Mrs Woodcock flinched at the raising of Ginny's voice.

Tears welled up in Edna Woodcocks eyes, then she looked up at her daughter sideways and smiled sheepishly as she dunked her rich tea biscuit. Ginny Gillard sighed heavily 'What am I going to do with you?' she said, putting a comforting hand on her mother's arm before turning to Andy and Ned. She sat down. 'Now, where were we?' she said brusquely.

***

It was dusk. Jack Dylan stood at the office window looking out into the empty backyard. He watched the light fade, and the world go grey. Revelations that fingerprints were recovered in the back of the taxi by Forensic had caused a stir – now they could check them with anyone who had a criminal record. The sky was clear, the night warm. He opened the top button of his shirt and loosened his tie. Headlights of a car came through the big metal gates at speed and glided into the parking space beneath his window. The driver turned off the engine and alighted, as did his passenger. Dylan went to make three cups of coffee.

***

Dylan sat and listened and as he did so he made notes.

'Ginny, the daughter told us that they didn't have a lot to do with her dad. She seemed bitter. He had promised her a partnership in his practice after she qualified,' said Andy. 'That didn't materialise.'

'His daughter's a dentist?' said Dylan. His eyes widened.

'And so is her husband. They both felt the need to move out of the area to practice. Mrs Edna Woodcock, she's been diagnosed with dementia. Her daughter tells us she has good days and bad. She can remember things from years ago but not what she did yesterday,' said Andy. 'She was telling me her dad was a dentist and he loved fishing but apart from that offered us little in the way of help.'

'Seemingly they went over to the family house at 15 Rock Villas very recently, after Mr Woodcock was taken into hospital and she was insistent that her husband had got rid of some of her things that had been given to him by her father,' said Ned.

'Then again she had reported her jewellery stolen this morning so...' said Andy.

'And was it?' said Dylan.

'Was it what?' asked Ned.

'Stolen?'

'No.'

'Vicky said there had been a report of theft from Mr Woodcock's address,' said Dylan.

179

'If it was from Mrs Woodcock you might want to take it with a pinch of salt,' said Ned.

Dylan twiddled his pen through his fingers. 'We need to find out who called it in. I'm sure Vicky said a man's name but maybe it was her son-in-law. She was going to follow it up and get a list of things that were thought to be missing,' he said.

'Anything happening here we should know about?' said Andy.

'Forensic have lifted some fingerprints from the back seat area of the taxi cab and we've had some people ring in to say they had been in his cab on the night he died. They've all volunteered their fingerprints for elimination purposes but if the killer had targeted Bell, as we believe he did, I don't think he would be careless enough to leave his fingerprints, do you?'

'I guess it's best not to leave anything to chance though,' said Andy.

'Exactly, that's why we aren't,' said Dylan. 'Believe it or not the camera in Alan Bell's taxi hadn't been switched on that night for whatever reason, so we've no recording. It's disappointing. What a bloody opportunity to nail our killer? However, we do have a recording of a person passing the doctor's surgery at the end of the road at a fast pace the night he was killed. The quality isn't magnificent and it's dark, but the team have secured a working copy of the tape.'

'Are you having the imaged enhanced?' said Ned.

'I don't know whether it's worth it to be completely honest. I'm awaiting advice from the force photographic department. If they can't help they might be able to recommend a company who can. But we have to consider the cost implication. Truth is, if you blink you'd miss it.'

'Do you think the person knew the camera was there?'

'I don't know. We've played it over and over. The person's hood is up so we can only see his face from his nose and below. Could be anyone if I'm honest.'

***

Dylan walked into the front office. It was half past nine and the night shift were starting to arrive for duty.

A middle-aged man stood at the desk, in front of the Desk Sergeant.

'A nice wood trunk came into the charity shop where my wife volunteers today,' he said. 'When I looked inside it's full of dynamite. It looks old,' he said.

'Where is it now?' said the Sergeant.

'It's in the boot of my car.'

'Okay, and where's your car,' he said looking slightly unnerved at Dylan.

'Just outside there,' he said pointing to the door of the police station.

***

It was one thirty a.m. when Dylan arrived home.

'What on earth did you do?' said Jen on hearing his news.

'Evacuated the station. You would have laughed though he'd only parked next to Hugo-Watkins' new Rover.'

'Hugo-Watkins was in at that time of night?'

'He'd been called in to do an extended detention for a prisoner in the cells, hence why he hadn't parked out back in his own parking space in the yard.'

'It turned out to be dummy training dynamite. Don't look so worried,' he said pulling her nice warm body towards him. 'Now go to sleep.'

Dylan's eyes closed and within seconds or so it seemed he was fast asleep.

Jen lay, eyes open in the darkened room staring up at the ceiling and thinking how this night could have turned out so differently. She stared at the clock three thirty a.m., the phone rang.

'Are you awake sir, it's the Control Room.'

'I am now,' said Dylan. 'What've you got for me?'

'Shades nightclub in the town centre?'

'Yes, I know of it.'

'A young man has been attacked outside and at this moment he's on his way to theatre for emergency surgery. He's a serious injury to his neck, but that's not all. The man who's been

181

arrested on suspicion of the attack has a tooth in his pocket and it's believed to be a human tooth.'

Chapter Eighteen

Jen sat on the edge of the bed and watched Dylan step into his clothes that she had selected for him from the wardrobe whilst he'd shaved. A cup of coffee half drunk and a plate with a slice of cold toast, half eaten, sat on the corner of the dressing table.

'There's a sandwich, fruit, and a bottle of water on top of your briefcase. I've put it by the front door so whatever you do, don't fall over it,' she said. She yawned loudly and throwing her legs onto the bed she snuck onto Dylan's side of the bed, pulled the duvet up to her neck and snuggled into Dylan's pillow. She watched her husband move around the room quietly. He looked like he was concentrating hard as he buttoned up the cuffs on his shirt. He moved to stand in front of the mirror and secured his tie.

'Thanks love,' he said distractedly. His eyes scanned the dressing table top.

'Handkerchief?' said Jen.

Dylan nodded.

'It's in your suit pocket with your mints.'

Dylan picked up his jacket, felt in the pocket and retrieving the sought after items he smiled at her, leant over the bed and put his hand on her forehead. 'Have I told you how much I love you lately?' he said.

Jen shook her head.

'Well I do,' he said.

'It's a good job. When I'm fat, forgetful, depressed and have bags under my eyes it'll be all your fault Jack Dylan,' she said. She closed her eyes tight and he kissed her on her puckered lips.

'You forgot the lack of sex drive.' Dylan gave a throaty laugh. 'I read that article too in your magazine. I'll see you when I see you,' he said as he walked towards the door. 'With some luck this lad they have in custody will be able to help us with our enquiries and it'll all be over very soon.' Dylan's voice had a tone of excitement to it.

'Thank goodness,' she said, turning over with a groan. Dylan walked down the stairs and stepped over Max. He ruffled the dog's ears and was rewarded with a swish of a bushy tail. His moan was long and low as he shuffled along the carpet to the door. 'Know how you feel mate,' he said. 'Go back to sleep it's not time to get up yet.'

***

As Dylan drove through the Sibden Valley and over the hill the landscape before him seemed to open up and end at the sunrise. It reminded him of the colour of bad blood – how apt that he was going to deal with a scene of horror.

Detective Sergeant Hardacre met him at the station, she was eating a banana and holding a glass of water in her hand.

'That bad?' said Dylan.

'Worse, I've had about two hours' sleep. Coffee's on,' she said with half-smile as she walked towards the kitchen. Dylan followed her. 'I thought you'd want to be contacted about this one. In brief, on the surface, there's nothing unusual about an attack outside a nightclub. The injured lad, in question, has been rushed to theatre with a gaping wound to his neck. Caused, we believe by a craft knife that was recovered from the pavement nearby. Oh, and by the way the bouncers are called crowd control safety officers now, in case you didn't already know.'

'What?' Dylan said.

'Bouncers, the terminology doesn't exist anymore they want to be called crowd safety officers,' she said, getting two mugs out of the cupboard. She grabbed the jar of coffee and stood with a spoon and the open jar in her hands at the breakfast bar.

'Okay, whatever. Bouncers are bouncers to me no matter how they want to dress it up.'

'Warren Derby, the lad who is in theatre is in the club with his girlfriend Jade Thomas right, when our local knob head Tony Morris takes a shine to Jade. He gets so annoying that witnesses tell us Warren and Tony have words inside the club which would have come to blows if it hadn't been for crowd control safety officers throwing Morris out. End of problem you'd think, but no fifteen, twenty minutes later,' she said with a shake of her head, 'Warren and Jade leave the club and are walking towards the Kashmir Curry House and they pass Morris in a shop doorway. He follows them. The couple purposefully stop to let him pass by looking in a shop window, but he comes up behind Warren and with one swift movement,' she said drawing her index finger across her neck, 'he reaches over his shoulder and cuts Warren's throat. Immediately blood starts pumping from the wound. Jade screams out for help as Warren drops to his knees with his hands to his neck and for good measure Morris put the boot in. Warren is kicked in the face, then his body... When we, uniform get there the crowd control safety officers who are standing outside the night club have come to the couple's aid and detained Tony Morris. Tony Morris is still thrashing around on the floor and has to be restrained.'

'That name, Tony Morris, it rings a bell. Am I right in thinking it's not that long ago, he bit someone else's ear off in a fight?' Dylan leant against the kitchen's breakfast bar, his arms crossed in front of him.

'Yeah he got a suspended sentence for the job. His brief argued that he was defending himself.' Vicky poured the coffee, added the milk, spooned in two sugars and stirred the drink, picking up the cups she offered one to Dylan who took it from her.

'Thanks. Well, maybe this time the courts will put him inside for some considerable time,' he said turning his back on her as he left the room. She followed him along the corridor to the incident room.

Dylan caught a glimpse of a girl walking past with a uniformed police officer, through the window to the adjacent corridor. It was obvious she had been crying. She reached out to the officer and he stopped. They turned to face each other. She held a tissue to her mouth, her hand was trembling, her eyes staring at his face.

'That's Jade,' said Vicky.

Dylan took another look, over his shoulder as he continued.

Jade was a tall slim girl who wore a short, tight, silky skirt with a loose lacy top over a camisole. She had a mass of auburn hair which she wore down. She was pale, her eye make-up had run and left heavy stains on her cheeks.

'The last I heard from the cells was that Morris was being seen by the police surgeon; he's got two badly swollen eyes.'

'What's this about teeth found in his pocket?' Dylan said as they stopped at his office door. Vicky took a step to one side, leant towards her desk and scooped up a transparent exhibits bag. She held it up to the light. Inside Dylan could see a tooth lodged in the bottom right hand corner. 'One tooth,' she said.

Dylan opened his door, flicked on the light which took a few seconds to judder to life and stepped back to allow Vicky to walk in ahead of him. He closed the door behind them and walked to his old leather chair, took his jacket off and draped it around the back. He turned the chair round to sit down. The exhibits bag with the tooth within lay between them on Dylan's desk. The two detectives leant forward, heads almost touching to study the contents of the bag.

'Has this guy Warren got any teeth missing do you know?' Dylan said. His eyes looked directly into Vicky's. 'Or could it be Morris's?'

'There's no suggestion from witnesses to say they saw him remove any teeth, neither do we know at this moment if Warren's got any missing... He was in a really bad way. Apparently, he lost a vast amount of blood at the scene. We think possibly the carotid artery was severed in the attack.' All was still and quiet. The two stared at each other.

Vicky's mobile phone rang, it made her jump and she sat up straight to answer it. 'Okay, thank you for that,' she said, her eyes never left Dylan's. She covered the mouthpiece momentarily. 'His parents have arrived at the hospital.' She continued to listen to the person on the line. Dylan could hear a male voice but it was so low that he couldn't identify its owner. 'And are you okay whilst I get some officers over to assist? The boss is here so I'll let him know,' she said. She put the phone in front of her on the desk, leant forward and grasped her hands tightly between her knees. 'Andy, he's at Harrowfield General Hospital, the medics lost their fight to save him. Warren Derby died a few minutes ago in theatre.'

Dylan rested both elbows on the desk and put his head in his hands. 'Bloody hell,' he said. He closed his eyes. Opened them again and looked up at Vicky. 'You always think that once they have them in theatre they're going to pull through don't you?'

Vicky put her hand to her mouth and nodded her head.

'Did the family arrive at the hospital before he died?'

'Apparently so, I'll get some officers over to help Andy...' said Vicky, standing. She shivered.

'You okay?' said Dylan.

'Yeah, just a goose running over my grave...' she said. Vicky pulled up the sleeve of her cardigan and showed him the goosebumps on her arm.

Dylan smiled. 'My mum used to say that all the time,' he said with a hint of sadness in his voice. 'I'll speak to the cells to let them know that at some stage you'll be nipping down to upgrade Morris's arrest to murder and I'll tell them to keep him under constant observation. Okay!' he said, slamming the palms of his hands on his desk. Dylan took a deep breath, 'Let's get some staff called in and make sure that Jade's got her parents here when the news is broken to her, she will, like his family, need our support.'

Vicky left the room.

Dylan picked up the phone and dialled the number of the custody suite. The phone rang and rang and when it was picked up the custody officer appeared flustered. 'Custody suite,' he snapped.

'Dylan, everything okay?'

'What a nasty bastard Tony Morris is,' he said. There was shouting and hollering in the background. 'Can you hear the commotion? Talk about kicking off.'

'I'm sure you'll cope. He's going down for a long stretch this time. It's just a shame they won't lock him up and throw away the key.'

'He's never been this bad before.'

'You know him then?'

'Knowing him, if he hasn't had a fight on a weekend he's not had a good night out,' said the Custody Officer.

'DS Hardacre will be down to upgrade his arrest from wounding to murder. They lost the fight, in theatre, to save the lad he attacked. I might just nip down with her to see the prat for myself.'

***

Tony Morris was a big muscular young man with a tattooed, shaven head. He was a sorry looking sight with two swollen, black eyes. He towered above the two officers who frogmarched him towards the charge desk where the Custody Sergeant, Dylan and Vicky were waiting for him. He was sweating profusely and gibbering under his breath. He might have had a menacing swagger and he snarled but the hideous paper suit and shoes that made him shuffle instead of walk took away some of that menace.

He stood before the Sergeant who was behind the charge desk. Vicky stood at his side facing the prisoner.

'You were initially arrested for wounding a man; the man you attacked has now died. So, we need to inform you that you are now under arrest for his murder,' she said.

The custody sergeant updated the information on Morris's detention sheet.

Tony Morris looked directly towards Vicky although since his eyes were virtually closed she did wonder how much he could see. 'Fucking shit happens,' he said with a cock of his head.

'Take him back to his cell,' said the Sergeant.

***

Dylan and Vicky walked into the CID office. 'We will open this incident room on the floor below Operation Saturn. I think this needs dealing with as a separate crime, unless evidence proves to the contrary,' said Dylan matter-of-factly.

'You don't think it's linked to our serial killer? What about the tooth they found in his possession?' said Vicky.

'Like I said before I want to know about any incidents that might prove connected to the serial killings but gut instinct tells me he isn't clever enough to be who we're looking for,' he said, screwing up his face. 'Tony Morris is a bloody aggressive idiot.

He's got a big mouth and he's handy with his fists; oh, and we now know he carries a knife but...'

Vicky raised her eyebrows questioningly.

'I'm not ignoring the fact that he had a tooth in his pocket on his arrest but until we know the origin of the tooth I want the incident treated independently.'

'You're the boss,' said Vicky, turning down the corners of her mouth.

'That's right Vicky I am,' he said with a nod of his head.

Chapter Nineteen

Apart from the tooth in Tony Morris's possession there was little found to suggest or connect him to the serial killer. Dylan was confident he could keep a watching brief on the Warren Derby investigation and let another of Harrowfield's Detective Seargeants, John Benjamin deal with it. That file would be straight forward enough. Back in the fold from training school the big black, gentleman detective would command this investigation as he had done with others, by his stature. This was routine, if there was such a thing as a routine murder investigation. Dylan would assist in the early stages with the family and media, after which, until they got the results on the tooth that he carried in his pocket he would just be on hand should he be required. John was a trusted colleague whom he knew would keep him updated.

This approach would allow Dylan, Vicky and Raj to remain focused on the hunt for the serial killer. He knew that the latest murder in Harrowfield would give more fuel to the fire for the media as to the town becoming increasingly violent. He could see it now. 'It's unsafe to leave our homes say Harrowfield Residents.' A press release was drafted and agreed with DS Benjamin who passed it to the press office for them to distribute. It was now time to go to the hospital to speak with Warren Derby's parents. There was nothing Dylan or John Benjamin could do to ease their pain. Another innocent life lost because of some idiot whose defence team at the later trial will make out had an unhappy childhood or that he had taken a cocktail of drink and drugs. They would end up trying to make the jury believe that he was also a victim. Who was Dylan to judge? He may not have had an easy life, like millions of others, but that didn't detract from the fact that he had committed a crime and in Dylan's mind he should serve the appropriate time in prison. His defence would have a hard time proving that this was 'out of character' looking at his history of offending, and all for the same crime: assault.

Dylan sat at his desk with a drink and his sandwiches; another working lunch. All was a hive of industry in the office outside. It was warm and he felt sleepy. With any luck the sustenance would keep him awake until he could go home. Pen in one hand and sandwich in the other he drafted the priority enquiries, as he saw them.

The initial interview with Morris hadn't given them anything other than, 'No replies,' and a 'V' sign every now and then, DS Benjamin reported. So, they were now dependent on a DNA profile of the tooth. A smile crossed Dylan's face. He could no more imagine Tony Morris extracting teeth carefully and skilfully than he could Vicky enjoying tea out of a china cup. Morris would rather knock teeth out and Vicky would rather have a swift half at the local. 'Our deceased didn't have any teeth missing. So, unless the owner is recorded, we may never know the identity,' said John.

Vicky walked in to Dylan's office. 'My God you look bright and breezy considering,' he said.

'Don't be fooled,' she said holding a can of Red Bull up at shoulder height. 'I've been in touch with Jim Woodcock, Timothy Woodcock's son. He's coming in to see me at five. I asked him about the burglary at his dad's home and he said it appeared to be primarily confined to his father's office.'

'He knew about it?'

'He reported it. He wanted to tell me about the things that are missing but I told him to bring the list with him. What was interesting though is that he did say his grandfather's fishing gear and his dental tools, left to his father by his father-in-law, are amongst the stuff that went.'

'Really? Now that does sound interesting, but let's not forget our serial killer is someone with experience and somehow I don't see an opportunist burglar having a go with the dental tools for the fun of it and finding in the process he has a gift in the art of teeth extraction, do you? But the fishing gear...?' Dylan's eyes grew wide.

Vicky nodded emphatically. 'And the dental equipment together is interesting.'

'Very interesting,' said Dylan.

'Ha ha! Never assume, you tell us,' Vicky said with a wink of an eye.

'I'm not and I'm always right because I'm the boss.'

'Yeah, whatever,' she said, taking her leave as Dylan's phone rang.

Jen was excited. 'Dad's just rang me, Thelma has bought a house in Spain for them,' she said.

'Spain?' said Dylan. His voice had risen an octave.

'Yes, Spain! And the best bit is she says we can use it whenever we want to.'

'We'll see,' he said. He scowled at the pile of papers that Raj brought in for him to read and sign. She smiled broadly, walked back towards the door, opened it and shut it quietly behind her.

'Any news on Thelma's missing purse or the money that was syphoned out of her bank account?'

'No, sadly not, nor have they captured the person responsible for the village's mini crime wave. But, they got an ear print believe it or not from the post office job. I don't know if it's good enough to get DNA from but if it is, and he is known to them now, or in the future they'll catch up with him with any luck. In all honesty I think that's what made Ozzy persuade Thelma to spend the money from the sale of her home and buy this holiday home in Spain for them all to use.'

'Why Spain?'

'Ozzy picked it up for her. It's a bit selfish of him because he's working there at the moment so he gets to use it. But, it's a nice place, Dad says, by the border in northern Spain and better still it was a bargain.'

'Have they been out to see it, this... apartment?'

'Villa.'

'A villa?' he said with surprise in his voice.

'Yes, they've just got back. Dad says it is truly amazing. They were invited around to their new neighbours and guess what, they own a yacht!'

'You never said they'd been abroad?'

'I didn't know till just now. Dad says it all happened very quickly. They had to go to get the papers signed to secure the property.'

'Buying abroad? Hope they've got a lawyer who specialises in Spanish land law. I've heard some horror stories from ex-coppers. I expected you to say they'd bought a timeshare – not a villa. How much did she get for her house on the Isle of Wight for goodness sake? Sounds iffy to me.'

Jen sighed once more. 'Why do you always have to put a downer on things? Not everything has to be dodgy. Sometimes nice things just happen to nice people,' she said. 'Dad deserves a bit of luck.'

'In my experience if something sounds too good to be true it usually is. I won't be going.'

'Well, me and Maisy might have to go alone then mightn't we?' Jen said, and he heard the click as the phone was put down. Dylan was tired. It made him grumpy. He shouldn't take it out on her. He made a mental note to apologise later, even if he thought he was right – this time.

***

Jim Woodcock arrived at Harrowfield Police Station promptly at five o'clock.

Vicky was called to the front desk. After introducing herself to him she invited him into a side room adjacent to the front counter in the foyer.

Mr Woodcock junior was not a big man. He had a long nose, receding chin and a full set of perfectly spaced square, white, teeth that he showed off to her in a broad, friendly smile. Vicky noticed he moved swiftly and easily on short stumpy legs.

He sat down in the clinically white room on a bolted down chair and frowned at the desk that he saw was also secured to the floor. 'Do you really think someone is going to walk out with them?' he said.

She closed the door behind them and sat opposite him. 'You'd be surprised,' Vicky said. 'That's when they not attempting to throw them at us,' she said raising an eyebrow at him. She saw

193

what she thought was a flash of admiration in his big dark, blue eyes as she put her paperwork between them on the desk.

'Really?' he said as he too pulled papers from a folder he had been carrying under his arm.

'Nice people you mix with,' he said.

'Tell me about it,' she said. Vicky noticed his mop of thin black curly hair that refused to be disciplined when he patted it down, which he did frequently. Although dressed in jeans and T-shirt he was clean shaven and exuded a smell of an aftershave she was familiar with. Her first impressions of him being a bit odd looking were soon dismissed by the easy way he had about him and his rich smooth velvety voice. She was disappointed that he kept his lips very tight so little of his teeth showed when he talked. He reminded her a bit of a ventriloquist in that way.

Jim Woodcock produced a piece of paper that he eagerly swivelled around on the table so she could read it. His little fat finger caught hers and it was soft and warm to the touch. 'I was summoned by my mother after her and the Gillards had been to visit. Father hasn't been well and... well basically, he's dying if I'm brutally honest.'

'I'm sorry to hear that,' said Vicky.

'Don't be, it's his own doing,' he said dismissing her sympathy instantly. 'Mother has a problem with her memory but she's not daft. She can remember things from her childhood as if it was yesterday.'

'You said the Gillards? That's your sister and brother-in-law who your mother lives with in St Annes, right?'

'Oh yes, she's with the prodigal one. I'm the black sheep. I was adopted. I've written down what mother told me was missing. I don't think they're of any value, it's more about the sentiment. The thing is the parents' divorce was not an amicable one, after his little misdemeanour at work, so we don't really know what father might have got rid of since mother left. I've visited father in hospital and in his lucid state he tells me the items should still be there. But, who knows?'

'Do you have regular contact with your mother and father?'

'Not really, you see I was a bit of a disappointment to the old man. I didn't follow the family tradition of becoming a dentist and as I am the only son to carry on the name... Well, it didn't

194

bode well. And my sister thinks I lead her husband astray so I'm not flavour of the month, any month in her house. Your fingerprint people have attended at father's by the way, but you are probably aware of that?'

'Lead your brother-in-law astray? What do you mean by that?'

'Father used to send me all over the world to dentist conventions with Devlin. It suited two purposes. He thought it might spark an interest in a dentist career for me – all it did was give me a love of travel. He also thought it might make my sister happy.'

'Why's that?'

'She's got a bit of a jealous streak has Gilly. Truth is it wasn't me who led Devlin astray. The old devil can do that all by himself. He likes the women does Devlin. She's a right to be suspicious of him. He's the bad influence on me.'

***

A skeleton staff manned the incident room. It was six thirty and Vicky walked into Dylan's office. DC Wormald was already there.

'Well, how did it go?' Dylan said.

'I'm just going to write up the Actions for inputting onto the database. You can't choose your family – luckily he can choose his friends,' she said.

'What do you mean?' said Dylan.

'Even though the family adopted Jim it seems that they have somewhat abandoned him to a certain extent – sad really. The allegation of the theft of the dental and fishing equipment is interesting. But, then again, Mrs Woodcock may have been having one of her 'moments'.

'Check the date that the burglary was recorded on our systems will you? It would be interesting to see if it was prior to the date the first murder was committed,' said Dylan.

'Trouble is we don't have specific dates of a burglary as the house has been unoccupied for some time due to Timothy Woodcock being in hospital,' said Andy.

'And it wasn't till Mrs Woodcock and the family went along to the house recently that the burglary was reported,' said Vicky.

'Fingerprints come up with anything?' said Dylan,

'No, CSI shows "no marks of value,"' Vicky said screwing up her nose.

'Jim Woodcock tells me that his father is dying. I'm going to check with the hospital and see if I can go and speak to him, if that's at all possible.'

'I've done that,' said Andy. 'The Sister said he'd welcome visitors. She doesn't recall him having any since he was admitted.'

'No, Jim Woodcock said he'd been to see his father,' said Vicky.

'Well, all I can tell you is what the Ward Sister said,' said Andy. 'Mind you she wouldn't be on duty everyday would she?'

'Are visitors listed on the hospital file for seriously ill patients do you think?' said Vicky.

'I don't know. Find out,' said Dylan.

Chapter Twenty

Dylan had finished his dinner and Maisy was lying on the rug in front of the hearth colouring with Jen. 'That's an orange one mummy,' Maisy said holding up a green pen.

'No darling, it's a green one.'

'No mummy it's orange!' she said. Jen's eyes flew up to Dylan and her nostrils flared. He bit his lip in an attempt not to laugh. Jen cocked her head and stared at Maisy and their daughter mimicked her mother's image.

'I think it's time for bed lady, don't you?' said Jen raising her eyebrow.

Maisy's eyes hooded and her mouth turned downwards. She rose, threw herself at Dylan and hid her face in his lap. Dylan picked her up and held her high. She squealed with excitement and he brought her towards him and kissed her chubby little cheeks before putting her down in front of Jen. She reached out, grabbed Jen's waiting hand and waved goodnight to him. He blew her a kiss and she blew him one back.

Dylan was putting his dirty dishes in the dishwasher when he heard Jen's footsteps on the stairs. 'She off already?' he said looking at her over his shoulder. Jen nodded and padded quietly across the kitchen to put clothes in the washing machine. As she got up and turned Dylan was standing with his arms open wide. 'Come here you,' he said. She did as she was told and rested her head against his chest. 'Tired?' he asked hugging her tight. She threw her head back to look up at his face and stifled a yawn. 'You could say that.'

'What's Maisy been up to today then?'

'Well, for starters she purposely tipped up her milk on the carpet when I was talking to Dad on the phone this morning – which meant I had to hurriedly cut him off and he was about to give me an update on the Spain adventure. Then not satisfied with the biscuit I gave her she started yelling, "Nack, Nack," and came back from the kitchen with a packet of crackers that she threw at my head! Hence, I didn't get to ring him back.'

Dylan stifled a grin. 'She's a surprising good shot for a nipper isn't she? She threw a shoe at me the other day when I was driving and only because she didn't want to be in her car seat. Maybe she'll bowl for England when she grows up?'

'Or might fly to the moon, why not?'

'If she fancies it...' he said with a little laugh. 'The world's her oyster.'

'Yes, well I'd like to know where my sweet little girl has gone. I think you'd better use your detective skills to find her because someone has replaced her with a little terror!'

***

At seven o'clock the next morning it was raining heavily. Dylan could hear Jen trying to coax Maisy into eating her breakfast as he dressed for work. 'Just one more mouthful...'

'No Mummy, go away,' he heard Maisy say as he reached the kitchen door. He put his head around the door frame. 'Daddy's home for breakfast,' she called out with glee and struggled to get off her child seat to get to him. Jen looked at Dylan and shook her head. 'Out of the mouths of babes,' she said as he lifted her in his arms, sat down and placed her on his knee.

***

Dylan travelled in the rain to Harrowfield Police station. As he drove into the back yard he saw Rajinder hurrying along. Her head was forward and her umbrella held like a shield. She ignored others, struggling as she was with putting her umbrella down, briefcase under her arm. He parked up. She disappeared into the building. A black cab drew up at the same door and he walked towards it. The rain glistened on its roof. Out stepped Vicky. Her face was pale and grey. Dylan looked at her, his eyebrows knit together.

'Great night boss,' she said sheepishly as she rummaged in her handbag. She paid the driver. Dylan followed her. She wore her clothes clumsily as if she had slept in them. They bagged at the elbows and the knees.

'Come on you, let's get in before that black cloud that's hovering above us bursts,' he said giving her a guiding hand as he looked up to the sky. 'We've got a long day ahead, at the mortuary.'

'Don't I know it...' she said looking up at him. Her husky voice seemed to come from a distance.

It was a day for them to be present whilst independent pathologists carried out a second post-mortem on Davina Walsh on behalf of any future defence team. Dylan's presence was required as a matter of routine in case the findings challenged the examination carried out by Professor Stow. In the next few days an inquest would be opened and closed by the Coroner until after an arrest had been made and the police had charged an offender.

However, this meant for Gary and Davina's friends the funeral could now take place.

The same process had to be carried out in respect of Carl Braithwaite and Alan Bell. The independent pathologists on behalf of any future defence would then write to the Coroner stating they were satisfied the bodies could be released for funeral purposes. Dylan was satisfied that the prosecution no longer required the bodies to be retained. The following couple of weeks would see Dylan with Vicky, Raj or John attending the funerals.

***

Dylan had learnt to deal with murder enquiries by not getting sucked into the emotion. But although his head told him such, his heart could not help being moved by a funeral service.

As he sat in the pew, next to Vicky at the back of the church at Davina Walsh's funeral he stared up at the high ceiling and the music filled his being. He studied the exposed wood beams. It reminded him of the ribs of a boat turned upside down. His eyes scanned the mourners, there were plenty. The uniformed presence reminded him of colleagues' funerals, men and women he had worked with. His heart felt heavy. Emotions were high and he dared not look at Vicky who he saw out of the corner of his eye wipe away a tear for another young woman whose life had been lost. He thought of Jen, the way he had laid next to that morning in bed just watching her and listening to her breathing, long before Maisy had woken her. He thought of her hair that had been on her pillow and draped down over her dimpled shoulders. He thought of her honest eyes, steady eyes, eyes that did not lie to him as others had before, making him untrusting in the opposite sex. And her air of deliberateness, fearlessness and her sensitive intuition that she clung to despite what had happened to her in the past. And then it was over. The coffin was carried out of the church and the young woman, with so much to look forward to, was put in a grave, six foot down in the ground.

'Do not stand at my grave and weep...' said the vicar.

Dylan and Vicky stood on the periphery of the group of mourners.

'How do you cope?' said Vicky wiping her eyes as they walked to the car.

'With funerals?' he said.

'With death...' she replied.

'We're all going to die one day. All we can do is try and make a difference whilst we're here and help preserve the life of others. How do I cope?' he said getting into the car. 'I believe that the body is a shell that is left behind when we die and our soul goes on.'

'So when you see bodies that are disembowelled, ripped open, faceless, horribly mutilated you don't see a human being?'

'No, but what I do feel is a passionate need to catch the person or people responsible and prove beyond doubt how that person died to ensure the perpetrator is put away for as long as possible. For the victim and for the families that are left behind to hopefully give them some sort of closure to help them move on. When my mum died the nurse opened a window to let her spirit go free. I liked that. It helped. Whatever we believe it has to allow us to get on with the job we are here to do.'

Vicky nodded her head and Dylan started the car. The next funeral would be Carl Braithwaite's which was to be a small family affair and proved not to be the public show of affection for the loner who was the taxi driver Alan Bell. Having no close relatives or partner his funeral was to be a celebration of his life, by those that knew him. A line of taxis would follow his coffin though the town centre which would bring Harrowfield to a standstill. Flags would fly and horns would blare, continuously.

Dylan was left feeling emotionally drained and guilty that these three people were buried and as yet, as the man in charge of their murder enquiries he had no idea who had killed them, or why.

***

It was late Friday evening and Jen waited for him with a bottle of wine in the fridge and a steak under the grill. Dylan walked in the door.

'Crap week?' she said with a screwing up of her nose. She walked towards him.

'I've had better,' he said, opening his arms to her.

She put a hand to his face. 'What is it you tell me? The funeral is simply to allow an outpouring of grief for family and friends, but you know, they know, the person has gone.'

'It's not that Jen. I feel as though I've let them down. I'm the person in charge of investigations. I want to give them answers and I can't. Should I have even gone to the funerals? Wouldn't the victims' family and friends expect me to be spending every minute I have trying to find the evil bastard that killed their loved ones?'

Jen gave him a quizzical look. 'You'll find them. You can't possibly work anymore hours and I think the families would be pleased you found time to attend the funerals. I know you won't give up until you have those responsible behind bars and one of these days you'll get the break you need.' Jen studied his face. 'Sometimes I hate the bloody job,' she said with tears in her eyes. Dylan held her tight. He planted a kiss on her head. 'Hey, don't you get upset,' he said. He licked a tear from her cheek. 'Why do tears always taste of salt?' he said.

She smiled at him despite how she felt but her look was fiercely serious. 'I just watch you become embroiled. You sink deeper and deeper into yourself as the days pass and the murders are not detected. You don't like to think that each one takes that little bit more from Jack Dylan... but it does, believe me it does.'

He understood what she was saying. 'Don't worry about me, I'm fine. Sometimes I have moments when it gets to me, but it passes.'

Jen leant forward and planted a kiss on his lips. 'There's no good trying to reason with you is there?' she said holding one of his large soft hands in hers. 'So I guess all I can do is try and look after you,' she said. He lifted his chin and planted a kiss on her forehead.

'Sounds good to me.' His smile reached his eyes and for a moment or two his eyes held hers.

She knew he was trying to offer her comfort but she also knew that although he appeared to take the heinous sights he saw and the investigations in his stride, the pressure to find the person(s) responsible got under his skin. She knew the hard face detective was a mask – Jack Dylan was a human being after all.

***

The TV was on but no one was watching. Jen was sewing the bottoms of Maisy's trousers. Jack had long since fallen asleep, sitting upright on the sofa.

'Let's go to bed, get a good night's sleep and pray that bloody phone doesn't ring,' she said sliding his mobile phone off the arm of the settee into her sewing bag. He sat up, yawned and retrieved his phone and looked at the screen.

'You're right. Time for bed,' he said with a smile. His eyes creased at the corners and made them look like those of a young boy.

***

Dylan met Vicky walking out of the police station as he walked in early the next morning. She talked at him and fast.

'I had a call from the hospital. Sister says Timothy Woodcock is able to speak to me today, so I want to seize the moment before the doctor does his rounds and puts a damper on it,' she said, jumping into her car. Dylan nodded and watched her leave with a determined look upon her face.

Timothy Woodcock lay in a side ward, alone. A young nurse accompanied Vicky into the room. All was quiet but for the bleeps that came from the apparatus at the side of his bed. His great white face was turned towards the window. She saw his eyes were wide open and she followed his gaze to a sloping lawn and claret coloured flowerbed interspersed with daisies. Beyond that was a copse of still, leaf filled trees. She was taken aback by his size. It appeared to be too much effort for the large, solemn looking man to lift his hand from under the covers. The nurse looked on at his feeble attempts and then did the deed for him.

'How are we feeling?' said the nurse brightly as she bent over and laid the palms of her hands firmly down on the starched bed linen. She didn't wait for an answer but continued to busy herself flicking switches on the apparatus and checking his drip bags were adequately full and the liquid was running freely through the tubes. Mr Woodcock appeared disinterested and his reply was nothing more than a pathetic grunt. 'Look here,' she said. 'I've got a visitor for you. If you won't talk to me maybe you'll talk to this nice young lady?'

Vicky was aware of Timothy Woodcock as a pair of eyes – eyes that were waiting, waiting for what she didn't know. His face was the colour of milk. The glassy eyes followed the nurse as she walked to the bottom of his bed. She motioned Vicky towards her and pulled her up a chair. 'DC Hardacre wants to talk to you about a report of a burglary at your home. Shall we try to sit you up?' she said leaning over the great bulk of the man. His illness made him appear ten years older than his actual age. With a swift well practiced action and great effort she lifted the heavily obese man to a semi-sitting position. Mr Woodcock panted at the exertion. Vicky sat down, her hands were crossed in her lap. He held her gaze with a strange, sulky stare. 'I'll be back shortly,' said the nurse. 'Call me if you need me,' she said quietly in Vicky's ear.

Vicky held on to a forced smile. She tried to engage with him. Her efforts appeared to be futile but her patience held.

'I'd like you to look at a list of items we believe may have been stolen from your property Mr Woodcock,' she said, offering him the document she retrieved from a folder. He didn't take the piece of paper from her but looked at it apathetically. Then he closed his eyes and forced himself back into his soft pillow. Vicky read the list out to him. He didn't interrupt her and when she finished she sat silent for a few minutes. She wasn't sure he had heard any of what she had said. He lay in a kind of voiceless anguish then in a laboured throaty voice he opened his mouth and spoke to her. His voice was husky at first.

'One of the reels might be worth a bob-or-two,' he said. 'The dentistry instruments were my father-in-law's. He left them to me. A break-in you say? I don't know nothing about a break-in.'

'Your son, Jim, he told you about it. Don't you remember?'

'My son? Is he back from Hong Kong? Why hasn't he come to see me?'

'I don't know...'

'Jim did try, bless him, but it wasn't in his blood,' he said with a little shake of his head. He raised his hand slightly and let it fall back heavily, and the gesture appeared to suggest his mood. He pressed his lips against his teeth. His mouth was clearly dry but he continued. 'Not like Ginny,' he said. 'She was always a natural.' His voice trailed off and he closed his eyes.

Vicky sat for a while but there was no response to her calling his name. She left the room and found the nurse. 'He seems very weary,' she said.

'Yes,' she said. 'He's a very poorly man.'

'Just out of interest, who have you listed as his next of kin?'

'We don't have anyone... it's sad. He talks about a son and daughter but.... We have no one listed.'

'There is a living ex-wife, a daughter, son-in-law and an adopted son that we are aware of. I'll get you their details.'

'Thank you,' said the nurse. 'It'll make someone's job a lot easier when the time comes.'

Vicky took a short cut to the car park and in doing so passed Mr Woodcock's window as she passed between a laurel hedge and the red-brick wall. Timothy Woodcock was lying perfectly still – ghost-like.

***

DS Raj, DS Benjamin and Dylan were in Dylan's office when Vicky approached it. It was something of a glass bowl and she could see them in animated discussion. She feebly knocked at the door, opened it and walked in. She sat next to Rajinder. Everyone's eyes were upon her.

Well, how did it go with Mr Woodcock senior?' said Dylan.

'Well, let's say I think it's safe to assume that he isn't our serial killer. He didn't appear to know about the burglary, although Jim Woodcock told me that he had informed him but who knows what he has been told and by whom... He's on so much medication I don't think we can take anything he says into account. He did say the fishing reels might be of some value but he also thought Jim was still abroad.'

'That's a pity. Did we get an update on the tooth that was found in Tony Morris's pocket? Surely they can give us something by now?' said Dylan.

'I'll give Beryl a ring,' said Raj, jumping up from her seat.

'Thanks,' said Dylan.

'And I need to get the nurse at the hospital Timothy Woodcock's next of kin details which the family haven't been forthcoming in giving them,' said Vicky.

◆

Chapter Twenty-One

'In respect of our would-be hard man Tony Morris,' said John Benjamin. 'According to prison liaison, since his arrival, he's been fighting everyone. He has a broken nose and several deep lacerations to his face which will no doubt leave him scarred for life.'

'He'll learn. No matter how hard or tough you think you are there is always someone harder and tougher,' said Dylan.

'Not him boss, I don't think he'll ever learn. Using his fists appears to be all he knows. He's not going to change. The sad thing is when he is released, others will suffer.'

'If he is ever released. Who knows what will happen in the next decade whilst he's locked up.'

'The tooth he had in his possession didn't belong to any of our victims so who it did belong to is anybody's guess...' said Raj.

Dylan shook his head. 'He never was bright enough to be our man. He's all brawn and no brains. He certainly isn't going to talk to us. We can eliminate him from our serial killing enquiries, but let's hope the trial Judge slams him because of his past record and the degree of unprovoked violence he used on Warren Derby.'

'I'm sure that would give the family some comfort.'

'Do we know if he intends to plead guilty?'

'At the moment he's going not guilty, but rumour has it he will plead on the day.'

'We can live in hope, John. If not Derby's poor girlfriend, Jade Thomas, will be the main prosecution witness and she'll have to relive the events of that fateful night when she saw her boyfriend killed in front of her.'

'So will his parents,' said Vicky.

'Could she cope with it do you think?'

'The court?'

Dylan nodded at John.

'She's only a young girl. She wouldn't find it easy. But, I think she'd do what she had to do and come across well to a jury.'

'Good, like I said before, let's hope the Judge recommends a nineteen year stretch for him. He may have quietened down by then. Thanks for that John.'

So Tony Morris was out of the running. Dylan never really believed he was the serial killer they were looking for, but he had slashed his victim's throat and had a tooth in his possession on arrest so he had to be put in the frame. Dylan's next update to the ACC would be to tell her that Morris was eliminated from the enquiry.

Dylan would be interested to hear what Forensic could tell him now and awaited results. There had been nothing more forthcoming from the offender profiler and Dylan knew it was only matter of time before the killer struck again. Although the team was working full steam ahead to prevent it from happening, not one person featured prominently on the radar as a likely suspect and that worried him. He was well aware the killer was still in control and that he got great satisfaction from the way he structured the crime scenes with no evidence being left behind to give the police any clues as to his identity. But ultimately, on a positive note, he was actually linking the crimes.

One thing the team had was the knowledge that the three crime scenes were confined to a relatively small area of Harrowfield. Dylan was more and more certain that the killer had good geographical knowledge of the town. However that didn't mean the killer lived on the patch. The canal/cycle path link appeared paramount to the crime scenes and Dylan asked himself the question. Did the culprit use these tracks to travel on? Maybe even secrete a means of transport nearby the would-be crime scene as a means of a quick and easy get away? Most of his route using two wheels or a boat would be covered by darkness, quick and relatively quiet and there was little in terms of CCTV cameras to catch him in the act of getting away.

This wasn't the first time the thought had crossed Dylan's mind. He had had the access routes searched after the murder of Alan Bell. Nothing had been found. This was not enough for

Dylan now, he had to do something, he had to do more, and the longer he waited, the more likely the killer would strike again.

'I want an action plan,' he told the team. 'We need to start being pro-active instead of re-active. We can't afford to sit back and wait for something to happen. I will implement a plan of action that we use for the cross-border problems we have with the travelling criminals. We will initiate a stop and check of vehicles on various routes that are significant to the investigations and hopefully their high visibility will deter would-be offenders from neighbouring counties. I know it's a bit pot-luck in detecting any crime but it appears to have been successful in the past and prevention is better than cure. I also want the canal/cycle paths on our plan but for these,' he told those present at the briefing. 'I want this to be done on an observation, followed by a stop and check basis. These checks will be carried out between midnight and five thirty a.m. which will fall in line with working shift patterns.'

There was a grumbling in the room. 'I know,' said Dylan. 'Davina's murder took place after five thirty a.m. but I am satisfied that the killer had been in the area for some time before he struck that day. After all he had found the used condom, this must have been something that he had looked around for to intentionally throw the police off the scent of what he was about to do. I also believe that in Davina's case, the murderer might have been watching her and untypical of how he appeared to come across Carl Braithwaite fortuitously, he may have latched onto her routine. Make sure we have the helicopter available for our "eyes in the sky,"' Dylan said. 'We need its ability to search areas which are in total darkness by using its on board thermal imaging camera.'

Dylan wanted a breakthrough and he wanted it now and his need was tangible.

One phone in the incident room rang, then another. Dylan ended the briefing. He could hear his phone ringing and DS Raj intercepted the call.

'Forensic sir,' said Raj. 'They have news. Do you want to take it?' she said.

Dylan went to his office hastily. 'What have you got for me,' he said. 'Something good I hope?'

Chapter Twenty-Two

Each murder scene was dealt with separately by Forensic too, ensuring no possibility of contamination.

'We know your culprit has removed teeth from three victims. One upper molar we have recovered at the Alan Bell murder scene has been identified as belonging to the first victim Davina Walsh, from which I think we can assume two things. It was either dropped accidentally or it was left on purpose by the killer. At the same scene a garrotte was recovered, and I can confirm it was made from very old braided fishing line. Along with two random sized newish pieces of kindling wood. We have tested the blood that was on the fishing line and as expected it has been identified as belonging to murder victim, Alan Bell. Tapings from the rear seat of the taxi have revealed lots of different fibres which we are wading through,' said Beryl.

Dylan raised his eyebrows at Rajinder who knocked at his door and walked in. He beckoned her to sit.

'Can you possibly date the fishing line for us?'

'Well braided fishing lines of this kind have been around since the nineteen thirties and since then have continued to be developed in several ways by braiding or weaving fibres of a man-made material like Spectra or Micro-Dyneema.'

'Braided fishing line is strong stuff then?'

'Oh gosh yes, you need a sharp knife or scissors to cut this. Many an angler will have a nasty scar on his hand, I dare say to prove it.'

'As always, I'm grateful,' said Dylan. 'And perfect timing. I was just about to review what we had with my detective sergeants. I just wonder if our killer will stop after he has achieved a desired number of teeth?' he said.

'If only we knew what was going on in his head,' said Beryl.

Dylan put his phone down on its cradle, slowly. His hand lingered for a moment. Then his eyes found Raj's big brown serious eyes.

'What are you thinking?' she said as she looked at his studious expression.

He picked up a pen and turned a page in his notepad before he spoke.

'What's interesting me,' he said putting pen to paper, 'is that our killer is taking a variety of teeth from the mouths of our victims.'

'And that matters because?'

'Let's see, he took incisors and an upper molar at the Davina Walsh murder.'

'He extracted molars from Carl Braithwaite's mouth and premolars from Alan Bell.'

'You're wondering if his aim is to get a full set aren't you?'

'Yes, but why on earth would he want a full set of teeth?' Dylan's mind skipped from one murder scene to the other.

'...And a totally perfect set of teeth,' said Raj.

'Mmm... I wonder?'

Vicky held an enlarged still photograph. She turned it to face Dylan. 'We may have got ourselves a witness to this man, near the Alan Bell murder scene,' she said pointing to the image of a man in a blue hoodie.

Dylan took the picture from her and putting it down on his desk he retrieved a magnifying glass from his desk drawer. The men's faces could not be seen clearly. The image showed one man dressed in dark trousers, possibly jeans and a hoodie; the other in a suit.

'It's a long shot but do we have anyone on CCTV wearing this type of clothing hanging about at the taxi rank that night?'

'Well, yes we have lots of guys in suits, shirts and smart trousers, jeans and t-shirts but... the man in the hoodie he looks sort of out of place. There appears to be a logo, mark, tear, burn, something on the left shoulder which could make it quite significant to us if we can trace it,' said Vicky.

'I want you to find me them both somewhere else on CCTV. Let's put more resources into the examination of the CCTV we have on the Walsh and Braithwaite murder too.'

Raj and Vicky left Dylan alone. He saw them gather their teams in the incident rooms. 'Listen up, you lot!' he heard Vicky shout against Rajinder's quieter approach. Dylan got up and closed his door. Maybe, just maybe this was an important piece of the jigsaw. His spirits were lifted.

Dylan proceeded to write in his policy book with a renewed vigour. When John Benjamin knocked at his door Dylan sat upright, arched his back, lifted his clasped hands to the ceiling, palms up and yawned loudly. DS Benjamin looked down at his boss.

'We've just had a call from the manager at the Forget Me Not charity shop in Harrowfield in response to your appeal. Would you believe she has just found antique fishing equipment and an old dentistry set together, on a shelf in the stock room, waiting to be priced up?'

Dylan was still for a moment. His mouth snapped shut. His arms fell to his side. 'How long has it been there? Does she know?'

'She can't say. Could be weeks, months. They don't take note of what's donated and by whom but she does know she wasn't working when they were brought in.'

John looked over his left shoulder. 'Andy took the call. He told her not to touch it and him and Vicky are off round there now.'

Dylan looked out into the incident room and caught sight of DC Andy Wormald putting on his suit jacket And Vicky scooping up her bag from the side of her chair. He watched as they hurried out of the office.

***

About half past five Dylan heard a commotion outside. He finished the witness statement he was reading, before he lifted his head and stood up. Seeing others gathered around Vicky's desk he put his pen down and went to join them.

'You've got them?' he said.

'Yes, nothing exciting really, it's just some old fishing gear and a case with a few old dental tools in.'

'Do you think they belong to Woodcock?' said Ned.

'How the fuck do I know,' said Vicky. 'I'm not a chuffin' psychic,' she said pulling a pair of disposable gloves from a box on her desk. She put the first glove to her mouth, turned her head away from the exhibits and blew into it. Talcum powder showered the carpet tiles. She placed the glove on her left hand before she did the same with another for her right.

'Vicky,' growled Dylan. He walked back to his office with his arm outstretched. 'Come on everyone, show's over, there's nothing to see, yet,' he said, waving his arms in a sweeping action. He looked around the room at people making their way back to their desks. There were a few downhearted grunts and groans. The team was getting restless and Dylan could feel it. An inclination that there might be a sniff of a lead in the enquiry was exciting enough to whet their appetite, but not satisfy their thirst.

'Keep your bloody hair on, I was only asking,' Ned said, holding some exhibit bags out to Andy who held the first one open for Vicky to transfer an item into it.

'An old fishing reel, still with fishing line on the spools,' she said. Andy made a note. 'Exhibit AW1,' he said writing it carefully on the exhibit label. Vicky sealed the bag and Andy attached the label.

The box that held the dental equipment was a similar size to that of a laptop. 'That's bigger than I imagined it would be,' Ned said as Vicky carefully opened the wooden lid to reveal a worn purple velvet interior. It also held within a small wrap of long thin dental tools, some scissor like pliers, two large syringes, a piece of piping, a small tin of denture adhesive powder, a larger tin of Clove Oil and indentations where other dental paraphernalia once lived.

'Pity it's not complete,' said Ned. 'I reckon there would be collectors out there that would pay a wad for it.'

'Wow! An antique expert now are we?' said Vicky.

'Hey, don't let this pretty face fool you, I'm an intelligent beast,' he said throwing her a cheeky grin.

'Keep telling yourself that,' she said without raising her head. 'Someone might actually listen to you one day,' she said as she put a determined full stop to the Connected and Miscellaneous Property Form information.

She turned her head towards Dylan's office. She saw him put the phone down and as he did so he pushed his chair back, stood and made his way towards them. 'Well, boss do you think they fit the description of the items allegedly stolen from Timothy Woodcock's house?'

'I wonder what happened to the missing items?' said Andy. He scratched his head.

'That fishing line is of definite interest,' said Dylan.

'Annoyingly the manager has no idea when they were brought in or by whom?' said Andy.

'Yes, she does,' said Dylan.

'She does?' said Vicky.

'That was her on the phone,' he said smiling. 'Luckily for us a volunteer who's just had a baby popped in and was privy to the conversation that she was having with another colleague. I've got the lady's contact details here for you to follow up,' he said handing a piece of paper to Vicky. 'Let's ask Jim Woodcock to look at the items and see if he can identify them as being his father's. I'd also like Professor Stow to see them to give us his professional opinion on whether they might fit the bill. We might be getting somewhere if we can prove they are about the right era for the tools that were used in the murders. First get hold of CSI and see if Sarah or Karen are working. We need to get the fishing tackle and the dentistry items photographed before we send them to Forensic for the fishing line to be checked against our garrotte that was recovered at Alan Bell's murder scene.'

'Good idea, we can use the photographs whilst the items are being examined at forensic for our enquiries,' said Ned.

'Keep me posted.' Dylan's voice was excited.

Chapter Twenty-Three

Vicky's phone call with Jim Woodcock was not as successful as she had hoped. He apparently didn't think that he could be much use in identifying the stolen items which he hadn't seen in a long number of years.

'But, if you'd just take a look. It might just spark some sort of childhood memory.'

'I'd rather not if you don't mind. Why not ask my father to identify them for you?' he said.

'I don't really want to bother him,' she said. 'I'm sorry to hear from the hospital today that his health has deteriorated.'

'Try mother then or the prodigal pair.'

'Pardon?' said Vicky.

'I'm sure Devlin will have seen them and Ginny for definite,' he said.

***

Dylan sat with his elbows on his desk and his chin lightly resting on his hands that were clasped together in a fist. He appeared to be reading something on his computer screen when Vicky joined him.

'It doesn't add up,' she said hurling herself down on a chair opposite him.

'What doesn't add up?' he said moving his eyes to look at her; his head remained still.

'Why would anyone burgle a house and then take the stuff they've stolen to a charity shop?'

'A would-be Robin Hood?'

'Do you know any burglar who has a charitable bone in their bloody body? And anyway why would anyone steal something if they didn't want it in the first place?'

Dylan's stare at the screen was persistent. His eyes flickered, then turned her way.

'Think about it. From a thief's point of view, even if in this unlikely of scenarios we have a charitable thief, it's another chance that they could be caught and more than likely by way of CCTV these days, isn't it? So wouldn't the alleged thief, in reality just dump them somewhere if they wanted to get rid of them?'

'It will be interesting if the volunteer who he handed them to can give us a description of the person who brought them in.'

'Mmm...' she said. 'Edna Woodcock is over in West Yorkshire today with her daughter so I'm meeting up with them to see if they can help with the identification of the recovered items. If not, I'll have to see how the land lies at the hospital to see if I can see Timothy Woodcock again. You seen Jen?'

'No, not since I left this morning why?'

'Oh, rumour has it that the powers that be are making all the civilians re-apply for their jobs.'

'Again? You are joking?'

'Nope. And Beaky...'

'Ms Avril Summerfield-Preston to you,' said Dylan with a lift of a brow.

'I only call people who I respect by their proper names. Beaky, she's causing an uproar upstairs in admin. Seemingly, she's strutting about telling everyone that her job is the only one that's safe here. Apparently, the cost-cutting doesn't apply to the holder of the title of Divisional Administrator.'

'Oh, and why am I not surprised? It's a bit like the desk job twerp that decides the rank of Inspector and above should take a rise in pay instead of being paid overtime because their job is nine to five, no shifts, no weekends, no call outs...'

'Jobs for the boys,' said Vicky.

The telephone rang. It was Jen. Dylan pulled a face at Vicky and Vicky smiled at him.

'Jen,' she mouthed. He nodded. She left.

'And as usual part-time workers will be the first to go, won't they?' Jen said.

'Not necessarily,' Dylan replied. 'They will probably keep part-timers on hoping that they will work more hours for the love of the job.'

'I'm afraid those days are long gone. Everyone knows the force has to save money but it's the way the hierarchy go about it. They must think we're stupid not to know what they are up to. It's so blatantly bloody obvious!'

Dylan couldn't help but smile. 'What will be, will be,' he said. 'You know as well as I do that the names will be on the doors of the people they have selected to stay on so there's no point getting yourself all worked up. It's a waiting game for those who don't want to leave.'

'You know what will happen next don't you? They'll send their puppets out from headquarters like they did last time to play lip service to us. No, to bloody lie to us.'

Dylan remained silent.

'Yes, well they shouldn't be allowed to get away with it,' she said.

'No they shouldn't, but they do, so it's not worth getting out of bed over. Maisy okay when you left her at Chantall's?'

'No, she cried and wouldn't let go of me and...'

'You know she will be fine the minute you left.'

'You're right, you're always right. Oh god, why the hell do I let them get to me? I think I need a holiday. Maybe we will go to Spain?' Dylan could hear the teasing in her tone.

'And maybe we won't,' he said adamantly.

***

Rajinder's hand was on the door handle of his office door. 'I've just been asked if we can go through to see some CCTV footage,' she said. 'It's a possibility we have our man.'

Dylan jumped up.

'The footage that is being examined is from earlier in the day of Alan Bell's murder,' she said, as side by side they walked briskly down the corridor.

The room where the CCTV footage was being viewed was known as the quiet room, due to the fact the officers worked behind closed doors in a quiet environment so they weren't disturbed, even momentarily. Each and every one of them in there knew only too well that the slightest distraction could mean they missed a vital piece of information.

Minutes later Dylan was seated next to a detective constable.

'Based on the fact that we had a fleeting glimpse of two men near the murder scene, one in a hoodie and one in a suit, I have been reviewing CCTV material covering the taxi rank from where Alan Bell worked for around an hour before he was murdered. I have found this.'

Dylan moved to the edge of his seat. Waiting anxiously, he looked at the officer's finger willing it to press the play button.

***

John Benjamin was in the incident room. The charity shop volunteer who had taken the fishing and dentistry equipment from the donator was on the phone. 'You want to know who brought it in?' she said.

'That's right,' said John. 'Do you remember?'

'Yes, I do, for two reasons. One, the man was very impatient and he leant over an elderly lady who was already standing at the counter to drop the black bag on the counter. And two, when I took a look inside the bag I remarked to the lady that it was surprising what people brought in for us to sell.'

'We think they may have been stolen, so it would be really helpful if you could tell us anything you remember about the person?'

'Oh gosh, I play the game Guess Who with my six-year-old granddaughter and she's better at it than me. Don't hold your breath...'

'I play it with the kids and I'm rubbish too,' said John. 'I appreciate it's not easy but if there is anything about them that you could remember, anything at all...?'

'The man wasn't young or old, he wasn't fat or thin, his hair wasn't blonde or black, he wasn't scruffy or posh. He was just an ordinary looking twenty, thirty something guy, wearing what twenty, thirty something men wear, t-shirt, jeans and one of those hooded thingies.'

'That's good,' said John.

'Really?' she said.

'Really.'

'Can someone come around to get a statement from you?'

'Well, they can, but I can't tell them anymore than I've told you,' she said.

'It would help if you would give us a statement,' said John.

'Okay then,' she said. 'No worries.'

***

Meanwhile Dylan was asking the detective in the quiet room to re-run the small amount of CCTV again, and again and again.

'There... can we stop it just there?' Dylan said. 'Get me that still.'

Chapter Twenty-Four

Dylan had just watched a brief glimpse of a man in a hoodie amongst others who were relatively smart. The guy in the hoodie appeared on CCTV from two streets around the taxi rank. He was riding a bike and this appeared to be totally out of place in the town centre at that time of night. He kept his distance from the revellers – appearing to be nothing more than an onlooker to their enjoyment. Dylan was shown CCTV footage of the same man but this time on foot, an hour later. He stood half-in and half-out of a shop doorway leaning against its wall and facing the window. Here he could see the distinct mark on the shoulder of his hoodie. What had he done with his bike? His face wasn't visible due to the fact he had his head down and his hood was pulled conspicuously forward. But it was a man in a suit who got into the taxi with the registration number of Alan Bell's taxi at midnight.

Dylan asked for the screen to be frozen, took a closer look and patted the detective on the shoulder as he got up from the chair. 'Good work,' he said. 'Can we get some stills for each time the man in the hoodie and the man in the suit is shown on CCTV and have those copied. I want a professional assessment to be made to show those two people are one and the same at each point.'

He felt slightly optimistic as he walked back into the incident room. He shared the recent development with the team at debrief emphasising that this news must remain within the room. The last thing he wanted was the killer disposing of clothing that could put him at the scenes; if he hadn't done so already. Dylan was confident, find the wearers of those clothes and he would have his killer.'

'The volunteer from the Forget Me Not charity shop has put a hoodie wearer as the man who brought in the items of interest.

However that appears all she can tell us. I will task someone with going to see her and getting a statement,' said John.

'Could this really be our man?' said Vicky.

'Who knows? Any update on Edna Woodcock identifying the recovered items?'

'No, they didn't end up in West Yorkshire. According to her daughter she wasn't having a good day,' said Vicky with a grimace upon her face.

'Okay, we'll call it a day. I'll see you all back here tomorrow morning for an eight o'clock briefing please.'

Ned looked across the room at Vicky. 'There's something about you that's different,' he said.

'No fooling you is there my son,' she said with a click of her tongue and a wink at her colleague. 'I've got my dancing gear on,' she replied eyes wide and bright.

'You off out tonight then?' he said.

'You should be a bloody detective when you grow up.'

'Funny ha ha! Can I come with you?' he said watching her walk down the aisle between the desks in her short skirt and high heels.

'If you must, but you'd better not show me up, lightweight,' she said.

'I'm no lightweight. I'll show you. Give me a minute,' he said reaching for his phone. 'I'll just ring the missus and tell her I've a job on.'

DS Raj picked up her shopping list for the supermarket. She rolled her eyes at Dylan.

'Aren't you just glad those days are over,' she said.

Dylan chortled. 'I sure am,' he said with a yawn. 'I'm looking forward to a good night's sleep. Make sure they behave Andy,' he said to DC Wormald as he passed the detective on his way out.

'I'm not going sir. I'm doing a double-bubble.'

'He's offered to do a double shift,' said Vicky. 'No one made him.'

'God help us tomorrow then,' Dylan said to Raj, shaking his head at Vicky and Ned who were heading for the door.

***

Maisy was in fine form, singing happily as she sat alone in the lounge. Too busy to acknowledge her daddy's homecoming while sticking stickers in a book. Dylan popped his head around the door. The smell emanating from the kitchen was delightful and he filled his lungs.

'I'm home,' he called as he opened the kitchen door.

His father-in-law stood up from where he had been sitting at the kitchen table. 'I thought it was about time you met Thelma,' Ralph said as he held his hand out to shake Dylan's. His tanned face was smiling as he turned to his partner.

Jen entered the kitchen from the adjoining dining-room, cutlery in her hand, she was beaming. 'Look who I found on our doorstep when I arrived home,' she said putting her arm around her dad's shoulders. She hugged him tight.

'I hope you don't mind the intrusion. We've just stepped off the plane from Spain,' Thelma said. 'My Ozzy had a delivery for a client in Harrowfield so we offered to bring it for him. And the best bit is I get to meet you three,' she said.

'And he was kind enough to pay for our flight,' said Ralph.

'A no brainer then,' said Dylan putting down his briefcase on the table. Jen instantly removed it and walked into the hallway, standing it on the bottom step of the stairs. 'Come on for your tea Maisy. You can watch the Nosey Paca's afterwards on the television, if you're a good girl,' she said.

'I'll just go and change,' Dylan said as he turned to leave. Thelma caught his arm and brought him to a standstill. He looked down at the seated little grey-haired lady. Two old, pale green eyes peered up at him. 'I have a lot of time for the police. My son, he was presented a good citizen award from Hampshire Constabulary recently.'

Dylan's face looked at her with a furrowed brow.

'I heard,' he said.

Jen scowled at Dylan.

'What did your son want brought to Harrowfield?' Jen asked Thelma.

'Oh, it's something to do with this business he's running for our new next door neighbours in Spain. Mr Reynolds: he treats Ozzy like a son he never had. He's doing ever so well. He makes pots, well the people they employ make pots.' Thelma gave a little laugh. 'I can't see Ozzy making pots can you Ralph?'

'No, no I can't,' he said looking at Thelma adoringly.

'And they export them from Spain to Harrowfield?' said Jen.

'All over the world I believe,' Thelma said.

'We've brought you a sample,' Ralph said digging deep into a carrier bag.

'We couldn't bring the real thing. The real ones are the size of me,' said Thelma.

'Ozzy was over the moon to get this new contact in Yorkshire. We've brought a case full of stuff for them – it weighed a bloody ton,' said Ralph. 'Aye, I have to give the lad credit. He seems to be doing well for himself now... who'd have thought his nomadic lifestyle would provide him such dividends in the end?'

Dylan caught the hint of sarcasm in his voice.

'I'm just pleased he's settled down,' said Thelma. 'At least I know where he is for once in his life.'

'Where is it?' said Dylan.

'Where's what?' said Ralph.

'The case he gave you to bring?' said Dylan.

'Oh, we didn't actually... He took it to the airport and arranged for someone to meet us off the plane so we didn't have to carry it,' said Thelma. 'He's being very thoughtful...'

'I'm not as young as I was. I couldn't even lift the bloody thing,' Ralph said. 'Nice chap he was, the man who took it off us at Leeds/Bradford; very grateful to us for bringing it over for him.'

Dylan held the miniature in his hand. He held it every which way studying it with undue interest. Jen took it from him.

'Thank you. It will look lovely on our fireplace,' she said with a scowl at Dylan.

***

It was nearly midnight and DC Wormald was scanning CCTV footage. The darkness outside was not the only indicator to him that it was late, as the telephones were exceptionally quiet. It was surprising how much work could be achieved in an incident room at a late hour. At that moment the phone rang and Andy pressed pause, leant over his desk and picked up. 'Andy Wormald CID,' he said. His eyes closed, his mouth opened and he yawned.

'Control; uniform require assistance. They've got a man trying to get into a house.'

'A burglar?' he said.

'No, a drunk.'

'A drunk and you're calling CID?'

'He's causing a bit of a disturbance. Uniform say he's frightening the poor woman inside and he's asking for you by name.'

'Me?'

'Yes, you! Can I show you attending?'

'I suppose so. Give me the address,' he said.

***

Dylan awoke the next morning as suddenly as if he had drawn back the curtain. He stretched his legs, got out of bed and stood. Jen was sleeping. The house was still. Unheard he padded downstairs in his stockinged feet, put on his shoes whilst sitting on the bottom step and reached out to ruffle Max's broad head. The dog lifted his head and looked at Dylan with gentle brown eyes. Max shook his pendant ears, groaned and stumbled to his feet. Dylan walked into the kitchen, Max followed. Dylan raised the blinds, put the kettle on and retrieved a cup from the cupboard, spooning in coffee and sugar before opening the door to allow Max to go out into the garden. He strode in to the lounge and pulled back the curtains. Turning he saw the cinnamon coloured pot on the fireplace. He walked over and picked it up.

'He makes life sized figurines as well,' said Thelma who was standing at the open door; she was a small figure against a dark background like a picture in a frame.

'Would you like a drink?' he asked.

***

In his inebriated state DC Granger had slept heavily but his waking had been as sudden as Dylan's. He lay wide eyed for a moment and tried to figure out where he was. His surroundings were familiar but this place was not his home. He moved his head and cried out in pain, the room spun.

***

'And,' Vicky was saying as Dylan walked in the office, her voice loud, her mood mischievous. 'Ned was only banging on the door of the house they had moved out of a month ago wasn't he?' she said to Lisa. 'Good job Andy was here otherwise he might have ended up in a cell.'

Lisa looked at Dylan over Vicky's shoulder.

'Ned's wife, she wouldn't let him in, in the state he was in,' Vicky said, as if by way of an explanation. 'He's such a lightweight drinker,' she said. Turning in haste she walked directly into Dylan. All was quiet.

'Where is he now?' said Dylan.

'Sleeping it off sir,' said Andy.

'What's he working?'

'He's working two p.m. till ten p.m., sir.'

'Tell him I want to see him in my office the minute he gets in,' said Dylan.

The mood was set for the day and the team worked in relative silence. Dylan's mood didn't appear to be one that would accept joviality.

Lisa informed him that the ACC had put a call in to the office to say she was back at work and would be over later in the day. His mood darkened. He had no good news to share.

Professor Stow teetered at Dylan's door before making the usual flamboyant entrance he was better known for. Lisa without being asked walked in almost as soon as he was seated, carrying a tray with two cups of tea and a plate of biscuits.

Before the tray was put down on Dylan's desk Professor Stow leant over and pinched a chocolate biscuit. 'Don't mind if I do,' he said, raising an eyebrow at Lisa as he popped the whole biscuit into his mouth and took another. 'Preferably with a little brandy?' he said with a mischievous wink.

'I'm sorry you'll have to make do with sugar today,' Lisa said. He counted four heaped spoonfuls into his cup. Dylan thanked her and asked her if she could arrange for the dentistry implements to be brought in. Professor Stow smiled which displayed his crooked yellow teeth.

'I haven't long, I'm due to lecture at the University,' he said, peering over his half-rimmed glasses at Dylan.

Professor Stow considered the contents of the dental case with great interest. He whistled through his teeth. 'Mon. Charriere, Collin, Paris,' he read. 'Holy Moses, these are probably worth a ruddy fortune,' he said.

'Incomplete?' said Dylan.

'Yes. There's about eight hundred pounds worth of tools here and if it was complete well... you're looking at a thousand five hundred maybe, at auction. '

'Really?' said Dylan. 'They've yet to be examined by forensic.'

'Don't worry. I won't touch. These are very easily identifiable, surely if they have been stolen someone would be missing them?' Professor Stow's mouth was still open in a perfect O. 'Wow, I've never seen anything like these, except in a museum that is... The tools that are missing are the elevator which helps rock the tooth back and forth until the periodontal ligament has sufficiently broken and the supporting alveolar bone has been adequately widened, to make the tooth loose enough to remove it with forceps, which are also missing, by the way. These here are,' he said pointing to one of the implements, 'tweezers, files and they are a very thin pair of dental forceps for use on a child.'

'Are they in your opinion from the same era as the ones our killer is using?'

'I'd say most certainly. And not only that, the items that are missing are just the type of implements he would require to do the professional job he does, with the know-how of course.'

Dylan explained how they came to be in police possession.

'I presume they'll also be examined for traces of blood?'

'Yes, of course,' Dylan said.

'The fine workmanship on the bone handles oozes quality. If you find the missing tools they will fit nicely into those perfect moulded grooves.' Professor Stow stood and proffered one of his hands towards Dylan. 'I must go, students to frighten,' he

225

said with a twinkle in his eye. 'Call me when he strikes again because he will if he isn't caught, mark my words.'

Stow looked back at Dylan from the desk where Lisa sat. 'If he ever takes you for granted, Sparrow, call me. You can come and work for me any day.'

'Glad to see you're back to your old self Prof,' said Vicky.

'And wouldn't you know it's down to beer.'

'Beer?' said Vicky. 'Beer?'

'I kid you not. It helps flush the kidneys and the bladder. Plus, the alcohol takes the edge off the pain.' Professor Stow's pink flabby cheeks wobbled when he laughed.

'Surely not?'

'Well it works for me,' he said with a wink of a twinkly eye. 'And I don't intend to have any more trouble now I know about the cure.' Professor Stow tapped his bulbous red nose.

Lisa scowled as she watched him leave the office, the echoes of his raucous laugh in his wake.

'He is joking, right?'

'No, seemingly it's all down to the hops... you've just got to avoid the beer if you're on antibiotics or narcotic pain medications otherwise you render the drugs useless and it will make you sick. He seemed perfectly serious when he told me,' said Dylan.

'He's a funny old man,' said Lisa.

'He's better for knowing,' said Dylan.

'Professor Stow?' said Vicky.

Lisa nodded her head.

'Yes, he is,' said Vicky who passed her in the doorway.

Dylan was writing, he stopped and his pen hovered over a piece of paper. 'They nearly killed him you know,' he said looking up from his work.

'What did?'

'The kidney stones.'

'Really,' said Vicky.

'Yes, what he didn't tell you is that when we saw him at the PM it was his first day back at work,' said Dylan.

'Oh my God,' said Vicky. 'I didn't know you could die of kidney stones.'

'Well, now you do.'

'Are you busy?' said Vicky.

'Just penning some things I want to cover with ACC Smythe. I don't want talk of her Hong Kong trip to derail us, whatever happens.'

'A quick update?'

Dylan nodded.

Vicky sat down hands together on her lap. 'I've just finished taking a statement from the volunteer at the Forget Me Not charity shop and guess what?' she said. 'She says the guy who brought in the fishing equipment and dental implements had a hole on the left shoulder of his hoodie. She recalls it because when she thought about it, he had the bag in his right hand as he leant over the old lady to put the bag on the counter and she saw the hole and thought to herself that they had better hoodies for sale.'

'We need to trace the hoodie and more importantly the wearer.'

Dylan's phone rang. He picked up.

'Dylan, it's Wendy Smythe. I'm on my way over for an update. I'm sure you must have been missing me.'

'Of course,' he said with a grimace.

'Thanks for the contact with Phil and Yin. I don't know what I'd have done if they hadn't been there.'

'Really?'

'I'll update you when I see you.'

'So you're on your way now,' he said looking at the clock. It was one thirty.'

Vicky physically shrank in the seat and crinkled up her nose.

'Look forward to it,' he said. 'I'll make sure the detective sergeants are available for you to speak to.'

A broad smile crossed Dylan's face. 'If I have to suffer, so do you.'

'Thanks for nothing,' Vicky said.

Raj put papers in front of Dylan to sign. No words were necessary.

'You need me to be available for what?' said DS Raj.

'The meeting in about half an hour with Windy-Wendy,' said Vicky.

'Vicky,' Dylan growled.

'Whatever you do don't mention the latest holiday,' he said. 'Where's John?'

'I'll tell him,' said Raj.

Chapter Twenty-Five

ACC Wendy Smythe strode into the incident room and headed straight towards Dylan's door. Dylan saw her and stood. He walked out into the incident room to greet her.

'Ma'am,' he said offering his hand. 'Roads busy?'

'I came on the train. It seemed like a good idea at the time but I guess I was lulled into a sense of false security having just come back from China. The Chinese could teach our railway operators a thing or two about punctuality, cleanliness and courtesy,' she said, with a sour look upon her face as she took off her jacket and brushed the back of her trousers. The ACC caught Vicky rolling her eyes at Dylan.

'Made in two days for me in Hong Kong this suit, I'll have you know. Great work ethic Tam's Tailors have. Something that is sadly lacking in this country DS Hardacre,' she said. She surveyed her surroundings with her nose in the air. Vicky brushed the sweet papers to one side of her worktop next to the cups of half-drunk coffee and stood with her back to her desk.

***

Dylan's office was functional and nothing more. It was no size for meetings of more than four people. The ACC sat next to Raj and DS John Benjamin, Dylan sat at his desk opposite and Vicky squeezed on to a stool in front of the shut door.

Not off to the best of starts, the ACC's briefing by Dylan in his office was to be long and in depth. Dylan pulled his Policy Book towards him and picked up his pen.

'This hoodie with this mark on the shoulder? I'm of a mind to give the information to the press. It will show the progress we are making and we might be lucky enough to get a name of the wearer,' said the ACC.

'Looks like we're going to have our first disagreement because that for me would be the wrong course of action.'

The ACC scowled at Dylan. 'Explain.'

'If the wearer is our man then he's going to get rid of the garment as soon as he is aware it is significant to our enquiry. The tracing of the specific hoodie wearer is the only continuity that we have on the CCTV in our possession. Personally I think we need to keep this under wraps.'

'But think of the publicity Dylan. This simple act may give us our man.'

'The profiler suggests, and for what it's worth I agree, our killer is a loner. We need that hoodie. Giving that information to the media, at this time, I believe, would be like throwing that piece of clothing into the incinerator. Even with the hoodie in our possession, and its wearer being known to us, that still only puts him in a location before and after one of the murders. Maybe he was also the person who deposited the items at the charity shop but we have yet to get supporting evidence. We could even place him at the charity shop, let's face it, but even then we still have no proof that the wearer of that hoodie is our serial killer. What this piece of evidence does suggest to me however is that if we can house him, with the hoodie, we are one step nearer in the right direction in the enquiry, maybe... Fibres recovered from within Alan Bell's taxi may also take us a step further, but at this moment I don't want any of this disclosed to the media. I don't even want it to become common gossip in this police station, let alone the force.'

'Okay, okay!' ACC Smythe said raising her hand. 'You've convinced me: for now. I'll hold off on giving out the information. But what about an intelligence bulletin within the force showing the still of this man in the hoodie, which we have taken from the CCTV footage, near to the taxi rank, with a description of what he was wearing? It may be that one of our officers can suggest a name for him.'

'I'll agree to that. John, can you get onto it?'

The detective sergeant was already writing down the action.

'Everyone out there seems to be industrious enough,' ACC Smythe said, fleetingly looking out of DI Dylan's office window into the incident room. 'And I've seen the snippets you have released to the media whilst I have been away,' continued the ACC. 'The press officer showed me the file. Thanks for your updates. Now I'm back we need to catch our killer, don't we Inspector? So how do you intend to do it?'

'All in good time. Once we have him, I want enough evidence to keep and charge him. It's a bonus for us that he has only struck three times given the speed with which he has killed already.'

'I haven't been back at work two minutes and already feel the need for another holiday coming on,' ACC Smythe said with a hint of melancholy in her voice.

There was a noise outside in the incident room that drew Dylan's attention to the outer office and almost in slow motion Dylan saw Ned stumble into Lisa's desk and her neat work trays tumble. Vicky saw it too and Dylan saw the panic in her eyes. Raj saw the message that flashed unspoken between them and since she was sitting close to the ACC she touched her arm gently and turned to speak to her.

'You must tell me about Hong Kong. It's a place I've never visited,' she said.

Dylan looked relieved. 'I'll just order some coffee,' Vicky said in what was nothing more than a whisper as she expeditiously nipped out of the door and closed it quickly behind her.

Dylan could see Vicky tug on Ned Granger's arm. His mouth was wide open and he stood solid. There were raised voices. Dylan's eyes went back to the ACC and he smiled an uncomfortable smile. John excused himself from the room. The ACC was undeterred, her face animated as she described her holiday to Raj.

'Well, for a start it's quite an experience watching the Chinese doing exercises on an aeroplane,' she said with a titter.

'It's nice to be able to stretch your legs and get a drink during the long flight isn't it?' said Raj.

'It is. You could eat your meal off the floor in the airport at Lan Tau, but the food markets are a different thing. A Chinese stall holder cut a chicken's throat in front of me and I was assured it was to show how fresh it was.' Wendy Smythe pulled a face. 'And some of the insects they'd have you eat... taste horrid.' It was Rajinder's turn to pull a face. 'I had to go to the dentist there too... First time ever abroad. Well, it's alright being able to speak tourist Cantonese but another to explain to a dentist which *yáchǐ*... That's how your friends got involved.'

Raj and Dylan looked puzzled.

'Tooth ... needed attention,' she said showing Raj a gap in the gum on her bottom jaw.

'Ouch,' said Raj. 'That still looks sore.'

'I'm sure you jinxed me with this with this bloody case,' she said to Dylan whose attention was still on the incident unfolding in the CID office. 'They were so helpful... your friends,' she said, her voice trailing to a whisper as she turned her head to look over her shoulder and see what Dylan was looking at. The office was empty. 'Am I boring you?' she asked Dylan with a frown and a good humoured smile.

'Yes, no, I was just wondering where John and Vicky had got to?' said Dylan. 'It's always good to have someone with you who speaks the lingo when anything like that happens isn't it?' he said, turning his attention back to the ACC.

'Yes, and Yin thankfully speaks fluent Cantonese. She took me to a dentist she knew and was chatting to him all the time he worked on me. I told her to tell him I was heading an investigation regarding a murderer who extracted teeth from his victims when he said he had to take out mine. He actually spoke very good English and he went on to tell me that they had a similar case in Hong Kong that he had advised the police on. Their killer was never caught. He suggested Yin speak to the person in charge, so you never know you might get an email from her, him, them. I can't understand why anyone would want to be a dentist though can you? Can you imagine looking in people's mouths all day?' she said. She shuddered.

'You and I know everything is a commodity,' said Dylan. 'In Hong Kong as well as over here.'

'How would you go about selling teeth and what does one do with someone else's?'

'Ned Granger,' said Dylan, 'tells me someone he knows makes jewellery with human teeth. His acquaintance buys them on the internet.'

'Ned Granger. I thought someone was missing. Where is he?'

Vicky returned at that precise moment to hear his name being mentioned. Everyone looked her way.

'Ned?' said Dylan.

'Yes he...' she said. Her eyes locked into Dylan's and she looked flustered.'...has taken some exhibits to the lab.'

The door finally closed behind ACC Smythe. Dylan, Raj and Vicky breathed a sigh of relief.

'What the hell's going on?' said Dylan.

'Ned's with John. He's not in a good way.'

'Hungover or not, tell him I want to see him!' Dylan said, his face was like thunder.

***

Dylan was a few minutes from home – DC Granger was on his final warning. Why the hell would some people never grow up? He had told his detective constable how disappointed he was in him. The man had cried. Next time Dylan would have no choice, he told him, he'd be out.

Dylan's head hurt, he took a sip of water. His mobile phone rang. He indicated and pulled in to the side of the road. The phone stopped ringing, no number available. He looked in his mirror, indicated. The driver coming out of the hospital entrance flashed his car lights to allow him out. The mobile rang again. He waved the good samaritan on. The driver of the car looked at him bemused as he went past and shook his head at Dylan. Dylan knew that face, but where from?

'Hello. Dylan,' he said.

Chapter Twenty-Six

'It's Beryl...' said the caller. 'The fishing line that was on the reels you sent across to me to be examined? It's a definite match to the garrotte recovered from the taxi in the Alan Bell murder enquiry.'

'So quick? Really?'

'Really. It's too late today, but tomorrow I'll be straight on it and look at the fishing line under higher magnification for the possible matching of wire cutting grooves.'

'Excellent,' Dylan said looking up at the clear night sky.

'We aim to please,' she said. Dylan could tell she also had a smile on her face.

'Thank you.'

'Don't thank me yet, but I thought it was a piece of news too good not to share. You have a good evening.'

'You too, no doubt we will speak tomorrow.'

With that the line went dead. Dylan held the phone in his hand for a moment or two. He realised his hand was sweating. Even without the killer or the hoodie the evidence trail was substantial.

***

Jen saw Dylan pulling up on the driveway. Dylan saw Maisy opened the front door. She ran out of the house and into his arms. 'Daddy's home! Daddy's home!' she called out in her high pitched, excited way. 'When did you learn to do that little lady?' said Dylan.

'Today!' she said with an eyebrow raised. 'What a nice surprise to see you home early for once,' said Jen as she kissed him on the cheek. 'Well,' she looked at her watch. 'Early for you,' she smiled. 'I'll get your dinner on before I bath Maisy.'

'It's been one of those days.' Dylan sighed as he sipped a coffee. 'But, things might be looking up. I've just had a call from Forensic. The fishing line wire on the reel we had handed in at the charity shop, is a match for the garrotte found in the taxi.'

'No?'

'Yes, and since it was the last murder that was committed by our would-be serial killer I am hoping we can prove beyond doubt that it was cut from the line that was handed in.'

'Pasta okay?'

Dylan nodded, unable to speak as Maisy, who sat on his lap insisted on putting her hands over his mouth.

'Pull a funny face Daddy, for Maisy,' she said, squealing with delight as he did as she asked. She turned his face to look in the mirror and attempted to copy him.

Dylan's mobile phone rang. Jen took Maisy. He picked the phone up from where it lay with his keys on the kitchen table. The smile on their daughter's face was immediately gone.

'Dylan,' he said, brusquely.

Maisy started to cry. Jen put her finger to her lips.

'Yes it's DI Dylan,' he said turning into the hallway where it was quieter.

'Sorry to trouble you sir. It's Geoff Painter, Coroner's Officer. I'm ringing you to inform you of the death of Mr Timothy Woodcock. He suffered a major heart seizure and there was a Do Not Resuscitate note on his hospital file. I understand that one of your officers, according to hospital staff, had been to see him so I thought I would let you know in case it was relevant to ongoing investigations.'

'He wasn't a suspect Geoff, but his home address does feature and formed part of an investigation. Thanks for letting me know. I'll ensure the incident room updates our records accordingly.'

The face in the car, he remembered it was that of Timothy Woodcock's son Jim. Maybe he'd called in to see his dying father.

Dylan returned to the kitchen. He smiled at Jen and held his arms out to Maisy. 'Come here you,' he said to his daughter. 'How about I read you your bedtime story tonight?'

'You're not going anywhere?' said Jen.

'No,' he said. He saw the relief on her face.

'The call, I thought...'

Dylan put his finger to her lips. 'I know what you thought. I see you jump when the phone rings and a look of sadness come into your eyes, don't think I don't. But not tonight; now, where's my dinner?'

Dylan growled at Maisy as he put her down on the floor and proceeded to chase the squealing child around the house.

***

Dylan dropped Maisy off at Chantall's the next morning. It was the first time he had seen Maisy's childminder since Maisy had been ill. At the door she was met by her friend Annabelle and the two little girls linked hands and skipped off without so much as a by your leave. He smiled. Dylan was well aware of the need to learn good social skills in life and the ability to make friends was one of the most important.

The morning briefing was over in twenty minutes. Dylan updated the team with regards to the death of Mr Woodcock senior. He also told them about his call from forensic.

'I want to know who our local burglars are? Who has admitted to burglaries in a twenty mile radius of the Woodcock's family home? Nothing from your informants Ned, Andy?'

The men shook their heads.

'I'm going to brief the ACC about the developments. I want you out and about and with your ear to the ground.'

The assembled team members left the meeting with a positive spring in their step.

Dylan didn't need to ring ACC Smythe to update her. She was already on the other end of the phone the minute he sat down at his desk.

'We need to speak Dylan. I've been thinking. I want to give the media pictures of this very distinctive fishing reel and dentistry set to see if anyone comes forward to say they recognise it?'

'Media involvement at this time would gain us nothing other than to alert the killer of the connection we have made.'

'But think about the PR Dylan and the reassurance that we would be giving the public by showing them we are making headway with the investigations. I'm coming over. I want to discuss this further.'

Dylan gritted his teeth. The receiver rocked in its cradle where he had all but thrown it. 'More about her bloody ego than in the furtherance of the investigation,' he said to himself. 'I won't let her do it.'

Chapter Twenty-Seven

DS Vicky Hardacre had been out on enquiries with DC Ned Granger. A few minutes after their return there was a noisy commotion in the outer office.

'What's happening?' said Dylan to Raj who delivered a facsimile from Forensic marked for his urgent attention?

'The latest teeth joke,' she said with a titter.

'Go on,' said Dylan.

'I'm not good at this but... The teeth say to the tongue. 'If I just press a little, you'll get cut.' The tongue replies, 'And if I misuse just one single word, all thirty-two of you will come out.'

'Not bad,' he said with a smile. 'Who's the fax from?' Dylan took the piece of paper from her outstretched hand.

'Looks like the rough cut edge of the fishing line, on the recovered reel is an exact fit to one end of the piece of fishing line used to make the garrotte found in the taxi.' Dylan eyes left the piece of paper and found Raj's for a brief moment. He looked back at the printed words and back at Raj. 'So we can say beyond doubt that the garrotte was made from the line that had been on that reel. That's excellent news. Brilliant work by Beryl and her team.'

The door of the incident room slammed shut and the room went deathly quiet. Raj turned to see what had caused the sudden mood change. The ACC stood at Dylan's door.

'I'll leave you to it,' she said.

'Tea, black with lemon for me,' ACC Watkins said. Raj looked at Dylan.

'Coffee, strong, spoonful of sugar,' he said as he watched her place the large designer Blue Shirt Bag atop papers on the corner of his desk. Dylan's eyes flashed upwards to meet Raj's. Don't ask if it came from Hong Kong, they pleaded. Raj left closing the door behind her.

***

They now had the murder weapon and it would be naive to think the two missing implements from the set of antique dentistry tools hadn't also been used in the fatal attacks. But who was the killer and why did he kill, for teeth?

'Who had access to Mr Woodcock senior's home other than a burglar?' said ACC Smythe.

'The deceased, who was a retired dentist, his estranged wife Edna Woodcock, who now lives with her daughter Ginny and her husband Devlin Gillard, also dentists. Their adopted son Jim.'

'What about the neighbours? If Mr Woodcock senior was in bad health did he have some kind of help around the home? It seems to me that solving this burglary is our priority. What are you doing?'

'It appears he didn't have any help, no. We are doing what we can. We've already done house to house enquires. I've got the team researching known burglars who operate in and around the area; it isn't a high risk area, and we've done a leaflet drop. I'm open to suggestions to whatever else you think we might do?'

Wendy Smythe sighed heavily and held the eye contact she had made with Dylan. 'I'm not happy. We need to talk through this media issue. I don't want to keep information back from the public anymore; that could quite easily backfire on us.'

'I agree, but neither do we want our killer to know the progress we are making. We would not only be sharing with the general public what we know but also with the murderer. If he thinks for one moment we are getting near to him, it might make him think he's got nothing to lose... He hasn't struck a fourth time – yet. Perhaps the influx of officers in Harrowfield has made him lie low, and if it has, we now need to find him before he gets the urge, or the courage to come out of hiding for his next unsuspecting prey.'

'But would the disclosure to the press not flush him out?'

'I'm not sure it would, no. I don't want to show our hand at this stage in the enquiry.'

'So what's the alternative? Give me your proposed strategy Dylan to capture to our killer, before he strikes again.'

Dylan's insistence on secrecy left Wendy Smythe poised above a precipice. She looked at the facsimile that lay in her hands. She was thoughtful and so was he. He got up and stood at the window looking out into the back yard. All was still. Wendy Smythe was aware of his strange stillness, the quiet strength within him. She appeared to him like the big black bird on the window sill, ready to pounce and to carry off something or someone in her claws. That someone was Dylan – off the enquiry.

'We both know he could strike at any time,' he said without turning to face her.

There was a gentle knock at the door and Lisa entered to put a tray of drinks on his desk. He looked over his shoulder and back before putting his hands in his pockets. 'Thanks,' he said.

Only when ACC Smythe had picked up her drink did he come back to sit opposite her. 'We are building up a profile and all the while we are gathering evidence. We know what he wore. The hoodie is distinctive because of this hole on the left shoulder. We know he has access to a pedal cycle and uses cycle paths. We know where the fishing line that he used as his garrotte on the Alan Bell murder came from, and we can safely say it is highly likely that the tools that are missing from the dentistry set in our possession are the tools he has used to extract his victim's teeth. We know he has had some training and knowledge of dentistry by the way the teeth are removed. And we know his prey are those with healthy looking, brilliant white teeth. So that's our nucleus, we now have to retrace our steps to see if we have missed anything. We also have an action plan in place should he strike again. We are on the right track,' he said. 'I'm confident we'll get there.'

Wendy Smythe held the cup to her lips. 'But when...'

'When, is the difficult question to answer,' he said.

'I can't say I'm not impressed,' she said. The cup remained in her hand but she rested it on her knee. 'But, is there anything at all we can feed to the press? I am overseeing the investigation and I feel like I should be doing more to inform the public. The press side of the enquiry I can handle, which I am hopeful keeps the journalists away from your door and allows you to get on with the investigation.'

His blue eyes stared. He sat in his old leather chair with a stillness that was like that of a rock.

Wendy ran a finger around the rim of her empty cup. Her lips moved, but no sound came from them.

'Our Family Liaison Officer on the Carl Braithwaite enquiry is PC Mitchell. Michelle tells me that the family are very pro-police and let's face it this maniac has murdered their son and he is still at large. They are desperate to do something to help. What if we can encourage them to do an appeal with you about how much the "not knowing" for them, is stopping them from moving forward with their lives? From the media's point of view they have had very little access to the families of the victims, this may just keep the press on board for now.' Dylan said.

She looked across at him. 'Okay,' she said, nodding. 'But from now on we need to review our position on a weekly basis and we need to regularly update the press to keep them on board.'

'Agreed,' said Dylan picking up his coffee cup and drinking its contents down in one.

ACC Smythe stood. Dylan was pleased, he had expected it to be harder to win her over to his way of thinking but he would never have given in to her request to give the media all they knew.

'Right I'm off Dylan to have lunch with your delightful Divisional Commander. I'll ask him what he's doing to assist in detecting these murders in his Division. That'll make him cough and splutter a bit on his big custard tart,' she said.

And with that she collected her bag and was gone.

Vicky came to see him, a pork pie in hand.

'What've you done now?' said Dylan. He eyed her suspiciously but nevertheless took it from her.

'It's not from me boss, Lisa got it for you from your favourite pie shop whilst she was out on lunch. Ned paid...'

'It's to be hoped he's learned his lesson this time. A team is only...,'

'...as strong as its weakest link,' she finished the sentence for him.

'And I won't have any weak links on my team,' he said with a frown that caused a deep line on his forehead. He took a bite of his utopia. The warm meat juices ran down his chin. 'Mmm... I'll be out in a minute,' he said as he retrieved his handkerchief from his pocket.

'He's okay now is he?' said Ned out of the corner of his mouth.

'All I can say is thank goodness for Paul Hopkins' pies at times like these. It's always good to know the boss's weakness,' said Vicky.

The team meeting was brief. 'I want you to go through all the house to house forms and questionnaires that were completed for Rock Villas. Do we know if there is anyone that is yet to be seen?'

Vicky had her head down busily writing. 'I don't know boss, but Lisa will be able to tell us at the press of a button.'

'Timothy Woodcock may be out of the enquiry but we need to eliminate his daughter Ginny, son Jim and the son-in-law, see if we can get an alibi for them for at least one of the murders. Let's have them under the microscope. We know very little about them other than two of them are dentists and Jim is a student.'

'And he has a nice laugh, good taste in clothes and he's well-travelled,' said Vicky.

'They all appear to have sailed under our radar,' said Dylan. 'Why?'

'I'm happy to put Jim under the microscope – I mean it makes sense doesn't it since I've already had dealings with him. I wonder if he'll be arranging Timothy Woodcock's funeral?'

'Well, he's definitely about because I saw him.'

'You did?'

'Yes, the night I heard Timothy Woodcock had died. He passed me in a car.'

'What kind of car?

'I don't know, just a bloody car. He was going to let me out into the line of traffic when Beryl rang me. I was distracted.'

'But I didn't know he had a car?'

'Why would you unless you asked? I knew I knew the face...' said Dylan.

'I've left a message on his mobile to ask him to let us know when his father's funeral is so we can go and show our respects,' she said.

'Arrange for someone to go along and take some discreet pictures of those attending; who knows maybe our killer might be amongst them. And, if Mr Woodcock junior doesn't reply to your call then ring Geoff Painter. The Coroner's Officer will be able to tell you who the funeral directors are and they'll tell you.'

***

Maisy was in the bath when Dylan arrived home. She looked very pink and clean. Jen dried her soft, blonde hair dry with a fluffy, soft towel and sprinkled talcum powder like salt and pepper over her tummy. Maisy giggled with glee.

Later Dylan crept past Maisy's door. He could see the dimness of the night light inside her room from the crack that the open door allowed. There was a shadow he could just make out of Jen sitting on the floor by the side of Maisy's bed reading her a bedtime story. On seeing Dylan Jen stood up slowly and crept to the door. 'It always amazes me how she goes from 'giddy kipper' to asleep in five seconds flat,' he said.

'Like father, like daughter,' she laughed as she swept up Maisy's discarded clothes that lay on the landing. She carried them down and put them in the washing machine. Dylan followed his wife into the kitchen.

'Good day?' she said.

'Not bad.'

'I'm told it's the funeral of the dentist on Friday at Brelland Crematorium.'

'How do you know that?' said Dylan.

'Ah, wouldn't you like to know Mr Detective?' she said tapping her finger on the side of her nose.

'Come on?'

'Vicky rang just before you got home. She managed to speak to the daughter, Ginny?'

Dylan picked an envelope up off the dining room table. It was addressed to Jen's dad Ralph.

'What's this?' he said.

'Pictures of their new place in Spain,' said Jen excitedly. 'I don't know why they've come here. Dad probably thought they might arrive before he and Thelma left but they didn't.'

'You've seen them?'

'Just a quick peek. It looks absolutely beautiful. Please say we can go, can we?'

Dylan sat on the sofa and pulled the glossy pictures from their wallet. Jen put his hot drink down on the coffee table, sat on the settee beside him, put her arm through his and lay her head on his shoulder.

'They have a pool?' said Dylan. 'It's probably just a shared one.'

'No, it's their own,' said Jen. 'What a waste; Dad doesn't even swim so I can't see him getting much use out of it can you? You'd love a pool and just imagine Maisy learning to swim in that...'

Jen pointed to the electric gates and the high fences. 'And, their neighbours have fearsome guard dogs Dad tells me, so no one is going to hang around are they?' she laughed.

'And these neighbours have a boat?' said Dylan.

'Yes, dad says so.... Malcolm and Juliana, she's Spanish apparently.'

'Is he?' said Dylan. His eyes found the miniature pot on the fireplace.

'No, he's English.'

For a moment Dylan felt he was travelling in a parallel universe. He was surprised Jen wasn't suspicious. How could he burst her bubble? He had to find out more.

He stood, walked the few steps to the fireplace, plucked the Spanish pot in his hand and took it into the kitchen. A rolling pin was swiftly retrieved from the drawer and he hit it hard. It broke in half showing a broad space between the outer and an inner lining.

'What the hell did you do that for?' said Jen.

***

The briefing was hurried. Dylan had a lot on his mind.

'There were only eight people at Mr Woodcock senior's funeral,' said Vicky. 'Only Jim and the son-in-law turned up to represent the family. There were no tears shed. Jim was polite to the others who attended – one a local dentist. I believe Timothy Woodcock mentored him. The talk was of the conferences in China they had attended together. Sounded a right laugh. He was hot...' she said with a wink at Raj.

'Who was hot,' said Dylan.

'Well now you mention it the brother-in-law and the local dentist. I'm thinking I might have to sign up to his surgery.

'Where is it?'

'I'm not that fast,' Vicky said.

'What'd he look like?'

'Who?'

'This local dentist?'

'He was tall. His hair was blonde and it stood up like a bristle of a brush. He had a cute turned up nose with a little mole on his left cheek.'

Dylan appeared distant.

'Earth to Dylan,' she said.

Dylan's head went back with a jerk. 'Sorry,' he said. 'So his ex wasn't there or his daughter?'

'Nope, but at least the lack of emotion meant I could talk to Jim and ask him to come in and see me. He wore a suit, I've never seen him in a suit before. He had a nice, neat little silky T-shirt underneath, no shirt or tie but he looked very swish and the material is guaranteed not to crease or crumple, so he said.' She looked down at the front of her suit jacket. 'I wish I could say the same for the cheap tack I can afford,' she said to Raj.'

'It might help if you didn't leave your stuff thrown around,' Rajinder said plucking Vicky's cardigan from where it had been thrown in the top drawer of the filing cabinet.'

'Point taken. But to be able to afford to buy suits that don't crease sounds like heaven to me. I asked where he got it from and he showed me the label. Dead proud of it he was. I don't know why. It was from Tam's Tailors. It doesn't sound that posh to me.'

'Tam's Tailors? That's where the Blue Shirt designer bag come from that the ACC had with her. 'Tam's Tailors is in Hong Kong. It's where the rich and famous go.' said Raj.

'Really?' said Vicky. 'You clever old thing.'

'Not really, I looked up where a designer bag like the one Wendy Smythe had come from.'

'So, Windy-Wendy's got taste? I'm impressed.'

Dylan gave her a warning look. 'And more money than bloody sense by the sound of it.'

'Yeah, a bag and a suit, sir?' said Vicky. 'Probably nothing to her on her wage. It'd be like me going to Harrods and buying a face flannel.'

'Did you see the guy we had at the funeral taking photographs?' said Dylan.

'Yes,' she said. 'He said to tell you they will be in the internal mail tomorrow.'

Lisa handed Dylan a large envelope that had been delivered by external mail which was marked 'STRICTLY PRIVATE' FOR THE PERSONAL ATTENTION OF D.I. DYLAN – OPERATION TANGENT'.

'Wonder if the contents are as interesting as those beautiful stamps on that envelope?' Vicky said.

Dylan finished typing the internal Minute Sheet to Interpol and took his dagger letter opener from his drawer; slipping the tip beneath the signed seal he heard the rasp as it opened.

Chapter Twenty-Eight

The PIs at JJ Associates International, as promised had come up with the goods and in front of Dylan were details of a murder enquiry that had occurred on Tung Lo Wan Road, Hong Kong two years previously. 'The area boasts an upmarket wine bar called the Blue Lemon, where Fan Huang had been drinking until two a.m., before the attack,' Dylan read, thankful Yin had already translated the documents for him. What he read captivated him. The young Chinese woman was known for her radiant smile, as could also be seen from her picture. She had been strangled and four teeth removed after death. The case remained undetected and the media had reported the murder, at the time, as a possible ritual killing. There was no description of a possible suspect.

Dylan passed Vicky the file. 'Have this information put on our computer system will you.'

'What is it?'

'A murder in Hong Kong.'

'Oooo... Will I have to go?' she said. Her face lit up. 'Where did Windy-Wendy stop? Oh the illustrious the Metropark Hotel...'

'I didn't know you spoke Chinese?'

'Well... I didn't say... but I could meet up with your friends and I've never been disappointed with a takeaway I've bought off a Chinese menu.' Vicky laughed.

'You're a trier, I'll give you that. Jim Woodcock's suit was from Tam's Tailors in Hong Kong. How long ago was he there and didn't Timothy Woodcock think his son was still there?'

'He did but then again he was fairly out of it on his meds. He didn't say anything that we could rely on in court,' she said with fingers in the air marking quote symbols.

'When Jim Woodcock comes in I'd like you to ask him straight out if he's been to Hong Kong.'

'He must have been mustn't he if he had a suit made at Tam's Tailors.'

'Ask him and ensure you get a DNA swab and take his fingerprints whilst he's here.'

'Okay,' she said shrugging her shoulders. 'But I think you're barking up the wrong tree. Mrs Woodcock tells me what a caring boy he is and intelligent with it. Sounds pretty much like the man I've had dealings with. It's a pity he doesn't seem to get on with his sister.'

***

The next morning Dylan was standing unpacking his briefcase when Andy walked in. The clock in his office showed him seven thirty. 'You asked to be informed of anything that came in, in relation to dentists sir?'

Dylan looked at his colleague and moistened dry lips. 'What've you got?'

'The body of a Harrowfield dentist has been found at his surgery in Trinity Place, this morning. The Coroner's Officer and uniform are in attendance,' he said.

'Murder?' Dylan said gingerly.

'Suicide is what they are intimating sir. Slashed wrists... throat. He was discovered by the cleaner.'

'Have uniform protected the scene?'

'Yes sir, that's my understanding, once he was certified dead by paramedics.'

'I need to go. Who is the on call scenes of crime supervisor this morning?'

'Jarv.'

'Would you ask her for a rendezvous at the surgery? John Benjamin is early turn, isn't he? Can you mobilise him. Do we have a name for the deceased?'

'A Martin Crossfield, thirty-five years old.'

'Thanks, let control know I've been informed and reinforce the need for sterility of the scene until I get there. Tell them I should be with them in the next thirty minutes.'

He heard Vicky's dulcet tones in the incident room. She tapped on his open door and walked in.

'This one's a suicide right?' she said.

Dylan hadn't taken off his coat. He sat upright on the edge of the seat of his old leather chair, typing on his keyboard. His eyes didn't leave the computer screen. 'Sounds like it but...'

'We never assume,' she said. 'You don't think...?'

'He's the killer?' said Dylan.

Vicky looked at him intently. He lifted his head and turned to her.

'It had crossed my mind, but somehow I don't think our killer would take his own life. Not yet anyway, he's still toying with us... enjoying what he's doing. The game isn't over for him yet.'

'Want me to come with you?'

'I've already asked Andy to mobilise John. He's early turn,' Dylan said.

'He said he was going straight to Forensic to beat the traffic didn't he?' she said.

'Damn, I forgot. You'd better get your coat.'

***

The large, terraced, period villa on Trinity Place, to the west of the town, overlooked a deep grassy verge. Once big family houses, the majority were now used as a mixture of residential and commercial properties; a solicitors, holistic centre and the well-established dental practice among them. Dylan recalled the illuminated sign above the dentist's front door from a bygone age. During the long hours of darkness it had been a welcome sight on beat seven. If only he had a pound for the number of times he had checked that big, shiny, ornamentally furnished black door to ensure it was secure; all part of the job as a patrol officer on nights, in those days. He'd sheltered under the villa's big stone porch in the rain on many occasions in his helmet and Gannex police allocated raincoat, watching and waiting for the Inspector's white Hillman Avenger to drive towards him along Trinity Road, to check his pocket book, through the window's letter box sized gap that he wound down to allow the procedure to take place. There were no flies on the military-style way of the

Inspectors in those days – they weren't about to get their uniform wet.

Dylan and Vicky stood poised on the edge of a pavement, waiting for the traffic to give them an opportunity to cross the busy road. He saw the chance, grabbed Vicky's elbow, and took it. A few moments later they were passing under the crime scene tape and walking through the gates of the dental practice. The outer scene seemed crowded with authorised personnel however there was little noise; concentration on doing the job in hand etched on everyone face.

CSI Supervisor Sarah Jarvis slammed the rear door of the scenes of crime van and walked their way. Outside number 7, Inspector Stonestreet updated them collectively as to the discovery of the body. The uniformed officers who had responded to the 999 call were in attendance.

Dylan, Vicky and Jarv were directed towards the reception area. When the corpse was revealed Dylan was conscious of a gasp of anguish that appeared to come from the officer by his side. Vicky looked up at him with disbelieving eyes. Her lips moved; the colour drained from her lips. She put her hand up to her mouth. Dylan stood hesitant. 'What?' he said.

'It's the man... The one that I told you about... the dentist at Mr Woodcock's funeral,' she said.

'You okay?' said Dylan as she grabbed hold of his arm.

Vicky nodded and swallowed hard. 'I will be,' she said.

'Breathe in,' said Dylan. 'One, two, three, hold... and out, one, two, three...'

Vicky closed her eyes and appeared to sway but on opening them breathed out through pursed lips before giving him a weak smile.

There was a vast amount of blood.

'Where's the lady who found him?' said Dylan.

'We took her home,' said Inspector Stonestreet. 'I've made arrangements to get a statement from her. My officers have also obtained details of the paramedic who pronounced him dead and likewise a statement will be obtained from him later today.'

'Good. So, who has been inside?'

'The cleaner sir, the paramedic, Tracy and myself,' said PC Lucy Jordan who looked sheepishly at the Coroner's Officer.

'Geoff? Tell me you haven't?' Dylan said with an accusing glare.

'A look, that's all it was... just a look. Hands in the pockets. I didn't touch anything,' he said.

'Jarv, Vicky get suited up. Geoff, a quiet word please.' Dylan said moving a few yards away from the others. Geoff Painter followed him. He stood scratching his grey beard with hesitant fingers, Dylan stepped into his own protective clothing. Jarv and Vicky looked at Dylan and Painter.

Jarv cringed. 'I wouldn't want to be in his shoes,' she said brushing aside a lock of blonde hair that fell over her forehead. Vicky looked at her with deep blue eyes.

'My God is he in for a bollocking,' she said under her breath to her colleague.

Dylan spoke softly, his back to the team. 'Why the fuck do you think we put these on?' he said, as his shoe caught in the protective suit and he tugged furiously at the leg. 'It's a potential crime scene you bloody idiot.'

'But..'

'Best you don't say anything. Those cavalier days are long gone and you bloody well know it.'

'Sorry sir,' he said, bowing his head.

Dylan walked back towards Vicky.

'Those bollockings, the calm ones, they're definitely the worse,' said Vicky screwing up her nose.

'I'll get some foot plates out of the van, boss,' Jarv called over her shoulder as she headed for the van.

'Do you need a hand?' called Dylan.

'That would be good,' she called.

'No problem, Vicky's stronger than she looks,' he said winking at Vicky as they walked towards the vehicle together.

The metal footplates were the size of a paving slab. The three laid a pathway to, and around the body which lay spread-eagled on the floor. The blood had spread across the vinyl floor covering. Now the scene was duly protected, the three stood looking over the body at close quarters. The scene showed them deep cuts to both wrists and forearm which had severed the dentist's radial and ulnar arteries and there was a deep wound to his throat. Dylan looked up and saw an empty bottle of whisky and an upturned glass. The word sorry had been scrawled in blood on the floor close to the dead man's right hand side.

Leaving the body for a moment they took a look around the surgery which adjoined the reception room. It housed one dental chair, two stools, a sink, work surface and cabinets. It was laid out differently from Dylan's own dentist's surgery, although the contents of it were the same. He puzzled as to why this seemed unusual. Dylan's eyes were drawn towards two dental implements, which lay side by side on the dentist's bracket table, upon a tray on top of a pristine green drape. He pointed with his gloved hand.

'They look like exactly the same shape, size and design as the tools that are missing,' said Vicky.

'Do you think he's our serial killer boss?' Jarv said.

'He'll have saved the country a lot of money by topping himself if he is,' said Vicky.

Dylan was resolute. 'Hold on you two. Think about it. Would the killer really have left them on display for us to find if he was going to commit suicide?'

'Maybe, what with the funeral and the drink he decided to do the decent thing?'

'Perhaps he actually used them on his patients?' said Jarv,

'But wouldn't his dental nurse have questioned that?' said Dylan.

'He seemed like such a nice guy at the funeral,' said Vicky.

'No, no, this doesn't feel right,' said Dylan.

Dylan looked around him, his eyes were like two slits. 'The more I ... I'm getting a really uncomfortable feeling about this scene,' he said. 'There are a couple of thoughts going through my mind. It is either straightforward and he has committed suicide and he is the killer or does someone want us to believe he is?'

Jarv was busy taking photographs around the scene. The detectives watched her. The antique dental tools were taken in situ, then seized as exhibits. The CSI supervisor then concentrated on the body and the blood distribution that surrounded it.

'Boss,' she said thoughtfully looking up at Dylan from where she crouched next to the body. 'I'm pretty sure whoever wrote the words "sorry" here was wearing gloves. Look at the swirl pattern on the letter S here,' she said pointing to the writing on the floor with her own gloved finger. 'I would have expected to see our deceased's fingerprint in that blood.'

Dylan knelt down beside her.

'Also, look here,' she continued. 'Blood splashings that resemble blood being sprayed out of a spray can, at the side of the arterial blood which suggest he was facing the wall with his back to the entrance.'

'So what you're telling me is that we are right to be suspicious?'

'What I'm saying is that in my opinion this is not a suicide. Someone has spent time here staging this scene.'

Industriously they continued to gather evidence. Dylan pulled Vicky to the side.

'We need to find out more about Mr Crossfield. Get a few more of the team down here. See if we can locate CCTV in the immediate vicinity, if so retrieve and seize it,' he said quietly. 'For now, I want to keep a lid on what we know. I've spoken to the press office and they are aware to share nothing more than we are attending what is believed to be a suicide of a dentist in Harrowfield. The press will be told no more for now. When others are privy to the activity in the area no doubt we will have reporters here in a flash though, so we need to keep the scene secure. Identify an exhibits officer for seizing and recording relevant samples alongside Jarv. You and I will have to go to Crossfield's home address. Can you ask control if Mr Crossfield is on our key holders list for the dental surgery alarm call out, because if he is we will have his home address details available to us immediately.' Dylan's eyes flashed in the direction of the red alarm box that stood proud from the wall above the door. Dylan turned to Jarv. 'Will you make sure those dental implements are present at Martin Crossfield's post-mortem. Professor Stow will be informed of the developments. It will be interesting to hear what he has to say.' Dylan looked as though a thought had just occurred to him. 'Has he a car?'

'Well he drove one to the funeral. It was a dark blue Merc.'

'Peter,' Dylan shouted to Inspector Stonestreet, 'Will you get your officers to have a quick look to see if there is a blue Mercedes on the street outside please?'

Inspector Stonestreet moved towards him. 'We'd better get them to use the automatic retrieval number plate recognition on all the cars nearby. He might have more than one vehicle at his disposal,' said Stonestreet.

'Good thinking,' Dylan said.

Dylan's mind was skipping from one line of enquiry to another. He wanted to miss nothing. Only at times like these did he feel like the proverbial cat on a hot tin roof as he hopped from one thing to another.

CSI Jarvis was no longer alone, she had been joined by CSI Viney. They would remain at the scene until they were satisfied they had gathered every piece of evidence they could from the inner cordon. This procedure would take a few hours. Then and only then would the body be removed to the mortuary. A police officer would travel with Martin Crossfield's body to the morgue for continuity purposes.

***

Recently separated, Martin Crossfield lived on his own in a semi-detached house on Park Road which was within walking distance of the dental practice. As Dylan and Vicky made their approach they could see his dark blue Mercedes on his driveway. They passed the information to Inspector Stonestreet over the airways. Mr Crossfield's neighbour was very helpful to the detectives, informing them that his older sister was his next of kin and it was ascertained that she lived in Devon. From keys that had been in Mr Crossfield's coat pocket Dylan arranged for Crossfield's house to be searched.

Time was moving on and Dylan needed to try to either link him to the serial killings or eliminate him. He wondered which that would be. Or could it be that there had been more than one person involved in the murders all along?

The post-mortem examination was booked for six thirty.

'Do you think it's your man,' asked Professor Stow.

'I don't think it's as simple as that,' said Dylan. 'I'll explain when I see you at the PM.'

There were numerous messages left on his answering machine from ACC Smythe as well as several missed calls from her number. She would have to wait. It was three thirty p.m. and the detectives hadn't had a drink let alone a bite to eat and the adrenaline was pumping.

Chapter Twenty-Nine

Dylan and Vicky travelled over the ornate, Victorian, Stan Bridge into Harrowfield town. They drove on familiar roads through the town centre. Without the police canteen they both knew they were in for a long day without food being readily available to them. Dylan pulled up outside his favourite pie shop. A warm P & I Hopkins pork pie and a can of Coke would have to sustain him; there was no indication as to how long the working day would be. Dylan's phone rang as they stood in the queue looking longingly at the pies inside the glass-topped display cabinet.

'Dylan,' he said, turning away from the other customers.

'Boss, it's Jarv. When we moved the body we've found the print of a small toe section of a training shoe in blood beneath him.'

Vicky was in the queue and facing Dylan. His eyes found hers and he held her stare.

'This confirms what we already thought. This isn't a suicide. Our deceased is wearing smart, leather shoes.'

'Thanks. Look, we'll see you back at the incident room when you've finished up there. I'll get uniform to protect the scene for a further twenty-four hours, just in case we need to return to it after the post-mortem. At this moment I won't be updating the press.'

Dylan and Vicky ate their food in the car. 'I don't understand, why was Martin Crossfield selected as a victim?' Vicky said. She wiped the meat juice from her lips with the back of her hand.

'Because he's a dentist maybe? I think someone wants us to think he's the killer,' Dylan said. He finished his drink, screwed the paper bag in a ball and handed both to Vicky in a carrier bag.

'Thanks,' she said.

***

The minute Dylan entered the incident room Lisa handed him a note. He took it from her outstretched hand. She was on the phone. 'Ring ACC Smythe IMMEDIATELY !' he read. He raised his eye brows as his eyes met hers. 'Sorry, my fault, I told her you were on your way back to the station,' she said in a whisper, before going back to her call.

Dylan briskly pushed the door open that led into his office, stuck the note on his blotting pad, took off his suit jacket threw it on his desk and flopped into his chair. He took a deep breath before picking up the telephone.

'About time! I've been trying to get hold of you for two hours and as the person with overall charge of this enquiry you are well aware that I need to know exactly what's going on!' she said.

Dylan stared at the amount of enquiries listed on his wall chart, turned in his chair to face the window and screwed up his eyes. 'But ma'am, everything is not quite as it seems,' he said. 'Hence the delay in me ringing you, but things are now moving along at a pace at the scene. We have recovered two dental tools which may, I repeat may, be the ones missing from the set we have in our possession.'

'So it's him? Has he left a confession?'

'Well he has, but no, not really. The word sorry is scrawled on the floor, in blood.'

'His blood?'

'It looks like that but that hasn't been verified as yet. CSI are still at the scene.'

'What more do you need Dylan? We must have been getting too close for comfort,' she said with an air of self-satisfaction. 'I'm coming over there. We need to let the media know and reassure the public. Have you spoken to the press office? I can do that for you.'

'No, not so fast it's...'

Dylan heard the distinctive dialling tone that told him ACC Smythe had hung up. No doubt she was already on her way, imagining the crimes solved which Dylan knew was far from the truth. He looked downcast at Lisa. 'Need a caffeine fix?' she said.

'I need to tie the ACC down when she gets here and pin her bloody ears back. That's what I need,' he said.

Vicky raised her eyebrows at Lisa, 'Kinky eh?'

'I can think of nothing worse,' said Dylan, when he saw Beaky walking towards his door with the monthly budget statistics.

'What did you say boss,' said Lisa with a smile.

'Touché!'

***

Dylan opened his messages on his computer. Interpol's reply email to the Spanish intelligence he had submitted was swift. Force Intelligence was now liaising with them and they thanked him for the information on the Spanish pottery business and its owners which they were looking into. Dylan hoped his gut instincts about Ozzy's business dealings were unfounded for Ralph and Thelma's sake but only time would tell.

Dark and earnest eyes fixed upon Dylan's face when his office door flew open and the ACC entered. 'I haven't long Dylan. I'm a busy woman. We need to discuss this press release. I've asked the press office to be prepared for an update.'

Lisa stood behind Wendy Smythe. Dylan nodded at the enquiring look on her face. She turned to the ACC, 'Can I get you a drink too?'

'Green tea with half a squeezed lemon,' ACC Smythe said without taking her eyes off Dylan.

'We've got Yorkshire tea with a spoonful of sugar, or not...?'

'Whatever,' she said with a face that looked like she had sucked the lemon.

Dylan waited for Lisa to close the door. He was quiet, he was still, his face was more serious than usual. 'When we spoke earlier, you hung up on me before I had chance to finish.' Dylan's eyebrows raised in an invitation for her to sit down. 'You may like to make yourself comfortable and listen to what I was going to tell you before you go ahead.'

This was more of an instruction than a request. She sat with a sharp bending of her knees, while her back remained as stiff and straight as a poker. 'What's going on?' she said with a stare that was persistent and aggressive.

Dylan took a deep breath. 'Before you ask any questions, let me go through this morning's events. I'll tell you what we've discovered and then we can discuss a strategy.'

ACC Smythe's face grew red, and her eyes cold and stony. 'Well, yes, I suppose so, but I've... the Chief needs updating.'

Dylan lifted up his arm and showed her the palm of his hand. 'Stop!' he said. He saw her lean bony hands clench together on her lap. 'You need to hear what's happened. All is far from what it seems.'

She gave a jerk of her head, but Dylan carried on with the brief regardless. She listened.

Lisa brought the drinks in on a tray and offered a plate with biscuits to the ACC. She shook her head and waved her away. 'I think I need to just clarify the situation with the Chief Constable,' she said.

'It is only due to careful examination of the crime scene and the experience afforded us by Sarah Jarvis and her team that this important evidence was uncovered. Our killer did a good job. He wants us to believe Martin Crossfield is our serial killer. I'm satisfied that he isn't, but we have to have the necessary evidence before we move on.'

'Well, who the hell is the killer then?'

'If I knew that I'd tell you. But, it may be we are closer than we think and he's trying to divert the attention away from himself.'

'What a bastard,' she said, with a snarl, 'So, how do we play it then? What can I say to the press? Something along the lines of, "Officers from Operation Tangent are investigating the death of a local dentist whose body was found at his practice. This investigation is very much in its infancy?"'

'If you must say anything at all... You do know you'll get bombarded with questions about the serial killer don't you?'

'Obviously, but we're keeping an open mind, aren't we, and we are continuing to look closely at incidents that may or may not be connected to the series of murders? I can't name the deceased yet can I?'

'No, we have sent an out-of-force enquiry to Devon & Cornwall Police and they will go and inform his sister of his death, but we have not been updated to say that action has been completed. Local people in Harrowfield will obviously know who the dead man is so the editors of the newspapers etcetera will decide whether or not to run with it as a story until they have been formally given the information. They'll have photographs by now of the officers guarding the scene in Trinity Road and I wouldn't be surprised if the television camera crews are on our patch. Inspector Stonestreet is the duty inspector. He has plenty of experience. He taught me most of what I know, so I'm not worried on that score.'

'Contrary to your belief I'm here to help, not hinder,' said ACC Smythe. 'I've every confidence that you'll catch the evil bastard otherwise you would have been replaced by now,' she said with flaccid smile.

'How's your Chinese by the way,' he said opening his drawer and retrieving a brown A4 sized envelope.

She cocked her head. 'Pigeon, why?'

'Remember Phil and Yin telling you they'd send me a report on the Hong Kong murder that had a similar MO to our serial murders?'

She nodded.

'Well, they've come up trumps,' he said wafting the paperwork in front of her before laying it down on the desk before her.

Wendy stared at the envelope but it remained untouched by the ACC. She groaned, closed her eyes and shook her head from side to side. 'No! Haven't we enough crimes of our own to solve,' she said opening her eyes to give him a look of contempt.

'I think we are very lucky that they have their ears to the ground. As worldwide private investigators I don't think there is a lot we could teach them about the sharing of information. At least our murderer hasn't been given the label of a ritual killer by the media.'

'Oh, absolutely!'

'Jarv is the Crime Scene Supervisor on this one so once she's finished, which shouldn't be that long now,' he said looking at his watch, 'she will be updating me. Do you want to be present for that? We can walk through the scene together and you'll see the effort someone has gone to, to make us believe that this guy has taken his own life. We will be taking the two antique dental tools that we believe are from the set already in our possession to the mortuary with us for Martin Crossfield's post-mortem later.'

'Yes, that would be helpful but I can't stop too long.'

'You don't want to come to the post-mortem?'

'No,' she said visibly shrinking back in her chair.

'Feel free to wander around the incident room. The team will be very pleased to see someone of your rank taking an interest. Believe me it doesn't happen often.'

ACC Smythe looked perplexed. 'That's only because in my experience Senior Investigating Officers are complex characters and take what are meant to be constructive comments by us personally.'

He smiled, 'You can say what you want but in my experience you'll find that most SIOs and CID officers are dedicated officers who spend most of their lives on the trail. Ask my wife Jen she'll tell you.'

'I might just do that. It would be interesting to see what her take is on the SIO's role.'

'One thing for sure she won't pull any punches. She works here in the admin department and they have just been advised of major cuts.'

'Really?'

'In fact, look she's walking through the incident room now.'

Jen hovered around Lisa's desk. Dylan got up, walked towards his office door and opening it he invited her in.

'I don't want to disturb you,' she said. 'I've just been sorting the post and there's a letter marked urgent, for your attention so I thought I'd bring it down personally.'

ACC Smythe stood and held out her hand to Jen. Dylan winked at his wife. It gave her reassurance.

'Would you like to join me in a drink,' the ACC said to Jen. 'We'll leave Dylan to get on with what he does best.'

'Well, I don't know about... I'll have to square it with my boss.'

'Oh, I'll sort Avril Summerfield-Preston,' she said. 'I've heard she's a bit of a dragon with you ladies,' she said with a raise of her eyebrow at Jen. 'What's her nickname, Beaky isn't it?' Wendy Smythe turned to Dylan. 'I'd hate to think what mine is.' Dylan's smile was lopsided. Jen was impressed with the ACC.

Dylan walked with them as far as Lisa's desk in the incident room when his phone rang. To his surprise Wendy Smythe walked off with Jen, chatting like old friends.

'That's it, my career's over,' he said winking at Lisa.

Dylan leant over his desk and snatched the phone off its cradle.

'Boss, John, Jarv and the others are just finishing up here and we will be back with you and Vicky in the next twenty minutes but that's not the reason for the call. Claire Booth, Martin Crossfield's senior dental nurse is here with us. We've got a background statement. She's been a dental nurse for a long number of years in the area so I thought she might be useful to us to put some names to the faces in the pictures we had taken at Timothy Woodcock's funeral?'

'Great idea, they've just arrived,' said Dylan pulling the pictures from the envelope Jen had handed him. 'Will you tell the others the ACC is here and wants to be present for the scene update.'

Chapter Thirty

In all probability the only person who would be identified at Timothy Woodcock's funeral by other officers, from the pictures, would be his adopted son Jim, the son-in-law Devlin Gillard and the deceased Martin Crossfield.

Dylan studied the bundle of images in his hands and flicked through them slowly one by one. They didn't mean anything to him but he would wait for Vicky to return to get her views. If it was possible he wanted all those in attendance identified as soon as possible. He put the pictures down and pushed them to one side before picking up his policy book. Pen hovering, his eyes were drawn back to the photograph that sat on the top of the pile. The photograph was taken outside the crematorium. The men were smoking. Martin Crossfield stood out amongst the others because of his height, blonde hair and model-like looks. Dylan picked the picture up once more and studied it. 'Left handed or right handed?' he said to himself.

Mr Crossfield was holding his cigarette in his left hand. The others in their right.

***

Senior CSI Sarah Jarvis, John and Vicky gathered. They waited with Raj for Dylan and ACC Smythe. The room was in half-darkness, a storm was brewing outside and daylight diminished.

Lisa switched on the lights where the meeting was to take place; the empty boardroom on the top floor, a sanctuary for them from unnecessary interruptions. All was quiet and still, the window had been left open and a cool breeze blew in bringing with it fresh air. She laid down the tray with glasses and a jug of ice cold water on the big table around which they sat. She left them alone. Dylan arrived just before ACC Smythe, writing materials in hand. ACC Wendy Smythe took a seat at the head of the table. She opened her notepad and put on her glasses. 'I'm ready,' she said leaning forward and crossing her legs.

Dylan sat back in his chair and poured himself a glass of water at the opposite end of the table. He offered the jug to the others, all but Jarv declined. Slowly and methodically they went through every minute detail of the discovery of the dentist's body. At the point in the discussions when the body was first shown to them Vicky sat back and Jarv took over.

'Before we moved the body I took this three hundred and sixty degree video. If I play that to you, you will see the exact position the body was found,' she said.

'Excellent,' said Wendy under her breath.

Raj stood and went to the window where she busied herself pulling down the blind. The black cloud had quickly passed and the sun had come out. Its rays were immediate and strong. There would be a rainbow somewhere she thought as she scanned the landscape from the front of the police station building which she rarely saw.

'To the untrained eye the first impressions at the scene of the body are that this is a suicide. We have the empty alcohol bottle, the smearing of the word sorry in blood – you can see here, coupled with the slash wounds to each wrist, and the one to his neck. Bearing in mind we have no forced entry,' said Jarv.

Lisa tapped on the door and John let her in. A tray of hot drinks were put down on the table before them. She turned with little fuss and left the room, shutting the door behind her.

'A substantial find is this partial mark, of the front of a training shoe in blood beneath the body of the deceased,' Jarv said. 'I would have expected at least a partial fingerprint in the word sorry that was written in blood, on the right side of his body. This is not evident but what we did find was evidence of what I am confident are glove marks that the scriber wore.'

'Do we know if Martin was left handed?' said Dylan. 'The reason I ask is that on the photograph taken at Timothy Woodcock's funeral he can quite clearly be seen holding a cigarette in his left hand.' Dylan lifted the picture and pointed to Martin Crossfield. 'Now, correct me if I'm wrong but the way the word sorry is smeared in blood on his right side suggests to me that he was supposedly sitting on the floor, when it was written, before he lay down to die. In that case wouldn't the inscription be on the left of his body?'

'I'll check that with Claire Booth,' said Vicky.

ACC Smythe drew her head back and frowned.

'His dental nurse,' Vicky said. 'That's a thought. I wonder if there are dental tools specifically made available to left-handed dentists? Maybe he could not have used the antique tools with such precision if he is left handed?'

'Check,' said Dylan. 'We also need you to try and get names for the others at the funeral,' Dylan handed Vicky the envelope containing the funeral photographs. 'If you can't help maybe Claire or someone at the dental practice can?'

Vicky gave a little nod of her head as she wrote the action down.

'John, do you want to tell us about the blade used and the dentistry tools found?'

'Yes sir,' John cleared his throat. 'We recovered a red handled craft knife at the scene. This we understand belongs to the dental practice.'

'I've got it on my to-check-list with Claire who is in charge of stock control,' said Vicky.

'Sorry to interrupt. We will also need to speak to everyone at the practice with regard to their background and whereabouts in the early hours of this morning,' said Dylan.

John continued. 'On a working surface, placed on a green drape on a plastic base that is used in the practice, were two antique dental instruments. These instruments are known as forceps and elevators. These have identical markings on the handles to those in the set we have in our possession that belonged in the first instance to the deceased Timothy Woodcock. These were recovered from the Forget Me Not charity shop. We can't think of any other reason for these being on display in Martin Crossfield's surgery unless they were deliberately put there by someone who wished them to be found by us.'

'Professor Stow will be looking at those to see if he can identify the striation marks left by these particular instruments at the murder scenes of our serial killer. The instruments will then

265

be sent to Forensic and treated as a priority. ACC Smythe will be releasing a press release today via the press office which will let the killer think, for a short time at least, that we are going along with the suicide of Mr Crossfield. Martin Crossfield did not have any extracted teeth on his person.'

'Do you think that was an oversight on the murderer's part?' said Vicky.

'Maybe,' said Dylan. 'Or maybe he might have thought that was going a bit too far for credibility.'

'Probably didn't want to waste any more extracted teeth on us,' said Vicky.

'I will remind the Force to remain vigilant,' said the ACC.

'The idea for this is that maybe the killer will think that the extra patrols we have advertised are in place will be stepped down.'

'Giving him a false sense of security?'

'Exactly,' said Dylan.

***

Avril Summerfield-Preston teetered on her high heels along the top corridor. The briefing room door was thrown open and Dylan allowed the four ladies out past him. The ACC stepped into the Divisional Administrator's path.

'Ah, ma'am.' Avril smiled sweetly. 'I've been looking all over for you. I saw you talking with my personnel officer earlier when I was otherwise occupied with the Chief Superintendent, talking budgets. You know how it is. Were you looking for me by any chance?'

'You shouldn't have put yourself out Avril,' said Wendy Smythe. 'I'm sure you have more important things to do than chase after me. The ladies in admin answered everything I needed to know.'

'Oh, well, we will have to catch up over a G & T sometime,' she said. 'And I won't forget the lemon.' Avril Summerfield-Preston raised her nose in the air.

ACC Smythe turned to Dylan who was putting a wedge in the door. 'I'll speak with you later,' she said.

Dylan walked towards the CID office.

'Dylan!' Avril Summerfield-Preston called from behind. 'How many times do I have to tell you to turn off the lights!'

Dylan turned, looked over his shoulder at Avril and sniggered. 'Why does that woman always look as if she is sucking a bloody lemon?' the ACC asked.

Dylan shrugged his shoulders.

'And now I know how she gets the nickname Beaky.'

'That's not for me to comment on ma'am,' he said.

'You are diplomatic,' she said. 'It's much more fun listening to the admin girls' gossip. The admin is always a bit of normality in this mad world.'

***

The afternoon's office briefing was short. Dylan needed to be at the post-mortem. He reinforced that whilst the latest information regarding the murder of Martin Crossfield was a positive line of enquiry it was far from being the only one and that everyone needed to remain open-minded. 'I know from experience sometimes a route that looks very positive often comes to a dead end. If you pardon the pun...' he said in conclusion.

'And that's why we never put all our eggs in one basket,' said Vicky to Ned.

'You talking to me?'

'If the cap fits,' she said.

'Whatever.'

***

The time for the post-mortem of Martin Crossfield was looming and Dylan knew this one wouldn't be over quickly. It would be a late night for all concerned and because of that he sought Jen out before he left the building.

'I'm sorry to land you with the ACC earlier,' he said, catching up with his wife in the admin office.

'Don't apologise we had a good chat. She's got Avril weighed up. Did she show you her impression of her?'

Dylan shook his head.

'She didn't? What a scream? She should be on the stage.'

'So should most of them in the Headquarter's ivory tower.'

'Dylan?' Jen said with a scowl.

'Have you felt the daggers in your back yet?' said Dylan.

'We admin girls are tough. We can cope. We know what Beaky's like. Better the devil you know as they say. The ACC asked us in confidence to tell her our views on all the changes that are afoot and what we thought about the process they are using to save money for the force in reducing the support workers... And how we felt we were being treated.'

'And I bet you lot didn't hold back?'

'What do you think? Actually, it was refreshing to be treated like a grown-up for once and not like a school child by a member of the command team. Wendy Smythe said she was fed up with people like Beaky paying her lip service.'

'That is refreshing. Look, I'm going to be late tonight so don't wait up. I'm off to the mortuary next and then we've scheduled a late debrief.'

***

The trip to the mortuary was an uncomfortable one and not because of the thoughts of the imminent post-mortem but because dusk was falling, a warm summer dusk. The tar on the roads was sticky and it seemed everyone was seeking shade. As Dylan walked through the car park to the mortuary the air was full of the scent of roses, the garden full of a sad silence; and as he went up through the thickets and looked towards the vines that clung to the old building he remembered each body he had seen in the last few weeks and his heart sank. When would he get the breakthrough he so desperately needed? Soon he hoped as he looked up to the sky. He stopped and took one last deep breath before opening the big, wooden door.

The air conditioning in the mortuary was broken. All the windows were open but the place was extra pungent. Engineers were hard at work, they wore hideous masks that looked as if they should be in a war zone but he couldn't blame them. Dylan dug deep in his pockets for his mints.

Professor Stow arrived, took out his handkerchief wiped his forehead and held it over his big, loose mouth with its flabby pinkness. 'My goodness,' he said, 'I think I'll be keeping my mask on today.'

Dylan explained the circumstances of the discovery of Martin Crossfield's body and their subsequent findings at the scene. He allowed the professor to peruse the photographs of the body in situ.

Professor Stow didn't interrupt him but listened intently until he had finished. His half-rimmed glasses glittered in the light from the fluorescent tubes. The usually remarkably jovial man had become suddenly very solemn.

'So let me be sure that I understand exactly what you are telling me. On face value this death would appear to be a suicide. You have an apology written in blood on the floor where he lay and the implements left on display suggesting that this person is your serial killer. Mmm... Can I take a look at the dentistry tools?'

Dylan threw him a glance of caution.

'Don't worry. I appreciate that they have to be forensically examined,' he said.

He was passed the dental implements which were individually wrapped in see-through containers and secured within.

'Well,' he said. 'if I was a gambling man Inspector Dylan I would be putting quite a bit of money on these. Right era, right pattern and once I am able to I'll check them against the striation marks data we have already acquired. So let's start with the examination of this chap, shall we? Murderer, victim, or impostor?'

Chapter Thirty-One

Martin Crossfield's body was laid out on the examination table before them. The room was now pleasantly cool. The team gathered for this post-mortem stood around him, booted and suited. Professor Stow's half-rimmed glasses rested on his rosy, red cheeks just above the face mask and as his head was bent downwards they fell slightly to the ridge on his nose. He pulled his sleeves of his gown up slightly at the elbows with his gloved hands and stood with his arms extended outwards. Dylan saw from the rise and fall of his gown at his chest that he was breathing slowly and deeply as he focused on the corpse in front of him.

Crossfield's clothing was removed carefully and searched where relevant. Each of the dead man's clothing items was put into separate exhibit bags as they were removed. His shoes, like any article in pairs, required two bags which were offered to the mortuary attendant in quick succession before the bags were given to DC Wormald for them to be sealed by the exhibits officer and a label attached. In this case the exhibit forms would be signed by Professor Stow and not the officer at the conclusion of the post-mortem. There was no time to think about the smell of the mortuary now – there was a job to be done.

It seemed to Dylan that Stow took a while to visually examine the naked man's body. Whilst the corpse lay on his front he asked for the back of his head to be shaved and a photograph taken.

Professor Stow spoke the obvious for the sake of the recording.

'The only visible injuries are cuts to the throat and both wrists.'

Samples of hair were cut and plucked from the body, along with samples of blood and urine. Stomach contents were necessarily taken and these were immediately put into a container, sealed and the labels attached. Stow looked very closely at the injuries to the wrists.

'Did you say to me that Mr Crossfield was left handed?'

'Yes, that has been confirmed by his dental nurse,' said Vicky. 'For future reference, when a dental surgeon is left handed the surgery is set up the opposite way around to a right-handed dentist.'

'I knew there was something different about Martin Crossfield's surgery,' said Dylan.

'We learn something new every day,' said Stow. 'Look here, I would suggest the way each wound tapers off that these injuries were made by a right-handed person and not by himself.'

The professor turned his attention to the dentist's mouth. He spoke to no one in particular as he continued. 'No teeth missing?' He raised his eyebrows. His lower lip stuck out as he looked up at Dylan. 'However, looking at those gorgeous gnashers they may very well have attracted our killer. Okay, let's open him up.' The mortuary attendant stepped forward to hand him a tool and he proceeded to make the cuts to the chest and trunk.

The mortuary attendant removed the skull cap to expose the brain with an electric saw.

'I remember them using a small hand saw to cut through the bone at one time,' Dylan said, his eyes never leaving the procedure taking place.

***

'The cause of death is down to the severing of the carotid artery which means the poor man bled to death from the neck wound. Again, I don't think due to the depth of the wound that he did this himself. This would be difficult as these arteries are protected by the windpipe. The cuts to the wrists are pretty superficial only cutting the vein... With his professional background, if he was intent on killing himself I would suggest he would have slit the vein vertically.' Stow peered over his glasses at Dylan. 'I asked for the back of the head to be photographed when it was shaved and that is because I wanted to record the reddening and bruising of the skin on his scalp. This is significant because it confirms to me that someone grabbed a handful of his hair and yanked his head quite violently, I would suggest, backwards. Most probably at the same time as they cut his throat. So Inspector in my professional opinion this is not a suicide, but murder.'

'And like we thought, in your opinion, our killer wanted us to think it was suicide?' said Vicky.

'Another little test; not unlike the way he has tried to fool you before at the other murder scenes?' said Stow.

'Extracting the Michael then not a tooth?' said Dylan.

'I do the jokes Inspector,' Stow chuckled. His belly laugh was unlike any other that Dylan had ever heard. His joviality was always infectious. 'Now did you hear the one about the dentist who planted a garden? A month later he was picking teeth!' he said to Vicky as they walked down the corridor to the office.

Dylan's job was to ensure priority exhibits such as the recovered tools were taken to the Forensic laboratory for examination. On his mind was also what needed to be sent now as a matter of urgency due to the post-mortem findings. In silence Dylan and Vicky walked out of the mortuary building. It was always such a wonderful feeling to fill the lungs with fresh air after the confines of a post-mortem.

'Can I cadge a lift?' she said. 'Andy is going back to the nick via the hairdressers.'

'He's still courting then?'

Vicky laughed at Dylan. 'You are so old-fashioned sometimes,' she said.

'Nothing wrong with being a gentleman,' he said.

They walked towards Dylan's car in silence by way of an avenue lined with trees. The air was still and calm. It was suddenly very qui

The two detectives reached the car. There was a change in the air. There was a loud bleep as Dylan turned off his car alarm and he and Vicky opened their doors simultaneously. Even though it was quite dark, or as dark as it gets on a summer's evening, above Vicky's head Dylan saw a line of dark clouds ominously appear on the horizon.

'Those look like they aren't fooling around,' he said pointing in the clouds' direction.

Doors closed, Dylan started the engine as the first fat raindrops fell on the windscreen. As they drove out of the car park the cloud seemed to burst right above them and Dylan pulled into the filling station, as much to shelter from the deluge of rain that he couldn't drive in as to fill up with fuel.

'What's there to laugh about?' said Dylan throwing her a whimsical glance.

'Where did the dentist get his gas?' said Vicky, laying her head back against the headrest as she turned to face him.

'This is one of Stow's jokes, right?'

Vicky nodded, her blue eyes were laughing.

'Then I have no idea,' he said with half a smile.

'At the filling station!' she squealed as if she had been about to burst.

'But that isn't even remotely funny,' said Dylan.

'I know and that makes it even funnier,' she said with tears now streaming down her face.

Dylan shook his head. 'You really are crazy, do you know that?' he said.

***

Fifteen minutes later Dylan turned his vehicle into his parking space at Harrowfield Police Station.

'Martin Crossfield must have gone straight to his dental practice after the funeral,' said Vicky thoughtfully.

'Why do you say that?' said Dylan.

'Well, if he didn't, he had the same clothes on. Do you think the killer accompanied him then?'

'He might have, or he might have just arranged to meet him there?'

Dylan closed his car door and looked up towards the sky. He was thankful for the freshness the rain had brought. He waited for Vicky to alight and gather her belongings. They walked across the yard together.

The incident room was quiet. The night shift was working. Lisa was still sitting at her computer.

'Haven't you got a home to go to?' Dylan said.

Lisa's eyes looked red rimmed and sore.

'Anything new?' Vicky asked. She stifled a yawn.

'A message on your desk from Jim Woodcock. He's cancelled his appointment with you.'

'Why?' Vicky said. Her eyebrows knitted together.

'He said he's not ready to talk to anyone yet. He needs time to come to terms with his father's death,' she said.

'He seemed perfectly okay at the funeral,' she said looking at Lisa over the top of the note she held.

'Well I suppose a lot of people can appear okay on the surface but sometimes it takes just a little something... Maybe the funeral has just made him realise that he'll never see his dad again,' said Lisa.

Vicky crinkled her nose at her colleague. 'I wouldn't have thought... but I guess you never know... and of course now with the death of Martin Crossfield... his friend?'

At the rear of the office the doors swung open and in walked John and Ned.

Ned went straight to his desk and John followed Dylan into his office. He felt in his breast pocket for his pocketbook. 'According to the cleaner, boss the door was locked when she arrived. The cleaner tells me he's very particular and his flat is always spotless. So clean in fact, that you wouldn't think anyone lived there. With regard to the photographs, Claire Booth has named some of those present at the funeral for us. She can't think of anyone who had a grudge or a bad word to say about her boss.'

John turned to leave.

'Thanks John, will you send Vicky and Raj in please?'

'It's time we were at home but I want one of you to arrange to go and see Edna Woodcock. I want to know all there is to know about her adopted son and her son-in-law. Do we know if Mr Woodcock had any other children we should know about?'

'Why do you ask?' said Raj.

'I just think we ought to be certain there are no more siblings knocking about.'

Dylan picked up the report from JJ Associates that was close at hand. He turned to Raj, 'There is something niggling me about this,' he said passing the document to the sergeant.

'The two dentists and Jim Woodcock went to a conference together. I want to know dates, times etcetera. It may be that they were out of the country for at least one of the murders which would give them an alibi without us doing any more digging,' said Dylan.

'What about the other people at the funeral?'

'Put them into the system to be traced, interviewed and eliminated. Were any of them a close friend of Martin Crossfield?

'The receptionist said the dentist was a hard worker who kept himself very much to himself. They all knew each other more than likely.'

'A dentist, a loner... If we didn't know otherwise Martin Crossfield should be a suspect. How come his name hasn't come into our investigation?' said Dylan.

'I guess as a dentist in the area he will be on a list for someone to interview at some point but a visit to him was obviously not deemed as important as some of the other leads we are following up sir,' said Raj.

'Whoever our murderer is it is obvious he isn't going to stop until we find him,' said Dylan. 'And once the media know the truth about our latest murder they will be on our backs like a pack of hungry wolves.

Chapter Thirty-Two

Jen stirred slightly at Dylan's homecoming but only to throw off
the duvet. The heat in the room was such that it felt hard to
breathe comfortably. Dylan pulled back the curtain slightly to
enable him to open the window wider. He turned to see her
sleeping face and bent to kiss her forehead. She flinched as if a
fly had landed upon her face but didn't wake. He walked to his
side of the bed, took off his clothes, threw them over the chair
and slipped in between the sheets. He reached out for Jen's
hand, it was moist with sweat. He held it tightly and wished she
was awake; to talk, to listen. He closed his eyes and willed
himself to sleep but pictures of the murder scenes played
through the darkness one by one like a silent movie; the post-
mortems, the sequel to the night terror. What was he missing?
Eventually he fell into a fitful sleep in which he was running
between yellow, hazy streaks that turned out to be sand dunes,
deep as trenches. There were grey, dimpled, faceless beings
above him, pointing the finger; guilty, guilty of what? He was
running for his life, he could barely breathe and in that moment
he went over the edge of a cliff and into an abyss. He was falling,
falling into a deep, dark sea. Dylan felt a strong jolt in his chest
and he woke. His body was bathed in sweat and his heart beat
was erratic. He lifted himself up on his elbow. He was panting.
There was light through the gap in the curtain from the street
lamp outside which afforded him the relief of seeing his wife's
sleeping face, content in her peaceful slumber and he felt a surge
of love.

He lay back on his pillow. His head sank into the damp
hollow. The bedside clock showed three a.m. The phone rang.

'Sir, Force Control,' a voice said. 'I have been asked to advise
you by the Night Inspector at Harrowfield that he has

implemented the area sweep action plan in conjunction with Operation Tangent.'

Dylan sat up as if he were a puppet being pulled by invisible strings. 'What are the circumstances?'

'A lady unlocking her pedal cycle at the side of the China House restaurant where she had just finished her shift. She was hit from behind. Fortunately she had already put on her cycle helmet which broke the force of the blow but it still knocked her to the ground. One of our regular callers, Eddie who operates the council night road sweeper turned into the alley way and the attacker fled.'

'She was lucky.'

'She certainly was sir.'

'Who's the Inspector?' said Dylan.

'Stonestreet.'

Dylan breathed a sigh of relief.

'At this moment the lady is in A and E and the Inspector has sent an officer to be with her. The scene is taped off. The static observations are in position and the helicopter is airborne. So with a bit of luck... we'll locate our attacker.'

'Can this Eddie give us any description of the attacker?'

'Male, dark trousers, possibly denim jeans and a dark hooded top. He only got a brief glance but he does recollect white trainers or they may have had some sort of neon strip that caught his eye. Whether the incident is connected with your murders or not is yet to be seen but Inspector Stonestreet has a grip on it.'

'I'm sure he has. Let him know I'm turning out will you. I'll head to the scene at China House so will you let on duty scenes of crime and the night detective know I'll see them there. Also can we ensure that any CCTV known to us in that area, especially in the direction he was heading is seized?'

'Consider it done sir, all that has been added to the log.'

Dylan was up, shaved and dressed. Jen stumbled out of bed towards him.

'Are you just coming home or going out again,' she said in a sleepy voice.

'Going back out. I'll ring you later.'

'But...'

'Shh... it's okay someone's been attacked and the culprit has run off. I'll have to go,' he said giving her a kiss on her cheek as she yawned.

'Make sure you put some fruit and a cereal bar in your briefcase....' The door was closed and her words were silenced by the sound of his running feet on the stairs.

Dylan got into his car. He sat for a moment and listened. Everything was so very quiet and still. He switched on his lights. Driving in the middle of the night, when he had had little sleep felt like living in a dream world. Often the nightmare proceeded when he was faced with the horrors of the imminent scene he had been called out to appraise. As he drove through the Sibden Valley towards Harrowfield he passed the dim shapes of farm buildings, Sibden Hall and the speckled show of lights above the town at the peak of Harrowfield Old Road; a welcome sight. As the car gathered momentum on the descent some creature ran out in front. Dylan's foot hit the brake and the suddenness of pressure brought about a loud screech of brakes. The car was broadside at a standstill, in the middle of the unlit road. Dylan wound his window down. His heart beat rapidly. He couldn't see a thing around him except the drystone walling he had barely missed, in his headlights. Breathing more freely he wound down his window. Close by a rusty wire fence trembling caught his eye as a creature of the night vanished over it. Was it good luck or bad to see a black Manx cat had crossed his path? He couldn't remember but, it was definitely lucky for the feline.

Dylan's car emerged from the darkness as the road lighting now led the way into town. What seemed like moments later he was at the scene of the attack; 'the circus' was already there and what was night was now day thanks to the police dragon lamps illuminating the scene.

'Sir,' said DC Ned Granger who presented himself to his boss. He had kept somewhat of a low profile since his misdemeanour and was obviously keen to impress.

'What've we got Ned,' said Dylan.

'The victim is a Rachel Nicholson, she's twenty-two years old, a wannabe singer who works part-time as a waitress. She travels to and fro from her home address to her workplace on a regular basis, on her bike. She always locks this with a chain to the drainpipe at the side of the premises. I am told that there had been no previous problems. What struck me is that this girl, it is said by the restaurant owners, is known for her beautiful smile and brilliant white teeth,' he said.

Inspector Stonestreet joined them. In his arms he carried a small black cat. 'I wonder if Miss Nicholson stooped down to stroke this gorgeous creature?'

Ned looked bemused.

'It's said to be lucky to touch a black cat,' said Inspector Stonestreet.

'Well, she was lucky that's for sure,' Ned said.

'This is the work of our killer Peter isn't it?' Dylan put his hand out to stroke the cat. 'I guess we could all do with a bit of luck right now in this investigation couldn't we? Have we got an update on her?'

Peter Stonestreet kissed the cat between its ears and as if it knew it was being dismissed it leapt out of his arms and onto the floor. It was in no hurry to leave him however, brushing up against his leg in an adoring way. 'Slight fracture to the skull, she'll be detained. No doubt about it though her helmet saved her from serious injury, possibly death.'

'I want the headgear seized as an exhibit Ned along with the clothing that she was wearing. Have you seized the CCTV at the restaurant?'

'Yes sir,' said Ned. 'But, it only covers the front of the premises according to the owners.'

Inspector Stonestreet was distracted by the running commentary of the observer in the Force helicopter that could be heard over the airways. 'The helicopter has a man in its sights. He's running on the canal bank towards Waterford Road in a westerly direction.'

Ned retrieved his pocketbook to record the description being given: shorts, sleeveless vest, white trainers.

The jogger was running at pace now on the canal bank but they were staying with him. A few yards on and the jogger had stopped. They'd lost him amongst the bridges and the mill. However a few minutes later he re-appeared. He had his hands on his hips and he was bent over the canal. The commentary continued.

'He looks like he may be vomiting. The jogger is up and running but we've a lot slower pace. He's now walking, and within five hundred yards of our officers. Man now being checked by patrol officers. We will continue to search the area.'

'Inspector Stonestreet to Control. Can you ask the officers who are doing the checks on the jogger to keep me updated please. I am with the SIO at the scene outside the China House Restaurant.'

DS Vicky Hardacre joined the group.

'Couldn't sleep?' said Dylan.

'Wet her bed more like,' said Ned flicking the baseball cap off her head.

'Who says I was in my bed?' she said with a nod in the direction of a police car that was leaving the scene as she picked her hat up off the floor.

'Well, by the way you're dressed ...,' he said raising an eyebrow.

'That's enough,' Dylan said. 'What do you already know Vicky?'

'It's okay I heard what's going on en route, sir,' she said.

They stood quietly around Inspector Stonestreet, waiting for an update from Force Control.

'New member of the team?' Vicky said looking down at the black cat that sat patiently watching them from the branch of a nearby tree that stood in a pot on the precinct pavement.

'That's the second I've seen today,' Dylan said. 'The other was lucky it didn't end up under my tyres.'

The cat raised its head, turned and precariously walked along the branch.

'You know what that means don't you sir?' she said seriously.

'What?'

'It's bad luck to see a black cat early in the morning and for it to walk away – OMG that's the worst...'

Ned looked at Dylan. 'It's official. She has lost her chuffin' marbles.' He turned to Vicky, 'You have, you're bloody nuts!'

Inspector Stonestreet's radio crackled and a voice came over the airwaves.

'PC Jordan,' said the officer at the canal scene. 'Our jogger is still trying to get his breath back. He reckons we shocked him so much he can't talk to us yet. At present he's only given us that he's in the habit of running when he can't sleep... He looks in a bad way truth be told. I can't think he runs very often.'

'Is he out of earshot?' said Inspector Stonestreet.

'He is sir, yes.'

'Give me a description of what he's wearing.'

'White shorts, vest and trainers.'

'Any ID on him?'

'No, but that's not surprising, dressed as he is. He's just giving his name to Tracy... he says his name is Carl Bell, twenty-nine years old and he says he lives at Flat 4, Gillingham Place, off Hanson Lane.'

'His description?'

'Short, slightly built, brown hair, Yorkshire accent.'

Inspector Stonestreet listened intently as the Force Controller interacted. 'At present we can't verify that any person with that name is registered at that address,' he said. Peter's eyes found Dylan's face. He held Dylan's gaze.

'What're you thinking?' said Peter.

'If the officers with him haven't got back-up get them some now,' said Dylan.

'Carl is the name of one our murder victims,' said Vicky.

'And Bell another,' said Dylan.

'Trying to create a diversion for us do you think?' said Vicky.

'I think he's playing with us... He's dangerous,' said Dylan.

'Then again, it may just be a dodgy jogger boss,' said Ned. 'The road sweeper says the attacker was dressed in dark clothing.'

'His outer clothing could be easily discarded for shorts and vest,' said Vicky.

'I want him arrested,' said Dylan.

'On what grounds,' said Peter Stonestreet to Dylan.

'Suspicion of wounding but tell your officers to wait until back up arrives before they try to detain him in cuffs.'

'That's a brave move. It's only circumstantial evidence,' said Stonestreet.

'At the moment it is but trust me on this one,' said Dylan.

Inspector Stonestreet moved away from Vicky and Ned but he was within earshot as he spoke to the officer at the canal scene. 'Back-up is on its way. DI Dylan wants him arrested on suspicion of wounding.' He turned back to join the group, looking every bit his age. 'I wish I was there...' he said. 'The two officers at the scene are nought but young kids.'

Dylan could see his kindly face was drawn, his jawline fixed.

'I'm sure they'll be fine,' said Dylan. 'They've had a good teacher.' Dylan winked at the older man.

Lucy Jordan didn't question the command. 'PC Petterson is talking to him but he's getting agitated, she said.

'I told Control to ask officers attending to treat the severity of the call as officers needing immediate assistance,' said Stonestreet.

There was a shout over the radio. 'Tracy, PC Petterson, she's down.'

The attacker was running and they could hear by the sound of her voice that PC Jordan was in pursuit. 'Nearing Copley Bridge, PC Petterson is back on her feet, in pursuit, behind me,' Lucy said. Her words were spoken in between short, jerking breaths.

'Control to all units, PC Jordan and PC Petterson in pursuit of a man heading towards...' was the update over the airways.

The group turned to see all available police cars disappearing. Redirected to help their colleagues.

'Damn and blast,' said Dylan. 'I hope they don't bloody lose him.'

'Not on my shift Dylan they won't, you know that,' said Stonestreet with a gentle nod of a proud head.

Chapter Thirty-Three

'Man arrested on suspicion of wounding and assaulting a police officer. Prisoner en route to Harrowfield cells,' came the somewhat relieved voice of PC Jordan over the airways.

The assembled officers gave a collective sigh – none bigger than the one Inspector Stonestreet gave. 'Well, all you need is the evidence now Dylan,' he said with a twinkle of an eye and a grimace hanging on his lips.

'Where's that bloody black cat? Let's hope the luck we've had tonight continues. There's going to be a lot of searching done in the next few hours and his custody clock will soon be against us... Get control to call DS Raj and DS John Benjamin out will you.'

Vicky and Ned climbed in Dylan's car and left Peter Stonestreet at the scene. 'We need to find the bastard's clothes. He must have dumped them somewhere between here and the arrest site,' Dylan said.

'They could be in the canal. We might never find them...' said Ned.

Dylan looked in his mirror and proceeded to reverse the car briefly making eye contact through the glass with Ned Granger. Dylan's look could have cut steel.

'And then there's the little problem that this guy could actually be an innocent jogger' Ned continued.

'Shut the fuck up will you Ned.' Vicky turned on her colleague in the back of the car.

Dylan steered his car out of the car park. He put his foot on the brake and looked back at Ned as they reached the exit. 'Anything positive you'd like to offer as to the way forward, officer?' he growled. He put his foot down on the accelerator and the car leapt forward. The black cat jumped out of nowhere.

'Nooo,' squealed Vicky. Dylan hit the brake. There was a moment's silence before the cat strolled casually out from Dylan's side of the car. Vicky took her hat off, turned it around backwards and marked the windscreen with an X.

'What the fuck are you doing now?' said Ned.

She turned to Dylan. 'It's okay. You can go now,' she said. Dylan wasn't about to dispel any superstition no matter how crazy they seemed – not on a night as important as this.

'The minute we get back to the station I want you to make arrangements for the collection and viewing of any CCTV we recover from premises between the China House and Copley Bridge,' he said, flashing Ned a momentary look in his rear view mirror.

He nodded.

'Within the same area I want a visual search carried out. We are looking for abandoned clothing or anything close to the scene that looks remotely out of place... Something, anything that looks as if it could have been used as a weapon in the assault. Speak to the cells and get the prisoner's clothing, including his footwear seized Vicky. Raj and John should be joining us very soon.'

By half past six the organised search teams were briefed by Dylan and out walking the route that the would-be jogger was thought to have taken. After his arrest Carl Bell was sticking to his story that he was of that name, but had now changed his place of residency to no fixed abode. He was unemployed – he said.

'If this is our man do you think he might have attended Timothy Woodcock's funeral?' said Vicky.

'I don't know Vicky but let's remember our prisoner is under arrest at the moment for the wounding of Rachel Nicholson and we need to find evidence to prove it, otherwise he's going to walk.'

'But you think he's our killer don't you?'

***

The local duty solicitors Perfect & Best were called from the old Co-Op building offices by the Custody Sergeant in the cells at the prisoner's request. Apart from this he had refused everything else offered to him. 'He insists he's done nothing wrong.'

Dylan asked that he be notified when the on duty solicitor named as Yvonne Best arrived.

'Let's us have a sneaky look at the prisoner without him seeing us,' Dylan said to Vicky.

The pair waited for him to be taken from his cell to his meeting with his solicitor. In a side office where they stood they had a good view of him being walked past. Vicky could hardly contain herself when she saw him. 'Bloody hell, I don't believe it. It's Jim bloody Woodcock,' she said.

Dylan's eyes widened. 'Things might be more positive than we thought. All we need now is that little thing called evidence,' he said with a frown. 'It's going to be interesting to hear if he tells Ms Best his correct name and address.'

'We'll find out pretty soon now won't we?' said Vicky.

***

The cell area was empty when Dylan approached the custody suite desk.

'Anything on him when he was brought in?' said Dylan.

'Two keys,' the Custody Sergeant said.

'Keys? Where are they now?'

'Still here with the prisoner's property.'

'Can you get them and sign them out to me?'

***

Dylan sat at his desk staring at the keys that were in a clear, sealed evidence bag. One key looked like a door key and the other like Dylan's own briefcase key.

'Do you want a coffee and a sandwich boss?' said Raj. 'I bet you haven't had any breakfast seeing as you were called out at a ridiculous time.'

'Thanks. I'm so glad it was Stonestreet who was the Night Inspector. If he hadn't put the Operation Tangent sweep plan into action the officers seeing our man jogging on the canal bank may well have taken his fake name and address to follow up and allowed him to carry on.'

Raj shut Dylan's door quietly behind her. She saw him pick up the phone and key in a number. In her experience that phone call would be to ACC Wendy Smythe informing her of the arrest and relevant background details. She wondered as she strolled through the office if they would see the ACC in the office that day – then she reasoned with herself; it was highly unlikely and even more so as it was a Saturday.

***

As staff arrived in the incident room the atmosphere became more and more electric.

'I want any intelligence on Jim Woodcock that's out there. Which school did he attend? College, university; isn't he supposed to be studying something? What is he studying? Does he claim grants or have financial assistance? We need to house him, find the clothing he discarded, look for a weapon he used to assault Rachel with. He must have dumped it somewhere en route. I want an FLO to liaise with the family who are still at the bedside of the victim keeping a vigil at their daughter's side. Who's on?'

'PC Burkett is the on duty Family Liaison Officer.'

'Get her in to see us. His detention clock is ticking. Our first deadline according to the Police and Criminal Evidence Act, as you are well aware is twenty-four hours.'

***

It was warm, Dylan was sweating, he picked up his ringing phone and he loosened his tie.

'Sergeant Clegg sir,' Simon said. 'You'll be pleased to know we've already had some success.'

Eyes to the ceiling Dylan breathed out through pursed lips and when he looked down again Raj was staring at him.

'Approximately eight hundred yards from where Rachel was attacked, in the direction the attacker was seen running, we have come across an old wooden police truncheon. I don't know whether this could be the weapon that was used in the attack but it just seems totally out of place where it is, and it's relatively clean.'

'Forensic will be able to match it to the helmet Rachel was wearing if it is the weapon we are looking for. Have you seized it?' said Dylan.

Raj's look was one of surprise.

'We'll have it photographed in situ before we recover it then continue with the search, sir,' Simon said.

Dylan put the phone down. 'A find already?' said Raj.

'A truncheon,' he said.

'Strange thing to be found on the street?' she said with a furrowed brow. 'Yvonne Best is ready for the interview with her client,' she said. 'You're interviewing with Vicky I believe?'

'Yes, can you give her a shout for me I'll meet her in the cell area?'

Dylan was deep in conversation with the solicitor when Vicky arrived. They were standing outside the interview room, the door firmly closed on the prisoner.

'Is he still using the name of Carl Bell?' Dylan said.

Ms Best looked puzzled, then her look turned to anger. 'Oh no, you're not telling me he has he given me a stiff name are you?'

Dylan raised his eyebrows.

Her lips formed a tight straight line. 'Damn and blast, I've filled in all the legal aid forms which I am now going to have to do again. Oh, joy!' she said. 'As if we haven't enough to do. Go on, tell me, what's his right name?'

'Our prisoner is a James (Jim) Woodcock and he is twenty-nine years of age. The address he has given us is false too, we believe.'

'Give me another ten minutes with him will you?' she said. Yvonne put her hand on the door handle to the interview room and when it didn't open, with a face like thunder, she put her shoulder to the heavy door, pushed, and it opened wide. Slowly it closed after her but not before Dylan saw the prisoner at the table.

Dylan stood looking out of the window into the back yard from the corridor. It spoke volumes to him that Jim Woodcock had not given his solicitor his true identity. After all, he had asked for her help in securing his release. Dylan's eyes flew upwards to the bright blue sky. An aeroplane flew overhead. Would they fare any better in interview or would he make them prove every point right down to the minor details? 'Is this the supreme test?' Dylan asked himself. Woodcock was about to meet his match Dylan was fired up and ready to go. He turned as the door opened. They were all ready to begin.

Chapter Thirty-Four

The pathetic looking figure of Jim Woodcock sat back in his seat as far as possible, in the interview room.

The white coverall suit provided was larger than required and it made him look feeble. It was the first time Dylan had met the prisoner in person but since Vicky had already had the pleasure Dylan chose to change his plan and do the first interview with DS Rajinder Uppal.

The introductions for voice recognition, for the purpose of the recording of the interview, along with a video was completed and the caution administered by Dylan. The prisoner appeared unfazed as he sat pulling hair from his already wild, fine and wispy mane.

Dylan spoke first. 'Would you tell us your full name please?'

Unexpectedly, Woodcock smiled at Dylan and looked him straight in the eye. 'Yes, of course.' He shuffled in his seat and sat up straight leaning towards the detectives. 'I'm genuinely sorry. I now realise...' he said with a sideways look at his solicitor, '...that, that was very stupid of me.' Woodcock bowed his head and looked at his hands. He put them palms down on the table before him.

'Your full name please?'

'James Woodcock but everyone calls me Jim.'

'And can we call you Jim?'

Woodcock gave Dylan a quick half-smile. His lips were pressed together.

'Is that a yes?'

He nodded.

'Mr Woodcock is nodding in the affirmative,' said Raj.

'For the tape please could you speak your answers in future? So, tell me Jim why would you be jogging along the canal in the middle of the night?'

Woodcock cleared his throat and Dylan leant forward maintaining eye contact.

'I go running when I can't sleep.'

'So, tell me why you couldn't sleep last night?' said Dylan.

Woodcock stroked his chin. 'I think it was probably because I ate late. A cold curry isn't the best food to go to bed on is it?' His lips curled down at the edge of a smile.

'Okay, but what I don't understand is why you would assault a uniformed police officer in the line of duty and then try to run away?'

'They shocked me, jumping out in front of me like that, in the dark. I told them I was out for a run. Then the police officer said they were investigating an attack on a woman that had occurred earlier in the town centre.'

'And, what happened then?'

'I asked her why she was asking me. Was the person who attacked her dressed like me? I couldn't think why else she would have stopped me. The officer spoke to someone on the radio and the other officer started pushing me around. She said I wasn't to behave like a smart arse and kept demanding that I gave her my name. I was out of breath. I could hardly speak. She annoyed me. I'd done nothing wrong so I didn't see she had any right to be so threatening, uniform or not so I lied.'

'And you thought pushing her out of your way and running would help in what way?'

'Well, I guess it was a poor effort on my part to get on my way once I had lied. But, they had just put the fear of god up me. She pushed me so I pushed her back and she fell to the ground. I panicked when I saw her fall and I ran. The pair ran after me and the next thing I knew I was being wrestled to the floor and handcuffed. Now I find myself here and for god's sake I'd only gone out for a run. Wish I'd stopped in bed now.'

Woodcock pulled his hands back and placed them on his knees. He raised his chin.

'Okay,' said Dylan. 'But once you arrived here, you continued to lie to the custody sergeant and your solicitor? Why would you do that if you were not guilty of something?'

'I've already apologised for that. I know it's absolutely idiotic, but once I'd started lying... Let's say it just seemed like a good idea at the time.'

'But Ms Best is your solicitor. You asked that she be called out to help you. How can she do that if you lie to her about something as simple as your name?'

'If I'd have told her,' he said nodding sideways in the solicitor's direction, 'I knew she would be obliged to tell you lot.'

The detectives were quiet. Woodcock avoided any eye contact and started tapping the pads of his fingers on the table. 'It was wrong, I know that now, but I have never been arrested before have I and I thought they'd just take what I told them at face value and let me go on my way. Again...' he said making eye contact with Dylan, '... stupid I know. I didn't have time to think it through.'

'Where did you set off from, for your jog?' Raj asked.

Woodcock fidgeted in his seat and adjusted his clothing. 'Home,' he said.

'Where is home?'

'Flat 1, St Matthew's Square, Harrowfield.'

'So the address you gave the officers was also false?'

'Yes,' he said. He rubbed the back of his neck and looked down at the table.

'Did you go anywhere near Harrowfield town centre last night or early this morning?'

'No,' he said lifting up his head. 'Absolutely not.'

'Why did you choose the name of Carl Bell as your made-up name? Is that the name of someone you know?' said Dylan.

'No, they're just names that came into my head.'

'Do you regularly jog on the canal? Why the canal?'

'Yes, it's less pressure on the knees than running on the roads and it's quieter.'

'The keys you had on your person at the time of your arrest, what are they for?'

'Door key and the other's a padlock key.'

'What's the padlock for?'

'A locker.'

Dylan was perplexed. Woodcock had managed to answers all the questions put to him without hesitation and his responses were plausible. He didn't appear intimidated or nervous in interview. What Dylan did notice was a peculiar idiosyncrasy that he had of speaking with his mouth almost closed. Only occasionally did he see the tip of Woodcock's upper two large front teeth that appeared to be buck teeth like a rabbit.

Dylan terminated the first interview and Jim Woodcock agreed to provide his fingerprints and DNA swab.

The two detectives returned to the incident room.

'How did it go?' said Vicky eagerly.

'He was very plausible,' said Raj. 'Wasn't he?' she said turning to Dylan.

Dylan nodded his head but his face looked troubled.

'I just know he's lying. He's enjoying the attention he's getting. I get the impression that he thinks he's much cleverer than we are.'

Vicky's eyes were smiling, she tilted her head and opened her mouth as if to speak.

'No comment,' Dylan said.

'Hey, you didn't tell us he had huge buck teeth? I half expected them to be perfect his father being a dentist and all,' said Raj.

'I'm sure he didn't?' she said with a frown.

'I think you'd have noticed?' Dylan said laughing.

'Maybe I wasn't looking at his teeth?' said Vicky.

'I think maybe you need your eyes testing.'

'Maybe they protrude more when he's lying,' said Raj, raising an eyebrow.

'Quite an unusual form of body language but worth looking out for,' said Vicky. 'Maybe he has false teeth, shall we ask him?'

'We need evidence of this attack first and until we arrest him for at least one of the murders I don't want teeth mentioned to him in interview, do you hear?'

Raj frowned at Vicky. 'Anything new come in while we've been interviewing?' she said.

'What would you like to have come in sir,' said Vicky.

'CCTV of Jim Woodcock discarding his dark clothing would be heaven-sent right now,' said Dylan, rubbing his neck. He undid the top button of his shirt.

'Impossibilities I can do boss but miracles take a little longer,' said Vicky. 'However, there is a very nice looking young man waiting for you in your office sir, from the National Crime Agency. Feel free to give him my number,' Vicky said with a wink before peering around her boss towards his office. She lifted her chin, cocked her eyebrow and gave him a cheeky smile.

'How long has he been here?' said Dylan looking over his shoulder.

'Only about five minutes, Lisa's just made him a brew.'

Dylan strode out towards his door. Seated in his visitor's chair he could quite clearly see Gary Warner. He opened his door, walked in and shut it behind him. Vicky saw Dylan reach out to shake the other man's hand. He had a broad smile upon his face. 'Wouldn't kick him out of bed in a hurry,' she said to Raj.

'You're a hussy,' said Ned.

'A hussy what DC Granger?' said Vicky flicking her long blonde hair over her shoulder.

'You're a hussy, boss,' he said.

Vicky smiled broadly. 'Now he...' she said nodding in Gary Warner's direction, '...could call me anything he wanted,' she said, winking at Ned. 'I'm off to make the boss a coffee.'

***

'How the hell are you? Long time no see,' Dylan said, squeezing behind his desk and the piles of files surrounding it and sliding into his big, comfy chair opposite Gary.

'I'm good thanks. Last time we spoke you were running that drugs job...' he put his hand to his brow. 'Operation Whirlwind, wasn't it? Liz Reynolds and Frankie Miller ended up dead.'

'And her husband Malcolm is still on the loose.'

'I often wonder if it was him who killed Larry Banks,' said Dylan.

'Who knows,' said Gary. 'DS Banks's warrant card and bank cards were found on the corpse when it was pulled out of the river and later ID'd by DNA but we can only assume who killed him...' Gary looked towards the door as its handle was turned. Vicky walked in with a coffee for Dylan. He looked at her and smiled.

'Service, with a smile,' he said. 'Wouldn't mind a job here myself boss.'

'Oh, I'm sure he can arrange it,' Vicky said touching Gary's shoulder. 'Can't we sir?' she said raising her eyebrows at Dylan. He shook his head.

She stood at the door, her hand rested on it. She turned.

'Thank you DS Hardacre, that'll be all. Close the door behind you,' Dylan said, turning his attention back to his visitor.

Vicky frowned and left but as she did so she looked over her shoulder at Gary, who was watching her.

'Yes!' she said, to Ned biting her bottom lip and raising a fisted hand. 'The girl's still got it.'

He curled up his nose. 'Got what?'

Vicky shook her head at her colleague. 'I worry about you sometimes,' she said.

Ned's eyes were wide. 'That's rich coming from you,' he said.

***

It had been a long day and Dylan's mood was not getting any better.

'It had been such a shock to lose a close colleague, especially someone I had considered a friend. But, it was more of a blow to find out his death was as a consequence of his own actions... and not only that I hadn't realised he was bloody corrupt. A bit of a lad, yes, but not a wrong 'un. Anyway...' he said with a sigh, '...it doesn't do to dwell on the past. What can I do for you?'

'I'm here to update you actually,' Gary said, sitting up in his chair and leaning towards Dylan.

'Update me?'

'The information you submitted to Interpol in relation to a possible drug syndicate in Spain?'

Dylan's eyes rounded. It was his turn to sit up and lean forward. 'Go on,' he said.

'Oswald Moore, better known to his friends as Ozzy, has been on the radar for a number of years. He's always been on the periphery of some dodgy drug deal or other but there has never been anything to connect him officially. He's a slippery one, never stops in one place, or with one gang long enough to nail him. Give him enough rope though and, he was always bound to settle down.' Gary Warner's eyes lit up. 'Thanks to you we now have a permanent address for him and due to your information we know from our enquiries and subsequent surveillance that he is on the payroll of a significant drug cartel. We also believe that the head of that organisation is a Malcolm Reynolds, his next door neighbour. He will be desperate to clear his name for the Larry Banks saga and stay squeaky clean on the drugs front – maybe we will be able to bag them both this time.'

'Tell me, what can I do?'

'We have been reliably informed that Ozzy is on his way back to England. Did you know?'

'No, the last I heard was when the father-in-law and Ozzy's mother were asked to bring catalogues and samples of the pottery they make back to Harrowfield for a potential supplier which was when I put the intelligence in. At that time he was in Spain.'

'We've started covert surveillance today on their address on the Isle of Wight.'

'Jen's father's address is under surveillance? Do you think they're at risk?'

'We've done the risk assessments and we don't think there is a risk to them, but you've got to trust us that we've got it covered. As you can appreciate we need to gather as much information as we can before we strike. My boss wants to keep up the surveillance on Ozzy for as long as possible. He believes that Ozzy could take us to the drugs and lead us through the distribution network. We need to catch them with the goods to get a conviction. You know how it is...'

'Okay,' said Dylan. His phone bleeped. He took it from his pocket and looked at the screen. There had been six missed calls from Jen and now a text. He read it. 'Ozzy has been arrested whilst under the influence of drink or drugs on the Isle of Wight and he is now in police custody,' he said. 'I guess your lot will be liaising with Hampshire and the Isle of Wight Constabulary now.'

'Shit!' said Gary. 'That's all we need.'

Dylan picked up his phone to ring Jen. Gary sat quietly. 'I'll see what I can find out.'

Jen was distraught.

'So, he's been arrested before he got to your dad's?' said Dylan.

He nodded to Gary.

'Yes. My dad will be absolutely mortified. Can you do something?'

'I'm sorry love, if I could do anything... but as long as we know Ralph and Thelma are okay?' said Dylan. 'Keep me updated,' he said before putting the phone down.

Dylan put his elbow to the table, laid his head in his hand and rubbed his forehead. He looked up at Gary whose expression hadn't change. 'God...if only she knew.'

How could Dylan protect them? His hands were tied. All he could do was rely on his colleagues to keep them safe. 'If I'm not supposed to know about a job, then don't tell me,' Jen had always said to Dylan. 'That way if anything is leaked you will know I never said anything... not that I would... not that you would.... but...'

'We don't have secrets,' he said to Gary. 'This is so hard for me. You are absolutely sure they aren't in any danger aren't you?'

Gary nodded.

'He'll be bailed now won't he?' said Dylan.

'Yes. We'll have to get him bailed to ensure we can continue to tail him.'

'And it is likely he will go home to Jen's dad's?'

'I would have thought so as that is the most likely address he will have given the police – even if it is just to get his head down for the night.' Gary hesitated. 'You do know I am sharing this with you in confidence?'

'Of course. Don't worry, it'll go no further.'

***

PS Clegg's search team had found a pedal cycle fastened by a padlock to railings on a pathway that led to the canal.

'Vicky, take Andy, get down to the search team with the keys that are in Woodcock's property will you?' said Dylan

He paced the office like an expectant father. Numerous scenarios running through his head. Would the smaller of the keys fit the lock? If so what did that actually prove? He picked up his ringing phone, Jen was on the other end. 'I'm going to the Isle of Wight,' she said. Her voice was shaking.

'No, no, you can't. Think about it... Beaky will have a bloody fit if you leave her in the lurch. You know she's running with a skeleton staff due to the summer holidays.'

'And when have you ever thought about what bloody Beaky thinks? I've got to do something,' she cried. 'Dad is beside himself. He's taken his arrest personally... he's so ashamed. Will they search his house do you think?'

'I don't know... if they think he might have drugs there...' he said. 'I'm sorry, I can't talk right now but think about it logically. What can you do if you do go, and what will you do with Maisy?'

'I'll have to take her with me won't I?'

'No Jen, listen, please listen to me. Promise you'll wait until I get home. We need to talk. I'll be home as soon as I can,' he said. 'I promise.'

Dylan could hear the telephones in the incident room almost jumping off the tables. There wasn't enough personnel to answer them. Raj held one telephone in one hand and one in the other, she shouted out to Dylan.

'Boss, the bike has been photographed in situ and the key fits the lock. Can they remove it?'

'I really have to go,' Dylan said to Jen. 'We'll speak later, yes? Don't go anywhere,' he said. Dylan put his phone down and strode out with a purpose into the outer office. 'Yes Raj, and reiterate as careful as they possibly can. This has potentially been used on one or more of our murders,' Dylan said coming to stand at Raj's side.

'Did you hear that Jarv?' she said.

Rajinder's face didn't change. 'Why would Woodcock tell us the key was for a locker if it obviously wasn't? Surely he would know that we would check?' she said as she put the phone down on the CSI supervisor.

'He didn't bank on our tenacity. He knew we'd have to find the bike to disprove his evidence and link it to him, didn't he? Then he knew we would also have to have the presence of mind to check if that key he had in his possession fitted the padlock. Like we have always said he thinks he is cleverer than we are.'

'In his head I believe that he thought purporting to be a jogger would be more plausible than a man pedalling a cycle on the canal towpath in the middle of the night and that's why he ditched the bike.'

'But although this is all good evidence. It still doesn't prove he's our attacker does it?' Dylan said.

'Does this even prove it is his bike?'

'If I'm playing devil's advocate the Crown Prosecution will need us to look at the quality of the lock to see if more than one key would unlock it. It will have to be proved beyond any reasonable doubt that he is the only person who has a key that fits the lock for the evidence to count, in a court of law.'

Dylan wanted and he desperately needed more evidence to put to Jim Woodcock in his next interview that was scheduled for three o'clock. In this interview he would use DS Raj and DC Andy Wormald. He would be watching via the link to his office. They were close, they were very, very close, he could feel it. Woodcock was his man. Although there were many jigsaw pieces still missing to create the full picture. He would now have to have the canal checked, no matter how time consuming. He needed to find Woodcock's discarded clothing, sooner rather than later. Then and only then he perhaps would have the upper hand...

Chapter Thirty-Five

Dylan successfully updated the press office regarding the latest attack and made an appeal to the public. 'We believe our attacker may have discarded some of his clothing when he left the scene and therefore I would like to hear from anyone who comes across clothing that looks as if it has been recently abandoned,' he said. He knew it was a long shot but if someone did come across it he didn't want them to ignore it. It was imperative to the investigation that they secured all evidence to secure a conviction. He wanted there to be no way the Crown Prosecution Service could dilute the case against Woodcock. He wanted to put all the evidence before them in such a fashion that finding him guilty was inevitable. Then the judge could, he hoped, sentence him accordingly with recommendations that he served a minimum of twenty to thirty years. After all Jim Woodcock in Dylan's eyes was a grave danger to society.

In the Detective Inspector's years of experience Woodcock was one of the strangest people he had encountered.

The second interview with him was underway and Dylan watched from his office with interest as DS Raj got stuck into his ribs. He denied owning a pedal cycle and when he was told that a key found in his possession on arrest, fitted the padlock to which the cycle was secured to railings near the canal path, his response was quick coming.

'Is that the best you can do? Don't you know everyone has one of those padlock keys?' he said slouching back in his chair.

Dylan closed his eyes for an instant. He knew that was coming.

'I've told you, that key is for a locker. I've a degree in psychology and I'm studying criminology. I know what you're doing.' He put his hands behind his back, stretched and yawned loudly. 'I'm bored,' he said turning to his solicitor.

DS Raj continued. 'We've recovered what we believe to be a weapon near to the attack outside China House restaurant,' she said.

'And what has that to do with me? Nothing, absolutely nothing,' he said. His eyes were hooded. His shoulders dropped.

The solicitor at Woodcock's side watched him with interest. Her head tilted to one side. Jim Woodcock was becoming increasingly unresponsive and he yawned again. She turned to Raj. 'I'd like to request that my client has a couple of hours rest,' she said. 'He was up very early this morning.'

'Weren't we all,' Dylan said under his breath.

Woodcock's head that had been bowed turned to his solicitor and Dylan saw him smile at Yvonne Best weakly. The officers had no option but to grant the request as anything other than that cause of action may have shown the police to be unreasonable, and the interview or parts of it could be excluded from evidence, if deemed to be obtained by oppression.

***

Dylan clenched his fists and leant back in his chair. He looked through the half-glass door into the incident room. He got up and turned his computer off. It was time to see how the search was progressing and he was keen to speak with the officers who were scanning the CCTV footage that had been seized.

Dylan stood over Ned Granger. Ned had one hand through the handle of a freshly made mug of tea and another on his computer mouse. His eyes never left the screen.

'We need something Ned...' Dylan said in a whisper. He drummed his fingers on the desk. 'Have you got anything we can put to him in the next interview?'

'I've got a man running from the direction of China House. He's wearing dark clothing that covers his head. It may be a hoodie, with some imagination,' he said. 'The quality is abysmal.'

'Nevertheless, get me a still of that frame,' he said pointing to the computer screen. 'It's better than nothing. Keep at it,' he said with a fatherly tap on Ned's shoulder.

***

ACC Wendy Smythe had travelled from HQ to Harrowfield incident room and was hovering outside Dylan's office when he returned.

'Vicky Hardacre has updated me. Is it him?' she said.

'I think so, we just need the evidence.'

'What's he saying?'

'He's playing the game at the moment. There is no doubt he's savvy, he knows we haven't got the evidence or we would have arrested him for the murders. He more or less just told Raj so in interview.'

'Nothing new then?'

'No. I haven't put Vicky in interview with him yet. She's met him on a couple of occasions. I think we'll see if he is more forthcoming with someone he knows next.'

'Have you searched the place where he's living for his clothing? Could he possibly have gone home after the attack, put on his running gear and gone out again to see if there was any police activity in the area.'

'He wouldn't have had time but it was obviously his intention to get rid of the clothing he was wearing and maybe he wanted to get himself arrested knowing we had nothing on him. In fact he was actually making himself the distraction to already stretched resources. His flat is due to be turned over within the hour.'

DS Raj knocked on his door and walked in. 'Did you catch what Woodcock said after we finished interviewing him?'

Dylan shook his head from side to side.

'He asked us if we would feed his fish when we searched his flat!'

'So, what does that tell us?' said the ACC.

'He knows our next move is to do a search and is confident we're not going to find anything ma'am,' said Rajinder.

'Cocky bastard.'

'Tell Vicky, John, Andy and Ned I want them to go in now,' said Dylan to Raj.

'Are we alright as far as staffing levels go,' said Wendy Smythe.

'At the moment we are.'

'What results are imminent?'

'His training shoes have already gone for blood and the sole pattern analysis in respect of Martin Crossfield's murder.'

'Anything you need from me?'

Dylan looked at Raj. She shook her head. 'Not at the moment. I'll let you know immediately if we get any evidence to arrest him in connection with the murders.'

'I'll be in the building for a while. I've a meeting with Hugo-Watkins. If I hurry up I might just get Janet to cut me a slice of the large custard tart he has with his afternoon tea,' she said. 'Let's see how the Division is faring with all the cutbacks shall we? I'll get from under your feet.'

**

Using the key Woodcock had on him when he was arrested Vicky, John, Andy and Ned suited and booted entered the flat belonging to the prisoner. Jim Woodcock's flat was very clean and tidy.

'He must have been expecting us?' said Ned.

Vicky flared her nostrils. 'Bleach,' she said.

The small living space was dominated by a large four foot fish tank, which contained two very large fish.

'Just look at the size of them!' said Vicky.

'I expected to find a couple of goldfish in a bowl,' said Andy.

'What the hell are they?' said Ned.

'I don't know what they are but I do know who they are,' said Vicky. 'Look at their name plaque, Ronnie and Reggie,' she read. 'Named after the Kray twins do you think?' She turned to the others.

'They look like piranhas to me,' said John.

'Whatever you do don't put your hand in. I heard a piranha can snap a finger off if you trail it in the water,' said Ned, turning to Vicky with a grimace.

'Our lad's doing a project on them at school,' said John.

'Brilliant,' said Vicky. 'So what do you know about them?'

'Nothing, I haven't had the time to read it.'

'You're a rubbish dad,' said Vicky.

'I know,' said John. 'The downside of being a detective... I'm never at home.'

'Let's just leave the fish alone for now shall we?' said Vicky, but her attention was drawn to them many times during the search which turned up nothing untoward. A passport was found and the places visited were marked by an array of stamps from far away countries.

'I'll seize it to take back for the boss, shall I?' said Andy.

'Good idea,' said Vicky. She was distracted again by the room's illuminated feature. 'Reggie and Ronnie,' she said purposefully walking backwards and forwards across the room. 'Have you noticed that they follow you?' she said to Ned as she walked once again to stand at the tank.

'You probably look like a hearty meal to them, that's why.'

'You're right they might be hungry we haven't fed them.'

'Dropping to her knees she opened the cabinet below to find container after container labelled with different dried foods. 'Crayfish, worms, small insects, grasshoppers, crickets,' she said. She looked from the container in her hand to the fish swimming at the bottom of the tank, its eye was firmly upon her. 'What d'you fancy buddy?' she said. The fish spewed a heap of gravel out of its mouth, it made a loud noise as it hit the glass. She jumped backwards. There was a pause. Vicky's mouth dropped open.

'Holy shit!' she shrieked.

'What?' said the men who gathered at her side.

'Look! Is that what I think it is?'

Chapter Thirty-Six

'Oh my god it is! It's a tooth!'

Dutifully one of the fish once more dug deep into the gravel with its lower jaw and scooped another mouthful of gravel. It proceeded head first to the front of the tank.

'I don't believe it. It's eaten it,' she gasped. 'The bloody article! It's eaten the tooth.'

No sooner were four faces up close to the tank than the fish spat the gravel out forcefully at the glass.

'There it is,' Vicky shouted, her splayed fingers pressed hard against the glass.'

'Blimely O'Reilly, I think she might be right,' said Ned.

'We need a net or something to get it out quickly before it moves it again,' said Andy who already had his head in the cupboard below.

'Can't you just put your hand in and pick it out?' said Ned. Vicky was rolling up her sleeves.

'I'm sure I once read it takes three to five hundred piranhas to actually eat someone,' said Ned. 'Go for it.'

Vicky hesitantly went to lift the lid. No sooner had she done so but both fish propelled themselves with a flick of their strong tails to the top. Water went everywhere. The group jumped back. The lid snapped shut. The men laughed. Wet as she was Vicky tried once again, all the time keeping eye contact with one of the fish through the glass. This time the ferocity of the attack made her withdraw her hand in fear. The water was becoming cloudy, one of the fish was agitated and alert. The other lay close to the glass in the bottom corner.

Ned was doubled up laughing, so much so he could hardly speak. 'Woodcock certainly named them well...' he said wiping tears from the corner of his eyes.

Andy passed Vicky a small net he had found. She squeezed the wire together and fed it through the feeding hole in the roof of the tank. Very carefully she tried to steer it in the direction of the tooth. The fish appeared to back off until the net was fully submerged and her fingers were laid bare to him and then it struck with force, attacking the handle of the net and yanked it from her hold.

Vicky's hand safely out of the water the team watched the net slowly float to the bottom of the tank and settle upon the gravel, covering the tooth.

'They certainly mean business,' said Ned.

'I think we need to identify what breed of fish they are before we do anything else,' said Vicky. She wiped her hands and picked up her phone. 'Boss,' she said. 'We need your help.'

'Can you take a picture on your mobile and send it to me?' said Dylan.

'If anyone will know what the fish are, it'll be Ralph, Jen's dad,' he said.

Dylan forwarded it onto Ralph's mobile with the relevant question in the text.

'I'm pretty sure they're Oscars,' Ralph said by return. 'A word of warning, they might try to jump out of the tank given the chance. Tell your officers not to attempt to pick them up without covering them with a towel first. They have razor sharp fins.'

***

'Get me a towel will you, just in case,' John said peering at the tooth jewel, in its gravel crown. Ronnie and Reggie had backed into a corner. Without hesitation he put his hand in the tank and with a forefinger and thumb pincher movement he picked up the net, discarded it in the fishes' direction as a would-be shield, and gently, as if in slow motion to those watching, with bated breath, he moved the gravel in the water to locate the tooth. Picking it up he withdrew his hand sharply.

There it was. The human tooth for all to see was in the palm of John's large hand. For a few moments the observers were silent. Then they looked from one to the other.

'Do you think there'll be more?' said Ned, he looked over his shoulder to the menacing stare of the Oscars.

'We're going to have to drain it to see,' said John.

'How can we? What're we going to do with the fish?' said Ned.

'Do I need to ring the boss?' said Vicky.

The tooth placed inside an exhibit container, John held it out to Andy.

'Yes, it has got to be his call,' said John.

***

'We need photographs of the fish tank and the fish in situ. I'll get CSI to you directly,' Dylan said.

DS Raj scanned the internet for a local tropical fish retailer and arranged the removal of the fish for their safe keeping. Once this was done the water would be ready to be drained by the officers at the scene.

Ned stood close to CSI Jarv. They were both booted and suited. He offered Vicky the end of a plastic tube, the other he held under the water, in the tank. She ignored him. He threw a plastic bin at her feet. It bounced on the sterile sheet and toppled over. Sarah Jarvis picked it upright. 'Come on, it's right, you've got to put your mouth round it to get it flowing,' he said to Vicky '... and suck hard.'

She shook her head and smacked her lips together. 'I might be blonde but I'm not that bloody stupid,' she said giving him a sideways glance. 'Just get on with it will you...' she said.

They removed the gravel by the handful and as they did so teeth were picked out one by one.

Vicky's phone rang. 'Is there any sign of any dental tools at the flat,' said Dylan.

'No boss, nothing of use other than the passport.'

'Myself and Raj are going down to the cells, to arrest him for the murders and see what his response is.'

'We have recovered so far, what we believe to be fourteen human teeth. We'll get a quick confirmation from a pathologist, then we'll have the DNA checked. The gravel needs checking too in case there are smaller fragments we've missed.'

The cell area was empty other than for Ms Perfect, Woodcock's solicitor, a partner at Perfect & Best who had been summoned to the police station. Dylan disclosed to Ms Perfect their intention to arrest him with regard to the recovery of the teeth at her client's flat. In the charge room Dylan told Jim Woodcock, in the presence of his solicitor. 'Apart from the attempted murder for which you are under arrest. I am now arresting you for the murders of Davina Walsh, Carl Braithwaite, Alan Bell and Martin Crossfield.' He cautioned him.

James Woodcock didn't flinch or make comment. He was led into the interview room.

Dylan opened the questioning after the formalities of voice recognition and caution.

'You have just been arrested, apart from the attempted murder of Rachel Nicholson, which is why you are in custody but also now for four other murders those of Davina Walsh, Carl Braithwaite, Alan Bell and Martin Crossfield. Is there anything you want to say about that?'

'I'm astonished and appalled that you could even think I was capable of such things,' he said. Neither his body language nor his manner showed opposition to the charge that he professed.

'Well, one of the reasons that we have charged you is that we have recovered fourteen teeth from your fish tank. Which we believe to be human. As we speak they are being taken for further examination.'

'So, on that basis alone you have arrested me for murder?' he said. His brow held a frown as he looked sideways at Ms Perfect.

Dylan and Raj remained silent.

'I bought them on the internet Inspector?' He shook his head in little jerky movements. 'Didn't you know you can buy everything over the internet these days?'

'So explain to me why you would put them in a fish tank?'

Jim Woodcock sniggered. 'They're a feature. Unusual decoration don't you think?'

'Really?' said Dylan. His mouth turned downwards.

'Tell me Inspector. What have you done with my fish? I know you wouldn't have got the teeth out if you'd not removed the fish first,' he said.

'Don't worry they've been moved to safety. Do you have someone you wish to nominate to look after them for you in the long term?'

'Long term? You're hoping aren't you?' Jim Woodcock laughed. 'If anything happens to them, I'll sue,' he said with a more serious look on his face.

'You know it's only a matter of time before we get DNA results, so let's put a stop to this nonsense now, shall we?'

'I think you might be a bit premature Inspector. You may find yourself releasing me soon.'

'We'll see. Tell me. Why didn't you go into dentistry Jim? Your mum, Edna says your dad was disappointed you weren't interested in following in your father's footsteps. Did you not aspire to be a dentist like your dad when you grew up?'

Rajinder was eyeing Jim Woodcock's mouth with interest. 'Your two front teeth,' she said. 'They just don't look right...'

Jim Woodcock opened his mouth. 'Good observation skills,' he said, and with a simple hand movement he pulled out two teeth from the front of his mouth. Saliva ran down his fingers and dripped onto the table. He put them down on the desk in between himself and the detectives. Next he snatched them up together and swallowed them. He wiped his mouth with his forearm.

'And the purpose of that was?' said Dylan.

'What evidence?' said Woodcock, taking out a top plate. He smiled a wide, gummy, wet smile and laughed at the expression on his solicitor's face. 'If my father was still breathing he'd take great delight telling you what a disappointment I was to him. Even he couldn't ensure I had nice teeth. I developed anodontia at a young age – much to his disgust. The son of a dentist having no teeth – shock horror! He wanted me to be a dentist – spent hours showing me the ropes before he became a sad old lush. But why on earth would I want to look after other people's healthy teeth when I didn't have any of my own?'

'So why kill people to take out their teeth?'

'Those are your words, not mine Inspector. And now maybe I've swallowed all your evidence. Now that's sad isn't it?'

It was Dylan's turn to smile. 'It's not a problem to us Jim,' he said. 'We have a drugs toilet in your cell that's available for you to use when you're ready. You aren't going anywhere. You're not unique. We are quite used to people like you trying to swallow evidence in an attempt to conceal or get rid of things.'

Jim Woodcock looked perturbed and made no comment.

'We are used to people telling us lies too, but our job you see is to be patient. We are evidence gatherers. Then we put the best available evidence forward at a court of law. I'm sure as a psychology and criminology student you will be well read on these subjects, won't you Mr Woodcock?' Dylan said. 'Or haven't you got around to those points of law yet?'

'Maybe I am... But do you know what? I need the toilet right now,' he said and proceeded to try pull off his coverall.

Dylan ended the interview and he was escorted back to his cell.

Chapter Thirty-Seven

Dylan had missed several phone calls whilst they had been arresting Woodcock for his involvement in the murders, most of the calls were from Jen. Before he returned those calls he was duty bound to let the ACC know of the arrest status of the prisoner.

Granting the extension of detention to keep Woodcock for a further twelve hours wouldn't be an issue for the Divisional Commander. Dylan knew after this time had elapsed, if necessary, he could apply to the court to extend this for a longer period of time and it would be granted.

Dylan's head was buzzing. The team was working flat out. The most important aspects of the case were prioritised by him. Lisa brought in a coffee and put it down on the corner of his desk.

'Will there be a debrief tonight?'

'Yes, just tell everyone to give me a minute will you. I'll only be a minute,' he said. Picking up the telephone he dialled home.

She nodded and closed the door behind her when she left.

***

Maisy's face was growing increasingly dim as Jen sat watching the sleeping child. When she moved, the light from the lamp behind her opened up the bedroom. As she rose from her daughter's bedside she reached for Maisy's hand and enveloped it in hers. She leant over her and kissed her fleetingly on her forehead and put the storybook back on the shelf. When the phone rang Jen ran down the stairs. Jumping off the bottom two steps she ran into the moonlit lounge and picked it up.

'Jack?' she said. 'I've been waiting for you to ring. I'm sorry. I know you're busy but the Hampshire Police have had a DNA hit on the swabs they took from Ozzy. Dad told me Ozzy's been arrested for the burglary at the post office and his friends' house in Godshill. I've told him they'll probably search the house. I'm right aren't I?' The room dropped into darkness in an instant as a cloud passed over the moon.

There was a finality in Jen's voice. Dylan rose and stood by his window, and was just able to distinguish the shape of the officers whose stooped tired bodies were making their way hurriedly towards the police building anticipating the debrief and being dismissed to go home to their beds.

'Yes, it's procedure for them to search the house if he was arrested for driving under the influence of drink or drugs, should he have any drugs at home.'

'Dad can't deal with this on his own; he'll not cope with the shame of it. He needs me there.'

Dylan turned, took a step towards his desk when a rap came at his door. He looked up and made a gesture at Vicky to leave him be. 'No. Jen. Listen to me. Think of Maisy. Please don't go rushing off. You don't need to go. Thelma is with your dad. It's her son. He's nothing to do with your dad.'

'Will he be released on bail, back to Dad's house?' she said directly.

Dylan looked up at the full moon that hung in a blackened sky. What could he say that meant he did not lie to her? He said nothing. He knew Ozzy would be released on bail. The National Crime Agency would see to it.

'He will be released back to my dad's won't he?'

'Yes, I would think so unless he has some other permanent residence? Look, I can't... I don't know all the facts and right now I'm needed in a debrief. We've arrested Jim Woodcock for the murders.'

A cold clarity seemed to possess Jen. 'This will kill my dad. Honesty, integrity, it's all what dad's about...' A sob caught in her throat.

'Jen, I'll be home after the debrief and we can talk then.'

***

Dylan slept fitfully; like a fierce but tired animal, and next morning Maisy had woken at five o'clock and Jen's hands had been full entertaining their daughter. He was out of the house before dawn. He found it very difficult to be distant with Jen but there wasn't anything he could say to alleviate her anxiety and since nothing had been forthcoming from the Isle of Wight he could only assume that Ozzy was yet to be bailed.

The incident room office phone was ringing as he entered the room and looking around him he realised there was only him there to answer it.

'Detective Inspector Dylan,' he said.

'Are you the man in charge?' said a man with a rasp in his voice.

'I am. How can I help you?' Dylan fingers ran fluidly through the papers in the in-tray on the desk. This had all the hallmarks of a crank call. The line went quiet for a moment or two. 'You still there?' Dylan said cocking his head on one side as he looked at the inside of a file. He paused, took the phone away from his ear, looked at the receiver and was just about to put it back on its cradle when there was a high pitched scream.

'Is everything okay?' said Dylan with a furrowed brow.

'Sorry, damn cat dragging a bloody dead mouse into the office. Our tea lady, she'll never get used to dead vermin appearing all over the place. I keep telling her the cats are either wanting to feed her or show off their hunting skill and in return they only want a bit of fuss, don't you Smudge?' he said. Dylan could hear a distinctive, loud purring. 'But she won't have it will she?' he said kindly. Dylan was about to hang up. 'Broadstairs, it's Ted Broadstairs I'm night security man for Ventrix Mill on Waterford Road,' he said. The man grunted and in Dylan's mind's eye he had bent and placed the cat on the floor. 'I heard on the local radio last night that you were looking for some discarded clothing in relation to an attack on our patch.'

'Yes, that's right, why?' said Dylan a look of optimism caressed his face. He picked up a pen and pulled a blank piece of paper towards him.

'I, well, I found some clothing rolled up on the landing of the fire escape at the back of the mill, canal-side. It's only recently been put there. I know because I have to check the fire exits daily for obstructions,' he said.

'You've not moved it?'

'No, not yet I haven't. I have checked the security CCTV footage and it shows a bloke leaning onto the landing and placing the clothing there – then he clears off. Bloody suspicious I think... Thought you'd like to know about it.'

'You're right, I do. Do you keep your CCTV on twenty-four-seven?'

'Too right we do and the tapes are stored in chronological order for easy retrieval, if need be.'

'Thank you. Can I ask you to leave the clothing in situ and someone will be with you in...' Dylan lifted his arm and pulled back his shirt sleeve to look at his watch, 'in the next half an hour,' he said.

***

Vicky pulled up a chair, straddled it and with her arms crossed on the back of it she didn't take her eyes off the clothing that was being shown to Dylan from inside an exhibit bag. Dylan had to stop himself punching the air. The rolled up pair of trousers were wrapped inside a blue hoodie. In the inside pocket of the hoodie were found two shiny dental tools.

'From Martin Crossfield's surgery do you think?' Vicky said.

'Maybe,' he said. 'He would have needed something to replace the ones he had left behind wouldn't he if he had intended to carry on with the killings?' Dylan briefly closed his eyes. 'Please God,' he thought.

The CCTV that had been seized would be, as a matter of urgency, copied. This would then be their working copy which could be used for viewing. As a priority the master copy would be sealed and retained for evidential purposes.

Dylan sat with Vicky and Raj to view the tape. For what appeared like forever the three looked at an empty fire escape. Then as if it was a rat that was finding its way down a sewer pipe a hand was seen feeling around the step and onto the landing. A few seconds later a man's head appeared. The head was topped with dark flyaway hair. He disappeared. Those present watching the tape groaned. But before long he lifted himself up by his arms to look on the landing. Now his eyes could be seen. Again, his image fell away. With one big push they saw his chin come into view but it was skywards and all that they could see was his neck until suddenly, plain to see, there was a perfect full screen of Jim Woodcock's face.

The email addressed to ACC Wendy Smythe was urgent. On receipt she picked up the telephone and rang Dylan.

'With that sort of luck you should buy a lottery ticket,' she said. 'So what time's the interview?'

'Nine thirty,' said Dylan. 'But, once I disclose these findings to Perfect and Best I wouldn't think it's going to happen until at least ten o'clock.'

'You've enough ammunition I'd have thought to sink an armada now with this. It'll be interesting to see if he talks. I'll be over sometime this afternoon. I've a discipline hearing to attend in the next thirty minutes but I'm sure you will still be talking when I get out. Keep me updated. And Jack...'

'Yes?'

'Well done,' she said before putting the phone down. Dylan was still smiling when his phone rang a few seconds later.

'Dylan,' said Gary Warner. 'I've a bit of bad news. They've released Oswald Moore on bail, for reasons already known to you. The home where he was living, Jen's dad's house has been given as the address where he will reside so it is expected he will go there.'

'Promise me you keep a close eye on his whereabouts won't you?'

'Yes, we will.'

'Jen is adamant she wants to go down and take our daughter Maisy with her.'

'No need. Our source reckons Ozzy will be on his toes within the hour, and the surveillance team will be behind him. Hopefully he will lead us right to the team bringing the drugs in and ultimately the stash.

'You're sure everything is going to plan.'

'I'm sure.'

Dylan put the phone down. Vicky walked in his office. His face was sombre.

'I thought you'd be bouncing off the walls,' she said. 'Rachel Nicholson has been released from hospital.' Vicky frowned. 'What's up?'

He pondered. Was a trouble shared, a trouble halved?

'Nothing. It's going to be another late one. Let's get some breakfast inside us while we have time,' he said. 'At least before we rain on Jim Woodcock's parade. It should be game, set and match to us today with any luck.'

Chapter Thirty-Eight.

DS Raj and DI Jack Dylan sat in the interview room with a toothless James Woodcock. His solicitor sat to his left but very slightly behind him. Without turning his head she was out of eye contact with her client. Vicky watched and listened with John Benjamin from the monitor established in Dylan's office.

Woodcock was reminded that he was still under caution.

Dylan started the questioning by disclosing the finding of the clothing, showing him photographs of each item, referring to each with an exhibit number. He showed him the dental tools and then a still photograph from the CCTV tape which was a picture of the person placing the clothes onto the factory's fire escape landing.

'Is that you?' Dylan asked the prisoner.

'I don't need to say anything do I?' he said turning to his solicitor. Ms Perfect shook her head with two short, jerky movements

'She's right. You don't, but we all know it is you isn't it?'

Woodcock made no reply and slowly leant as far away from the table as his chair would allow.

'I believe Mr Woodcock that you attempted to murder Rachel Nicholson by hitting her over the head with a wooden truncheon. Fortunately for her this time you were disturbed and ran away. You collected the bicycle you used as transport into Harrowfield and at this time discarded the weapon. When you reached the canal, which you thought was far enough away for us to suspect you were involved you abandoned your bike, took off your outer garments to suggest to anyone you came into contact with that you were out jogging and put your clothes in what you thought was a safe place, until you could collect them later. You then commenced to jog along the canal where you came face to face with the two uniformed officers. Your intention was to kill Rachel Nicholson and remove some of her teeth wasn't it?'

Jim Woodcock made eye contact with Dylan and shifted his body slightly to face him full on. He leant forward, his shoulders dropped. His face sagged, his eyes were dark, and his direct look piercing. 'Yes,' he said, with a controlled slight up turning of his lips. 'Well done. Checkmate to you I think Inspector.'

Dylan felt Raj's body recoil beside him. The professional mask still didn't slip.

'Credit to you and the team Inspector that I'm here so soon,' he said. 'That was not my intention.'

'Thank you, but if you would, I'd now like to talk to you about each murder.'

'Understandable,' he said with a nod of his head. 'As you rightly said before, I'm not going anywhere.' Woodcock shuffled in his seat.

'Comfortable,' said Dylan.

'Perfectly,' said Woodcock

'Okay, so let us begin. The first killing that we are aware of is the young lady cyclist Davina Walsh? Do you want to tell us any different?'

'Yes, she was my first. Her downfall was routine. It was me who decided which day I would end her life,' he said with a wink of his eye. 'I was in control... father was dying... I had the power. I wanted a new set of teeth...'

'You used a garrotte?'

'Kindest way I thought. Silent, quick and clean,' he said, drawing a hand across his neck. He made a rasping sound.

'Then you removed her teeth, quite skilfully, I am told by the experts.'

'I could have made a good dentist.' Woodcock screwed up his face. 'I just didn't fancy it. But I did learn how to make my own dentures. I had to kill my victims so that they didn't move whilst I executed the procedure. Lovely white teeth she had. Don't you think there is something wonderfully clean and exciting about white teeth Inspector? The extraction of a tooth is such a wonderfully exciting ultimate procedure for someone like me. My father would have been proud. I was a natural. He used to say to me when I was young. "teeth are nice and white when

317

new. They make for a smile and help you chew..." to try and get me to wear the dentures he had made for me.'

'The used condom did throw us for a while...' said Dylan.

Woodcock grimaced. 'Dirty bastards, and in a police car in a public place too. I hope they got what they deserved. Everyone to their own. I'm not homophobic but... there is a limit to what people can stomach isn't there?' Jim Woodcock shuddered.

'What about Carl Braithwaite? Remember, the murder in which you staged a robbery scene for us'

'It was just one of those nights when I couldn't sleep. He came out of the nightclub as I walked past. I asked him the time. He was nice, polite, he had lovely white teeth. Jealousy really is such a horrible thing...'

'But you didn't use a garrotte on that occasion, any reason?'

'I didn't have it with me. This one wasn't planned. I found the weapon as I walked behind him down the snicket. I whacked him over the head.' Woodcock's eyes went up to the corner of the room. 'The noise... it echoed... real eerie it was. About the only time I actually felt scared that I'd be caught and I hadn't gained the label of serial killer.' It was evident that Woodcock was reliving the moment. He looked back at the detectives with a smile. 'Didn't stop me pulling his teeth though. Some teeth are easier than others to pull out you know.' Dylan knew full well he was talking through his fantasy but as long as he was admitting his crimes the detectives would listen.

'You must be very good to be able to extract so many teeth so quickly. Yet again the experts told me that the extractions were done very professionally.'

'Of course. I am a professional,' he said. 'If I don't do it right, I don't get the same feeling of satisfaction either.' With a cock of his head Woodcock's eyebrows knitted together.

'Who was it next?'

'You know very well who it was Inspector, don't tease me.' Woodcock smiled on one side of his face coyly at Dylan. 'Alan Bell The number of times I've travelled in his cab just to see those lovely white teeth of his. He stinks, terrible choice of aftershave, has the most annoying personality traits but his teeth are truly to die for.' Woodcock's face lit up. His eyes smiled. 'Ha ha! I made a joke,' he said looking directly at Rajinder. 'To die for! He stopped, his face took on a frown. 'Why are you not smiling?'

'Let's move on. Was dropping the garrotte...'

'...an accident? Yes, it was,' he said with a slow nod of the head. 'I had to leave pretty quickly on that occasion. His fare came back out of the house. But not before planting one of the cyclist's teeth for you to find.' Woodcock pulled a face. 'I didn't really want to part with it but I didn't want to let anyone else take credit for that murder. You see now, after three murders, I knew I would be given the status of a serial killer – not only in the newspapers... but also that woman, your boss, she went on TV talking about the murders. Fame at last!'

Dylan was conscious that the forty-five minute long tape was about to run out. If Woodcock and his solicitor agreed to carry on with the questioning the evidence would be admissible in a court of law. The tape was changed quickly by expert hands. It was sealed and signed. The detectives didn't want Woodcock to dry up on them, not now. A new tape was installed and the interview continued. Dylan reminded Woodcock he was still under caution.

'I'm intrigued,' said Dylan. 'How did you choose Martin Crossfield as one of your victims?'

'Ah, Martin... we met for the first time in Hong Kong a couple of years ago. I'd gone with Devlin the devil, my brother-in-law to a dentist conference. Father always paid for me to go, long after he stopped working. He never did give up on me becoming a dentist. I did let him down. Not because I didn't become a dentist but because he lost his job because of me. You see, he collected the teeth they found at home for me... because he had let me pull them out. It also made my paranoid sister happy to know her husband wasn't up to anything he shouldn't be... Oh my god if only she knew... he was worse than me! He gets bored very easily. We went looking for a bit of excitement in Hong Kong.' Woodcock raised his eyebrow and then winked at Dylan. 'Devlin likes a bit of fun with the girls, but that got a bit out of hand and hey presto I found another way of collecting teeth! Martin, Devlin and I went to Tam's Tailors together and got a new suit made. We thought we'd put them to the test. They really can make a suit up in a couple of hours,' he said. 'We got talking about the fun we'd had on that trip at Dad's expense at his funeral. Martin and I were both wearing the suits we had bought out there that day, funnily enough. Now, Martin has got the ultimate teeth for anyone with a teeth fetish. He didn't need to pay the girls for their services, handsome creature that he is... was... We got chatting. Devlin had to get home. He's under the thumb,' he said with a snigger. 'Martin said he'd drop me off at home but he needed to go back to the practice. His surgery has just been refurbished, and he asked me if I wanted to go back with him to take a look. Now, I wasn't about to look a gift horse in the mouth, so to speak, was I?'

Woodcock's eyes clouded over. He scowled. 'He poured me a drink. Then he started mocking me about my condition... He told me I didn't have what it takes to be a dentist ... He said you couldn't be a dentist without perfect teeth. He even offered to fit me dentures. That really was a step too far... I'd just buried my tormentor I didn't need another.'

They had seen him angry, but never such anger as they saw now. His face appeared to swell, his mouth open, his eyes were like dull glass.

'Could you explain to me again why you take the teeth?'

'I use the teeth, only perfect teeth mind, to make my own dentures,' he said, his lisp becoming more prominent. 'And it excites me to do the extraction in double quick time... quicker than the others who said I would never be a dentist...'

Raj had remained silent until now. 'When and how did it all start?'

'My teeth never developed. Like I said I was a huge disappointment to my father. I suffer from a rare genetic disorder known as anodontia. I think at one time father thought I was his big life challenge... Or I had been sent by God to test him. He used to be a religious man my father did, until his misdemeanour – then I guess he couldn't really face them... Although of course it was me not him...' Woodcock's eyes were as round as saucers. 'He had dentures made for me when I was young. They were good ones. Uncomfortable as hell. I refused to wear them. He hit me but he would not break me. The ridicule I suffered....didn't have friends. Instead I spent all my time following my father around. He taught me all about teeth, in an attempt to get me to accept my condition I guess. I studied taxonomic science for a while. When I got older he'd even let me do extractions when the patient was unconscious. He liked doing extractions too my dad did. It made him happy.

'What made you start killing people for their teeth?' said Dylan.

'Teeth are nice and white when new.
They make a smile and help you chew.
In your skull long after you're dead,
I'd like to remove them from your head...'

'I don't follow?' Dylan said. It was his turn to frown.

'Don't you see? I've never had a relationship with anyone other than my overweight drunken father – useless as he ended up being, he gave up everything for me and was all I had to aspire to. He told me often that I would never find anyone to love me because of the way I looked, if I didn't wear my dentures. After visiting him when we had been told he was terminally ill I went back to the family home and into his office. The old tools – they brought back fond memories.'

'So am I to understand that these were sexually motivated crimes? Would we be right to use the terminology odontophilia?'

'The terminology you're looking for is exodontia Inspector!' Jim Woodcock stood. He banged his chest like a monkey.

'Teeth are nice and white when new.
They make a smile and help you chew.
In your skull long after you're dead,
I'd like to remove them from your head...'

He sat with a bump on the chair. The detectives' masks still didn't slip.

'They were a lovely feature in the fish tank don't you think?'

'We appear to have more teeth in our possession from you than we have knowledge of taken from victims we know about. Are there more we don't know about?'

'More teeth or more victims Inspector?' he said with a raised eyebrow. 'You think you're so clever don't you Inspector. I wouldn't want to spoil your fun. You tell me. I've been labelled a serial killer. Which is all I want? How many more I've killed doesn't really matter does it?'

'It does to their families Jim. Their loved ones may be dead but they will carry the life sentence. Could you not bring yourself to at least try to give them closure?'

Woodcock looked Dylan straight in the eye and slowly he shook his head in short jerky movements.

'No matter what people call you, or what label they attach to your crimes you are nothing more than a sadistic killer with a strange perversion who shows no remorse to his fellow man.' Dylan said. He waited for a fall out from his remarks.

'Perhaps some would say that, others may say I was true to myself. Remember teeth are everlasting wherever they are... Like me, a survivor. Your wife has nice teeth Inspector doesn't she?'

Dylan didn't respond but it made him think. Had he seen Jen or was he just lashing out? He would never know.

Dylan terminated the interview.

Woodcock sat looking down at his hands. He sang quietly to himself over and over again the poem he had recited earlier in the interview...

'Teeth are nice and white when new.
They make a smile and help you chew.
In your skull long after you're dead,
I'd like to remove them from your head...'

Then he laughed... throwing his head back and opening his mouth to reveal his barren gums. Saliva escaped from the sides of his mouth and formed spittle that gathered at the corners and remained.

The officers left the interview room and his solicitor followed them.

'Charges soon?' she said. 'What would you say? Mad, bad, or a bit of both? I guess we should never be surprised in our line of work should we?' said Ms Perfect.

Dylan arranged for Raj to charge him.

ACC Wendy Smythe was waiting for Dylan in the incident room. 'Shall I contact the press office?'

'If you like. A man will appear charged with four counts of murder and one count of attempted murder,' said Dylan.

'Can I name him?'

'Crown Prosecution Service may not like it but I think the public would like to know. Speak to Jacki Stanley and see what she says,' he said. 'I'll update Professor Stow, Beryl and the team at the forensic laboratory. Update PC Mitchell, PC Bullock and PC Burkett will you Raj, the victims' families need updating.'

'On it sir,' she said.

'I've spoken to Yin at JJ Associates. According to his passport he was in Hong Kong at the time of Fan Huang's murder,' said Vicky. 'And with what he has just said in interview it may be that her murder may now be detected.'

'See if there is a DNA match to her with any of the teeth that we have found will you? We will need a statement from the tailor's too where the suit was bought. The dentist that Yin took the ACC to may be able to help,' said Dylan. 'Get Woodcock's brother-in-law in. If he was at the dentist conference like Woodcock said he was we'll need a statement from him for corroboration. I'd like to hear what he could tell us about the trip to Hong Kong and his possible contact with Fan Huang.'

'Will do, boss,' said Andy.

Dylan headed for the Divisional Commander's suite. 'I hear ACC Smythe is in with him?' he said to Janet his secretary. She nodded.

'They're having a meeting with Dorothy the duties clerk and Avril Summerfield-Preston in relation to staffing levels,' she said busily putting a china tea pot and cups and saucers on a silver tray.

'They must be taking it seriously if they've invited the duties clerk supervisor,' Dylan said.

'It's about the cuts. We have to make the spending meet the proposed budget and it looks like the thin blue line is going to get even thinner for us all,' she said with a look of sadness on her face. 'I worry for our officers. They look so very young to me these days.' Janet opened a cake box. Dylan watched her carefully place three cream buns on a plate and take one large custard tart out of a paper bag and place it on its own saucer.

'Hugo-Watkins,' Dylan said. 'I swear one day he'll pop behind that desk with all the tarts he eats.'

She took a receipt from her pocket, stapled it to a claim form and put it to one side on her desk.

'The hospitality budget not taking a hit I see?' said Dylan.

'No,' she smiled. 'Mr Hugo-Watkins wants to impress the Assistant Chief Constable. We don't see the likes of her rank at our station very often do we?'

Gary Warner came to the secretary's doorway. 'They said you were here boss, can I have a minute?' he said.

Dylan stepped out into the corridor. 'You'll be pleased to know my source tells me that Ozzy Moore has left the island without returning to the address he gave us in Godshill on the Isle of Wight.'

'He has a conscience then.'

'Maybe, but probably not, he might just be in a hurry. We have surveillance on him and are in no doubt he is travelling to Dover where we believe he will board a ferry this evening. Intelligence tells us that he is travelling to Spain to meet with goods that are scheduled to leave there in the next couple of days. Our counterparts in Spain will take up the surveillance from the ferry when it docks and we will be on him now until he meets with his transport. Once they have them in position the whole gang will be stopped and arrested before they leave the country.'

'Good. So there is no imminent danger to Jen's dad and Ozzy's mother then?'

'No. I told you. The next thing you will hear is that he has been arrested and he will be facing a long jail sentence.'

'And you're here to arrest this end?'

'Yes, we have made contact with the person whom Jen's dad and Ozzy's mum met up with to hand over the suitcase at the airport.'

'You'll need to speak with them at some point about that won't you?'

'Yes, in due course we will need a statement from them and we will ask them to ID the man whom they handed the case over to.'

'I for one know Jen's dad will be mortified when he finds out the extent of Thelma's son's crimes.'

'No one can be responsible for their adult children's actions. We can only hope that the way we bring them up means they will turn out to be well balanced adults,' said Gary

***

A drink to celebrate the arrest of the serial killer Jim Woodcock would have to wait until another night, after the court appearance. Dylan needed to see Jen.

Her mood was a sombre one as opposed to Dylan's elation and it was hard not to show his great relief that Jim Woodcock had been caught and admitted to his crimes. However, he was in turmoil to watch his wife suffer knowing what he did about Ozzy, her dad and Thelma's ordeal. No matter how much he assured her that her dad was going to be okay without being able to share the details until the arrest of Ozzy Moore it would not be enough. His knowledge that the arrest was imminent helped but until then he could only support them and he had to stay silent. And would they capture Malcolm Reynolds this time around? Only time would tell.

'The court will be packed with reporters when Woodcock appears briefly. I wonder what label he will get in the town Jen,' he said. 'All the experts will be out in force with their diagnosis of him.'

'Why would we care as long as they keep him locked up and throw away the key,' she said.

Dylan went to the fridge, took two glasses from the cupboard and poured a large glass of wine. Jen put her hand over the second glass to stop him. Dylan looked down at her puzzled.

'No! You never are, are you?' he said.